Praise for Dreda Say Mitchell

'As good as it gets' Lee Child

'A great read written by a great girl' Martina Cole

'A truly original voice' Peter James

'Zippy, twisty plot. . .and a bevvy of memorable supporting
goodies and baddies' *The Sunday Times*

'Thrilling' *Sunday Express* Books of the Year

'The most authentic chronicler of crime and punishment in
multiracial London' *The Times*

'Strong and Provocative' Barry Forshaw, *Independent*

'Awesome tale from a talented writer' *Sun*

'Mitchell outguns Marina Cole for pure, shocking East End
gangster grit. *****' *Mirror*

'Fast paced and full of twists and turns' *Crime Scene*
Magazine

'Fas

Born and bred in the East End of London, Dreda Say Mitchell has seen it all from the inside. After a string of jobs as a waitress, chambermaid and catering assistant she realised her dream of becoming a teacher. During this time she saw a new generation of East Enders grappling with the same problems she had but in an even more violent and unforgiving world. Dreda's books are inspired by the gritty, tough and criminal world she grew up in. She still lives in London's East End. For more information and news, please visit Dreda's website:

www.dredasaymitchell.com
Follow Dreda on Twitter: @DredaMitchell
Find her on Facebook: /dredasaymitchell

Also by Dreda Say Mitchell

Running Hot
Killer Tune

The Gangland Girls trilogy
Geezer Girls
Gangster Girl
Hit Girls

DI Rio Wray series
Vendetta
Snatched
Death Trap

The Flesh and Blood series
Blood Sister
Blood Mother
Blood Daughter
One False Move

Blood Mother

Flesh and Blood Trilogy Book Two

Dreda Say Mitchell

HODDER

First published in Great Britain in 2017 by Hodder
& Stoughton An Hachette UK company

A CIP catalogue record for this title is available from the British Library

Paperback ISBN 978 1 473 62569 3
eBook ISBN 978 1 473 62568 6

Typeset in Rotis Serif by Hewer Text UK Ltd, Edinburgh
Printed and bound by Clays Ltd, St Ives plc

Hodder & Stoughton policy is to use papers that are natural, renewable
and recyclable products and made from wood grown in sustainable
forests. The logging and manufacturing processes are expected to
conform to the environmental regulations of the country of origin.

Hodder & Stoughton Ltd
Carmelite House
50 Victoria Embankment
London EC4Y 0DZ
www.hodder.co.uk

To all the fantastic readers who have
supported me for years. Cheers!

Prologue

2003

'What's taking them so long?' Jen asked her two sisters impatiently.

Tiffany shrugged. 'You know Mum, she's probably still putting on her slap.'

Their half-sister, Dee, was watching the increasingly restless crowd. People had been waiting for things to kick off for quite some time now.

'Oi,' she called, spotting someone she didn't know. 'Get your mitts out of the mini sausage rolls. No one starts on the nosh until she gets here.'

The person quickly whipped their hand away; Dee Black was a woman who didn't stand any nonsense.

Dee turned back to her sisters. 'I told you we should've had it at an upmarket venue. Somewhere plush and cultured.'

Tiff rolled her eyes. 'Bloody hell, you're not still rabbiting on about that? Give it a rest will ya.'

Dee blinked her false eyelashes furiously. 'Everyone's so low rent here. Look at 'em.'

The crowd was a motley crew of people, mainly from The Devil's Estate.

Jen said, 'This is where a lot of her mates are.' She leaned forward and whispered, 'It must be that surprise we laid out on the way that's keeping them. I bet Mum's gobsmacked.'

They all looked as pleased as Punch with themselves at the thought of the surprise.

Nicky, Dee's boy, who was keeping a lookout, suddenly and dramatically raised his hand, signalling for silence. But then he frowned and said, 'Hold up.' He peered through the window. 'That can't be right . . .'

His mum snapped, 'What are you going on about? It's either them or it ain't.'

'It's . . .'

Before he could finish, the door opened and Jen's daughter Courtney came in. Alone.

'Where's your Nanna Babs?' Jen asked. Then she looked closely at her daughter and scowled. 'Where's your coat?'

Courtney swallowed, her face pale. 'I fell . . . it got dirty . . . Nanna Babs kept it.'

'So where's your grandmother?' Dee asked her. 'Are you alright? You look a bit peaky.'

Courtney swallowed again as she nodded. 'Nanna said she's just coming over.' She looked up at her mum. 'Can I use the loo?' She scarpered without waiting for an answer.

Jen stared after her. 'She didn't look right. Maybe I should–'

'She's coming! She's coming!' Nicky called out excitedly.

The lights popped off and they fell silent.

Half a minute later, the door opened. The lights flew back on and the crowd gathered at Babs Miller's surprise fiftieth joyfully cried, 'Happy birthday!'

But the happiness was sucked out of the room at the sight of the blood on her face and white dress.

'Something terrible has happened,' she said, 'someone needs to call the coppers.'

PART ONE: 1972

'You could do worse than Stanley Miller. A lot worse.'

One

'You're a whore! And a murderer!'

As if the spitting rage of the normally quiet and gentle Doctor McDaid was not enough, there was worse to come. Babs Wilson had, unfortunately, left the door to his surgery open as she fled out of it back into the waiting room, and now several rows of patients could all hear him tearing a strip off her.

A few minutes earlier she had been sitting among them, waiting her turn, fists clenched white, hoping against hope that there was some mistake in the test results she'd got yesterday. But Doctor McDaid had soon killed that off; fear and last-minute hope had quickly turned to horror. Then, when he'd turned on her in fury, she'd gone into shock. Now she stood in front of the other patients like an actor who'd forgotten her lines.

Some of her audience looked away in embarrassment while others watched with curiosity. Among them were several proper gossips who were already eagerly trying to work out what was going on so they could spread the word. She could imagine what their malicious patter would sound like once it started doing the rounds:

'Did you hear about the Wilson girl? I was down the quacks when Doctor McDaid called her a whore and a murderer. Ol' Jim

McDaid was in a right two and eight, I can tell you. I wonder what that was about. As if we didn't know . . .' Babs caught the eye of the Jackson woman, aka Dirty Laundry Jackson, who lived on her street. She'd be straight to work on the gossip mill, no doubt adding her own poisonous flavour to the story. The old bitch.

Babs was nineteen, a proud girl from a proud family. Her father had always told her to keep her head up and walk tall, no matter what. So she raised her head, stared down the gawpers and tried to take his advice. But when everyone heard the doctor call out again, to no one in particular, 'Whore! Murderer! The shame of her honest family!' she caved. Her shoulders sagged and teardrops stung her cheeks.

The receptionist called out, 'Mrs Donovan? Doctor McDaid will see you now. Could you remember to close the door on your way in?' Then she gestured at Babs with her head to tell her to sling her hook.

Babs moved with gathering speed. Out on New Road in Whitechapel, she pulled in gasps of air. Without realising it, she found herself wandering into the traffic. A car slammed on its brakes and squealed to a halt a few inches short of her. The driver shook his head and pointed at his eyes before driving round her. For a brief moment, Babs wished the motor had hit her and dragged her down the road into oblivion because she was a young woman in Big Trouble. In fact, she was in Big Trouble twice over.

She might have been able to cope with one or the other, but not both.

She couldn't go home to her parents' house and she couldn't go and see her friends. But as she tramped the streets of the East End, she realised she didn't have to. She would just go and see Neville straight away. He would sort her out. It was almost his catchphrase. 'There's nothing I can't sort out, baby. Nothing – you only have to ask and I make it happen.'

She hadn't seen Nev for a week or more. He was busy at the moment and couldn't fit her in. But she was proud of that. He weren't a lazy sod like some of the lads she'd grown up with. No, her Nev had prospects. Ambition. Babs perked up and began the trek, crossing over Commercial Road to the Bad Moon boozer in Shadwell where Nev held court most lunchtimes, although he'd never taken her there himself. He would sort things out. She whispered to no one, 'He'll have to, won't he?'

Nev was Babs' fiancé. Of course it wasn't official; Nev didn't do 'official'. He didn't buy engagement rings or hold celebration parties; that wasn't his style. He went his own way and lived by nobody's rules but his own. That was one of the things she loved about him. But it was 'understood' that they were engaged. When she stopped outside jewellers and gave lingering glances to the array of silver and gold rings, Nev would squeeze her arm and say, 'No need to rush things, baby. We're happy as we are. All in good time. Everything comes to him who stands and waits.'

So she'd waited. And waited. And waited.

When Rosie Wilson clocked old Ma Jackson coming down her street, wearing her trademark black hairnet, she speedily got off her knees to get into her house before the meddling old crone collared her and wasted her time spreading malicious natter. The big slob of a woman was legendary for sticking her snout – misshapen and red from years of stout and gin – into any and everything that wasn't her business.

Rosie had been cleaning her front steps. She got down on her hands and knees every week to scrub them with water, a capful of vinegar, some Vim, Sunlight Soap and her faithful wooden scrubbing brush. The Wilsons were a respectable family, unlike some who lived in the streets behind the Royal

London Hospital in Whitechapel. That's why she didn't care for back-fence talk. Besides, most of Dirty Laundry Jackson's gossip was made up anyway.

But the old dear was too quick for her. As Rosie reached for her door, Jackson caught her on the doorstep.

'Hello, Rosie, luv. Long time no speak. How's the family? Everything alright?' Then she added with a snide smirk, 'How's your girl Babs getting on? Everything OK?'

Rosie looked in the old woman's spiteful watery eyes. Jackson had a manner like a door-to-door salesman. She was that annoying. Rosie cut her short. 'We're very well, thank you, and Babs is fine. Now if you'll excuse me . . .'

But Jackson wasn't to be fobbed off so easily. She was an expert at this game. 'Oh, that's good, that's very good. So Babs is alright then, is she?'

Rosie pursed her lips, annoyed as hell that this woman wouldn't take her loathsome business elsewhere. 'Yes, Babs is fine. I just told you.' She pushed the door open.

Jackson moved in for the kill. 'Are you sure? You know me, dear, I don't like to spread gossip . . .'

Rosie interrupted with leaden sarcasm, 'No, I know you don't.'

'. . . But I was down Doctor McDaid's this morning and your Babs was there having a right old barney. He was in a fair state. Thought he was going to burst a blood vessel for sure. Effing at Babs, he was, while your girl was giving it back to him like a proper fishwife. He was calling her all sorts of vile names that I wouldn't like to repeat – then Babs marches out of the surgery giving him the old Harvey Smith.'

Rosie rolled her eyes dramatically. She couldn't imagine her darling Babs sticking two fingers up at anyone, like that show jumper Harvey Smith had done the year before.

But Ma Jackson cracked on. 'I've never seen the like in my life. So I thought to myself, there's something not quite kosher here; I mean, old man McDaid is always as quiet as a mouse and your Babs is such a nice girl . . . usually.'

Rosie kept it zipped. The mud that this poisonous old toad liked to sling around was always embroidered. Sometimes, there was a root of God's honest truth in there somewhere, but Rosie found this particular bollocks story impossible to believe on any level.

Fortunately, they were interrupted by the appearance of a stunning young woman dressed in flared slacks, a cheesecloth blouse and platform heels.

'Hello, Mrs Wilson, is Babs in?'

'Hello, Denny luv – no, she's out I'm afraid.' Denise Brooks was her Babs' best mate and Rosie liked her. She was a sweet girl, unlike many of the young ones around there who were growing into loud-mouthed replicas of their parents. The only problem with Denny was the unfortunate 'lights on but no one at home' expression she usually wore.

Rosie could see that Ma Jackson was eagerly hoping that this new arrival could shed some light on the incident at the doctor's. She was disappointed when Denny looked surprised and said, 'Oh? That's a shame; she said she'd be in. I thought we were going to the pictures later to see that *Steptoe and Son* film. Can you tell her I called?'

Rosie nodded. Denny turned, sadness clouding her face as it often did lately, and walked back in the direction she'd come.

Ma Jackson put the needle back on her stuck record. 'So, Babs is alright? You know me, if there's a problem and I can help in any way . . .'

Rosie stepped inside her house. 'I think you must have got the wrong end of the stick. Now, if you'll excuse me.'

'Of course, dear.'

Rosie closed the front door behind her. Her husband George was in his armchair in the sitting room, reading the *Evening News*.

He looked up at her. 'The miners are going on strike. Says here that Ted Heath and his lot are gonna have a state of emergency. They're talking about cutting the electric. We'll have to stock up on candles—'

'Stuff the Prime Minister.' With a mixture of alarm and anger, she asked, 'Have you seen Babs today? Did she say she was going down Doctor McDaid's?'

'No, I haven't.' Now George appeared concerned. 'What's she going down the quacks for anyway? She's not ill, is she?'

'That's what I'd like to know.'

Rosie walked around the house and pretended to do a few things before marching back into the sitting room and shouting, 'Where the hell is Babs, anyway?'

TWO

Even before she pushed open the door of the Bad Moon gut instinct told Babs her fella wasn't there. 'I'd Like to Teach the World to Sing' played around the few punters, while the stocky barman and the busty, hard-faced landlady wiped down surfaces. As soon as she reached the bar, the landlady stopped polishing and asked, 'What can I get you, pet?' But she didn't seem very pleased with her new customer. Babs knew the Bad Moon was a bloke's pub. That was why Nev always took her somewhere else.

'Has Nev been in today?' Babs knew her voice sounded desperate, but she couldn't hold her emotions back.

'Nev? Don't know any Nevs.'

'Yeah, you know – Neville.'

'Oh, him.' The landlady looked at her with sympathy. Babs' stomach rolled – this woman had already guessed what the deal was, the way landladies do. 'I haven't seen him around for a while.'

Babs' desperation grew as the other woman got back on with the cleaning. While there had been some hope, she'd kept things under control, but this was her first port of call and already hope was draining away.

'What do you mean, you haven't seen him?'

The landlady looked back up, her eyes as tough as stone.

'What I say – I ain't seen him. It's not a very complicated sentence, is it?'

Babs clenched her fists. 'You're a liar. He's always in here. I know.'

The landlady put her dishcloth down and placed her palms on the bar. Her fingers twitched ever so slightly, showcasing knuckles that said she knew a thing or two about the hard knocks of life. 'Look, I'm not taking any lip from a slip of a girl. He's not here and we haven't seen him for a while. Now – do you want to order a drink or what? Otherwise I have to ask you to leave.'

Babs looked around at the patrons nervously. They were staring at her in the same way as Doctor McDaid's patients earlier.

She left.

So she never saw the barman shift up and ask, 'Who was that?'

'Some dopey bird looking for Neville,' the landlady answered, pulling out a Virginia Slim and lighting up.

And Babs never saw the barman burst into laughter. 'Silly bitch. Her and half the other scrubbers in the East End.'

Once she hit Commercial Road again, Babs caught a bus to Limehouse. When she'd met Nev, he'd had a pad there. In fact, it was there they'd first had sex, later the same night. She'd gone up the Reno nightclub in Stoke Newington with her mate Denny; they'd heard it had a classier clientele than the usual wide boys, spivs and pretend bank robbers they met on a night out in the East End. At first it seemed that wasn't true, but that was before she met Nev. He hadn't been that interested but when she turned him down for a dance, he suddenly became very attentive indeed. Nev wasn't the kind of bloke who took refusals lightly. He spent the rest of the night pursuing her, chatting her up. Once he had his big strong arms wrapped around her for a slow dance in the small hours, she didn't remember making any more decisions. She'd followed him in a dreamlike state to a cab, then to his flat and then to his bedroom.

Babs had had other guys of course, but Nev was different. He was tall, he was strong and he was cool. He didn't show off or play act because he didn't need to. The hard boys in the Reno all got out of the way for him. The manager and the bouncers all knew him by name. She knew no geezer was going to lean out of a car window and shout 'Oi darlin', show us your tits!' while Nev was around. Not if they wanted to keep a matching pair of ears. He was so polite. And as Babs knew, guys like that were at a premium down her neck of the woods. She wasn't going to let him go without a fight.

So the morning after the Reno, after she'd waited patiently for him to arrange to see her again, she got angry when she was finally forced to ask, 'Are we going out together then, or what?' – and he didn't seem to understand the question. She got even angrier when he said nothing in reply. She'd shouted, 'I'm not a fucking tart Neville,' so loudly the neighbours must have heard.

He'd gifted her with his one-hundred-watt smile. 'Yeah – sure we're going out.'

Afterwards, she apologised for getting on his wick. It was obvious later he was just upset that she'd even asked the question in the first place. And that was the first excuse she'd made for her new boyfriend.

As Babs looked out of the bus window at the estate in Limehouse, she realised in the pit of her guts that she'd been making excuses for him ever since.

She'd never seen the estate in the light of day before. It was one of those old-style Thirties estates, already on its last legs, dirty and dingy. She walked up to the fourth floor. At first Nev had claimed it was his flat but later he'd admitted that he was looking after it for a friend who was on remand for something that he totally and absolutely hadn't done. Of course, she'd believed him. She knew Nev wasn't at the flat any more but kept her fingers crossed that he might have left a forwarding address.

Whoever was occupying the flat now had a poster in the kitchen window that said, 'Demand The Impossible!' She guessed they might be squatters. The same poster had been in the window of a squat on the street where she lived with her mum and dad. That was before the rozzers had come round and dragged the squatters out by their long, greasy hair, given them a good kicking and chucked them in the back of a Black Maria.

The lock on Nev's old flat had been kicked off. It was a squat alright.

Babs tapped on the door. It was opened slightly by a young man with long straggly blond hair that was nearly down past his nipples. He wore flared jeans and a Che Guevara T-shirt.

'Wha'cha want?'

'I'm Neville's fiancée. He used to live here. Have you got a forwarding address?' Babs realised how stupid she sounded, standing at the door to this flat, on this estate, asking for her 'fiancé'.

'Never heard of him . . .' The door slammed shut. But a few moments later it opened again, more widely this time. 'Neville, you say? Wait there a minute.' The freak disappeared again before returning with a handful of mail. He passed it to Babs without a word and the door shut again.

As she slowly made her way downstairs like a mourner at a funeral, she looked at the envelopes, each addressed to Neville but with various surnames. There were final demands, summonses and threatening letters about unpaid loans and overdrafts. Nev had always told her he was 'in business'. That he had various 'irons in the fire'. That he was looking at 'investment options'. Now it was clear why he was so well dressed and could afford such expensive gear. He wasn't actually paying for anything but living on the never-never.

Then there were the postcards. She'd cried no tears since her visit to Doctor McDaid hours earlier. Now they erupted again: acid ones that stung her face.

Hi Nev! Found a great spot for some nudy sunbathing! Can't wait to get back and show you my new all-over tan. And I mean all-over! Loads of love! Tania!!!

Another one from Petra in West Berlin.

Baby! Course finish next week. I'm in London from Monday. I call. Petra XXXXXXXXXXXXXXXXXXXXXXXX XXXXXXXXXXXXXXX ps but please don't call me Nazi any more, yes?

Babs checked the postmarks on the cards. They'd both been written after she'd met her guy at the Reno club.

All those nights the little bastard was 'busy' or doing 'business'. Or he was 'seeing his family'. Of course he'd never asked her to meet them. It seemed that Nev had taken the same view as Doctor McDaid all along – she was a whore. What a fucking proper moron she'd been. And worse, what a fucking moron he must have thought she was.

When she got down to the courtyard below, Babs scattered the envelopes and letters in the gutter. But she took the postcards, tore them into tiny pieces, spat on them and threw them on the ground, before grinding them with her heel in fury.

She was done weeping and wailing. Her back straightened and steel set in her spine. She raised her head, more determined to find Nev than ever. She was Barbara Wilson. And no one was going to make a divvy out of her.

As she walked on, she remembered something. One evening when she'd been in the flat upstairs, there was a knock at the door. After a brief chat on the doorstep, Nev had said he was popping out for ten minutes to discuss business with his visitor. While he was out, the phone in the flat had rung. She was absolutely forbidden to pick up Nev's phone and was sometimes ordered out of the room when he answered it. But as he wasn't there, she'd picked it up. The voice was smooth and Cockney. 'Alright, darlin'? Can you pop Neville on the blower?'

'He's just stepped out.'

'No problem. Can you ask him to call the Go Go Girls Modelling Agency in Soho? We've got some work for him. He's got the number, but I'll give it to you anyway.'

Babs had got a bit excited because Nev had mentioned that he did a spot of photography for a modelling agency. 'OK. Can I tell him who called?'

The man seemed amused. 'Me? I'm the proprietor, luv. My name's Stanley Miller.'

Three

Twenty-two-year-old Cleo Clark closed her Bible, shut her eyes, took a deep breath and enjoyed her little moment of peace in the house in Mile End. Cleo was a cross between Diana Ross and her namesake Cleopatra – black, beautiful and a diva, if she needed to be. She let the hard realities of her life slip away as her soul was bathed in a world of angels singing and soft golden light. A world of beauty, gentleness and truth. But her precious moment was interrupted by a man downstairs bellowing, 'Come on then! Come on then! I'll take you all on.'

With a groan, she opened her eyes and was back in the real world, which didn't include beauty, gentleness and truth at all.

'Not again, Pete,' she moaned, as the shouting got worse. 'Why can't you behave like a paid-up member of the human race for once in your miserable life?'

There was a sharp tap at the door. 'Oi. Are you in there, Cleo? Come on, sweetheart, I've got a job for you to do. This ain't a doss house.'

Cleo knew what this particular job would involve. When she wasn't having sex for money in the knocking shop her other job was 'taking care of Pete'. And taking care of Pete was pretty much a full-time job on its own.

She looked around her grotty room, in the grotty

Georgian three-storey house where grotty people lived. Although those people were far better than the grotty Herberts who paid cash up front for her to take them squealing to heaven and back. She sighed, kissed her Bible and put it back in her bedside drawer. She turned the key and then put it in the locket she always wore, even when she was on her back working.

There were many light fingers in the brothel but Lord help anyone trying to nab her Good Book. She'd rip their mitts clean off. It had been a christening gift and whatever else she'd won and lost over the years, the book had stayed with her. The pastor at her mum's church had explained, 'Read a little every day, it will help you on your way!'

And Cleo needed all the help she could get.

The hammering started up again. 'Open the bloody door. Our friend Pete is really creating down there.'

'Keep your drawers on, I'm coming.'

Cleo stood up, popped her bouncy caramel afro wig on and smoothed down the tight blood-red latex dress. The top half of the dress was a lace-up corset, and the back had two holes so that her bum cheeks stuck out. She despised the dress. It made her hot and sweaty and squeezed her like a clenched fist. But it got the geezers who came through the door frothing at the chops, so she didn't have any choice but to wear it. With a tired sigh, she ran her fingers through the wig and finally opened the door.

Dorothy Sure, called Daffy by one and all, stood outside, leaning on her black walking cane. She was small and dainty with a dyed flame-red Twenties bob and a few lines on her face that made most people mark her as around thirty. It was the sharp lines that popped around her lips when she was pissed off that showed her age. Cleo didn't know what that age was, and Daffy wasn't the type of woman to tell. But the walking stick she used to support her right leg said more about the rough life she'd once lived than her telling the tale.

'You ain't shooting up in there, are ya?' Daffy asked, her eyes squinting in warning. She ran the place with an iron fist and had a thing about her girls getting strung out.

Miffed at the question, Cleo kissed her teeth and stuck her fists on her hips. 'You know I'm a clean living girl ...' She scowled as she looked around. 'Apart from this joint, obviously.'

'I know you are and that's why I need you now. We've got a problem.'

'I've got a pair of ears; I can hear the silly sod from here.'

As if on cue, banging and crashing sounded on the floor below. It was always the same with Pete, he moved from verbals and threats to slogging it out pretty swiftly.

'He's on the sauce again and causing havoc.'

Cleo looked at her watch. 'It's only three in the afternoon. How can he be smashed outta his skull already?'

Daffy put her arm around Cleo's shoulders and began to lead her towards the staircase. 'When it comes to the booze, his mouth has the same slogan as the old Windmill Theatre in the West End – *we never close*.'

Cleo dug her heels in. She was tired of this carry on. 'No – why should I do it? You're in charge, why don't you tell him to put the top on the bottle and go sleep it off. Or – this might sound a little crazy but stick with me – why don't you get the guys to chuck him out and tell him to sod off for good?'

The place had a few hard boys on the door so the punters got the message to behave loud and clear. Or else ...

Daffy lowered her voice. 'You *know* why we have to keep Pete sweet. Without him there wouldn't be any of the *specials*.'

Cleo sighed heavily at the reminder of her, Daffy and Pete's other business, which none of the other girls had a clue about. A very murky business indeed, but one she needed if she was ever going to get out of this shithole. Daffy hadn't originally been part of it, but when she'd caught them one night she'd demanded a cut of the money to look the other way.

Daffy continued, 'Plus he won't listen to me; he won't listen to anyone except you.' She ran her hand persuasively down Cleo's arm and lowered her voice. 'Come on, luv, go and use some soap on him and tell him to pack it in. Shag his brains out if you have to, just stop the bastard tearing the place apart and scaring off the trade.'

Cleo stood her ground. 'No. I'm a tart, not anyone's mum.'

Daffy reached into her pocket, took out a couple of nicker and stuffed the notes down the cleavage of Cleo's rubber. 'Come on babe – help me out.'

Cleo patted the notes and hissed, 'OK, but you've got to put the kybosh on this once and for all. It has to S-T-O-P. One of these days he's going to do someone or himself a mischief and fuck up our business arrangement. Maybe you should have a little word with the owners to straighten him out.'

Cleo still wasn't sure who the owners of the knocking shop were, despite working there for two years.

Daffy looked away. 'If I knew who the owners were, I would.'

Cleo didn't believe a word of it. Daffy wasn't the sort of woman who ran an outfit like this without having the full S.P. on the money men behind it.

Downstairs, Cleo walked into a reception room that had been converted into a bar; a place for the punters to meet the girls and get their motors running before going upstairs. The room had once been in the neighbouring house but it had been knocked through to create one big sex-for-sale establishment.

Sure enough, good ol' Pete was going into one, spit and fists flying. Without the drink in him he was a good-looking fella, all blond hair and blue eyes, but once the booze hit he was a dead ringer for an orangutan being denied his dinner. The two heavies from the door were trying to stop him attacking two terrified punters, trapped in a corner of the room. The barman behind the makeshift bar had his arms around bottles and glasses to protect them from Pete's wild fists.

As soon as Cleo appeared, one of the bouncers desperately mouthed, 'take care of the fucker.' Normally they wouldn't hesitate to dole out a proper kicking to any out of order geezer before heaving them down the stone steps outside. But they were under orders to take it easy with him. Orders from whom, Cleo didn't know.

Pete had started as the manager about a year ago, but Cleo knew it was all a front. The real reason was to get the specials racket started. But Pete's love affair with the bottle was starting to put a crimp on everything. He'd turn up at all hours getting into it with the girls, the customers, the staff and the bouncers. Then he'd end up bladdered in someone's bed, on a chair or on the floor. Every now and then a bloke called Mickey – who Cleo suspected was the brains behind the specials – would come down to check on the premises and Daffy would raise the 'Pete problem' with him. But Mickey's only response was to help himself to a bunch of banknotes from the cash box and say, 'Pete? Don't worry about him, he's a pussycat, he just likes a wet once in a while, don't he. Who doesn't?'

It was hard to work out what would set Pete off. But there was always something.

He staggered forward, shouting the odds at the scared customers. 'I'm not having a couple of benders coming in here, as easy as you like, and running their mouth about my girls. I've got fucking standards, ain't I? Now square up, boys, and let's take it outside. I'll show you how we deal with wankers like you in the East End.'

The bouncers bunched in front of him to stop him in his tracks. Pete turned on them instead. 'What's the matter? Do you want some too? I could take on two plastic hard men like you any day of the week, no fucking problem; now get out of my fucking way.' Pete threw a punch in their general direction. He had strong arms and big fists but his swing had no power and he was caught firmly by the wrist before he could do any damage. They secured his other arm and told him, 'Cool it, OK? Calm down.'

Pete looked like he was about to burst a blood vessel. 'I'll give you fucking calm down, you pair of penguins.' He began to struggle but he was massively out-powered.

After a moment, he hung his head in shame. 'Sorry. I'm out of order. Let me go, eh? No hard feelings.'

But when they did, he went off like a firework, launching himself at the men cowering in the corner. 'Come on, then! How do you like it now, eh?'

He aimed a big punch towards the nearest man, but he was too pissed, and the two men scarpered towards the door. Pete yelped with pain as his fist hit the wall and he reeled backwards. When he realised his quarry was gone, he went bananas, tearing the room apart. Cleo and everyone else took cover. A leather sofa was overturned. One arm sent bottles flying and the other scattered glasses. He grabbed a chair and crashed it against the wall.

Powerless, the bouncers looked on, before one turned to Cleo. 'Well?'

She tutted before hurrying over, doing that wiggle-jiggle walk that Pete loved so much. 'Petey! My precious Petey! Baby-baby! What's the matter?'

His face lit up like a little kid when he saw her and he

instantly dropped the chair. 'There you are. Where you been? Look at this mess. Why is it me who's always left to sort things out? Why can't anyone else cope? You tell me that, eh?'

The harder he found it to cope, the more Pete whined about others coping. She put her arm around his waist. 'What's happened? Tell your little Cleo all about it.'

All the rage drained out of him. 'I'll tell you what's what. Two blokes come in here causing trouble and those two over there don't wanna know, so it's left to muggins here to sort it out.' He yelled at the bouncers, 'Thanks for your help, boys. If you've ever got a problem in future, don't call me, I'm not interested.'

It was clear the patience of the men was nearly exhausted. Cleo jerked her thumb to suggest they leave. She turned back and carried on schmoozing the dumb idiot. 'I know, baby, but there's no need for you to take things on. Look, park yourself down and I'll get you a snifter.' She gave him a saucy wink. 'One of Cleo's specials.'

But there was nowhere to sit down and the drinks were a wet mess on the carpet. Cleo upended the sofa and drew him down on it. When she sat next to him, he leaned his head heavily on her shoulder, blowing whisky fumes all over her. 'Why don't you tell your baby exactly what happened?'

Then Cleo switched off while Pete prattled on non-fucking-stop. When he finally stopped for air she jumped in with a whispered, 'I can't believe our two guys left you in the lurch like that.'

Tears appeared in his eyes. Tears meant her job as his sob sister was nearly over. Cleo's heart lurched. She hated seeing him crying. When he wasn't smashed out of his nut, Pete was such a bang-up bloke. He wailed, 'You're the only one who understands me.'

Cleo nodded with true sympathy, but she also wanted to

wallop him a good one to knock some sense into him. Instead, she got up and began looking for a bottle that wasn't broken. When she found one, she half escorted, half carried her charge to the stairs, doing the wiggle-jiggle all the way. She threw Daffy a squinty-eyed meaningful glance as she went.

In her room, she flopped Pete down on the bed and patiently spoon-fed him Scotch like a baby. She made clucking-caring noises at the halfwit babble spewing from his gob. It took a good half hour and a good half bottle before the witless twat finally passed out.

When she heard him grunting and snoring, Cleo shook her head sadly. 'You tosspot.' She caressed his cheek affectionately and smoothed his tousled hair away from his eyes. 'What am I going to do with you?'

Cleo so desperately wanted out of this life, but she needed readies for that and this place paid a pittance after she coughed up for her keep. She really should've listened to her mum years back when she'd told her point blank that the guy she was with was no good. 'No good' hardly did justice to the battering she'd taken from him once he'd started pimping her arse out to his mates. Cleo had managed to flee literally with the clothes on her back. She'd been too ashamed to go back home. Besides, her mum had already cursed her out as a Jezebel fit only to dwell with Satan, so what else could she do but go on the game?

But she didn't have to do it for the rest of her life, did she? What she needed was money. And fast. That's why she had to keep Pete nice and happy – because of the specials that brought in extra cash. And if she was truthful she had a soft spot for him.

Cleo went downstairs again, but hid when she saw Mickey had turned up. He was deep in it with a ranting Daffy, shouting as she put him straight, thumping her cane against the wooden floor. 'You need to do something about that clown Pete and you need to do it fast. We get influential guests in here and if he shows 'em up or takes a swing, you lot are going to find yourselves in very deep water indeed.'

Four

Caffs, snooker halls, clubs . . . Babs had been to the lot, with no sign of Nev. Worse still, she was palmed off with variations on the same story.

'Never heard of him.'

'Haven't seen him around for a while.'

'Neville? I heard he moved in with the blonde up Westbourne Grove.'

'Neville? I heard he moved in with the brunette down the Elephant.'

Babs was properly pissed off and her feet were screaming bloody murder by the time she only had one more place to check out – the Go Go Girls Modelling Agency run by this Stanley Miller fella. It was up West, in Soho, a place she'd never been. Her dad had once warned her, with a shiver, that that part of London was full of aggro; a cesspit infested with pimps, tarts and foreign criminals. Babs suspected it was a fool's errand anyway; the slippery Neville would probably have cut out of there as well. In fact, given how much time he seemed to be spending on his various birds, it was amazing the two-timing berk had the energy to work at all.

Despite feeling washed out, she took the tube to Piccadilly Circus and started towards Soho. *You prat*, she thought as she froze in her tracks, *you ain't got a clue where you're going.* So she hailed a black cab and asked the driver to take her to the Go Go Girls Modelling Agency.

The cabbie burst out laughing. 'Modelling agency? Everywhere's a modelling agency round here – if you know what I mean?' But when he clocked the grim look on Babs' pale face, he turned serious. 'Alright, let me see what I can do.'

When he saw a cab coming the other way, he tooted his horn and leaned out of his window to talk to the other driver. 'Do you know the Go Go Girls Agency, mate?'

After a brief chat, he turned back to Babs. 'It's on Chancery Row.' He frowned hard at her. 'Are you sure you wanna go there, sweetheart? You seem like a nice, respectable girl to me.'

Babs read between the lines of what he wasn't saying – Chancery Row was not nice *or* respectable. She swallowed and then nodded before she lost her nerve. 'Yes, I do.'

He turned back around. 'None of my business, of course.'

As they drove, the streets of the West End turned from theatreland and cinemas to sleazy places advertising non-stop striptease, massages, saunas and dirty mags. It made Babs feel uncomfortable, but a thrill of excitement went through her all the same. This was a naughty world where good girls like her shouldn't be.

When they reached Chancery Row, a seedy street in the back end of Soho, the driver refused to take her money, just told her to take care, like she was his own daughter.

Babs shook in the daytime chill as she walked up and down. There was no sign of any modelling agency. But there were other things creeping her out – sex bookshops, 'private' cinemas and tatty cards with women's names handwritten on them sellotaped next to doorbells. And rubbish, piled up in doorways. In despair, Babs came to a halt outside an empty building and stood motionless, unsure what to do next. Then a heavy door swung open and a middle-aged woman appeared, caked to her hairline in make-up and wearing an outfit that Babs considered the fashion equivalent of a dirty mag.

'Sorry, luv, you can't tout your business there – that's Sasha's patch.'

It took a few moments before the penny dropped. The nerve of the woman! 'I'm not a ... err ...' Babs stopped faffing around and got on with it. 'I'm looking for someone.'

The woman sashayed onto the street. 'Looking for someone? You ain't the filth, are ya?' Then she looked Babs up and down, laughed and answered her own question. 'No, of course you're not. Who do you want?'

'Stanley Miller at the Go Go Girls Modelling Agency.'

The woman gave her an arch look and then pointed a cherry-red fingernail down the road. 'See that barbers? It's the black door next to that. Give it a knock, but don't necessarily expect an answer.'

Babs trudged down the street to the black door. Her luck was in; it was wedged open with a brick. Behind was a flight of wooden stairs leading up to a landing. Babs walked up the stairs like a condemned prisoner mounting the gallows and found a door with the agency's name pinned on it. She turned the handle and entered an office. It was empty except for a desk with a black telephone and a transistor radio on it. Behind that, a woman sat filing her nails and humming along to David Bowie's 'Life On Mars'. She seemed to have been pickled in the Sixties, sporting a beehive, Biba knock-off blouse, mini skirt and a pair of white vinyl go-go boots.

'What the hell do you want?' she asked roughly, flapping her huge false eyelashes.

'I'm looking for Neville.'

Babs knew what she was going to say before she said it. 'Never heard of him.'

She changed tack. 'Stanley Miller?'

'Ain't heard of him either – how the hell did you get in anyway?'

'The door downstairs was wedged open.'

The woman looked upwards with an accusing glare. 'It's about time I had words with that lot on the second floor.' Then she turned back to Babs. 'Well, ta-ra and sorry I can't help. Shut the door on your way out, there's a good girl.'

It was the end of the line. Babs wasn't taking this shit from people any more; there was only so many brush-offs a girl could have. She'd gone from pillar to post to find Nev and brainless Beehive wasn't going to fob her off. 'I'm not going nowhere until I see Stanley Miller.'

Hatchet-face stood up, fixing a menacing stare on her unwanted visitor. 'Alright, little girl, you've had your bit of fun, now sod off. Or would you like me to have you thrown downstairs?'

She looked like she meant it but Babs didn't care. 'I want to see Stanley Miller.'

Clearly pissed off, Beehive marched around the desk and grabbed her by the scruff of the neck, dragging her across the floor.

All the day's anger, fear and despair exploded in Babs' fist as she took a swing at her attacker and caught her one on the cheek so hard it sent the woman flying. She landed on her back, legs all over the place and beehive wobbling to the side. Shocked, she looked up, touching her bruised face with her fingers. Then she clenched her fists and growled, 'Oh? Like a ruck, do you? I'll give you a ruck, sweetheart ...' Then she flew at Babs, getting her hands round her throat, shaking her like a rag doll.

'What's all this, then?' a man's voice boomed.

Babs only saw who it was when the mad bitch loosened her hands and her vision came back into focus. Her breath caught in her throat. Gordon Bennett, this geezer was a right sort. Tall, decked out in an immaculate three-piece navy blue suit, a silk hanky in his pocket and handmade leather shoes. He smelt of Brut, her favourite aftershave, and sported a carefully Brylcreemed feather haircut. He could have been a Hollywood star.

Beehive told him, 'Don't look at me like that, Stan. This bitch came in here looking for trouble, so I gave her some. She asked for it, believe me.'

So this was Stanley Miller. Now she'd clocked him, no way in hell was she going anywhere until she got some answers.

He ignored the other woman, giving Babs his full attention. 'What's the problem, darlin'?'

Weariness caught up with Babs. She crumpled on the floor blubbing her heart out. Through her tears, she was impressed that Stanley Miller got on the case straight away, ordering the other woman to get a glass of water. Then, with a gentle touch, he helped her to her feet and took her into his office.

Babs' mouth fell open. The room was a proper knockout. A beige chair with dips and curves like a woman's body sat behind a gleaming mahogany desk. There was a leopard-print sofa, a pink and purple lava lamp, a globe minibar with drinks and glasses inside. Babs had never seen anything like it in her life. It was glamorous with a capital G.

Stan sat her down on the sofa and then poured her a glass of brandy from a crystal decanter. He parked himself next to her and asked her name. 'Alright, Babs, don't upset yourself. What's the problem? How can I help?'

'I'm looking for Neville. He said he worked here sometimes.'

Stan looked blank, leaning back slightly. 'Neville? I don't know no Neville.' Babs got deflated all over again. But she brightened up as Stan tapped his fingers to his forehead.

'Oh ... Neville. That Neville. Yeah, I'm afraid he don't work here no more.'

'But he told me he was a photographer.'

Stan shook his head, but grinned. Flippin' hell, what a killer smile. 'A photographer? Neville's been called a lot of things but I've never heard him called one of them before. I had to give him the push. He was a bit unreliable. What do you ...?'

His eyes drifted to her belly and only then did she realise that her hand was laid protectively over it.

Stan lost the killer smile. 'Put you in the club, has he?' Babs started crying again. Stan hugged her like a father. 'Look, there's a lovely place around the corner. Why don't you let me buy you some nosh and then I'll get you a cab home?'

Babs stuttered, 'Alright.'

'Hold up a minute,' Stan said. From the knowing expression on his face, Babs knew he'd put two and two together. 'Neville's a coloured boy – does that mean you're carrying a coloured baby?'

Babs stopped crying for a moment and looked down. That's why she was in Big Trouble twice over – she was up the duff and the daddy was black.

Stan clasped his hands together. 'My word. You are in a pickle, aren't you?'

Five

Melanie Ingram sat on the bonnet of the Jag, resting her arms on the bodywork so she could lean back like a model, turning her face towards the watery sun. She was wearing the beloved knee-length mink coat she took every opportunity to flash around town in, even when the weather wasn't right. The car was right and the coat was right. It was only the road that was wrong. A shabby street in Mile End wasn't the right spot for a classy bird like her. At least, that's what Mel told herself. She belonged in the south of France – not parked up by a row of knackered terraced houses boarded up with corrugated iron. She dreamed of a world where blokes wore navy blazers, peaked caps and drank dry martinis with those green things in – not one where van drivers slowed down, looked at her tits and shouted, 'You don't get many of them to the pound!'

A man came round the corner and stopped in horror. 'Oi – what are you doing sitting on my jam jar? This ain't the fucking motor show.'

Mel turned her head and peered over her psychedelic sunglasses at Mickey. That was another thing. She had the wrong husband as well. They'd both grown up in Bethnal Green, in houses too packed to have enough space for themselves, so they'd had to make their names on the street. She'd been nifty with her fingers as a young 'un, lifting stuff from pockets, shops and residences as well. But what she'd loved most of all was the rush she got from doing the old five-finger discount in jewellers. All that glitter and sparkle got her heart going just thinking about it. Mind you she'd almost come a cropper that time she'd palmed a ring belonging to a South London Face's missus, which was in the jewellers being mended.

That was how she'd met Mickey properly. Despite them bunking off the same school she'd only really seen him around, never been given a proper intro. People had told her to see Charlie Dalton if she wanted to get the Face off her back, so she had. He'd done the business on her behalf and she'd started seeing him between the sheets. But she'd also taken a shine to his mate Mickey. She was soon seeing Mickey on the side as well, until Charlie caught them bang to rights – banging. She really should've stuck with Charlie, or John Black as he'd started calling himself: she'd heard he was going places. Upmarket, dodgy places. Ah well, a girl could dream . . .

'You took your effing time,' she griped at Mickey, chucking him a dirty look.

They got into the Jag and he drove away at speed; he didn't like people seeing him near the knocking shop. When she repeated her complaint, he looked unhappy. 'Yeah, well, I had a problem to sort out, didn't I?'

Her tone turned bitter. 'Let me guess – has the gas been cut off? Are the neighbours playing music too loud? Am I getting warm?'

Mickey ground the gears. 'Don't take the rise luv, it don't suit you.'

In fact, it suited her all too well. 'I can't think what else it can be . . .' She stuck her finger in her mouth and stared into space like she was having a good old think.

'Ummm, let me have another guess . . .' She brightened. 'Oh,

I know! Has Pete been on the sauce again? Is he going round taking a swing at the punters and the Toms before falling over in a puddle of his own piss again?'

Mickey growled, but kept his eyes on the road. 'Pete just likes a few wets. He's alright.'

Mel fished in her handbag for some lippy. 'Alright? He's gonna kill someone one day – you know that, don't you? And who's gonna be left to clear up the mess? Mickey Muggins, that's who. You've got to tell his brother the drunk's got to go. If you don't, I will.'

'I can't do that. He sticks up for Pete. He's about the only person in the world he looks out for. He won't do it.'

'Oh, give over, the slimy little weasel doesn't care about anyone.'

Mickey shook his head and sighed. 'Nah, it's different with Pete, it's a family thing.' He looked in the rear view mirror as if worried that someone might be listening. 'They're a funny family. The mother is a nutter and their old man was a drunk who used to slap them around all the time. Pete used to stick up for him. When he was old enough, he knocked their twisted old man out and the kickings stopped. He owes Pete. That's how it is. To be honest, it's about the only human thing in him.' He glanced in the rear view mirror again before adding, 'Don't tell him I told you that. He's very sensitive about it.'

Mel sneered back. 'My heart is breaking. It doesn't help us, though, does it? Why doesn't he get Pete a job as a traffic warden? He knows people on the council.'

'Don't worry about it. There's a girl called Cleo up there who knows how to handle Pete. She keeps him out of mischief. It's all sweet.'

Mel pulled down the vanity mirror and began touching up her pale-peach lipstick. 'Sweet? The cretin's a menace. Pete's

got to go before he gets us all into some major league bovver.'
She knew Mickey was fed up, but the fact he wasn't doing as
he was told only goaded her more.

'What am I meant to do?' he fumed. 'I've just told you, he
can't boot Pete out of the business. It'd be like me telling you
to sling your hook. Anyhow, he knows he's gotta sort Pete out.
Drag him onto the wagon if he has to.'

Mel huffed, not convinced one bit. 'He won't be sorting
nuthin' and that's typical of the way he treats you – like he's
got you on a lead, yanking you every fucking which way he
wants.' Once Mel got started, she couldn't stop. 'Whose business was it to start with? Who put up the front money? You
did. Then flash moosh comes along and starts chucking out
orders. He's swanning round the West End like Lord Clore
while you're down here with your sleeves rolled up, elbow
deep in all the dirty work.' When Mickey didn't answer, she
snapped, 'Where's your fucking self-respect? Do you even
know what he's up to in that office of his? Probably plotting
to diddle you out of your own business, that's what.'

Mickey's driving became more Jackie Stewart as he upped
his speed, bending under the weight of Mel's handbagging.
She pressed on. She knew why her old man was getting the
nark and why his defence of his partner was becoming so
desperate. Mickey secretly feared that she was right and she
was determined to keep beating him around his nut until he
finally grew a pair and did something about it.

'Please – give it a rest, will ya? I know what I'm doing. He's
got a good brain on him; you know he has. He takes care of
the admin. I'm better at the practical side. It was the same
when me and him were at school. He could do sums, I was
good at woodwork. That's how it is. It works.'

Mel angrily shoved her lipstick back in her macrame purse.
'Oh, he's clever alright, I'll give you that. He's too fucking

clever – that's the problem.' Her voice suddenly screeched, 'Watch the fucking road!'

Mickey pulled on the steering wheel, only just avoiding a lorry coming the other way. He slammed on his brakes and pulled over, shoving his finger in Mel's sour face. 'Pack it in! I've had it up to here with your moaning and nagging. Leave me to look after my business – you get on with preening yourself like a good wife should. I know my mate. We go way back, a lot further than you and me, and don't you fucking forget it.'

Mel almost went for him again but if she overdid it he might twig she was trying to jerk him around like a puppet.

Instead she turned her voice all delicate and gently stroked his arm. 'Right you are. You'll speak to him about Pete?'

'Yeah, I'll speak to him, OK?'

She said nothing and he got the motor on the move again. She meant to keep it shut but was unable to resist softly twisting the knife. 'You know what he's up to, don't you? Have you noticed how he never takes no interest in what you do? Bet he doesn't chat to Pete about the knocking shop either. Your mate's keeping his back turned on your side of the business for a reason. You mark my words, one day the Old Bill's gonna kick in the door and he's going to pretend it was sod all to do with him.'

Mickey kept it schtum. He wasn't arguing. Mel barely managed to keep her glee at bay. She'd nearly convinced the dopey sod that she was right. Months of hard work were paying off. It was just like chopping down a tree. Lots of hacking away and then one final blow and, Geronimo, over it went. Now all she had to figure out was how to get rid of Mickey's toerag business partner once and for all.

Six

'I never realised I was in the family way,' Babs blurted out, her face bright red, as she stared at Stan over her mouth-watering steak and chips in the Lilac Club. 'Doctor McDaid told me I'm about four months gone already.'

She hadn't realised she had a bun well gone in the oven? Stan was constantly reading that trendy long-haired teachers were scrapping old-fashioned education and encouraging teenagers to get their leg over with anything that moved – and this kid didn't realise she was expecting? And fancy being taken in by an obvious smoothie like Neville.

'I weren't on the pill but I borrowed some from a friend because old man McDaid won't dish 'em out unless you're married. Perhaps they didn't work . . .'

Stan nodded with sympathy. He'd known a girl who'd bled to death during a botched backstreet abortion because her quack wouldn't give her the pills women's libbers insisted all birds had the right to have.

'And then when I asked McDaid if it was too late to get rid of it . . .' Babs burst into tears again. That was all he needed, everyone thinking he'd made her turn the waterworks on. He had a rep around here as a man who got on with folk, especially the ladies. Stan quickly checked out the other diners, but they were too busy stuffing their faces. He took out his silk hanky and passed it to her. 'Here you go, don't upset yourself.'

'He called me a murderer!'

Stan nodded sagely. 'Catholic, is he? That's probably why; they're like that. It's all sin and sackcloth to them. Put it out of your mind, sweetheart.'

When she'd finished her story, she looked at him as if he were a wise old man who could solve her problems with a few words. In fact, Stan had discovered he wasn't that much older than her. She was nineteen to his twenty-five. But compared to her he really *was* a wise old man, and she was just another chump that the East End spat out like grape pips.

He looked across at her as she waited expectantly to be told what to do. He took out his silver cigarette case and lit up. He offered one to her and her gaze caught his finger. Half of his index finger was gone. He hoped that she didn't ask about it; he wasn't in the mood to tell the story he'd made up to hide the truth.

She kept her mouth zipped, which he appreciated, and took a fag. Her fingers shook as he lit it and she coughed as he considered what to say next.

He leaned across the table. 'Look, Babs-babe – it happens. Girls like you are a dime a dozen. My mum was in the pudding club with my older brother when she was your age. Will your people get the nark? Maybe, maybe not – but they'll get over it. Life goes on. Go down the council and get yourself a flat – they're putting up some lovely new estates in the East End. Your family will fall into line. And then you'll meet some nice fella and he'll take the kid on and everything will be sweet.'

Babs' eyes widened. 'But Neville's coloured – and my mum and dad don't like white people from south of the river, never mind coloureds. When they find out my kid's half-caste, they're gonna go fucking spare. And that's after they've gone mental because I'm expecting.'

Once again, she looked hopefully over at him. He shrugged and decided to tell it to her plain and straight. 'Yeah, they probably will. You can't blame them, can you? I know it's 1972 and we're all brothers under the skin these days and everything, but it's a bit much. If I had a little girl and she got preggers by one of my coloured mates, I wouldn't exactly be throwing a party would I?'

Tears swam in her eyes again. He didn't need her boo-hooing again, but he knew what it felt like to have your back pinned against the wall. He took her hand. The poor kid was shaking like a leaf. He decided to help her out. 'Look – I know a woman who can solve the problem for you . . . She's clean and discreet.'

Babs shook her head. 'I just told you . . .' She looked down protectively at her tummy. 'It's too late now anyway.'

'Get it adopted, then.'

Babs looked back up at him with deeply troubled eyes. 'And what am I supposed to do in the meantime?'

'You've got no choice, girl,' he insisted. 'Go home and spill the beans. Take the grief and work your way through it. I'm a businessman, I know about these things. Sometimes life deals you a duff hand and when you can't walk away from the table, you just have to play it out and take a hit. That's how life is.'

'They'll chuck me out onto the streets. I've got no job; I've got no eff-off money. That's too much of a hit for me.'

Stan was starting to like this girl. Under all that weeping and wailing he sensed guts and determination. And that's when the spark of a plan started lighting up in his head. His dragon of a mum had taught him a number of rules – mostly with the back of her hand – to help him get on in life. One of which was never show kindness to strangers.

'They take advantage of you, son, they take liberties – show anyone your neck and they'll bite it, you mark my words.'

Even as a nipper, Stan had his doubts. If his mum knew the rules of life so well, why were they shacked up with the rats in a tenement in Bethnal Green? Why did she send him out to steal veg from market stalls? Why did he have to rummage through dustbins outside sweatshops to find offcuts of leather to stuff inside his shoes?

As Stanley had discovered, his witch of a mum was arse about face, as usual. Acts of kindness to strangers meant you could take advantage of them, not the other way around. It meant they owed you. And anyway, he was a nice bloke, a cheeky chappie, an East Ender. He prided himself on it. But he'd found combining being a nice bloke with a little wrinkle worked well.

Stan seized the moment. 'I might be able to sort you out there. My modelling agency has a position available and I need a good girl to fill it. And I can see you're a good girl, despite your situation. How would you like to come and work for me? That old slapper you got in a barney with is only a temp. I'm looking for someone permanent, with a decent head on her shoulders. It's good money, the work's easy and if you need time off for the quacks and that, I can help you out.'

Stan had formed the impression that this girl already trusted him completely. But the look on her face suggested otherwise. 'A modelling agency in Soho? I don't know about that . . .'

Oh, Stan thought grimly – *she's not that dozy*. Still, he didn't need someone with half a brain working for him. He sent her a blinding smile that seemed to make her blush down to the bump in her belly. 'I'll level with you; I can see you're not a div. I run a completely respectable modelling agency. It's all fashion work for magazines. We don't do none of that porn or nude rubbish. My girls are well looked after and I run a tight ship. Would I rather be based in the Kings Road or Kensington? Of course I would, but I'm not some mug. I won't pay silly rents or drive a Roller round and then go bust in six months, like some of my competitors. In my line of work, you have to be in a showbiz area and Soho still counts as showbiz. I have to do deals with a few dodgy sorts, but that don't make me a crook.'

His voice turned to steel. 'But I'll tell you this. In five years' time, I'm gonna be living it up in one of those big offices in Mayfair and flying Mick Jagger and Jackie Onassis out to my island in the Caribbean for holidays. If you want to be part of that, I'd be delighted to have you on board. I think you'll fit right in.'

'Mick Jagger? Jackie O?' Babs let out a quivering breath. From the light in her eyes and the way she was clutching his hand, she was buying into it. 'Alright then, you've got yourself a new receptionist.'

They sealed the deal with a handshake and a grin. It was the first time he'd seen her smile and he had to admit she wasn't a bad-looking sort.

Outside, Stan gave her a peck on the cheek and told her to report for duty at nine on Monday morning. He advised her to tell her folks about her kid and not hold anything back. Then he went to his office. Bev was long gone, so he took a seat at her desk, put his feet up and lit one of his Turkish fags. He rang his receptionist at home and told her he was absolutely disgusted that she'd attacked a pregnant teenager, in his office of all places. She was given her cards with immediate effect. When he put the phone down, Stanley Miller had a well pleased smile on his face. He didn't need that old slapper any more. He had Babs instead.

Seven

When Babs left Soho, she was riding high, feeling confident. Stan was right. So she was expecting. So what? It happens. So the kid's dad wasn't white. Who cares? It happened. Everyone would get over it eventually. Her mum and dad wouldn't like it but Babs was their only kid and they loved her to bits. When they started seeing straight again, they'd be on her side.

But when she emerged into the early evening darkness outside Whitechapel tube and began to trek home, through the leftover rubbish from the street market, Soho and Stanley Miller seemed a long way off. Babs was a bundle of nerves.

At her house, she decided she would have to tell her parents whatever happened, so it might as well be now. But as she turned the key in the lock, she decided tonight wasn't the night. She was totally done in and couldn't face the grief. Tomorrow was another day. Or maybe after she'd told them she had a bang-up job – although not that it was in Soho. Her dad would hit the roof at that. She'd definitely mention the colour thing later, after they got used to the idea of having a grandkid about the place.

But as she crept into the hallway, she knew something was up. The lights were on but there was no noise, no TV, no radio playing. The house was in complete silence, as if someone had died.

'Babs? Get in here.'

It was her mum, summoning her in a frozen tone. Babs very nearly fled back into the street but her mother appeared in the hallway, arms folded. One look at Rosie Wilson's stern face told her there was trouble brewing. Her mother marched her into the sitting room like a prisoner.

The room was clean and smelt fresh from the flowers on the table in the corner, which Rosie got every week from Columbia Road Market up Bethnal Green way. Rosie prided herself on keeping a spotless and respectable home. They were lucky to be renting this cosy Victorian house from the council when so many had been condemned and bulldozed down, their residents now living in new estates and – some would make the sign of the cross next – those homes in the sky.

Babs spotted her dad. George Wilson was a decade older than his wife and looked it. The years spent working his fingers to the bone as a tailor until he made it to foreman had weathered his skin and taken a toll on his hair. He sat bolt upright in his armchair near the blazing coal fire, his wire-rimmed spectacles pushed high on his nose, looking like a judge. Babs realised she was about to be tried, although she didn't know what for. She crossed the fingers of her free hand behind her back, praying that this didn't have anything to do with her very delicate situation.

Her mother led the interrogation. 'Where you been all day, young lady?'

Babs nearly wept with relief. Was that all? 'Out.'

'Yes, I know that – where?'

'Just out ... you know.' When her mother's stare remained stony, Babs added, 'With Denny.'

'Oh, I see,' her mum snapped. 'Funny thing is, your mate was up here earlier looking for you.'

Babs avoided her mother's eyes. 'I'm not a kid, I'm allowed out on my own.'

'Yes, we know that.'

After another silence, Babs begged, 'Is that it then?'

Her mother drew closer. 'Not quite. Are you ill?'

Babs felt the ground giving way beneath her feet. She desperately wanted to sit down. 'No. Why?' Technically, that was true; being up the duff wasn't the same as being sick.

Her mother was only inches from her now. 'Only I ran into that evil old bitch Mrs Jackson earlier. She seemed to think she saw you down McDaid's surgery this morning.'

Babs desperately tried to cling on to the life she had, which was disappearing before her eyes. 'Well, she's fibbing outta her hairnet and you know it.'

Her mother pressed on. 'Perhaps. But it's difficult to see why she'd lie about that. She had something else to say. She said you had a slanging match with the doctor. Would you like to tell us what that was about?'

Babs tried hard to think of an explanation but she had nothing left in the tank. 'Alright, I was down there, but I weren't shooting my mouth off.' Technically true again; that old fart had been the one blowing a blood vessel.

'No row?'

'No.'

Her mother sighed. 'OK, then. Fair enough. It wouldn't be the first time Dirty Laundry Jackson's poured acid in other people's drinking water.' For a few moments, Babs thought she'd survived. But then her mother added, 'But I'll find out tomorrow. I've got to go and get a prescription, so I'll have a word with old McDaid myself. See what his version is.'

Babs was horrified. 'You can't do that. It's private.'

Rosie folded her arms. 'You're my daughter. I've got a right to know.' Babs sank down onto the sofa while her mum choked out, 'You're in the family way, ain't you?'

Babs had no tears left She saw the bitter disappointment in her mum's eyes and looked away because it hurt.

Her dad spoke for the first time. 'Oh, Babs, we thought you were better than that.' But he didn't sound angry; just disappointed and resigned. Her dad had been through the Blitz; it was going to take something bigger than finding out she'd got herself into trouble to make him fly off the handle.

Her mum wasn't finished though. 'So who's the father?'

Crikey O'Reilly! No way on this earth could she tell them about Nev. Not yet, anyway. So Babs told them about someone else. 'My fiancé. He owns a business in the West End and he's very ambitious. He's planning a move to Mayfair.'

Her mum was unconvinced. 'Is that so? She walks out of the house this morning a carefree nineteen-year-old and comes home with a bellyful and a fiancé who's moving to Mayfair. Well, la-di-da.'

Her dad snapped, 'Alright, that's enough, Rosie luv. Don't bully the girl. She's carrying our grandchild.'

Babs was the apple of George Wilson's eye. He and Rosie had given up on ever having a kid after the terrible miscarriage Rosie had had. They'd given up hope and then, like a golden penny, their Barbara had come along. And what a beautiful baby she'd been.

Her mum pursed her lips and shook her head. 'Well, you'd better get this fiancé round pronto because we want a word with him. If he thinks he can have his bit of fun and then swan off into the night, he's got another think coming.'

Upstairs, Babs found a gorgeous lime green and bright yellow handbag on her bed. Her dad was always bringing her back goodies from his job, making sure that she was decked out in the latest fashions. He spoiled her something rotten, which made her guilt at not telling them the whole truth stab harder. She should stop bottling it and go downstairs and cough up the rest. That there was no fiancé, who the father really was and what colour her bundle of joy was going to be. Her dad was already coming round to the idea of a baby and her mum hadn't completely blown her stack.

Babs walked past her poster of gorgeous hunk George Best and out onto the landing, ready to take the plunge. She summoned up everything she had and went downstairs. As she neared the sitting room door she heard her parents talking, clearly worried, but not about her.

'I'm going out of my mind. It'll be us next,' Rosie said.

'We're safe, pet. This house is owned by the council and they aren't going to chuck us out. When the rent man comes calling his money's always ready. We've never missed a payment in our lives.'

'But paying their rent on the dot didn't stop the landlord sending his bully boys around and kicking the Dempseys out in the middle of the night. And her with a baby and all. Plain greed, that's what it is.'

Her father tutted. 'It's a wicked world that puts out families in the dead of the night to make an extra bob or two. You mark my words, the council will never get away with behaving like that.'

'Mum, Dad,' Babs interrupted cautiously.

Her dad gave her a half smile. Her mum looked pensive but there was no malice in her stare.

'What is it?'

'Umm . . .' Babs prepared to tell the truth but her tongue had other ideas. 'I'm really sorry. So sorry.'

Her dad got to his feet and pulled her into his arms. Babs sagged into him. It felt so good to be in his warm embrace.

George Wilson soothed her hair and whispered, 'It's gonna be alright, luv. Don't you worry about a thing. Me and your mum will see you right.'

Eight

'Open up! It's the police!'

Beryl Bradshaw crouched behind the front door of her house in Whitechapel. The clock in the hallway said midnight but it was always stopping and starting and she couldn't be sure. It could be later. She'd put the kids to bed after *Please Sir!* – her brood were crazy about that show, which was strange since none of them had taken to school – and then she'd had a lovely steaming cup of Milo with a drop of gin before calling it a night. She'd been fast asleep when the hammering had started. She'd reached across to the other side of the bed to rouse her sleeping husband, but her hand had flopped back when she remembered. Pneumonia had taken her Phil unexpectedly the previous year. She'd taken his going hard. Still couldn't get it into her head that he wasn't blissfully snoring away next to her.

Now she was wide awake, scared out of her wits, the kids crying upstairs. She waited. Hoping they'd got the wrong house or would get bored and sod off.

'This is your final warning.'

Beryl opened the letterbox. She could see two, possibly three men. Her voice shook. 'Who is it?'

'Are you deaf? We're the police. Now open up or we'll kick the fucking door off its hinges.'

'What do you want?'

Her answer was the door shaking as it took a kick. Beryl knew it wouldn't take much pressure, so she opened it a fraction. But that was enough for the men outside. She was thrown backwards like a paper bag as they crashed their way in. Beryl was too scared to scream. There were four of them. All dressed to scare the living daylights out of her, in leather jackets, black trousers and bovver boots. She watched two march into the living room while the other two stood sniggering in the hallway. One of them said, 'Alright luv, get your things together. You're moving.'

'Moving?'

'Yeah.' He handed her a badly folded sheet of paper. 'It's all official. Your house is being repossessed for non-payment. The details are all on there.'

Beryl was outraged. 'I pay my rent like clockwork every week.'

They found her excuse highly comical. 'Do ya? Oh dear. Must be a clerical error then, you'll have to take it up with the landlord.'

'You're not the fucking coppers,' she dared to argue.

One of the two jokers swiped the other across the chest. 'Did you say you were the police? You little fibber, you.'

'Don't blame me; my mum couldn't afford to send me to Sunday school.'

From the front room there was the sound of furniture being turned over and things crashing on the floor. Beryl got the picture – the pair in the hallway were the brains and the other two the brawn. She rushed into the room to find them throwing her possessions about like they meant nothing. She grabbed a vase that one of them was about to throw on the heap.

'Get out!'

The two jokers had followed her in. 'Don't interfere with the course of the law. We've got the right.'

Beryl caught her breath and yelled, 'The right? You're well hard, ain't ya? Attacking a defenceless woman and smashing up her things.'

One of the jokers pretended to be wounded. 'Oh that's nice. The boys are just trying to help you move. If you don't want their help, I suggest you get a suitcase and get a fucking move on!'

Beryl, still clutching the paper they'd given her, looked at the four men staring at her in silence. 'I'm not going nowhere until I've spoken to my solicitor.'

'You ain't got a brief, you silly moo. People like you never do.' He looked at his watch. 'You've got ten minutes to get everything out and then whatever's left is going out the window. It's your choice. And tell them kids to shut it. Think about the neighbours.'

Beryl threw the vase at their feet where it crashed into pieces. She ran upstairs, got her howling kids and packed up what she could. When they were all downstairs again, dragging suitcases like a family of evacuees from the war, she got them dressed in hats and coats as the four intruders looked on.

'And where am I supposed to go?'

'We don't know, do we?' the brains of the outfit bit out, his patience clearly running thin. 'We're not fucking estate agents.' He turned to his associates. 'Alright boys, change the locks and fix the windows. We don't want any reprobates coming in and squatting on the landlord's property.' He turned back to Beryl. 'Pleasure doing business with you. Now piss off.'

The evictors went back to a transit van parked down the street, near a wall where someone had scrawled in white paint:

DECENT HOMES FOR LOCAL PEOPLE

The two men took not a blind bit of notice. As they waited for the house to be secured the smaller one lit up a Manikin cigar and the other opened a small silver box and sucked menthol snuff up his nose. Outside, a bewildered Beryl and her children sat lost on the pavement in the frosty night.

'You might almost feel sorry for them,' the shorter one said and puffed out a smoke ring.

The other one sniffed as the snuff made his eyes water. 'Yeah, you might do, but you don't. There's two types of people in the world, the kickers and the kicked out, and I know which one I'd rather be. Do you wanna drink?'

'I'm driving.'

'I find it improves mine. You don't worry so much about pedestrians when you've had a couple.'

'Go on then. Just the one.'

When they saw their boys emerge from the house and slam the front door, one said to the other, 'Well, that's another one ticked off. The boss will be well pleased.'

They both nodded.

'Anyway – nice work, Mr Horner.'

'Nice work indeed, Mr Cricket.'

Nine

Babs left the house early the first day of her new job and took the tube up West. She made very sure she didn't bump into her parents on the way out. She hadn't fancied more earache from her mum, plus her tummy had been playing up something chronic. She was still trying to come up with a good cover story about the colour thing. If she told them her fiancé was a black musician, rather than a general nogoodnik like Neville, that might sweeten the pill. Her dad had played the piano down his local, and she'd noticed they didn't seem to mind coloureds when they were singing and dancing on the telly. She'd even seen her dad squint with appreciation at Mary Wilson when the Supremes were on. Her dad had a load of Motown and Stax records and her mum was a Nat King Cole fan. It was just in real life they didn't like them very much.

Babs thought she'd leave it for a few weeks and then tell them her fiancé had gone to America on tour and she wasn't sure when he was coming back. She knew it was a bollocks plan but it was all she had and it might buy her some time.

When she got to Chancery Row, she realised that there were a series of bells on the black door, one of which had 'Go Go' written by it. She pressed it and a cheerful Stan Miller threw the door open a minute later and escorted her upstairs. He wore an immaculate brown whistle, chunky navy tie and a matching hanky in his top pocket. Babs did like a fella who was nicely turned out.

He gave her the grand tour of the tiny kitchen, his office and the main office. Babs was dead excited. Fancy her working up West. She sat down at the desk that Brawler Beehive had once called home. Stan perched on the side of the desk and explained her duties. He gave her a piece of A4 paper with a list of names written on it.

'If someone asks to speak to me whose name's on that list, put the call through. If it ain't, tell them you've never heard of me and put the dog and bone down. If the doorbell goes, find out who it is and then report back to me. I'll take care of things from there. OK?'

Babs didn't want to sound suspicious on her first day but she couldn't help thinking this was a funny set-up. Her face had clearly given her away because Stan was chuckling. 'Look – it's like I was telling you in the Lilac Club. You get some dodgy types and time wasters in this line of work. I don't want to be bothered by people like that and I don't want you bothered by them either. See?'

Babs nodded. It made sense. 'And what do you want me to do if any girls ring up looking for modelling jobs?'

Stan shook his head. 'They won't. This office is the admin side of the operation. There's a studio where all the practical stuff goes on, the hiring and, unfortunately, sometimes the firing. And that's about it.' He stood up. 'I'll leave you to it.'

'That's it? Answering the blower and the door? You don't want to me to do any typing or filing or anything?'

Stan shook his head again. 'Nah. I've got other staff on other sites to take care of that kind of thing. You just sit there and look pretty. Listen to the radio, file your nails, do the crossword. Have a nap . . . I told you this job was easy, didn't I?'

Babs said nothing. She wasn't complaining; it wasn't like she was working for the Bank of England. Stan walked over to his office but before he went in he asked, 'How did you get on with your mum and dad?'

Babs shivered when she remembered the scene. 'I told them. They weren't happy.'

'And what did they say about the black and white thing?' When Babs broke eye contact, he gave her a pointed stare. 'They're gonna notice something's up when that kid's born. All that curly hair for a start.'

She didn't answer; he wasn't telling her anything she didn't already know.

Stan drifted back towards her desk. 'Oh yeah – there's one other thing. You might notice some interesting characters coming in and out. The modelling world's full of 'em. You might hear some things, a bit of verbal every now and again, see some things and think to yourself – *I don't like the look of that*. But I have to deal with the world as it is, not as I'd like it to be. I'm running a legitimate outfit here but not all the people I work with are. That's how it is. You get me? So whatever you see and whatever you hear – you ain't seen or heard nuthin', OK? And if you've got any concerns, bring them to me.'

Babs nodded. She liked Stan. Trusted him.

He took five new tenners out of his wallet. 'Here, get yourself something nice on the way home.'

Babs was alarmed. She might need the money but she was no charity case. 'I can't take that.'

'Course you can.' He picked up her bag and shoved the money inside. 'Consider it an advance on your wages.'

When Babs was alone, she took out the notes. It was more money than she'd ever handled in her life. She looked around, then rolled up the money and put it back.

She made herself a cuppa and then returned to her desk. As the morning wore on, she did that a lot. There were no phone calls and no rings on the bell. At first she played the radio quietly, feeling guilty as she did so. But as time passed she turned it up. She'd brought a Harold Robbins novel from Whitechapel Library to read on the tube, so she took it out and read. Occasionally, she heard a phone ringing in Stan's office and his voice as he answered it, but hers was silent. At one point she picked up the list of approved names in the hope that she might recognise someone from the papers but she was disappointed. There was no David Bailey or Twiggy – only a list of people who sounded like patrons of a boozer in the East End. There was Mickey and Mel, Jimmy, Freddie Q, C&H, Fast Jacky, Bertie Steptoe, and a lot of other nicknames. But she thought she recognised one name. Lord Tilgate. She was sure she'd heard the name on the telly. Wouldn't it be something if he was related to the Queen?

As she read, she heard footsteps on the wooden stairs. The door swung open and a man in his twenties stepped inside. How the hell had he got in? He hadn't rung the bell. He wore trendy black cords that were way too tight and an orange shirt left halfway open to reveal a St Christopher's medallion, a hairy chest and the top of a paunch. He was unshaven and had unkempt long hair. He looked very much like one of the interesting characters Stan had warned her about.

He looked at Babs and mumbled, 'Wotcha darlin',' before doing a double take and demanding, 'Who the hell are you?'

Babs was alarmed. He looked like he wanted to do serious damage. 'Babs Wilson.'

'Right. And what are you doing here?'

'I started work today. I'm the receptionist.'

The corner of the man's lip started to twitch in a very nasty way. 'What happened to Bev?'

She shrugged. 'Dunno.'

'So Stan's hiring and firing, is he? We'll have to see about that. Don't make yourself too comfy, sugar, you might be leaving pronto.'

The man walked over to Stan's office and went inside. Babs heard Stan shout, 'Oi – have you ever heard of knocking?'

'Why? You're not having a wank, are ya?'

Then the door was slammed shut. Babs shuddered.

Stan was reading what he called his golden list when his visitor marched unannounced into his office. The golden list held the names of all the people Stan needed to turn his business into an empire. Councillor Joseph Carter was going to be easy, but Lord Tilgate was proving more problematic. *Patience, son, patience*, he told himself.

He put his list down as his visitor helped himself to a large one and sat lolling around on the other side of his desk.

'What do you want, mate? I'm busy.'

'For a start, I want to know what happened to my cousin Bev and why that gormless kid outside is sitting in her chair.'

Stan sighed and shuffled some papers. 'I had to get rid of Bev. She was trouble; she attacked a pregnant woman in my office. I can't have that, can I?'

'I'd be the first to admit she's a bit lively with her fists. I saw her knock a bloke out once in a pub in Poplar. Broke his jaw.'

'There's your answer then.'

'Alright, fair enough. So who's the new bird?'

'That's the pregnant girl your Bev knocked around.'

His visitor almost snarled, obviously not happy. 'You're hiring a girl who's up the stick? Have you banged your head? She'll be gone in months. She looks as thick as a docker's sandwich. I don't get it.'

Stan put his papers down and glared. 'Of course you don't.

That's the difference between you and me. I'm always one step ahead of the opposition, while you're always one step behind. If life was a game of Monopoly, I'd be bagging hotels on Mayfair and Park Lane, while you'd be going directly to jail without passing go. Now what do you want?'

'You reckon you're ahead of the game, do ya? Well, here's your chance to prove it. We've got a problem that needs sorting because if we don't, everyone will be going to jail without two hundred quid – including you.'

After Stan had escorted his lairy visitor off the premises, he asked Babs, with a smile, if she'd had a good morning.

'Yeah. Apart from that bloke. He had a right cob on about me being here.'

'Is that so? The little prick.' He muttered the last under his breath. 'Take no notice of him, Babs-babe.' Babs blushed; she liked it when he called her that. Made her feel warm and special. 'He's all mouth and no trousers. If he gives you any more jip, tell me and I'll sort him out. Unfortunately, he's an investor in this business, so I have to humour him for the time being. But I'll be buying him out shortly; I don't like working with prats.'

'Who is he?'

'He comes from down your way actually. Goes by the name of Mickey Ingram.'

Ten

As soon as Babs saw her best mate Denny down the packed Drum and Whistle pub off Vallance Road, she knew something was up. Denise was a head turner, with such stunning cheekbones and hazel eyes that usually at least half the men would be eyeing her up, but tonight there was none of that. She looked plain worn out and sad.

Denny and Babs had been best friends since school, since the time Babs had chased off a group of kids taunting Denny about her torn second-hand dress. Babs hated bullies. The first time she'd taken Denny home, her mum hadn't been happy. But it had nothing to do with the poor girl; Rosie thought her stepdad was an 'utter bollocks skiver.' But Denny's gentle well-mannered ways had soon won Rosie over.

'What's up? You look like a proper wet weekend,' Babs said as she sat down. Denny already had a glass of Babycham with a glacé cherry lined up for her. Babs wasn't much of a drinker, her dad having lectured her for years about the evils of the demon drink, but she did like a bevvy with a bit of fizz.

Denny smiled; it was her way to be sunny and happy most of the time, but there was no hiding from Babs. She could see that something bad had happened.

'Is it your bloody stepdad again?' That man had been giving

her poor mate grief since the day he'd slipped a ring on her mother's finger.

Denny's face paled, which worried Babs. 'He ain't belting you one, is he?' If he was, Babs was going to go around to Denny's and give him what for.

But Denny brushed her off. She whispered, 'What did the doctor say? You've been keeping yourself scarce for a week.'

She was right. Usually Babs would've been on the blower to Denny straight off, but this time she'd wanted some space first to absorb all the changes in her life. She looked around to make sure no one was earwigging and then turned back and nodded.

Denny's mouth fell open. 'Hell's bells, Babs. What you going to do?'

'I'm four months gone so there ain't nuthin' I can do except have the baby.'

Denny frowned. 'But it's Neville's kid.'

'I know it's his kid—'

'I mean is he's . . . you know . . .' Denny mouthed, 'Black.'

Babs didn't have a problem with that and she hoped her mate didn't either. That would be so disappointing.

Denny went on, 'What are your mum and dad going to say?'

Babs took a large gulp of her drink, the sweet bubbles bursting on her tongue. 'I've already told them about the baby.' Denny's eyes nearly popped out of her head. 'My mum was proper pissed, but she didn't do her nut and my dad's already come around.'

'And—?'

Babs shook her head. 'I ain't told them about *that* yet.'

'But I don't get it, those pills I gave you should've sorted you out.'

'There must've been something up with them, or Neville was packing some super spunk.'

They both howled with laughter. Babs knew it was no laughing matter, but it felt good to indulge in a little tickle again. God knows the life she had stretching before her wasn't going to be a stroll in the park.

'Is Neville going to do right by you?' Denny asked as she finished her drink.

All Babs' anger at the rotten pig came flooding back. And the humiliation. She felt ashamed to have to admit that some man had made a right monkey out of her.

'The bastard's nowhere to be found. Plus, he was two-timing me behind my back while he had me on my back.'

'I ain't surprised. He tried to cop off with me when you went into the loo at the Reno.'

Babs fixed her friend with a furious gaze. 'You what? Why the bloody heck didn't you let me know? No way would I have given him an in if I'd known he was chasing after you as well.'

'I didn't want to disappoint you. You looked so happy.' Denny tugged nervously at her bottom lip.

That was the problem with Denny, always wanting to keep everything hunky dory. That sweet trusting nature of hers was going to get her into big time bovver one of these days.

'Hold up,' she said with a twinkle in her eyes. 'Geezer alert at four o'clock.'

Babs looked over on the sly and checked him out.

Both women giggled and said as one: 'Chirpy, chirpy, cheep, cheep,' which was their way of saying the stranger was a tasty sort. Still, to Babs, he didn't have a patch on Stanley Miller. Which reminded her . . .

'It ain't all bad news. I started a top job up West today.'

'The West End?' Denise practically had stars in her eyes. Up West was a big exciting world for both of them. They didn't go there often, most of the time preferring to stay local, but when they did venture into town they were like two kids in a sweetie shop. 'You haven't got a gig in one of the department stores?'

Babs shook her head. 'It's in Soho.'

Denny frowned, clearly worried. 'It ain't dodgy, is it? I hear it's full of dirty old geezers with wrinkled knobs.'

Babs thought about handsome Stan Miller, looking natty in his business suit. Stan, a dirty old man? Wrinkled dinkle? Not bloody likely. 'It's a reception job in a modelling agency—'

'Get away,' Denise trilled in disbelief. 'A flippin' modelling agency?'

Babs pushed her chest out. Her best mate no longer felt sorry for her, but was green with envy. 'It's all above board. The man running the outfit, Stanley Miller, is a total gent. He knew Neville was a wrong 'un so he took me on to help me out.'

But Denny was lost in her own world. She softly breathed, 'I've always wanted to be a model. Everyone keeps telling me I've got the looks for it.' She looked desperately at Babs. 'You couldn't put in a word with this Stanley and fix me up with a job? I could get my own place then.'

Although Babs said she'd see what she could do, secretly she wasn't so sure. She'd only done one day's graft there and remembering that Mickey made her tummy churn. She didn't want to land her mate in the crapper if the place turned out to be part of the sleazy cesspit her dad said all Soho was.

Eleven

'Tra-la-la boom dee-yay.
   My knickers flew away.
   They came back yesterday.
   I didn't know what to say.'

A group of girls sang happily as they skipped a few feet away
from the house where Mel Ingram was mixing Bacardi into
baby Tommy's bottle. That should shut the little bleeder up. He
had a gob on him that Aretha Franklin would kill for and it
was driving her around the twist. Even though she'd shut him
up in the bedroom she could still hear him going at it.

Mel was fed up with having to live in the poxy East End.
Her Mickey had his fingers in property all over the place but
where did he plonk his nearest and dearest? In a two-up, two-
down in Shadwell, round the back of the bloody Highway. She
was getting sick to death of it. Mickey had better get his head
set on moving them up in the world.

'Mum, can I have some cheese and onion crisps?' asked her
eldest, four-year-old Donna. She was sitting on the eye-
watering patterned lino in the hallway, playing with a doll.
Her face and hands were sticky from the blackcurrant jam
sarnie Mel had made for her a half hour ago.

'I only fed you a while ago and still you want more. Fucking greedy, that's what you are.' She bent down and peered in the little girl's face. 'Repeat after me, "I'm a greedy girl."'

Little Donna looked up happily. 'I'm a greedy girl.'

Mel couldn't stand the sight of her daughter and the reason was simple – she was the spit of her father, in ways as well as looks. Always grasping for more and with an empty noodle on her shoulders.

Mel ground her teeth as she fed the baby – who guzzled down his milk – and waited for Mickey. What was taking the big ape such a long time? All he had to do was tell that rat bastard Stan who was running the show. It reminded her of all the times she'd waited patiently while Stan Miller made a monkey of Mickey in that modelling agency he ran. Or, as she preferred to think of it, Mickey's modelling agency that Stan had mysteriously taken over.

The longer she waited, the more likely it was that Miller was running rings around the wally again. Mel had given Mickey a simple task – tell Mister Fancy Pants that his brother Pete was out of the business. Simple. But nothing was simple with Mickey. He was a bang-up geezer, but he was unbeliev-ably thick. He knew how to give a bloke a good hiding but as soon as anyone started using long words, he was all at sea. No bloody wonder she had to do the thinking for both of them.

She'd been down the boozer on the day that smug wide boy had first asked Mickey if he could find Pete a position because his brother was at a bit of a loose end.

Of course Mickey had said yes. 'I could use someone down at the knocking–'

Mr Wriggly had jumped in quick. 'That's alright, bruv, I don't need to know the details. Just find him something to do.'

Mel had said with a sneer, 'what's the matter, Stan? Is Mickey's side of the business beneath you? Too busy having tea up the Ritz with Little Lord Fauntleroy to worry about where the real money is coming from?'

Mickey had put his oar in. 'Oh come on luv, that's not fair, is it?'

Stan had paused for a moment and cracked, 'Oh, don't you worry, face ache. I know exactly where the money's coming from.'

And that was another thing she couldn't stand about Stan. The way he called her 'mad bird', 'Aunt Doris', 'droopy drawers' and any other little put-downs he could think of to avoid using her real name.

But she wasn't going to take it like Mickey did. 'And how is your brother? Still like a snifter in his Sugar Puffs?'

Stan puffed on one of the stinking foreign fags he smoked to prove he was cooler than anyone else. 'Pete likes a drink now and again. So do I. So does Mickey. And let's be honest, bird, so do you. I seem to recall us having to carry you out of Hammersmith Palais when you'd had a sherbet too far. Wasn't that the night you threatened to clobber a copper? I'm sure it was.'

Mickey had laughed his stupid head off, the cretin. That was loyalty for you.

Mel had stared at the pair of them, beaming at each other like schoolboys. That was another thing she resented about Stan. He was a bit too close to her husband for her liking. She knew they went way back and had been through a lot together but she was still suspicious. If it wasn't for Mickey demanding his conjugals off her twice a week on Tuesdays and Saturdays, she might even have suspected there was something a bit funny going on between them. Soho was notorious for that sort of thing.

'As long as he's not going to show my Mickey up.'

'He can handle his booze.'

Mel shook her head. 'Dream on. Your brother's piss has so much alcohol in it I'm surprised he doesn't drink it.'

Mel had been proved right as usual. Pete had hardly arrived at Mickey's place down in Mile End with a brief to keep the punters sweet and everything ship-shape before he was causing all kinds of mayhem. By tea time he was usually unconscious somewhere, so the girls and their customers were left in peace, but by midnight he was up and about, like Dracula, costing them business. Mel had had enough. She was determined Pete was going. And Stan along with him.

Seething at the memories, she looked up to find Mickey coming through the doorway with Donna in his arms. She hadn't even heard him come in. He seemed pleased with himself. He whispered in his daughter's ear, loud enough for his wife to hear, 'Daddy's been a very good boy and got the job done.'

The child giggled, making Mel hate her even more. Sometimes she thought Mickey loved that kid more than he did her.

'Hop it,' Mel ordered Donna roughly. She put the now-sleeping baby down.

'You got some tea in the offing?' Mickey asked.

'Fuck your dinner. Has Pete been shown the door?'

'Yeah, Stan's going round his mum's later and he'll speak to Pete then.'

Mel needed to hear him say it in black and white. 'To tell him he's got the boot?'

That wiped the smile right off his face. 'Well, yeah . . . Well, not exactly – I mean he's got to give the geezer a last chance, hasn't he? It's his flesh and blood.'

Mel rose to her full height, her face contorted with rage. 'Last chance? What's the matter with you?' She stomped out into the passage to put on her mink. 'I'll tell you what, I'll break the news to him myself.'

Mickey's big paw gripped her arm and he marched her into the sitting room and shoved her down onto the settee. 'No, you won't. I don't need any bird to do my work for me. I've told Stan straight. Any more trouble with Pete and I'll park his bum on the street myself. That's final. Stan understands and he won't create. Now then – what about some nosh?'

Mel decided to leave it; she knew when she couldn't go too far. 'Give Bev a little tinkle for me. She can give us the lowdown on what's happening in that office of his. Anyhow, I haven't seen her for a while, we can catch up.'

Mickey avoided her eyes. 'Bev? Nah, we can't do that. Bev's left.'

Mel realised straight away what had happened. Her anger wasn't hot any more, it was cold, steely and quiet. 'He's given her the push, hasn't he? Your own cousin and he's sacked her without so much as a by your leave. Who the hell gave him the right to do that? I know Bev can be a bit of a handful but Stan's taking the piss. You can see that, can't you? He's laughing at you.'

To her surprise Mickey started looking like he was finally putting that brain of his to use. His next words were music to her ears. 'Yeah. I can't pretend I was very happy about it . . . Stan's got a bit up himself lately . . . got a little cheeky.'

Mel drew breath. 'It's not just Pete we need to get rid of. It's his brother as well. And we need to do it fast, before he does it to us. That means we need to find out exactly what Stan's up to.'

'Oh yeah? And how are we going to do that?'

Mel's mouth hardened into a grim line. 'You leave that to me.'

Twelve

'Go on then! You trying to get me?'

Even before the door at his brother's local had closed behind him, Stan knew a ruck was either starting or finishing. It was that kind of pub. And he knew Pete would be in the thick of it. He was that kind of bloke. A drunk and a brawler.

Despite that, his older brother was the only human being Stan truly loved. As a youngster, Pete had been more of a man than a boy, protecting Stan when their drunk dad beat them and sticking up for Stan when it would have been safer to have kept his head down. Stan had idolised Pete. Now their roles had reversed; Pete more boy than man, veering between sozzled fists and self-pity. Deep in his heart, it hurt Stan to see his beloved Pete turning into their old man.

The place wasn't packed, so it was easy for Stan to zero in on his brother. There he was, foaming at the mouth, squaring up to two geezers at the bar. Both men looked like proper toughs, eager to get in on what passed for entertainment in this spit-and-sawdust gin palace.

Stan walked up to Pete, grabbed him by the scruff of the neck and pulled him backwards. 'Oi, I want a word with you.' He turned to the two monkeys gearing themselves for a punch-up and declared in a bored tone, 'The fight's off, duty calls.'

But the two blokes weren't having it. They gave him the

once-over and one wrinkled his face. 'If you're looking for a gay boy's pub, there's one up the road.'

His mate sniggered, 'Nah, I reckon this bloke here's the boyfriend – he obviously ain't that fussy.'

Pete lunged at him but Stan had a tight grip on him like a dog on a chain. The other punters went silent, waiting to see where this was going and when to dive for cover. Stan smiled at the two Herberts. 'Sorry, lads, not today. If you want a beating why don't you go and bang your heads on the toilet wall. Cut out the middle man?'

But they weren't letting go. 'I'll say this for your boyfriend. At least he's up for it – he's not a bottle job.'

Stan looked around the pub. He didn't recognise anyone but he couldn't be sure word wouldn't spread that he'd ducked out of a fight. He didn't care what anyone thought, but he knew that was bad for business. Anyway, he could always buy a new suit. He was good for it. He let go of Pete's collar and reached for a chair. 'Alright then, you wankers!'

The other customers got out of the way as he swung the chair in a quick arc. It smashed into the neck of the first guy, who crashed into the second like a skittle at a bowling alley. He'd found extreme force, loud noise and the virtue of surprise was always the key to a successful rumble. While they reeled with shock, Stan moved in to take advantage. He punched the second guy in the face so he fell backwards and took a bottle from the bar to club the first over the head.

Pete was weaving around like Andy Pandy, throwing aimless punches that weren't connecting with anything or anyone. Stan pushed him out of the way. The second guy still had a bit left in him so Stan bashed the chair against the bar until a leg came off and hit his cheek with his makeshift baton. The guy's face broke and cracked, sending a spray of blood across Stan's jacket like the foam from a champagne bottle.

Stan looked at his jacket in disgust and whacked him again. 'That's for the fucking dry cleaning bill.'

Stan was satisfied with his work but it wasn't quite over yet. He still had one more dickhead to go. He grabbed Pete by his lapels and dragged him out of the pub.

Pete was angry and resisting all the way. 'Come on, we ain't done yet. Let's take them all on. Make a proper ding-dong of it.'

Stan rammed him against a brick wall. 'You really are a little prick. Have you got nothing better to do with your time than pick fights in pubs? You're worse than the old man.' He pulled him away from the wall and began frog-marching him down the road. 'Now, I wanna word with you and you're going to listen for once.'

All the spit and fire drained out of Pete. He knew when his brother was serious.

'Pete! Petey! What the fuck's happened?' an alarmed Shell Miller barked as she clocked her two sons on her doorstep.

Shell Miller lived near the Londoner in Limehouse. That was how people identified where they were, not by the place's actual name but by a well-known nearby pub. The Londoner was Limehouse, the Blind Beggar, Whitechapel, the Boleyn meant Upton Park and Princess Alice signified Forest Gate.

Stan was holding Pete up after he'd taken a drunken tumble. He'd cut his face on a paving stone. Pete had lost his key and Stan didn't have one. Nor did he want one.

Shell was horrified. She touched Pete's cheek with her fingertips and put her arm around him. 'What the fuck's happened? Come in and let your old mum get you a cuppa and patch you up.'

Stan stared at his mother with contempt. He always felt she looked like a vulture with badly dyed feathers. Her hair was grey with some brown streaks and she had a nose like a beak. When he thought about her – which he did as little as possible – he always imagined her perched on a lamppost waiting to descend on a victim, wings flapping.

She led Pete inside, fussing sympathetically all the way. Stan was left on the doorstep. But that was kind of right. He'd been left standing on the doorstep of this house since he'd been old enough to walk. He closed his eyes, took a deep breath and gritted his teeth. He was not going to be provoked.

He followed them into the front room. The house was a total tip as usual. Unwashed dishes on the corner table, monkey-nut shells littering the floor, a Guinness and cider bottle perched by his mum's armchair. On the black and white telly, Mrs Slocombe was talking about her pussy on *Are You Being Served?* Shell fussed over Pete, who lay on the sofa clutching his cheek. She turned on Stan, her bloodshot eyes spitting fire. 'Was this you? Well, was it?'

His brother's voice was faint. 'No, Mum, don't blame Stan. He started a fight down the boozer and I had to step in and help out. It weren't his fault.'

Their mum's face contorted with fury. 'You had to step in? You should leave the little ponce to fight his own wars. Look at him – not a mark on him. I suppose he ran off while you did battle?'

Stan stiffened and unconsciously rubbed his half-finger.

'It weren't his fault,' Pete insisted.

'Likely story. Stop sticking up for the little bastard. That's your problem; you're always sticking up for him.'

Stan rubbed his face in frustration. But he refused to be baited and asked, with mock sweetness, 'You alright, Gladys?'

His mum's real name was Sheila – most folk called her Shell – but Stan always called her Gladys because that's what she was, a right Gladys. He never called her 'Mum'. She'd lost the right to be called that a long time ago.

'Mind your own soddin' business,' she snapped back.

'That's good then. Glad to hear you're coping.'

From across the room a voice chirped. 'Fuck off, son! Fuck off!'

Stan turned with a big smile to mum's mynah bird, on its perch in a cage. The bird squawked its welcome for a second time. 'Fuck off, son! Fuck off!'

Stan poked his half-finger through the bars. His voice softened as he whispered, 'Hello, Charlie, how are you, mate?'

The bird looked at his finger but decided not to peck it. 'Fuck off, son! Fuck off!'

Stan reached into his pocket. 'Ere, look, I've got you something.' He produced a piece of cuttlefish, which he pushed through the bars. 'There you go.'

His mum noticed. 'What are you giving my Charlie?'

'It's a present.'

She reared away, outraged. 'A present? You never bring your own mother presents. Some fucking son you are.'

'That's because Charlie's the only person in this house you can have a sensible conversation with.'

Stan loved the bird. Charlie might have been trapped in his cage but he'd kept his self-respect. Whenever his mum had visitors she would gather them around her mynah and demand, 'Go on, Charlie! Say something! Say something! Pretty Polly! Pretty Polly!' But the bird would sit with its beak shut and look at her with an expression that said, 'Why don't you say something instead, you silly cow? I'm not a circus act.' Charlie only talked when he felt like it.

Stan noticed something and let rip at his mum. 'Why don't you ever change Charlie's drinking tray? I've seen water in the Royal Docks that looks healthier than this.'

She huffed, 'What am I? A fucking zookeeper? He's not complaining.'

'Of course he's not complaining, he's a bird, you stupid woman.' Stan fetched the tray out. He walked into the kitchen, emptied it into a sink stacked high with washing up and carefully scrubbed it clean. He deliberately avoided looking at the block in the garden that most people mistook for a shed, but which was in fact their old outdoor toilet. His mum had a working indoor lav but she kept the one outside because it reminded him of the horrors of his childhood. The malicious old bat.

Stan shook off the past and filled the tray up. As he put it back, he said, 'Ere you go, Charlie – have a drink on me.'

There was a mallet under the cage. He picked it up and held it until his knuckles turned white. It had been his mum's favourite instrument of torture. More than once he'd been chased up the street with it when he'd upset her for some minor reason. Even their dad had thought that was going too far. His preferred weapons were his fists and boots but at least he'd dished out batterings to both sons. With Gladys, it was only him. Pete was her little mummy's boy. And he'd been her little mummy's boy ever since.

Stan put the mallet down and turned around to face the less interesting animals in the room. He was glad his old man was dead. It was one less useless git to worry about.

Pete was drifting away. His eyes were closed and the first pig-like noises were beginning as he began to snore. The plaster their mum had stuck to his face was already coming away.

He grabbed Pete by the scruff of his neck and shook him. 'Wakey-wakey, bruv. Me and you still need to have that serious chat.'

Pete opened his eyes and gave his brother a long stare, before closing them again.

Stan shook him again. 'Oi! I mean it!'

Mumbling, muttering and whinging, Pete began struggling upwards. 'Nag, nag, nag, you're just like my fucking wife—'

'You ain't got a wife, you prick. There are plenty of thick birds around here but none of them are thick enough to marry a soak like you.'

'Moan, moan, moan . . .'

Their mum was horrified to see her patient disturbed when she came back in the room. 'What do you think you're doing? Leave him alone, he needs to rest.'

Stan could feel his blood boiling. 'Rest? All he ever does is get pissed and rest, fight and feel sorry for himself. Now piss off. I want a word with Pete in private.'

'Anything you've got to say to your brother, you can say in front of me.'

Stan frogmarched his brother to the back room, slammed the door and pushed a chair in front of it so their mother couldn't get in, although he knew she'd be earwigging outside. He parked Pete at the table and said in quiet, clipped tones, 'Listen, I'm going to cut the crap because I want out of here as fast as possible. There are two things I've got to say and they're not up for discussion. Number one, the sauce has got to stop.'

Pete looked at his brother in disbelief. 'I don't know what you're going on about. I like a drink, so what? It's not like I'm an alkie or anything.'

For Stan, his brother's denial was proof enough that he was. 'Pete, you're making a total tit of your life. And it's affecting my business, alright?'

His tone seemed to be sobering Pete up. The wound on his face began to glow red. 'I know I ought to stop,' he admitted. 'I'm trying, I really am. But you don't know what it's like. It's hard. I only mean to have the one and then one thing leads to another and I'm all over the shop and things get out of hand. I know it's wrong, I know it's wrong . . .'

Pete was in tears now. Stan's heart nearly broke at seeing his brother in such a mess. Where had the knight in shining armour from his childhood gone?

Stan spoke more softly this time. 'The second thing is, I might need to arrange for someone important to come down to the knocking shop and I need you to do the usual special for me. If it's a goer, I'll give you a bell with the details.' Abruptly he grabbed his brother and pulled him up so they were face to face. 'This particular job is very important to me, so don't muck it up. If you do, I'll rip your fucking arms off.'

His brother's eyes narrowed. 'You've got a short memory. When our dad was ripping *your* arms off, you were grateful to me when I took him on. When I put a stop to it for good, you swore undying devotion.'

Stan loosened his grip but his face was still like flint. 'I know. And I love you, Pete. If I didn't – mark my words – I'd have cut you off ages ago.'

The brothers stared hard at each other, remembering the violence that had created the bond between them.

Stan let Pete go. 'If the special happens, don't fuck it up.'

Pete nodded. 'Don't worry about it. I'll sort it. There's a girl down there called Cleo. She always helps me and of course you know Daffy—'

Stan brought him up short. 'How many times have I told you I don't want to know about Mickey's sleazy empire? He's got his side of the biz and I've got mine and never the twain shall meet.'

And that was true, except for the little wrinkle he and Pete had cooked up behind thicko Mickey's back. There were reasons he kept well back from Mickey's other dealings. Partly, it was common sense to keep the two things separate, in case the coppers got involved. Stan wasn't going to get banged up; he was very sure about that. Plus, his only interest in Mickey's side of their world was the profits he could invest in his business.

But Stan was unable to resist asking, 'Is this Cleo alright?'

Pete's red face transformed into a sparkling smile. 'She's a stunning black bird. She's smart, she knows what to do and how to keep her gob shut.'

'As long as you're sure.'

As Stan knew only too well, smart people are at a premium in life. He made a mental note of the name *Cleo*.

As he rose, Pete said, 'I love you too, bruv.'

Stan nodded and made his way back to the sitting room. The telly wheezed and cut off as he entered. The TV was a rental and would only work with fifty pence coins popped into the money box on the back.

His mum groused, 'After all I've done for you, you can't buy your old girl a proper telly. The shame of it.' She turned to the door and yelled, 'Pete, the telly needs a ten-bob bit.'

Stan smiled. She knew better than to ask him. If she was waiting for him to buy her a TV set she'd be waiting for the rest of her miserable life.

'See ya later, Charlie!' he called warmly as he left.

The mynah bird hopped down off its perch and peered out of its cage.

'Fuck off, son! Fuck off!'

Thirteen

'Babs, you still haven't brought this so-called fiancé home to see us,' Rosie Wilson reminded her daughter.

It was a month later. They were out shopping in Whitechapel market for a few bits and pieces for the coming baby. Babs' belly was starting to show.

'Ain't that pretty,' Babs replied, picking up a stuffed elephant and trying her hardest to steer the conversation away from the non-existent fiancé.

But Rosie Wilson wasn't that stupid. She snatched the toy and put it back with the other knick-knacks on the stall. She made her daughter face her. 'Some man left a baby in your belly and we, as respectable and God-fearing parents, have the right to meet him. Now, if he's chucked you—'

'No way, Mum,' Babs jumped in quickly. Her mum and dad finding out that was exactly what had happened was too shameful for her to deal with. She knew they were going to find out sooner or later, but she preferred it to be later. Much later.

'So, when's he going to show his face?'

'Tell you what, I'll see if he can come over on Sunday for dinner.'

Now she'd gone and done it! Somehow, Babs had to get her hands on a 'fiancé' to bring home to meet her parents.

Daffy left the world of the brothel behind as she went out via the back door to see the man who was her closely guarded secret. She'd known so many men in her life, some of them leaving scars she would carry around forever, but this man was different. Just thinking about him turned her usually pinched features into a face brimming with pleasure. And what pleasure she would have when they met. She couldn't wait.

She caught the bus from Mile End Road, got off at Aldgate East station and took the rest of the short journey by foot. Daffy entered an alleyway and pushed past the bin bags until she reached a rusty back door. She walked into a warm workroom.

Her face lit up as the sight of her secret man puffing away at his pipe.

'I'm here,' she called out.

'Get your kit off then,' said a grinning George Wilson.

Daffy sent him a quick smile before she took off her dress and put on the overall he always laid out. Then she settled at the sewing machine he'd set up for her and got to work. Most people would roar their heads off if they learned that iron-fisted, knocking-shop keeper Dorothy Sure's only dream was to one day have her own boutique up West. She'd thought the fantasy would be forever out of her reach until the fateful night she'd met George. That night was so horrible she made herself not remember it. The only shining light had been George. He'd saved her life and she would never forget that. That gentlemen like him still existed remained a wonder to her. When she'd confessed her dream he'd pulled out all the stops to help her.

Now she sensed there was something troubling him. 'What's on your mind?' she asked.

His shoulders sagged. 'My girl has only gone and got herself in the club.'

This was where most women would shake their heads sadly, but Daffy knew all about the casualties of real life. 'It happens. It ain't the end of the world.'

'But me and the missus think she's stringing us along about having a fella. I think some bloke has left her high and dry.'

Daffy perched on the table next to him. 'I've been there and it ain't a good feeling. If that's what's happened, you and your wife need to give her double the amount of love to make up for it.'

He looked so sad it hurt her heart. 'But I had such high hopes for her—'

'It's wrong to live your life through your kids. All you can do is support her on her own path.'

He huffed and got to his feet. 'Right, let's see how you've got on.' They went over to check over the blouse she was making. George set her tasks like a teacher, his way of helping her learn the trade.

He pulled the blouse high. 'Sleeves good. Collar alright. But this stitching here is as wonky as the road my daughter's found herself on.'

'I'm trying my best here.' Her face came over all dreamy. 'You know what I'm going to call myself when I get my shop? Something that sounds all posh and French. Madam Dominique, that's who I'm going to be. I want a clean break with my past.'

She laid her hand gently on his arm. 'Whatever your girl's done, you can help her find a blinding future.'

Babs bit the inside of her cheek anxiously. She needed to find the right moment to talk Stan into posing as her fiancé. She was at her desk sorting through some invoices, but her mind wasn't on the job. Babs desperately tried to find the right words to persuade him.

'*I'm in a bit of a fix . . .*' No, that made her sound like she was really down on her luck.

'*Stan, you've got to do me an all-time favour . . .*' No, that sounded like she was telling him what to do.

Babs stood up in frustration. Going over and over it was royally winding her up. The best thing to do was just say what she needed to say and leave the rest up to him. Courage renewed, Babs walked briskly to Stan's office door, knocked and opened it without waiting for his response. She went into the room and ran straight into his chest.

His hands were around her in no time to steady them both. Babs inhaled sharply at the feel of his flesh against her skin. It was like an electric bolt jolting through her, making her feel all sexy and warm. *Stan* made her feel all sexy and warm.

Shocked to her socks, Babs glanced up to find Stan staring intently down at her. His hands tightened ever so slightly.

Flustered, Babs wiggled away from him and tried to get some control back.

Stan coughed nervously and then popped on his trademark charming grin. 'Something up about those invoices?'

Get on with it, girl! 'Can I ask a favour? Quite a big one, actually.'

Stan headed back to his desk. 'Sure, what is it?'

Babs nervously twisted her teeth into her bottom lip. 'It's a little bit delicate.'

'Don't worry about that – delicate's my middle name.'

She swallowed. 'The thing is, my mum and dad have been going on at me to meet the fiancé I keep talking about. But you know the problem there – I ain't got one. So I was wondering . . .' Babs drew out the last word, '. . . if you're not busy on Sunday, if you could–'

'What? Come over and do a Mike Yarwood as your fella?'

Babs would've normally chuckled at him comparing himself to the famous impressionist, but this situation was too serious. 'Exactly.'

Stan pulled a face. 'But I ain't black.'

'They don't know about my kid's colour at the moment, so it'll all fit.'

Stan tutted as he linked his fingers together. 'Babs, you're gonna have to spill the beans or it's going to end badly. Very badly.'

Babs' mouth went dry again. 'I can't deal with that now. I do have to – I know – but just not now. So, will you do it?'

Stan looked deeply into her eyes. 'I'd do anything for you, Babs. Anything.'

Babs expected him to start laughing or wink, turning his words into a joke. But he kept on staring at her as if she didn't have another man's baby growing in her belly. It hurt, really hurt, that she wasn't free to be with an upstanding man like Stanley Miller.

'But . . .' Stan went on.

Babs' picture perfect image of Stan dribbled away. She should've known there was a catch. 'What?'

He was back to smiling. 'You've got to do me a favour too.'

Babs' disappointment deepened. But he was getting her out of a tight fix, so maybe it was only right she did something in return. 'What do you want me to do?'

Stan leaned back in his chair. 'I'll let you know soon enough. But when I do, there's no backing out.'

A minute later Babs was back at her desk, her tone all chipper on the blower. 'Mum, guess what? My fiancé Stanley will be coming over for dinner this Sunday.'

'So are you gonna do this for me or what?' Denny asked Babs bluntly later in the Dog and Whistle.

Denny had gone from 'just remembering' that Babs was going to put in a word for her at the modelling agency to having a bite in her voice as she insisted that her mate help her out. Meanwhile Babs had gone from 'forgetting to ask' to increasingly unlikely excuses. Her latest was that Stan had gone on an assignment in Morocco and no one knew when he would be back. It was becoming a headache she didn't need.

'So there's no one else you can ask for me?'

Babs couldn't look her friend in the eye; best mates shouldn't string each other along. 'No. There's Mickey but he don't book models, that's Stan's job. I can't do nuthin' for you until Stan is back.'

'What does this Mickey do, then?' When Babs mumbled something about organising shoots and that, Denny cut her short. 'You're a crap liar, Babs. What's the matter? Don't think I'm pretty enough?'

That gave Babs the nark. 'I never said that. It's just, you know . . .'

'No – I don't know.'

Babs decided to tell her half the truth. 'Modelling ain't easy-peasy. It's flippin' hard work from what Stan says. It can chew girls up and spit them out. You don't want to get involved in that, do you?'

Denny slammed her drink down. 'Oh, right. Now we're getting down to it. You could help me out but you won't. Some mate you are.' She shook her head. 'I can't stop at home for much longer. I . . .' Her lips snapped shut.

Babs was concerned. 'What's up, Denny? Things haven't seemed right with you for a while. What's going on?'

Denny pursed her lips. 'I'll tell you what's up. My best friend don't wanna go out of her way for me.'

Babs knew she was cornered by her own promises. 'When Stan gets back from Spain, I'll ask him.'

'Spain? I thought you said he was in Morocco. Don't worry about it, I'll sort myself out.'

Babs was horrified. 'What's that supposed to mean?'

'What I said. If you won't help me out, I'll do it myself. There's more than one way to shine a penny.'

Fourteen

Bright and breezy on the Sunday morning, Mel went down to the agency. She used her husband's key to open up and then tried the door to Stan's office. She was sure he wouldn't be there; the whole of Britain shut up shop on a Sunday. She'd been meaning for ages to have a snoop around and find out what he was up to. Now it was urgent.

The door was locked. Mel scoffed at that. She pulled out a bobby pin from her bun, stuck it in the lock and wriggled it about for a few seconds before the lock sprang and she was inside.

She'd never had time to examine his office before. Whenever she and Mickey had dropped by, it was always on business. The room looked more like the kind of love-nest a rich bachelor would have than a place of work. And she should know; she'd been in enough.

Mel checked the globe drinks trolley, which seemed to be expensively stocked, and helped herself to a brandy. She sat on his plush leopard-print sofa, crossed her black crinkle boots and looked over the room.

She knew the little weasel was too crafty to leave anything incriminating lying around, but he had to be hiding things somewhere. But where? She drained her glass, placed it back on the drinks trolley and began looking behind his pictures for safes and levering the floorboards to see if any were loose. When she had no joy with that, she went over his desk. The drawers were locked. But that was no problem for a pro like her. She'd once been the squeeze of a burglar from Romford who'd told her, 'Drawers are just like houses, girl. Always go in round the back.'

There was a solid silver paper knife on Stan's desk. She used it to prise away the vanity panel to get at the drawers from the rear. They were heavy but she chipped away at the joints. So intent was she on getting in that she got the shock of her life when she heard Stan's chair squeak as it turned and a voice say, 'Morning Mel – I didn't know you were into DIY?'

Bollocks, she hadn't even heard him come in. She peered over the top of the desk to see Stan lighting up. Mel knew she looked straight-up stupid, on her hands and knees with a silver knife in her hand. 'I'm sure I dropped an earring in here. It belonged to my dear mum. I suppose I should have asked you but I didn't like to bother you on a Sunday.'

Stan blew smoke and pulled a face. 'Give over, Mel – you can do better than that. That's the kind of excuse your dick brain of a husband would come up with.'

Mel got to her feet and put the knife back. She pulled up a chair and sat down. He offered her a cigarette, which she took. Then he gestured at the room with his fag.

'If you want to know anything about my side of the biz, doll, you only have to ask. I haven't got any secrets from you and Mickey.'

She burst out laughing and choked on her smoke. 'It's me you're talking to, not my cack-handed Mickey.'

Stan shrugged. 'That's not fair. Me and Mickey are as thick as thieves. When we went into business together, we agreed we'd have no secrets. I'm sure Mickey's told you how we sealed the deal.'

Mickey had told her alright, but she'd had to drag it out of him in bits and pieces. Even he could see what a cheeky ponce Stan was being. How when he'd joined the business, he'd visited the premises in Chancery Row, wandered into Mickey's office and made himself at home in Mickey's swivel chair behind Mickey's big desk. Then he'd said, 'I'll tell you what, why don't you let me run the modelling agency? You stick to what you know and I'll take care of this for you.'

And like a mug, Mickey said yes, although on condition he still got first dibs on the birds to supply his other interests. Stan had agreed but Mickey told her the supply of girls had soon dried up. Whenever Mickey asked how the Soho business was going, Stan would reply, 'It's still ticking over.'

But was it? Shortly afterwards Stan had taken over Mickey's property interests in the East End to 'look after them' too. Of course it made sense to Mickey. Stan was smart, he knew all about contracts and council pen pushers and solicitors and how to persuade others to buy and sell. That was the trouble with Mickey. Everything made sense to him. He was so fucking thick.

'Yeah, he told me about your business arrangements. Trouble is, my husband's so busy he doesn't have time to keep tabs on what's happening up here.'

'Why would he?'

Mel hissed. 'Because you're up to something, Miller, that's why. There's no modelling going on here, we both know that. And this office doesn't supply us with girls no more—'

'You know this is my base for looking after Mickey's properties. People are more likely to work with you when you've got a West End address.'

Mel wasn't letting him off the hook. 'See, what worries me is what's going on with Mickey's houses and flats. I've given up counting the forms and documents you've asked him to initial in the past months, knowing he won't ask what they are. What's going on, Stan? What are you up to?'

She knew she couldn't trust his words or his face, but she could trust his eyes. And they were glinting.

'Nothing's going on; it's admin, that's all.'

'Fuck off. You're up to something.'

Stan lit another fag. 'Sounds to me as if you're accusing your husband of being too thick to read what he's signing.'

That was what she thought but instead Mel said, 'Not too thick – too trusting.'

'Trusting, thick. What's the difference?'

She'd blown it. In the unlikely event there was anything incriminating in his office, by the time she got another chance to look for it, it would be gone. But Melanie Ingram was no loser. She still had one card left to play. 'OK, fine.' She slowly undid her mink and coyly tilted her head to the side. 'So tell me, what's a girl got to do to get a drink around here?'

Stan sniffed the air. 'Already smells like you've had a snifter or two . . .' But he got up and went to his drinks cabinet. While he was pouring her a brandy, she undid her blouse to reveal her ample cleavage. After all, there's no talk like pillow talk.

When he put the drink in front of her, he didn't look at the flesh on display for more than a second before asking, 'Feeling warm?'

She lowered her voice to a husky whisper. 'Well, you know how it is . . . Sometimes a woman does feel quite warm, don't you find?'

Mel scooted up onto his desk and crossed her legs, letting her dress fall down over her knees. She took the hem and wafted it up and down. 'That's better, circulating some air . . .'

Stan leaned forward, looked at her legs, then back at her before saying lecherously, 'You know what you need, don't you?'

Gotcha! 'I think so . . .'

Stan leaned back again, deadpan. 'Some fresh air – and a better plan. You should know me better. I always keep business separate from pleasure. I'm unusual like that.'

Mel shook her hem down and climbed off the desk. If it had been any other bloke, she'd have been furious. But Stan was indeed an odd fish. She'd wondered whether he might be a bit ginger. It was probably working in Soho that did it. She picked up her bag.

At the door, she turned to him and said, 'You're running on luck, Stan. The trouble is, luck eventually runs out.'

'No, Mel. I run on talent and that never runs out. And do your buttons up, droopy drawers, or you'll have some sad sack on the street asking you how much it costs for you to give his cock a close-up.'

The rapid clunk-clunk of Mel's heels on the wooden stairs matched her fuming mood. That slimy bastard. Rotten cunt. Smug prick. Her mind cursed Stanley Miller every which way. If he thought he'd put her down for good, he didn't know the first thing about her. Ever since she'd been a not-so-innocent fifteen-year-old and rolled over her first guy by promising sex and then ripping the geezer off instead, Mel had made it her business to find men's weaknesses. And every man had one. Her Mickey's was their daughter Donna. And Stan's was . . .

Mel stopped. His weakness was so glaringly obvious he probably didn't even realise it.

His older brother. Pete. Why else would Stan go all out for a man whose nut was pickled in booze most of the time? Mickey had told her the tale of Stan's unhappy childhood. Stan probably thought he owed his brother.

'What a chump,' Mel whispered. In her book, one of the

golden rules was never owe anyone anything. Especially if they were your flesh and blood.

Now all she had to figure out was how to use Pete to get rid of Stan. She went out of the door and was caught up short by a real stunner of a girl loitering nervously nearby. She didn't look like the usual Soho tart, so Mel asked, 'Can I help you, luv?'

The girl hesitated as she gazed at Mel with enormous hazel eyes. 'I was looking for the Go Go Girls Modelling Agency but it don't seem to be here.'

'The agency? Funny time to come looking. It's a Sunday. No one works on a Sunday – I'm just off to church.'

The girl's face fell. 'Oh. I thought the guy in charge might be here, I heard he works on a Sunday sometimes.'

'The guy in charge?'

'Yeah, Stanley Miller.'

That needled an already needled Mel even further. 'You've been misinformed, darling. The gaffer is called Mickey and I should know – I'm his wife. Stan's just the office boy. Mickey makes all the decisions.'

'Oh.' She looked even more deflated. 'I wanted to know how to become a model.'

Mel should've known. What did girls hanging around in Soho always want? They were always the same – girls from nowhere who were as thick as a bookie's wallet.

Mel assessed the girl. Mind you, they could always use another pair of boobs down the brothel.

'You should go home and forget this modelling lark,' Mel told her. She didn't know why; she'd lost her heart a long time ago. If this girl wanted to end up on her back with men poking her for a living, what was it to Mel? But there was something innocent about the girl that reminded Mel of herself before life got its fangs into her.

'Get yourself home.'

The girl shook her head furiously. 'Home?' She begged, 'Please, missus, put in a word for me with your old man.'

She was desperate. All softness left Mel. She smiled, transforming her into the picture of kindness. 'I might be able to sort you out. No promises, mind. Let me have your name and address.' After this was done, Mel smiled again. 'I'll be in touch.'

She headed down the road, mind buzzing away, until she came to Luigi's café. She knew it would be shut so she headed around the back and knocked on the door.

A half-naked brunette with more paint on her face than a Dulux factory opened it. Her face creased into a smile when she saw Mel. 'You wanna word with Luigi?'

Mel shook her head. 'Nah, just need to use the blower.'

She entered a large backroom with a live striptease show on stage, men staring at it, glassy-eyed. While most of Britain had a day of rest on the Lord's day, behind closed doors Soho was still doing the devil's work. Luigi's served tea and muffins in the daytime and dished up strippers and muff at night and all day Sunday.

Mel found the call box outside Luigi's office. She dialled. 'It's me . . . He caught me at it . . . Calm down and keep your hair on . . .' Mel lowered her voice. 'I've thought of a better way to wipe out Pete and Stan. We need to think this through properly. There's this dosey-doe called Denny . . .'

Fifteen

'Your young man's not very punctual, is he?' Rosie Wilson complained in a clipped tone while they were waiting for him to join them for Sunday roast.

'Like I said, he's very busy with his company.'

Her mum snorted at that, and Babs couldn't blame her.

She was sitting facing her parents in the front room, her hands neatly folded in her lap. Inside, she was bricking it. *Come on, Stan.* What the bloody heck was keeping him? He was already fifteen minutes late. One slip-up and she was royally screwed. Her mum and dad had pulled out all the stops: got dressed up in their Sunday best and put on a spread fit for the Queen.

Mercifully the knocker on the front door went with a solid bang. About time! Babs started to get up, but her mum gave her the eye that clearly said this was her house and she'd be doing the opening of any doors.

Less than half a minute later, Rosie escorted Stan into the sitting room. He looked like the dog's bits, a total knockout. He wore a navy Norfolk jacket with patch pockets and a stylish belt, trim-cut, flared slacks and shoes buffed to perfection. He wore his clobber with such style that Babs wished for a moment that her fake fiancé was the real deal.

'You must be Babs' mum – I can see where she gets her

looks from,' Stan told Rosie. She blushed. What woman could resist Stan's killer smile? 'And these are for you.' He presented her with a large bunch of flowers, a box of Black Magic chocolates and a bottle of such upmarket vino Babs couldn't even pronounce its name.

Babs rushed over to Stan's side. He put his arm around her waist possessively as she introduced him to George.

'I'll call you *Dad,* shall I, now I'm family?' Stan said after the introduction.

'Yes, I suppose,' George muttered, not so easily taken in. 'Although, I'll tell you this, I was not best pleased—'

'George, dear,' Rosie intervened with a tight sweet smile, 'let's all go through for dinner, shall we.'

Stan praised the roast as 'one of the best joints he'd ever eaten' and then held court like he did in the office. Her parents chucked questions at him like booby traps, but Stan answered each and every one so convincingly, Babs was half believing it herself. She said nothing and let him get on with it. He was doing a bang-up job.

'My business? It always keeps the cash flowing if you've got your fingers in a number of pies. So I'm in import/export and I think there are some very interesting possibilities opening up on the continent, what with the talk of this Common Market. I've got a number of commercial partners in the Netherlands and West Germany I'm exploring opportunities with.'

Rosie looked at him as if he were talking German, so her husband took over. 'The Krauts?'

Stan tucked into his succulent beef. 'Yeah, alright, they did reduce the East End to rubble but fair's fair, they know how to do business. I'm not going to hold the past against them. My office in Soho—'

'Soho?' George jabbed his fork into a roast potato and drilled his gaze into Stan.

It was the first time he'd put a foot wrong and Babs held her breath. She'd warned him all about her dad's opinion of that part of London and to stay clear of it.

Stan laughed. 'I meant Southend. That's where some of my business contacts are as well.' He swiftly turned to Rosie, making a delighted *mmm* sound. 'Mum, this food is fantastic.'

Rosie preened, but George was not such a pushover. 'I'm still asking myself, s*on,* why it took you so long to find our doorstep?'

Babs' knife clattered to her plate. *Here we go!* She looked over at Stan, who turned to her father. 'The truth is, I was away on business and when I got back and my Babs told me the wonderful news I wanted to come over as soon as. But I had a few family problems.' Rosie made a little gasping sound of sympathy. 'But that's all sorted now, and me and Babs can look to the future.' He took Babs' hand and squeezed it.

'Babs,' Rosie said, looking very pleased with proceedings, 'let's clear the table and bring in afters.'

After the Angel Delight had been served, Stan produced two Havana cigars, one for him and one for George. He took a pair of solid silver cutters from his waistcoat and expertly cut the ends off.

'My word, you do like the finer things in life, don't you?'

'Only the best for me – that's why I wanted to marry your daughter.' He squeezed Babs' hand again and she blushed. She'd been hoping Stan would do a rush job, convince her parents and then clear off before they tumbled. Now she was wishing this Sunday would last forever.

George puffed blissfully on his cigar. 'I'll be honest with you, me and the wife weren't very happy that you jumped the gun, but you seem like a very nice young man.'

Before Stan could answer, there was a bang at the front door.

George got to his feet. 'I don't know who that can be,' he muttered. 'As far as I know we're not expecting any company.'

'Yoo-hoo!' a high female voice screeched from the passage after George answered the door.

'Oh no,' Babs and Rosie chimed together, one with an expression of dread and the other rolling her eyes.

A very glum George reappeared, followed by his cousin Valerie from Shadwell. Valerie had turned twenty in 1942 and it looked like that had been the last time she'd bought any clothes. Her whole look had a make-do-and-mend vibe about it. Her suit had clearly been black at one stage but the colour now varied like sun-bleached curtains. She wore a matching pillbox hat with a half-veil. For most people, the veil wasn't pulled down far enough. She always looked like she was on the way to a cheap funeral.

Since her Cliff had passed five years back she made a habit of dropping in unexpectedly on a Sunday. Babs knew she should feel sorry for the old girl – she was obviously lonely – but the woman was the definition of earache and careless talk rolled into one.

Cousin Val took in the scene and sniffed the air. 'Sunday spread. Well, I don't mind if I do.'

She had her hat and coat off in five seconds flat and pulled up a chair. She gave Stan the eye. 'This your fella then, Babs?'

Babs popped on a cheerful smile. 'He's my fiancé.'

'I'm glad to hear it. I was starting to wonder if that baby of yours actually had a father.' She let out a piercing laugh that had Rosie's special glasses shaking in the cabinet. Babs and her parents winced but Stan wore a gentle grin like he was having the time of his life.

Then Val wiped the grin from her face and she peered at him closely, her eye twitching. 'Don't I know you from somewhere?'

Babs' heart dropped. She glanced over at her wannabe fiancé, who remained as cool as you like. 'I would remember a beautiful woman like you, Cousin Valerie,' Stan informed her. 'I never forget a pretty face.'

Loving that, Val let out another glass-shattering laugh. She shifted her gaze to Babs. 'You've got a right one there, dearie. You want to hang on to him.' She helped herself to a slice of beef, talking away. 'It's nice to see a young man with such good manners. Back in my day . . .'

And she was off like the Grand National. Ten minutes straight she talked, without coming up for air. Babs was surprisingly grateful: it took the heat away from her and Stan.

But then Val stopped abruptly, halfway through a story about the Hackney Empire back in her day. Her gaze fell on the floor. 'What's that?' She leaned down and picked something off the floor. A small card.

Stan coughed. It was the first time Babs had seen him nervous. Bloody hell. 'I think that's one of my business cards. It must've fallen out when I got those cigars.'

He held out his hand, but Val lurched back. 'Ooh! A business card, not many folk have one of them. You must be doing alright for yourself.'

Babs face grew tight. 'Yes he is. He was telling Mum and Dad all about it before you dropped by.' She held out her hand. 'Now why don't you give me that?'

Instead her cousin held it close to her face and read it aloud. 'Stanley Miller Esquire. Pro . . . Pro . . . Pro-pri-e-tor. Go Go Girls Modelling Agency. Soho. London.' She was so wrapped up in her own world she never noticed the deathly silence around the table. 'When I was young everyone said I should've been a model. Said I looked like Rita Hayworth . . .'

Babs watched her dad's lips go thin. 'Soho?' he said.

With a smile laced with retribution, Rosie said, 'Stanley, Barbara, help me clear the dishes away.'

Stan sighed. As they dutifully trailed after her mum, he whispered, 'I should leave.'

'Please Stan—'

'There's a lesson I've learned Babs-babe – when the curtain falls, you should leave the stage.'

A minute later Rosie had Babs and Stan cornered against the Formica counter. 'Alright sonny, what's your game?'

Babs looked at Stan with pleading eyes. He faked good cheer. 'Sorry, Mum, I'm not with you?'

Rosie's lip curled. 'Don't you *Mum* me – what's a so-called respectable businessman like you doing with a modelling agency in Soho?'

Knowing the game was well and truly up, and not wanting to make Stan fib any more, Babs confessed. 'Stanley's not really my fiancé. He's a mate doing me a favour. He really is a businessman, though. And the modelling agency is a decent one, nothing funny. The truth is, the baby's dad did a bunk.' She hung her head in shame.

Rosie blew her top. 'Fine kettle of fish this is. Not only is our daughter no better than a Soho whore—'

Stan pulled himself tall. 'I have the utmost respect for you, Mrs Wilson, but don't be calling Babs that.' He clenched his teeth. 'I won't stand for it.'

Rosie was clearly surprised by his defence of her daughter, but she wasn't finished with Babs by a long shot. 'You think you can make fools of us in our own home? I taught you better than that, Barbara Patricia Wilson. Come on, out with it, who's the bastard who knocked you up?'

'Alright, dear, that's enough. We'll talk about it later,' George said quietly from the doorway.

She turned on him in fury. 'You're as much to blame for this as she is. If you were any kind of man, you'd have tracked the father down by now and shown him what for.'

Babs felt so humiliated. 'I'm so sorry.'

George came around and hugged her tight. 'Don't be daft. Plenty of girls have been taken advantage of by some worthless cunt.'

'George Wilson,' Rosie shrieked, scandalised by his unusually ripe language.

But he wasn't sorry. 'It's true. Men like that are the lowest of the low.' He eased Babs slightly away, to look in her face. 'What's done is done. One day you'll meet the man of your dreams, and in the meantime we'll always be there for you. There is nothing on this earth you can do that will ever make us turn our backs on you.'

A few minutes later, a washed-out Babs saw Stan to the door. What a right old muck-up Sunday roast had turned into.

'Maybe this is for the best,' Stan said. 'They were always going to find out that I wasn't your fiancé.'

Babs knew he was right, but she still hadn't been ready for the full force of her mum's displeasure. 'You're a stand-up fella for doing this, Stan.'

'Which leads me to that favour I wanted in return.'

Babs groaned inwardly. She'd forgotten all about his side of the bargain. Even though she felt like her legs weren't going to hold her up much longer, a deal was a deal. 'What do you want me to do? Clean the office from top to bottom? Wash your suits? Work every Sunday for the rest of the year?'

Stan laughed out loud. 'You can do all three if that's what you want, but that ain't my favour.' He pulled a small envelope from his pocket. 'Remember what I said, you have to do it.'

As soon as he handed it to a puzzled Babs, he was out of the door. She tore it open and pulled out a white card. Her jaw dropped.

She rushed after Stan and caught him on the street near a group of boys playing footie. She waved the card at him. 'Stan, it's from the council offering me a flat. I don't get it.'

Stan smiled with satisfaction. 'I had a little word with a mate on the council who sorted you out a nice spot on a new development down Mile End way. It won't be ready for a couple of months, mind.'

'I can't take this.'

He caught her hand. 'Remember our bargain. You have to do it. As much as I liked your parents, the one thing that stood out today was that you and the baby need a place to call home.'

Babs almost jumped on him, crushing him joyfully to her as the boys wolf-whistled.

'I was right,' Rosie said triumphantly as she and her husband watched their daughter and the young man she'd brought home in each other's arms. 'He fancies her.'

'Don't jump to conclusions, luv.' But George was grinning from ear to ear.

'He looked like he was going to clobber me when I called her a tart. He's protective of her and the baby. And she needs a fella—'

'Rosie—'

'I'm just saying.' Babs' mother smiled.

Sixteen

'So what are you running from, Denny?' Mel asked the other woman, as they sat in a café in Soho a couple of weeks later. It was their third time out together since meeting that Sunday two months ago. Mel needed Denny to trust her, so that when she and Mickey went in for the kill the girl would come like a gormless little lamb to the slaughter.

'You what?' Denny said, her hazel eyes wide with anxiety.

Mel carefully placed her cup in its saucer. 'If you'll pardon me saying so, a bird with your looks doesn't come down Soho way unless she's trying to leave something behind.'

Denny's cheeks reddened. 'I ain't running from nuthin'. My mum and stepdad think the world of me. It's just time for me to find my own place.'

Mel would have bet her pay packet – if she worked – that the girl wasn't even aware of the dread in her voice when she mentioned her stepfather.

She reached across and tipped Denny's chin up with a gentle finger so she could look her in the eye. 'I'm going to tell you a story which you can take or leave – it's up to you – but I'm going to tell it to you anyway.' Mel shook back her hair. 'When I was thirteen my mum married a bloke who seemed like God's gift. He'd buy us kids pressies, my mum flowers. He even had a car.' Her eyes bore deep into Denny's. 'I don't need to tell you what happened when he took me for drives to Epping Forest.'

Denny's breath shuddered in her chest, reverberating across the table. Mel carried on. 'I wish I could've stopped him, but that's foolish talk. He was bigger and stronger than me. That's why I became an independent woman; so no man ever had control over me again.'

Denny's face crumpled. Her voice shook when she finally spoke. 'The bastard's been after me for the last six months or so. Trying to put his disgusting paws on me any chance he gets.' She shook her head. 'If I stay in that house he's going to get me—'

'No, he won't,' Mel snapped. 'You know why? Because if he comes near you all you've got to do is scream your head off.'

'But my mum doesn't believe me. She said I'm a wicked girl for suggesting Darren would do any such thing.' Her head jerked up, her gaze fierce. 'But I ain't lying.'

'I know you're not.' *But I am. Filling your brainless head with my bollocks sob story.* Mel had never had a stepfather and if she'd had one who tried to play kiddie fiddler with her she'd have chopped his dick off.

Mel got on with the job. Now she knew Denny's secret it was going to be oh-so-very-easy to reel the desperate girl into her and Mickey's net. She was desperate for some kindness, a bit of safety, and Mel was up for playing Fairy Godmother with the magic wand of a modelling career.

Mel gripped Denny's hand. She leaned across the table and whispered, 'I'm going to make all your dreams come true. My husband, Mickey, who owns the agency, wants to meet you. Women like me and you, with the same experiences, need to stick together.'

Seven months pregnant, Babs got off the number 25 bus with her mum and Denny to see the flat in Mile End that Stan had wangled off the council. She would be forever grateful to him for getting her a spanking new two-bed on the Essex Lane Estate. They were becoming a real team. But neither of them had taken it further, though there was definitely something between them. Babs wanted to, but how could she, with another man's kid in her belly?

'I had a so-called friend who lived around here,' her mum sniffed. 'Turned out she was making a play for your dad behind my back.'

Rosie Wilson was not best pleased that her only child was finally flying the nest. She was desperate to play mother hen to both Babs and her baby, but her daughter couldn't seem to get out from under her roof quick enough.

'Come on, Mum.' Babs linked her arm into her mother's as if sensing her sad thoughts. 'Feel happy for me. I'm about to start my new life.' She almost laughed out loud. She still couldn't believe that she was going to have her own front door.

'I think this is the wrong way,' Denny said. Although her best friend had been chuffed that Babs was getting her own place, she'd also worn a 'wish it were me' expression. Something was up with Denny, Babs just knew it, but she wouldn't say what. Babs' gut told her it had something to do with that rancid stepdad of hers.

'You're right,' Babs said, realising that she'd directed them into a run-down square. The small garden in the middle must've once been something to behold, but now it was dried up, the grass a strange shade of green. But it wasn't the garden that caught Babs' attention, it was the larger-than-life Jag positioned outside one of the houses and the two teenagers who seemed to be guarding it. It was all a bit odd; the motor didn't fit into a place like Mile End.

'Let's get a move on,' her mum urged, steering them away from Bancroft Square.

A few minutes later, they were on the other side of Mile End Road and Babs had her first glimpse of the Essex Lane Housing Estate under a dull, cloudy sky. 'I like the look of this.' Even the baby kicked in approval.

Babs knew she was dead lucky to get a home here. When the estate went up there was a gold rush to get places. Everyone for miles around could see the frames of the new towers and smaller blocks slotting into place like a jigsaw puzzle. Everyone had heard about the trees and open spaces where the kids could play, instead of kicking balls on the street. When the locals peered over the fences, they could imagine these new buildings were like the country houses on *Upstairs Downstairs*. Word was they had the works: central heating throughout, fitted bathrooms, a community centre and even one or two boozers were to be provided. Terraced houses were yesterday's news.

They passed a group of girls playing two balls up the wall and singing:

'Oh, you never get to heaven, oh, you never get to heaven,
　As newlyweds, as newlyweds,
　Because the Lord ain't got, because the Lord ain't got,
　No double beds, no double beds.'

The kids looked happy, making Babs even surer that this was a good place to bring up her child. Her elation only grew when they got inside her new flat. It was all mod cons, two good-sized bedrooms and a sitting room. The kitchen and bathroom were a bit pokey, but all in all it suited her to a T. Rosie went from room to room on her own, muttering things like, 'You couldn't swing a cat in here,' 'The walls are paper thin,' while Babs and Denny plotted how to turn the place into a real home, giggling like two schoolgirls.

'When I'm a bit more flush,' Babs said, eyes sparkling, 'I'm going to put in a bar over there. And get Mrs Phillips – she's one of my dad's machinists – to run up some lovely curtains.' She placed her hand at the small of her back as it started to ache.

Denise leaned in close. 'Have you told your parents about *you know what*?'

Babs looked baffled. 'What?'

'You know – that the kid's going to be black?'

'Black?' Rosie yelled behind them.

Babs and Denny jumped apart. *I'm done for now*, Babs thought as she turned anxiously.

Denny did her best to rescue the situation. 'Err . . . black . . . yeah, I saw this programme where this couple had black carpets. It looked really cool.'

'Cool?' Rosie looked at her as if she'd totally lost the plot. 'My grandkid isn't growing up in a home with black carpets like something out of *The Munsters*.' She headed for the kitchen, muttering about 'young kids and their fancy-fool ideas.'

Babs grabbed her friend. 'Thanks a bunch, Denny, what did you go and say that for with my mum two steps away?'

'I didn't know she was that close.' A dreamy expression suddenly broke over Denny's face. 'I'm going to have a place like this soon.'

Babs' eyebrows furrowed. 'I didn't know that you'd put in to the council.'

'I didn't. Screw the council. I'll be getting my own private drum, probably up West somewhere.'

Babs gazed at Denny as if she'd grown three heads. Private flats cost the type of money you didn't get from working in a chicken factory in Bethnal Green like her best mate did. She was worried about Denny. She'd hardly seen her over the last couple of months. Denny was usually out when she called around for their weekly trip to the local. Even her mum didn't know where she was or who she was with and when Babs pressed her, Denny clammed up.

The time for beating about the bush was over. 'Denny, what's going on?'

Denny flattened her mouth like she was going to remain schtum, but then leaned into Babs, her dreamy expression getting stronger. 'I'm not meant to say a peep, but I'm seeing that photographer who owns the modelling agency you work at.'

Babs frowned. 'What photographer?' Stan had never said anything about being a snapper as well.

'Mickey. Don't know his last name.'

Mickey? Babs couldn't think who she was going on about. Then the penny dropped. 'Mickey? Mickey Ingram?' Any happiness she felt drained away. 'How did you link up with him? I never gave you the number for the agency.'

Denny shot her a resentful look. 'I'd been asking you morning, noon and night for the number but you didn't come up with the goods, so I used this for once.' She tapped her head. 'I met his missus. Ooh! You should've seen her, all done up in a fur coat. She's been telling me all about the modelling biz. She's ever so nice. Thinks I've got what it takes.'

Babs remembered the reception she'd got from Mickey at the agency and Stan's warning. 'I don't think he's the type of bloke you wanna be knocking around with.'

Denny folded her arms. 'What do you mean?'

'Just take it from me, he ain't.'

Denny flounced like she was already on the catwalk. 'Well, Mel's been really good to me. She's a proper lady, so her old man must be a real gent. I'm meeting him later today.'

Babs didn't like what she was hearing at all. She didn't want Denny anywhere near the thug. But from the stubborn expression on her mate's face, she knew that her mind was made up.

'Maybe I should come with you.'

Denny threw her hands in the air. 'Don't be daft, I'm not a baby. What's it gonna look like if I turn up with you as my minder? So ta, but no ta.'

A tap at the open front door pulled them into the passage. Two women were peering in.

'Are you the new family?' one piped out.

Both women were similar ages, wearing similar clothing. But one was large, with an enormous bosom, and the other was thin and as flat as an ironing board.

'I'm Beryl,' the thin one announced.

'And I'm Cheryl,' the large one added. 'Beryl and Cheryl, I know,' she finished off, laughing at the astonished look on Babs' face.

Beryl explained, as a curious Rosie came into the hallway. 'We moved here on the same day a couple of months back. Me and my family had to shift ourselves sharpish because our bas–' she coughed, 'no-account landlord chucked us out onto the street.'

Babs caught her mum's anxious expression and remembered how concerned her parents were about the disgraceful evictions they kept hearing about, how worried they were they'd be next.

'It's my daughter here,' Rosie nodded in Babs' direction, 'who's moving in. I'm Rosie Wilson.'

The women introduced themselves again – Beryl Bradshaw and Cheryl Parker.

'You don't need to be worrying about your girl while we're around,' Cheryl reassured Rosie, then noticed Babs' belly. 'Ah, expecting a new addition? So your other half will be along shortly?'

Wrong question. Rosie tightened her mouth in displeasure. Spotting the tension, Beryl and Cheryl winked at each other in an unspoken agreement. 'Husband, no husband, who the heck cares? Look at that Liz Taylor; she seems to be eating 'em for lunch most days,' Beryl said, lightening the mood.

It got Rosie laughing, though Babs still saw her mum sigh. Her mother wasn't happy about her moving out; she hoped that Rosie felt better now she'd met two cracking women who obviously weren't about to judge her.

'Well, we'll leave you to it.' Cheryl stepped back. 'But any time you need anything, don't worry about banging on our doors.'

'Nice ladies,' Rosie commented as they stepped back outside. 'Right, I'm off to measure the windows.'

After her mum had gone, Babs got back to her earlier concern. 'I ain't happy about you meeting Mickey.'

Denny got narked. 'I'm a big girl now,' she said with conviction. 'Whatever I've gotta do to get out of my mum's house I'm gonna do.'

As if sensing its mother's changing mood, the baby started turning in Babs' tummy.

She had a dreadful feeling about this.

Seventeen

'I ain't ever been to Park Lane,' Denny confessed, clearly out of her depth as Mel led her up the stairs to the third floor of the Imperial Hotel.

Mel plastered her special dopey Denny grin on her face. 'Mickey only uses the best places for his photo shoots. People are already calling him the new David Bailey.'

The Imperial was indeed a swanky hotel, but most people didn't know that the manager wasn't above taking a back-hander to rent out rooms to make blue movies. Everyone from the cops to the council was willing to make a little money on the side and a posh hotel in town was no different.

'Right, here we are,' Mel announced as they reached room 243. She turned to Denny. 'Now remember, Mickey is the real deal, so don't get up in his face asking all kind of questions. He won't work with chatterboxes.'

Denny nodded as Mel knocked on the door. A tall woman with flowing blonde hair in a raspberry-coloured maxi dress opened the door. 'Oh, hello, Mickey said you might be drop-ping in.'

Mel smiled. 'Alright, Linda. I've brought my friend Denny, she's looking to get into the business.'

Linda ushered them into the room. The wallpaper was mind-blowing: small beige circles threaded through larger brown ones. In the middle of the cream carpet a zebra print rug was laid out as if the animal had died there, and against the back wall was a huge waterbed with scarlet satin sheets. To those in the know it was a classic porn set, but to Denny it was the most stylish room she'd ever seen.

And there was Mickey, snapping away at a slim thing reclining on the black leather sofa. 'That's it babe,' he encouraged her. 'Now give the lens a really big smile, show your pearly whites.'

Pearly whites? Mel had to stop herself rolling her eyes. Mickey was meant to be a classy photographer, not a frickin' dentist.

'Mickey,' she called sweetly. 'I've brought that girl who—'

'Not now,' he growled. 'Can't you see I'm photographing Candice? This is art.'

Mel gritted her teeth. She'd give him bloody Candice if he didn't get with the programme. She kept her voice calm, but with enough sting that her husband would notice. 'But Mickey, you said finding new girls is a priority.'

With a huff he turned around, giving Mel the shock of her life. She'd told him to dress for the part, not to look like he'd crawled onto *The Sonny and Cher Show*. His shirt was unbuttoned to his navel, showcasing his incredibly hairy chest and a chain with a peace sign medallion. He wore a rainbow-coloured headband and a beaded belt hung around the waist of his bell bottom jeans. What a Class A prat.

He leered at Denny, and Mel was dismayed to see her little lamb stumble back. If Mickey fucked this up . . . She let out a breath when he started smiling. 'This the chick you told me about?' he asked.

Mel grabbed Denny's hand and tugged her forward. 'Isn't she something?'

Mickey swaggered up to her, his medallion bouncing like it

was trying to escape his chest hair. He said, 'hold up a minute!' Denny was clearly startled when he touched her cheek with his nicotine-stained fingers and tilted her head to one side. 'Lovely profile, darlin'. Just fantastic. I can see you now, wearing a gymslip, sucking on a lollipop in your gorgeous mouth ...' Mickey caught the warning in Mel's eyes. 'The camera's going to love you, baby.'

Mel rubbed Denny's arm. 'Didn't I say you were a born model?'

Denny just nodded, obviously heeding Mel's advice about speaking too much.

Mickey turned back to the other two women in the room. 'Right ladies, that's a wrap. I'll let you know when Vog says the pictures will run—'

Mel jumped in. 'Vog's Mickey's pet name for *Vogue*.' Couldn't the idiot remember anything? She'd coached him for the last couple of days.

'*Vogue*, yeah, yeah right,' Mickey agreed, looking slightly sheepish. 'What's your poison?' he asked Denny, waving at the drinks cabinet

As he led Denny to the sofa, Mel followed the other two women out of the room. As soon as they hit the corridor her smile slipped from her chops. She pointed her finger. 'Hop it back to the knocking shop. And if I find out that you've breathed a word of this to anyone ...' Mel knew she didn't need to finish. They knew the score. Mickey was not the type of man they wanted to cross on his good days, much less his bad ones.

Mel returned to find Mickey with his arm along the back of the sofa behind Denny and his legs spread like he was king of the castle. 'So you wanna be a model, princess?'

She nodded shyly. 'Yeah, I really do.'

Mickey looked pensive. 'Well, darlin', I'm gonna be straight up with you, it's a long and stony road to the top, full of setbacks. But with the right guy to hold your hand, it'll all be worth it when you get there. Do you wanna drink, Denny? I can call you Denny, can't I, babe?'

Mel stepped in. 'We've got some lovely champagne. Ever had a bit of fizz Denny?'

Of course the muggins hadn't, but Mel waited for the expected nod. Then she made a big drama of filling the glass. It was actually lemonade mixed with a touch of cider. Mel had filled an empty bottle of Bolly from the brothel's bar.

As Denny sipped, her nose wrinkling at the taste, Mel parked herself on a sofa opposite.

'So how long have you owned the modelling agency?' Denny asked.

While Mickey told her a bogus story, Mel thought back to how the agency had really come into their lives. Originally it had been owned by a Maltese bloke. In the Sixties it did topless shots for dirty mags and supplied actresses for blue movies. Mickey had been excited about winning the business in a card game, surprised that the Maltese didn't seem upset. But that was before he discovered the business was making about ten bob a year. He also learned that the modelling studio down in Vauxhall had a hole in the roof and equipment that a kid with a box Brownie would be embarrassed to use. Still, there was a girl called Brenda who knew how to keep it ticking over and Mickey let her get on with it until she'd left for greener pastures in Amsterdam. He'd realised it had another advantage.

He'd already been running the knocking shop, and soon put two and two together – a modelling agency equalled an endless supply of candidates for his establishment out East. He started sitting in on the interviews. He said nothing when Brenda asked questions about whether they were willing to do topless. That way, he soon redirected the ones willing to do a bit of modelling on their back, and the ones who needed some smack. He was more than willing to feed the habit – deducted from their wages, of course. He wasn't a charity.

Mel came back to the present to hear Mickey giving it the big 'un about his successful career. He reached into his pocket and pulled out a carefully constructed joint. 'What about a bit of Puff The Magic Dragon? That'll be your thing, won't it? Being a model and that, it helps relax you on a shoot.'

Mel almost shoved the thing down his gob. They had discussed this and agreed not to frighten the girl off.

And, surprise, surprise, Denny looked shit scared. 'I don't really smoke that much. It's bad for your looks, ain't it?'

Mel desperately tried to catch Mickey's eyes to tell him to lay off, but he was in full flight. He squeezed Denny's shoulder. 'I'm not talking about fags, darlin'. I mean a bit of blow, the old Jamaican woodbines.' He lit up, breathed in the smoke for a moment and passed it over.

Right, enough of this malarkey. Mel gently plucked the joint from a bewildered Denny's hand. She turned to Mickey with vengeance in her eyes. 'Denny's right, Mickey, she don't want to be losing her looks. Why don't I show her your portfolio?'

Mel took out a book from the large wooden sideboard. She'd nicked one of Donna's exercise books and glued in pictures from magazines. Now the trick was not to let Denny see they weren't real. Once she was back sitting down, Mel held the book a careful distance away and began to flick through the pages. Mickey distracted her with stories about film stars and fashion designers, about his adventures and travels and the time he pulled Sean Connery's girlfriend in St Tropez and Sean had never forgiven him for it.

Denny was shocked. 'You got off with Sean Connery's girlfriend?'

'Yeah – and if Sean don't wanna call me any more on that account, that's his loss not mine. No sense of humour. Mel, fill her up with more fizz–'

Denny gazed at her glass with obvious distaste. 'Err . . . no thanks–'

'Don't be daft,' Mickey said, 'you're going nowhere in the business if you don't knock the Bolly back. You don't want people to think you're from up North or something, do you? Plus it stops you from scoffing, keeps your figure nice and trim for the camera.'

Denny obligingly hit the fake fizz, determined to show she'd fit in.

After four glasses she asked tentatively, 'Do you think you'll take me on?'

He squinted and gave her a good looking over. 'I dunno–'

'Pleeeze. You won't regret it.'

'Tell you what I'll do. I'm away on a fashion shoot in Paris for a bit.' He pulled out a mountain of notes from his jeans and passed them to Mel. 'Why don't you let Mel wine and dine you, on me of course. My way of showing I'm interested. Then when I'm back, we can get down to business.' He winked. 'I'm gonna make you a big, big star. Believe me.'

When Mel got back from escorting Denny out of the hotel she found Mickey happily puffing away on the spliff.

Mel fetched the real booze out and knocked some Scotch back. Then she waved the bottle threateningly. 'You know what, you're a right twat.' Her mouth curled. 'Look at that get-up–'

'What's the problem? I could've told her I was Peter Pan and she'd have believed it.'

'*You* got off with Sean Connery's girlfriend? What a joke . . .'

Mickey was hurt. 'I might have done – why not?'

'Because you're a fat ugly prick who hasn't been on a day trip to Calais, never mind St Tropez – that's why.'

Mickey drew deeply on the joint. 'We shouldn't wait. The girl looked ready to me.'

Mel took another strong slug of booze. 'No, she ain't ready yet. I need her to be like putty in my hand. Her situation is ugly.' Her voice hardened. 'I want the dopey moo to think I'm the only person she can turn to.'

Mickey ground the joint into the ashtray. 'Your plan depends on Pete being in Mile End and completely pissed. You made me get Stan to read the riot act, so he might be on the wagon now.'

Mel moved towards the waterbed and pressed the vibrator button. It started jiggling like jelly. 'The only wagon Pete's going on is the one I'm building for him.' She started unbuttoning her blouse. 'Get your kit off. Thoughts of revenge have put me in the mood.'

Eighteen

'Close your eyes,' Stan ordered as soon as Babs walked into the office.

Babs rolled her eyes playfully instead as Donny Osmond sang sadly about 'Puppy Love' on the radio. Stan had his hands hidden behind the back of his emerald-green jacket. One of the things Babs loved about him was how impeccably turned out he always was.

'Go on,' Stan urged, 'shut your eyes.'

With an indulgent smile, Babs humoured him. She heard him move close to her desk. 'Right, open them.'

Babs gasped when she saw the pair of beautiful booties he'd put on the desk. They were crocheted, one blue, one pink, with a yellow flower on top. She picked them up, ever so carefully. 'Oh, they're absolute heaven.'

He sniffed, like he was embarrassed. 'I got them made special like. Since your sprog ain't made an appearance yet I got one blue, one pink, you know what I mean?'

Her lip wobbled in gratitude. 'Stan, you're a total sweet-heart.' And before she knew it she had her arms tight around him, hugging him to death. It felt so good to be in Stan's arms. Being this close to him made her feel like she was next to her mum and dad's coal fire. There were butterflies fluttering away in her tummy that had nothing to do with the baby.

She pulled her head back, mortified. 'Uh . . . Err . . . I . ..' But she never finished. Stan planted a killer kiss on her lips. She'd been dreaming of this for such an eternity. Babs pushed him onto the desk and took the kiss in a whole new direction. Bloody hell, she couldn't stop, he tasted that good.

Stan gently picked her up and turned her to face away from him. Babs leaned forward and braced herself on her desk. Most people had told her that pregnancy would kill her sex drive but when Stan was near it rocketed into outer space. She wanted this so much. So . . .

Babs let out a tiny squeal of pleasure. Bloody hell, he blew her mind.

Ten minutes later, they were a heaving heap on the desk.

'Is the baby alright?' he breathed into her ear.

Babs came crashing back to earth. The baby kicked her twice.

He pulled himself off her and she scrambled back, her hand flying to her mouth. 'I hope you don't think I'm giving it away for free.' The baby kicked again, as if reminding her she'd already done that once.

Stan smiled an easy smile. 'Don't be daft, Babs-babe. We fancy the pants off each other, nothing wrong with that.'

She felt crushed. 'But I'm having another man's kid.'

Stan's face turned serious. 'Look, let's not make a big drama out of it. Let's take a breather and when the baby puts in an appearance . . . who knows, eh?'

He caressed her cheek. She noticed his half-finger again and this time she didn't hold back. 'It ain't none of my business, but what happened there?'

For an instant his face clouded over. 'That, my girl, is the wages of a misspent youth. When I was a young 'un I got into a nasty ruck and got it sliced off.' Babs winced. 'That's when I realised if you want anything out of the world you've got to use this.' He tapped his temple before heading to his office.

Babs slumped into her chair. *What a prat! Fancy chucking yourself at him like that. The geezer probably thinks you're a division three slapper!* Babs couldn't stop beating herself up about it. Depression cloaked her until she noticed the darling baby shoes again. They were so soft and so teeny-tiny. She was seven-and-a-half months gone and couldn't wait to hold her baby in her arms. She had a new doctor in the modern medical centre on the Essex Lane Estate, a woman doctor, mercifully, who hadn't branded Babs a whore. She said that both Babs and the baby were hale and hearty.

The only hurdle left was telling her parents that the baby was going to be half-caste. How would she explain she'd been with a black bloke? It wasn't done round her way. But she took strength remembering the time her mum made a lemon drizzle cake for the Baileys, a black family three doors down from them. When Rosie had got back she'd smiled and said, 'Upstanding family.'

Babs swept all her fears to the side. She bent her head and whispered to her child, 'Everything's gonna be alright, baby-mine.'

Stan came back into the front office. 'I'm popping out for the rest of the day.'

After he left, Babs touched her lips lightly where Stan had kissed her. If only she'd met Stan before Neville.

Stan parked his motor in a side street in Bow. He went into the town hall and up to the third floor. A secretary at a desk was guarding a door behind her. Stan breezed past.

She shot up in alarm, spluttering, 'I'm sorry, can I help you?'

He shot her a lopsided smile, not breaking his stride. 'No, you're alright, I'll sort myself out.'

The secretary hurried to bar the way. 'I'm sorry, you can't go in there. There's a meeting going on.'

His smile widened. 'I know, angel, I'm invited.'

'I don't think you are.' Her alarm turned to suspicion. 'Who are you anyway?'

'Me? I'm one of Joey's ol' Chinas. Ask him later. He'll tell you.'

As Stan tried the handle, the woman tried to push him back. 'I'm going to have to ask you to leave.'

Stan grabbed her by the wrists. 'Why don't you let me go about my business? I don't want to turn nasty and it's against my principles to manhandle birds. Unless of course they're offering to be manhandled – that's different . . .' His remark made her eyebrows shoot almost into her hairline, but she said nothing further. Tangling with Stan was obviously more than her job was worth. He shifted her to one side and opened the door.

A meeting was indeed going on. A dozen people were gathered around a long polished table, a tubby man in a polyester suit, glasses and a comb-over presiding at the head. When Stan swaggered in, all eyes turned to him with a mixture of surprise and curiosity.

The tubby bloke looked stumped for a few moments before turning angry. 'Who the hell are you? This is a private meeting. Get out immediately!'

Stan was having none of it. He pulled up a chair, sat down and popped his feet up on the table. 'Oh, come on, that's no way for a councillor to talk to an old mate. You wouldn't want me to take a picture and share it with the *East London Advertiser*, would you?'

The blood drained from Councillor Joseph Carter's face. Stan carried on, 'Why don't you tell these good people to go and have a cuppa and a ginger nut. I expect they could do with a break after listening to you droning on all afternoon.'

With colour flooding his cheeks, the councillor addressed

the table. 'Could you excuse me for a moment, everyone? Only for five minutes while I have this gentleman kicked out.'

Stan nudged the woman next to him in the ribs. 'He's well hard, ain't he?'

The woman jerked away from him like a bad smell. She and the others shuffled out of their chairs and left, whispering all the way. For a fat bloke Joseph was out of his chair pretty lively, hurrying to make sure the door was firmly closed. He was sweating like a pig by the time he came back. 'What the hell are you doing here? I did what you asked, but I refuse to do another thing for you.'

Stan had been glad when Mickey had handed the admin work for his properties over. It made sense because paperwork, indeed writing itself, wasn't really Mickey's thing. Business wasn't really Mickey's thing either. His old mucker's preferred method was to try some bogus charm for five minutes, followed by threats of violence. Stan had no objection to using menaces but, like a golf player, he knew you had to use the right club for the stroke you were trying to pull. Mickey didn't understand that. In fact, Stan had been wondering for some time what exactly he *did* understand. But at least that meant that Stan was left alone to concentrate on the bigger picture. And Joey was definitely part of the bigger picture.

Stan took out his metal cigarette case and lit up. 'I understand why your nose might be a bit out of joint – and not just because it don't fit your face.' He tapped his ash into a glass of water. 'It's cheeky of me but I'm in a bit of a fix and I need a favour. Nothing too serious.'

'No, no, no.' Spit flew violently from the councillor's mouth. 'I'm not doing you any more favours. If that's all you're here for, I must kindly ask you to leave.'

Stan took a long drag on his cigarette. 'That's disappointing. But if that's how you feel . . .'

'That's how I feel.'

'OK. Fair dos.' He stood up and dropped his dog-end into the water. Then he put his hand in his breast pocket and pulled out a photo. He laid it on the table. Councillor Joseph Carter started shaking as he numbly gazed at the photo of himself: naked and having the time of his life as a black woman did the business on top of him.

'How's your fine wife and your lovely kids?' Stan quietly asked. 'Wonder what they'd think about you doing the dirty with a black tart?'

Joseph Carter slumped into a chair, his shoulders sagging, the picture of a broken man. 'Why won't you just leave me alone?'

Stan scoffed and went to the door. As he opened it he heard Joey's agonised plea, 'Please, Miller!'

What a fucking prima donna, Stan thought as he let a huge, triumphant grin spread across his face. He dropped the smile and sat down next to the defeated man, putting his arm around his shoulder. He played up the mock sympathy to the hilt. 'It's only a little thing, mate. I just need some help with planning permission on some houses.'

'I've got nothing to do with planning permission and you know it.'

'Of course not.' Stan tightened his arm. 'But I expect you know the blokes who do. Just put a word in for me. I ain't asking for permission to put a betting shop on Park Lane.' He slapped the other man on the back. 'And I forgot to say thanks for sorting out that flat for my mate. She's tickled pink.'

Joey winced, but said nothing. He didn't have to. His silence was all Stan needed.

Nineteen

The baby kicked away as Beryl and Cheryl took Babs on a grand tour of the estate. There was so much of it to take in. Her head spun as they pointed out one thing after another after another.

'That's Patsy's corner shop. Her son Big Marky helps her out along with his bulldog Sidney.'

'Around the back there is the post office. If you've ever got any problems just ask for Mrs Green.'

'That's the cemetery. No one's put to rest there any more, but you still wouldn't want to be there after dark.'

'Over there is the chippie. Oh, it does a nice bit of cod. Next door is the ironmongers.'

'Those two women we call Miss Mean and Miss Trouble. A right poisonous pair. Stay well away from them.'

They stopped when they came across a short bald man fixing the railings near the small park. Beryl and Cheryl waved frantically and yelled, 'You alright, Arnie?' Beryl added, 'This is Babs, who's just moved in. She's expecting a little delivery in the not-too-distant future, so make sure you keep a special eye out.' Arnie nodded respectfully in Babs' direction.

'Why do you want him to look out for me?' Babs asked as they moved on.

Cheryl explained. 'He's the caretaker—'

'There's a caretaker?' Babs had never heard the like. The Essex Lane Estate was a dream come true.

Cheryl obviously felt the same. Her eyes came over all dreamy. 'I know, fancy that. Find yourself in any bovver or need a little repair doing, just knock on his door. He can't talk, that's why he gave you a nod.' Her voice turned fierce. 'Don't treat him like a nitwit though. Just coz he can't speak don't make him stupid.'

Babs smiled. That's what she loved about her neighbours, they didn't just see the surface, they saw the person underneath. She'd forever be grateful to them for not judging her.

Beryl added, 'Although we've got Arnie, all the blocks have a list so each family takes it in turn to wash the stairs from top to bottom. We might be poor but that don't mean we have to live dirty.'

They carried on walking, Beryl and Cheryl jib-jabbering away, until they reached a one-storey brick building on the west side of the estate.

Beryl produced a large set of keys. 'This is where I work. I got the job to manage the place.'

Babs was confused. 'What is it?'

'Wait and see,' Cheryl piped up, the sparkle in her gaze suggesting Babs was in for a treat.

Beryl opened up and proudly announced, 'Welcome to the washhouse.'

They entered a huge room with white tiles and thick copper pipes on the wall. It was filled with large sinks and taps, wooden and glass washboards, mangles, two iron presses, laundry tongs, baskets and wooden rails to dry clothes on.

Beryl went into her manager's patter. 'This is for anyone on the estate, but it's understood that it's for us women only. It's free to use, all you've got to bring along is your dirty laundry and soap. One simple rule – no fighting. You got a problem with someone, you take it outside.'

They sat Babs down on one of the long wooden benches and got cosy with teacups of Beryl's homemade sloe gin.

'Soooo,' Cheryl said in a long, drawn-out tone, 'where's the bastard who left his bun in your oven?'

Babs started blushing, feeling again the humiliation of being chucked by Neville.

She didn't know what made her say it but she blurted out, 'He's coloured.'

The other women gave each other a look. Babs waited for their outraged condemnation, but it never came. Cheryl simply said, 'Well, you know what they say, it takes all sorts to make a world.'

Beryl sipped some gin. 'My Auntie Eileen ran off with a Chinese sailor from Limehouse. My Granny Lyn wouldn't talk to her no more, that's until she saw her grandkids, my cousins. Fell right in love with them.'

'I haven't told my mum and dad about the father,' Babs said sadly.

The women gave each other that look again and then Cheryl shifted her eyes to Babs. 'I'm going to talk to you like a mum would to her daughter. You've got to tell your people. At a time like this you need your family around you. Just tell them and see what happens. Honesty is always the–'

Beryl joined in. 'Best policy.' Abruptly she stood up, her gaze diving into a dark corner. 'Ere, what was that?'

Cheryl rolled her eyes. 'Not the bloody rats again. The council wanna . . .'

A small boy darted out and belted for the door. But he wasn't quick enough. Cheryl lunged forward, caught his jumper and hauled him back. Babs looked into one of the saddest faces she'd ever seen. He had one enormous dark brown eye visible behind National Health glasses. She couldn't see the other one: it was covered with a thick plaster to help correct a lazy eye. He was streaked with dirt and his jumper and trousers had holes in them. He didn't smell too bright either.

Cheryl gave him a shake. 'I thought I told you to keep your tea-leafing mitts away from here, Kieran Scott.'

Beryl shoved her fists on her hips. 'You should be indoors. Your mum will be proper worried about you.'

His head snapped up defiantly. 'No she won't. She's got some fella with her. Told me not to come back until the moon's in the sky.'

Poor thing, Babs thought, he looked like he needed a bath, some new clobber and some tender loving care. It broke her heart to see a child in such a state. 'Fancy coming over to mine for a nice bit of bread and strawberry jam?'

Cheryl gasped. 'You can't take him home. Probably leave nits all over your drum.' Beryl nodded in agreement.

But for once Babs ignored her neighbours. All she did was stretch out her hand and he took it.

'Flippin' hell.' Denny gawked, looking around the upmarket Bond Street clothes shop, eyes wide with wonder. 'This looks like something out of a film set.'

Mel had been seeing Denny on a regular basis, splashing out on her, taking her here and there, drawing her into her and Mickey's web. The girl might be a proper dim bat but, surprisingly, Mel enjoyed her company. Denny wasn't a girl who rabbited her head off. She was sweet really. A little bit of Mel regretted what she and Mickey were setting her up for. But only a little.

Mel grinned as she linked arms with the younger woman and pulled her close. 'This is the lifestyle you can expect if you become one of our models.'

For the next half an hour Denny had the time of her life, eyes nearly falling out of her head as she was presented with so many dresses she could hardly keep up. Choirboy dresses, shirt dresses, exotic glamorous coat dresses.

'And this is from our most exclusive range,' the manager declared, beaming.

Even Mel was struck dumb. An eye-grabbing emerald-green evening dress with a high slit that took *showing a bit of leg* into a whole new dimension.

'We'll take it,' Mel announced.

A shocked Denny turned to her. 'But that must cost a packet. I don't—'

Mel patted her hand. 'Don't you worry about a thing.' She turned to the jubilant manager. 'Have it wrapped and we'll come back after lunch.'

That wiped the smile off her face. 'You're not going to buy it now?'

Mel looked her up and down. 'Of course not. You can't take a beautiful dress like that into a restaurant. What if something spilled on it?'

'Of course, of course,' the other woman agreed. 'It will be waiting for you when you return.'

As soon as they left the shop Denny gushed, 'I can't believe that you bought that gorgeous dress for me.' She did an excited twirl in the street.

Mel wasn't about to burst her bubble and tell her the truth – that Denny was never going to wear it because Mel wasn't going back for it. She'd spin some tale about Mickey going to pick the dress up later. Mel had learned years ago that all you had to do to make desperate people do what you wanted was to give them a promise. The promise of a glitzy dress to show the world you were no longer poor. The promise of a modelling career to show that dreams really did come true for working-class girls.

'Denny, darling,' Mel said with mock excitement, 'I've got a surprise.'

Denny sucked in her breath. 'What?'

'Mickey's back from Paris.' Denny's face lit up. 'He's asked if you'll come to a showbiz party he's hosting next week Tuesday—'

'A showbiz bash?' The girl clapped her hands together, her eyes glittering. 'You mean famous people are going to be there?'

Mel clasped Denny's hands. 'Mickey knows all kind of faces from the entertainment world.'

'Where's the party? Soho? Mayfair?'

'Mile End.'

Denny pulled away abruptly. 'Mile End? That don't sound like the type of place famous people hang out.'

'Well, that's where you're wrong. Someone really famous has a house there. It's his secret hideaway, so the press can't find him when he comes to Britain.'

Denny could hardly contain herself. 'Who is it?'

Mel shook her head and tapped her nose. 'He wants to keep his hideaway all hush-hush, so my lips are sealed. But when you get there I'll personally introduce you.'

'I can't believe any of this,' Denny gasped.

You know what they say, if it's too good to be true . . . But Mel kept that sentiment to herself. 'Good girl. You can't tell anyone about it, OK. And Mickey has promised to get your modelling career in motion the next day.' Mel gave her a huge hug and whispered in her ear, 'You won't live to regret this, believe me.'

Twenty

'Wotcha Stan – it's Jimmy from the Threes. That bloke you came to see me about, the lord? He's playing blackjack at one of our tables.'

Stan pumped his clenched fist in the air and mouthed an ecstatic 'yes', like he did when Arsenal scored (although the left-footed twats had lost the FA Cup to Leeds). He'd finally tracked down his golden list's last name – Lord Tilgate. Pinning down Lord Tilgate was as difficult as finding a bloke who owed you a ton in the East End. A toff's name connected to his business was essential for the contacts that would help his empire rise and rise. Stan knew he'd never get into any of the gentleman's clubs Lord Tilgate frequented in a million years, so he'd followed a hunch that like most toffs, he enjoyed the seamier side of the entertainment that Soho dished out so well. His gamble had paid off.

'You done well. That drink I owe you will be waiting behind the bar.' The manager of the Threes had only been amenable if he stumped up some cash. Fair enough.

Stan went into the tiny toilet and splashed some water on his face. He considered going home to get changed but decided a crumpled suit and midnight shadow was the right look for the Threes anyway. The casino had originally been the Three Bells – till the owner got fed up with bankrupt punters calling it the Three Hells and changed the name. Then the gamblers started calling it 'that fucking bent casino' instead.

He walked the half mile to the back of Leicester Square and climbed up the casino's fire escape. Two likely lads were standing guard on a heavy door.

'Alright Stan. How's business?' one of them asked.

'Yeah, good. Is Jimmy in?'

'Yeah. Just got back from handing over the local Old Bill's winnings.'

Stan didn't blink. Paying off bent coppers was part of the landscape. Stan had been sixteen when he first realised that the Bill were up for a backhander. He'd been enjoying a jar in Limehouse when two men had waltzed in, easy as you please, and doled out a bone-crushing beating to a man at a nearby table. He'd later learned that the reason no one had stepped in to stop it – including the victim's mates – was because the two thugs were cops sent by a local Face to teach the geezer a lesson he'd never forget.

Stan went inside and walked over to the roulette tables. The club was spread over two floors and nearly pitch black. In theory that was to make it discreet, but really it meant that punters who weren't in the know couldn't see what was going on. As the owner liked to explain, his club attracted a very varied crowd; from West End gangsters to East End gangsters. But there were also hard-core gamblers, local workers who wanted a drink after hours, American tourists who couldn't believe London shut up shop by eleven and posh blokes who liked a walk on the wild side.

Stan found Jimmy not far from the roulette table, decked out like someone from the 1940s. Navy blue double-breasted suit, silk tie, high-waisted trousers with a spot-on crease held up by black suspenders and two-tone saddle shoes to polish off the look. And of course, a dark fedora hat worn at an angle.

'Stanley. Thought I'd be seeing you,' Jimmy said in a low, feminine voice. Jimmy was really a Jenny. Why she togged herself out in men's clothes and wanted to be known as a fella, Stan had no idea. That's what he liked about Soho – you could be who you wanted, no questions asked.

'Where's my guy?'

'Right in front of you . . .'

And so he was. Having abandoned blackjack, Lord Tilgate was now frittering away chips on the fixed roulette table. But Stan didn't feel sorry for him. He was good for it.

Stan went in for the kill. 'Blimey! Lord Tilgate! Fancy meeting you here. Mind if I join you?'

The honourable Jack Hampton, aka Lord Tilgate, had the reddened and slightly puffy skin of a man who liked a decent drink. He played the eccentric toff to the hilt with frayed cuffs and tweed trousers, a jacket that had seen better days, scuffed brogues and a trilby hat. If it hadn't been for the fuck-off diamond ring on his finger he might have been a bus driver blowing his wages on a habit he couldn't give up.

Tilgate looked up, confused. 'I'm so sorry, do I know you?'

Stan kept smiling. 'Yes, sir, of course you do. We met at Julie's in Hampstead.' Was her name Julie? Might as well have been. A month ago Stan had blagged his way into a cocktail party. After that it was simply a question of sniffing around and finding out who mattered and who didn't. He soon discovered Tilgate mattered. At least his honourable title mattered . . . to Stan.

'We've been planning to get together for a while.' He was lying of course but he was in the right establishment for it. 'To discuss some business. Let me refresh your memory – the name's Stanley Miller.'

'Ah yes – of course, I remember.'

Stan cupped his hand over his mouth and whispered, 'Try

the low numbers on the red, Lord Tilgate. I think you'll find them lucky . . .'

Stan was right – he got a dirty look from Jimmy for his trouble. This cheered the peer up a lot. 'So tell me, Mr Miller . . .'

'Oh please – Stan.'

'Stan. What line of business did you say you were in?'

'Property's my thing, your honour. I've got an extensive portfolio and I'm looking to take it up a gear. I understand you've got interests in that field yourself? I'd be interested in exploring some ideas . . . for our mutual benefit.'

'You mean you need a peer of the realm to put on your headed notepaper to impress the easily impressed?'

Stan was taken aback. He wasn't used to being spoken to in such a frank manner by one of the country's elite. In the East End, yes, but not by one of this crowd.

'Seeing as you've put your cards on the table, I'll lay mine out too. That's exactly what I'm thinking. If you look east, you'll notice something – whole tracts of East London are a complete desert. The docks are closed, the Krauts levelled entire areas and no one wants to live or work in what's left except people without a choice – the poor. Did you know Wapping High Street once had a hundred and forty pubs? Now you'd be lucky to find a beer bottle lying in the gutter.'

Stan's voice grew excited as he carried on. 'The East End is dying but one day it will rise again. If you buy parts of the corpse now there's going to be a lot of money to be made when it comes to life. I've got a map of all the places people will have to buy if they want to develop out East. At the moment you can get them for a song. It helps that I have friendly arrangements with a number of council officials down that way. And I have associates who can smooth paths and iron out wrinkles.'

Tilgate interrupted, his eyebrow raised. 'You mean criminals.'

Stan's nose was put out of joint. 'I doubt whether they're any more criminal than your associates in the City. They're probably a lot more honest about it.'

Lord Tilgate pulled a face. 'No offence, Stan, but I prefer not to get involved commercially with gentlemen who know how to play fixed roulette wheels.'

Stan paused for thought. As any burglar knows, you can get in anywhere if you're smart enough. It was just a question of finding an access point. A man's usual weaknesses are sex and money but Tilgate had plenty of the latter, so it would have to be the former.

As the chips piled up and the Scotch flowed, Tilgate seemed quite happy in Stan's company. He offered to introduce him to some local characters. There were a number of tarts at the Threes and Stan knew them all. He needed to find out what the toff's kink was.

'I hear that Colette is very handy with a cane . . .'

'I had enough of that at public school . . .'

After a while, Stan decided that women weren't his lord-ship's thing and introduced him to some young men instead. When he twigged what Stan was up to, Tilgate told him, 'I had enough of that at public school as well . . .'

Stan was baffled. Every geezer has his own perversion but Lord Tilgate was coming over like one of the Mary Whitehouse brigade. It didn't make sense. He seemed inter-ested in Soho lowlife but showed no sign that he wanted to join in.

'Where are you on cabaret, my lord? They do a very good floor show here.'

The peer was swaying slightly, but said, 'Those places expect you to pay through the nose for a drink.'

Stan chuckled. 'No need to put your hand in your pocket when I'm around.'

The floor show was in a back room. A small stage was lit by spotlights and revolving glitter balls. The scent of sexual tension was high in the air. A young woman called Luscious Lucy, dressed in a sparkling purple backless dress with a scarlet feather boa wrapped round her neck, was doing a sexy catwalk onto the stage. Lord Tilgate murmured, 'Oh I see – strippers.'

Blimey, mate – what were you expecting? Judy Garland?

Stan gestured at the stripper to tell her to put a special effort in for his guest. Mid-way through her act, dress abandoned on the stage, she plonked her stilettoed foot on their table, peeled her stocking off and wrapped it around Lord Tilgate's neck. She jiggled her tits for him and licked her finger and ran it down his cheek. Stan sat back in despair. His guy might as well have been listening to a speech on car parking in the House of Lords. Stan didn't like admitting defeat but he had to face it: his effort to find a way to set up this bloke had ended in failure.

But then he got a lucky break.

Squeezing through the tables was an Italian guy, an enforcer for various local Faces. He'd brought a woman with him. She was very tall, very scantily dressed and very black. As she squeezed her bum past their table, Tilgate was transfixed. When she took a seat a few yards away, he strained to see her in the darkness and shuffled his chair around to get a better view. He was the proverbial rabbit in the headlights.

Relieved, Stan whispered, 'Nice-looking bird, eh?' Lord Tilgate said nothing. 'Do you like the coloured ladies, Lord Tilgate?' The toff still said nothing. 'Not that I'm sitting in judgement of course – I've always said we're all equal.'

Tilgate got back in the saddle of his high horse. 'I don't

approve of race-mixing, Miller. That helped bring down the Roman Empire.'

Roman Empire? What was the old duffer going on about? Stan only just stopped himself suggesting Tilgate dressed up in a fucking toga and put leaves on his head. 'Of course, but it's not the same thing. It's more like sprinkling some on your cornflakes.'

Tilgate ran his palms down his lapels. 'It's rather academic . . . I don't meet many African ladies in my social circle.'

Stan played out his hand. 'Perhaps you should extend your social circle, my lord.' He tipped his head closer. 'I might be able to arrange it for Saturday night. Of course, there would be expenses involved.'

Tilgate cleared his throat and looked around furtively before resting his eyes back on Stan, his voice low. 'You have access to a lady at the darker end of the rainbow?'

'I most certainly do.'

Gotcha, you dirty old goat!

It was time to organise another special up at the house in Mile End.

Twenty-One

'You're one amazing chick, Cleo girl,' Cricket leered on Friday after he rolled off her.

Cleo wanted to spit in disgust, but knew she couldn't. Cricket's partner, Horner, was looking on with glazed eyes and a dirty smirk on his chops. God, she hated having to 'entertain' these two thugs. But getting to screw the fabulous Cleo was a perk of their job: evicting families on behalf of someone connected to the brothel. They always insisted on doing her one after the other, Horner liking her on top so he could maul her arse with his hands and Cricket wanting her beneath him so he was in charge. They were truly evil and she hated having to take care of their needs . . . but what could she do? She always put on a show for them in the executive suite, not her room. With a secret smile, she fixed her gaze on the far wall. She was going to have the last laugh one day.

Horner got up, starting to undo his trousers. 'That's got me all horny again. Someone ring the bell because I'm getting ready to climb on board. Ding! Ding!'

Not on your life, matey! He'd already had her once and that was his lot for the night. 'I'm a bit busy tonight, my friends. I've got to see a man about a motor, you know what I mean?'

Cleo got up without waiting for an answer, displaying the policewoman's uniform she wore. For some reason they got a real rise from the get-up. They even insisted she say, 'Hello! Hello!' when they first came into the room. It turned her stomach. What was it with men? Her previous punter had got a hard-on from her pretending to be a headmistress, in a cardie buttoned all the way up, tweed skirt, black, flat shoes and fake pearls, giving him a bollocking for not handing in his homework and beating him silly on his arse. The client before him got his rocks off from her saying the times table out loud and he always hit cloud nine on the same sum – eight times six. Just as well, she always got that one muddled up.

It was a million miles away from the life she'd grown up in. She'd been born in London after her family had come over from the Caribbean island of Grenada. They'd settled into the growing community of Grenadians and Trinidadians in Notting Hill. The place had been alive with parties and music but her family were hard-core church people. All Cleo had wanted was to be out there having fun, fun, fun, but her parents wouldn't have it, especially her mum. She'd started sneaking out. When her mother had cottoned on, she'd begun bolting the door to stop her. Eventually it had come to a choice – Cleo either stayed under her parents' roof and did what she was told, following the Lord's word, or she was out in the cold with Satan. She'd chosen the good life. But it had soon turned twisted and dirty; anyone who said otherwise didn't know what it felt like to have geezer after geezer on top of you night after night. Cleo wanted out. But even the specials she did on the sly weren't bringing in enough cash to get her on her way.

Once Cricket and Horner were gone she washed the muck and stink of them from her body, then popped on her silk floral dressing gown and sneaked downstairs for a soothing cuppa and some quiet time. She rarely touched the hard stuff, a leftover from the pastor's fire and brimstone words during her childhood.

In the kitchen she found Daffy at the small table, nursing a glass of sherry with her walking stick propped against her chair.

'Cleo, honey,' the other woman called out. 'I hope those two mutton heads didn't do anything too out of the way this time.' Cleo really liked this woman. What she admired most of all was that she never poured glitter over the filth they lived in.

Cleo didn't answer, just popped the kettle on the hob to boil. She turned back around and asked, 'Don't you get tired of this? The dangly bits, the smell, the ones who want you to choke as they shove it down your throat?'

Daffy pulled out an Embassy Gold cigarette and lit up. 'I was fourteen when I started in this business.' Cleo couldn't keep the shock from her face. Her boss only had a few rules: the biggest being, *no drugs, no kids*. 'The usual story – girl falls hard for an older man and before she knows it she's giving his mates a good time too. Older man dies in a knife fight and girl has to walk the streets and look after herself. She gets bottled, punched, knifed, kicked, raped, breaks more bones than she realised she had.' Cleo stood frozen stiff in horror, but Daffy's gaze remained cool, like she was telling someone else's story. 'She gets hooked on morphine from this doctor client of hers until one day she's so out of it she can't service customers and her Maltese pimp chucks boiling water all down her leg.'

Cleo put her hand over her mouth in horror. She'd always wondered how the other woman had ended up using a stick. She wasn't surprised it involved some poxy man.

'She must've passed out,' Daffy resumed, 'because she wakes up halfway to hell in a back alley somewhere.' She pulled in a long drag of smoke. 'Luckily this fine man finds her. Ah, George.' She smiled like a young girl. 'There was no side to him, he just wanted to take care of her burns. He wanted to take her to the ozzie, but she wouldn't have it. No point going to the plod; most of them think a working girl ain't worth the time of day.'

She had that right. Cleo remembered one of her cousins going to the cop shop to report a crime, years back, and getting banged up instead.

'She asked him to take her to this cathouse she knows. The madam there had been after her for a long time to join her girls. He was outraged, but did it when she insisted. The madam took a shine to her and showed her the ropes. The girl Sally Matheson died a long time ago and Dorothy was born. This is what I do, what I know. For now. If you want out, you know where the door is.'

Cleo felt an overwhelming ache of sorrow. Poor Daffy. 'Sometimes, I just want to go back home—'

'Then do it,' the older woman cut in, leaning forcefully towards her. 'Sally didn't have a home to go back to, but you do. By hook or by crook, use your time here to get what you want. You're not a div like a lot of the others. You've got a brain. That's why you're involved in the specials with Pete and me. Pete's brother—'

Cleo lit up with curiosity. 'Pete's got a brother?'

Daffy stubbed out her fag. 'Oh yeah. I know him very well indeed. But I ain't saying any more about him. I keep my snout in my business only, which is making sure this place runs like clockwork.'

'Pete won't like me going if I get the chance to bolt.'

'Fuck that soak. He'll forget about you when he's got more minge stuffed in his face. He don't own you.' She leaned back. 'Don't let any man ever own you, my girl.'

Sinful Simon, who specialised in both men and women, put his head around the door. 'Cleo, you've a customer waiting and Pete's on the dog and bone for ya.'

Cleo rolled her eyes tiredly. She'd forgotten about the client, the one who liked her to call him Big Dong Dildo Daddy. She hadn't even had time for a brew. As she left the room, she couldn't forget Daffy's words:

'*By hook or by crook, use your time here to get what you want.*'

She picked up the telephone receiver in the hall. 'This will have to be quick, Pete, I've got a punter waiting.'

'We need to get one of our specials ready tomorrow night.'

'*By hook or by crook, use your time here to get what you want.*'

'I'm up for that. But I want more dosh this time. Much more.'

'I says to him, if you ever go with another scrubber behind my back again, I'll shove my rolling pin so far up your jacksie you're gonna need surgery to get it out.'

Babs roared with laughter, along with the other women in the washhouse. Oh, she did love this place. It was like a club where all the women on the estate gathered not only to do laundry, but chat about their problems and have a good old giggle. Babs peered across at Kieran, who was chuckling away too as he helped her fold a sheet. The poor kid didn't have much to laugh about, so Babs had taken him under her wing. He spent most evenings roaming around the estate on his Jack, but any time he saw Babs he'd help her carry her shopping and she'd tide him over with a soft drink and some nosh. He loved it when she read him a story, but when she asked him to read for her he'd just shake his head and say, 'I like the sound of your voice, it's right sweet.'

Beryl got out her transistor, lengthened the aerial and turned the knob. The radio crackled for a bit until it found

Radio Caroline and Chuck Berry's naughty 'My Ding-a-Ling' belted into the room. All the women joined in with him.

They stopped abruptly when the front door flew open and in barged a very angry-looking woman. Her long hair and make-up were a mess and her belly was huge with the baby she carried. Kieran's mum, Lou Scott.

Her eyes darted wildly around until they froze on Kieran. 'Oi, you fucking little bleeder,' she shouted, making Babs and the other women suck in their breath. 'I thought I told you to ask Mrs Roberts for a coin for the lecky meter. I've been sitting in the dark like I'm renting a corner of hell.'

Before Babs or anyone could do a thing, she'd stormed over to her son and cuffed him one across the face. The boy didn't even flinch, obviously used to the back of her hand.

He might be this woman's flesh and blood, but Babs wasn't standing for that.

She went to Kieran and stroked his unruly hair, as if trying to take the hurt away. 'There's no need to take it out on him,' she protested. The place had gone deathly quiet.

Lou growled and her mean brown eyes squinted in displeasure. 'Well, you've got a brass nerve, thinking you can tell me what to do with my effing boy.'

Babs stood her ground. 'There ain't no need to show him up in public. He's such a nice kid—'

Lou barrelled right up to her. 'How would you know? You got a thing for kids?' She sneered, 'I've heard about people like you. I should report you to the coppers.'

Babs wasn't taking that from no one. 'You do that and I'll tell them all about how you're busy shagging shit you've found on the street while your lad is out and about at all hours, instead of being at home with a hot meal inside him.'

'You—' The other woman raised her hand.

'I dare ya,' Babs goaded.

They stood face-to-face, belly-to-belly. Instead of hitting her, Kieran's mum grabbed him by the shirt he'd worn for four days on the trot and practically dragged him to the exit. At the door she twisted around and bellowed at Babs, 'Stay away from my kid. He don't need another mum, he's got one at home, thank you very much.' Then she snarled as she scanned the other women's hostile faces. 'Look at the lot of ya, having to use a public washhouse. Some of us have got washing machines at home.'

Cheryl chucked back sourly, 'That ain't much use if you can't pay the electricity.'

Under all that warmth and kindness there was something hard about Cheryl: as if she'd been through troubles that had toughened her up. Kieran's mum must've seen it too because she didn't mouth off, just dragged her son into the night. Two hard slaps against skin were heard as soon as the door shut. There was no sound of Kieran crying.

'You alright?' Beryl asked as the women clustered sympathetically around Babs and her unborn baby.

She nodded. 'How can a mum treat her child like that?'

'Like I said the other day, pet,' Cheryl said quietly, 'this world is full of all sorts. But heed his mum's words – stay well clear of him. That Scott brood are a thoroughly bad lot and there ain't anything you can do to stop Kieran growing into their likeness.'

'We've got a massive problem. Pete's on the wagon,' a flustered and pissed-off Mel told Mickey from the phone box on the corner of Mile End Road.

Mel had been horrified when she discovered Pete had gone dry. Mind you, it was her and Mickey who had got the ball rolling by whinging about him to Stan. At first, when she'd bumped into Daffy down Roman Road market and heard that

Pete had been sober two days straight, she hadn't believed it. But when she saw Pete, he was twitchy, uncomfortable and unable to concentrate but also very clearly sober.

When she suggested, in a flirty-flirty manner, that they take a little trip to the local, he'd muttered something about being too busy.

Her old man burst out laughing. 'Give over. He ain't on the wagon. There ain't a wagon been built that could keep him on it. He'll be pissed again later.'

'You want to take the chance, do you? He's well on his way to being a teetotaller. If he kicks the drink, we're screwed.'

'Have you told the girl about the party?'

Mel swore, 'You know I have.'

'Get in touch now and tell the bint the bash is tomorrow night. Tell her if she doesn't show, she can kiss fuck off to her modelling career.'

Twenty-Two

The next day, Cleo was painting her toenails strawberry red when Pete opened the door and waltzed in. She waved her brush at him. 'Ever heard of knocking?'

He looked distracted. 'Yeah, sorry about that. Come on, look lively, you know we've got a special on tonight. It's a special-special. I can't afford any fuck-ups.'

She groaned and went to her wardrobe to select a Diana Ross-style wig. Then turned and really looked at Pete. His face was drawn and a touch haggard but his eyes had some of their old glitter back. Cleo hadn't seen him like that since way back when. 'If you don't mind me being blunt, you seem to be clear-headed again. That's every night this week. Have you given up or something?'

The redness of his skin deepened. 'I'm not always blotto, sweetheart; I'm just a party person. I wouldn't call that a problem – I'm not an alkie or anything.' He turned away to avoid her stare. 'Although I probably could do with cutting back a little. Who couldn't?'

Cleo caught his arm. 'I prefer you when you're on the wagon. You can be quite the little gentleman when you want to be, I remember from the first time round.' She leaned in and kissed him. He opened his lips and deepened the snog. Without the alcohol on his breath he tasted sweet and clean, just the way Cleo always imagined her dream man would.

She eased back and got on with business. 'So this geezer isn't a special-special because he's a perv, right?'

'Nah. I need you to make sure he has a good time. Put on a really eff-off show, if you know what I mean? Actually, this'll interest you; he specifically asked for a black bird.'

Cleo folded her arms and twisted her lips. 'How very flattering.'

'So you might want to play up the black angle for me.'

She kissed her teeth. 'What do you have in mind? Wearing a grass skirt and calling him master?'

'Oh come on, luv, give me a break. I hear he's very posh and loaded, he might slip something down your knickers by way of a tip. Along with the extra I'm giving you.'

'Oh great – it's knob-a-snob night. They're the worst.'

'There'll be trouble if anything goes wrong.'

Cleo arched her eyebrows. 'With your brother?'

Pete was alarmed. 'Who told you I had a brother?'

'Alright, don't get out of your pram; I just heard. I don't care about your relatives. The others are saying that Mickey and his missus have got some party thing going on tonight. You know anything about it?'

Pete shook his head. 'Nope. I've been keeping away from Mickey's old girl. She was acting a bit strange yesterday. All over me like a rash.' A visible ripple of disgust went through him. 'She gives me the willies.'

Cleo chuckled. 'Sounds like she's after your willy. If you don't want any bovver tonight, make sure you keep our special-special snooty snob away from that crowd.'

Pete changed the subject, his face turning shy. 'Do you mind if I ask you a question?' When she said nothing, he carried on. 'Have you ever thought of getting out of the skin trade? You don't really fit in with it – you know what I mean?'

Cleo sighed. 'That's all I think about, darling, all day and especially all night.'

'Here we are, sweetheart,' Mel announced in her most cultured voice as she and Denny reached the front door of the brothel.

Mel was dressed to the nines, minus her trademark mink. She wore a full-length black dress, lime green platform heels and a plastic rose stuck behind her ear.

'Do I look alright?' Denny asked, self-consciously smoothing her hand over her hair.

You look like a prat, Mel wanted to say, but kept it to herself. She despaired of the girl's rig-out. The psychedelic tunic that just about covered her bits, the long, yellow Isadora Duncan scarf and a snakeskin bracelet that made her a dead ringer for a Sixties hippy chick. It was the Seventies, for crying out loud. At least the way she'd styled her hair in two pigtails put Mel in mind of a young Brigitte Bardot.

She put her arm around the girl and hugged her close. 'You look a treat. There's no need for all this trembling. Stick with me and you'll have the night of your life. And don't forget you're here to impress Mickey.'

Mel knocked on the door, which was opened by a perky-looking Daffy dressed like a waitress. Daffy sent her a sour look on the side. Mel had had a stand-up row with her earlier when she'd told Daffy how to dress. Who did the bitch think she was? Bloody royalty? Mel had laid the law down and told her point blank if she didn't do what she was told, she was out on her arse. And where would a cripple like her find work then?

Mel quickly drew Denny into the VIP lounge so she didn't get too close a butchers at the rest of the house. The room was where the girls paraded around in little more than their birthday suits to entice the clients to take a better look upstairs.

This evening they were decked out in tasteful gear to give the impression they were models too. Simon, their only male tom, was doing a fake stint as a waiter alongside Daffy. Classical music by a composer whose name Mel pronounced as Chopping played in the background.

'Ah, there's my beautiful girl,' Mickey announced, waving his arm in the air.

Mel had personally made sure there was no fuck-up with his appearance this time, selecting a simple suit and tie.

'Come and sit with me,' Mickey carried on.

As soon as a clearly nervous Denny sat beside him he put his arm around her shoulder. Mel gave the other girls the wink and they all sat down and started chatting away. She'd warned them to keep the talk clean and above board.

Denny's eyes darted around. 'Where's the famous fella who owns the place?'

Mickey swung into action, squeezing her arm reassuringly. 'He's on a movie shoot. He'll be dropping in later specially, to meet my new girl.'

Mel nudged Mickey when she realised that Pete had come in.

Mickey raised his arm in an exaggerated greeting. 'Pete, you old bastard! Come and join us. I want you to meet my latest signing at the agency, the girl who's going to be on every billboard and magazine stand in The Smoke. Come and say hello to Denise.'

Pete stared at him. 'I can't stop—'

But Mel jumped in. 'Don't be silly. Surely you've got five minutes to say hello.'

Mel wriggled to make space, while Mickey began frantically winking at him. 'Pete mate, how's your new film coming on? Did Michael Caine take the part or can't your cheapskate studio afford that kind of money?'

Pete looked confused.

Mickey turned to Denise. 'Only kidding, baby. Pete could afford to hire Marlon Brando if the old ham's career wasn't going down the crapper.' He turned back. There was more winking. 'Isn't that right?'

Pete looked at Mel for support. She rolled her hand quickly to tell him to play along. Pete stammered, 'Err, yeah. That's right, we could afford him.' *Good man.*

Mickey patted him on the shoulder. ''Course you could. Remind me, what's your poison? Vodka martini?'

Daffy hovered in the background, her lip curling, until she caught Mel's glare and pasted a blinding smile on her chops.

Pete looked at her and then back at Mickey and stuttered, 'I'll have a barley water.' He patted his belly. 'Trying to shed a few pounds, you know.'

Mickey was horrified. 'Barley water? Have you turned ginger?'

Mel turned to Daffy. 'He'll have a vodka martini.'

The fake waitress mouthed, 'What's that?'

Mel angrily mouthed back in turn. 'Make it up . . .'

When the drink arrived, Mel and Mickey stared at Pete intently. 'Down the hatch, son!'

Pete took a few sips and a lump of ice into his mouth. Then let most of the liquid flow back into the glass. But Mel saw the eyes of a man who'd come home after a difficult few days away. Mel beckoned for Denny to follow her into the hallway as Pete picked up the glass again and cradled it in his hands.

It was getting late. Cleo began to think her nob was gonna be a no-show. The noise from Mickey and his wife's shindig downstairs was still going on. She'd declined Mickey's offer to join them – she would've if it hadn't been for the 'special'. She got off her bed and opened the window to take in some of the chill night air. The square was quiet and dark. Cleo had heard that Mickey paid the local kids a regular retainer of fifty new pence to knock out the street lamps with stones and keep it that way. But she wasn't sure he needed to. The lamps round here were out most of the time anyway and no one seemed in a hurry to repair them.

Then she noticed a car trying to work its way around the square. There was something strange about it; its headlights weren't on. It came round the square twice and came to a rest about twenty yards down the road before creeping forward and parking outside the house, its engine still running. It was a Bentley. A figure climbed out and then the car moved off to park on the other side of the square.

The man who emerged wore a long overcoat and a flat cap pulled down over his face. It was too dark to see anything else. He looked furtively around a few times before quickly going up the steps to the front door. Cleo heard a bang of the door downstairs, and sighed as she shut the window. 'That'll be Lord Nob then.'

But it seemed she was wrong. There was no sign of her special guest and no sign of Pete either. Pete had better not bloody well be lounging about downstairs in the party. She flopped back on her bed and began to doze. But then she was woken with a start. There was shouting and what sounded like a struggle on the stairs. What the fuck! She jumped up and went out onto the landing. At the top of the stairs two men were entangled and exchanging words. It was difficult to tell which one was supporting which. As Cleo went towards them, she realised one was the geezer in the flat cap from outside, and the other was Pete. He was swaying like a sapling in the breeze.

Cleo bit her lip with regret. She liked Pete. When he was clear-headed, he was one of the few men she did like. And now this.

'Can I help you two gentlemen?'

The nob introduced himself. 'Good evening, Miss. My name is Tom. This young man is supposed to be helping me find a lady called Cleo. But I seem to be helping him instead . . .'

Cleo took Tom by the arm and suggested he wait down the landing for a few moments. Then she grabbed Pete by his lapels. 'What the hell happened to you?'

He was gently rocking. His eyes looked desperate, but he sounded cheerful enough. 'I'll tell you what's happened bird – I've become a movie mogul. Go down and ask Mickey, he'll tell you! Ha ha!'

Cleo scrunched her face up at the nonsense, then settled her features into glamour puss mode as she realised Tom was taking a close interest. She seethed quietly, 'Look mate, if you're fallen off the wagon, that's up to you, but you've got work on here. You're supposed to be at the controls.'

'I know, I know, I'm going . . .'

'You better had.'

Cleo left him to it, fixed a sexy smile on her face and wiggle-jiggled down the landing. 'Sorry for the delay.'

Tom didn't seem interested in the delay. 'My word, you are a full-figured young lady.'

His lecherous eyes were already going over her flesh. There was a lot of it on show. She wore a red mini-dress with a plunging neckline and a pair of mauve platform shoes. She'd put on one of her mile-high Afro wigs after Pete had advised that her client liked 'African ladies'. His beady eyes bulged as if he was being strangled as he took her in. 'My word . . .'

'Why don't you join me in the executive suite to examine my full figure more closely?'

The executive suite was like all the other rooms in the house, except the carpet was a little newer and the curtains a little less stained. But it still smelt of mildew and rotten wood. As Cleo had discovered, a lot of men liked it like that. It was like they got off on the sleaze and dirt. While Tom made himself comfy in an armchair, she very slowly poured drinks to give Pete time to get the broom cupboard next door set up. She handed Tom a glass of cheap brandy and sat in his lap so her dress rode up her thighs. 'So you like black girls? What is it you like about them? It's just a colour, after all.'

Tom was flummoxed. 'Err ... well ... I suppose it's because ...' But he never got the chance to explain why. Through the wall came the sound of an almighty crash and a shout of, 'Oh fuck!'

Both Cleo and Tom were startled, but it was Cleo who guessed what had happened. She excused herself and went to investigate, rushing next door to the broom cupboard. Her suspicions were proved correct.

'You twat,' she cursed softly. In a corner she found Pete spread out on the floor, nursing a cut to the forehead. On a desk nearby were the controls he was supposed to be working. A camera was set up to film through a hole in the wall and there were a series of switches for microphones scattered around the room. She didn't know who had ordered the filming and recording – Pete was clearly the monkey, not the organ grinder.

'Pete?'

He struggled up, one hand clasped to his head. 'Don't worry yourself, this is easy, I'm alright. Go and ask Mickey, I'm a movie mogul!'

It was clear he wasn't up for doing any more work that night. His voice was too loud and Cleo began to worry that Tom would smell a rat rather than being one. She whispered, 'Are you sure?'

Instead of answering, Pete slumped to the floor with another crash. He called out, 'Stan thinks he's the clever one but I'm clever too. For a start, he's not a mate of Michael Caine like me. Ha Ha!'

In despair Cleo began to manoeuvre him towards the door as quietly as she could. She whispered, 'Stan?'

'It weren't my fault he was locked in the outside khazi and our mum didn't love him . . .' He hiccupped. 'But he blames me, see . . .?'

Stan was clearly the brother.

She got Pete out on the landing. 'Go downstairs. Talk to someone. Anyone.'

While he staggered down the landing, she went back into the broom cupboard.

She stared at the equipment. 'What a fucking balls-up.'

She didn't have a clue how the stuff worked, but she had a regular who went on and on about the films he made, including the boring technical bits. Cleo didn't want Pete getting into trouble. She flicked all the switches and was relieved to hear a tape machine begin whirring away under the desk. Next to the desk was the camera. She peered through the lens and could clearly see the bed next door. She could also see that Tom was starting to look suspicious and nervy. She hurriedly scanned the apparatus. When she pressed one of the levers, the camera hummed into action and the roll of film began to revolve.

She went back next door and sashayed over. 'Foxy momma is here to take care of her . . .' she kicked off her platform shoe, lifted her foot and slowly placed it on Lord Nob's hard knob, '. . . big baby bear.'

Cleo gave Tom a right royal seeing-to, making sure he lost his flat cap and gave the camera a good profile. Like many women, she was a past master at detaching herself from the act and focusing on other things. She had plenty to think about.

As she bounced up and down on the howling Lord Nob, she wondered – *who was Pete's brother, Stan? And what did he have to do with the specials?*

Twenty-Three

Bang! Bang! Bang!

'Hold your bloody horses,' Babs yelled as the knocker went like the devil on her front door.

Babs didn't really have time for a chat, so whoever it was had better state their business quickly. She didn't feel her best this morning. The baby had been using its feet like it was trying out for Arsenal all night and when she'd woken up she'd felt slightly off-balance. She moved to the door and was shocked to see who was on the other side.

'Have you seen my Denny?' a very distressed Maggie Brooks begged. Denny's mother was not a fashion plate at the best of times, but today she looked one step down from awful. Dark circles under her eyes, hair uncombed and greasy. The poor woman was shaking like she'd just been told she was dying. She stumbled into the passage and had to press her hand against the wall to keep upright.

'Denise! Denise!' she called out.

'She isn't here, Mrs Brooks.'

Tears spilled down her cheeks. Her eyes were glazed and wild. 'She's got to be. I've looked high and low and I can't find my girl.' Her voice ended on a shriek that turned into heart-wrenching sobbing. Her body bowed forward like she was about to break into two.

'Come on.' Babs held her as she took her to the sitting room.

Babs handed her a glass of gin and then sat next to her. 'I haven't seen Denny since last week. She was nice and chirpy—'

'Why?' Maggie's bloodshot eyes snapped to her. 'Has she got some fella hidden away I don't know about?'

Babs shook her head. 'You know she isn't that type of girl.'

Maggie gulped heavily at her glass. 'I know things haven't been easy at home. What with Darren trying . . .' She caught her words back in alarm.

Darren trying . . .? Babs suddenly understood what had been troubling her friend. That animal of a stepfather of hers had been trying it on with her. She should have guessed. The one and only time she'd been around Denny's, Darren Brooks had gazed at her with such blatant lust in his eyes she'd vowed never to go there again. Poor Denny.

Babs was angry and let it show. 'You should've slung that old man of yours out. Better still, you should've called the coppers on him. How could you have let him at Denny?'

Maggie's eyes turned bright with unshed tears. 'What could I do? I needed a man to help me with the kids. A woman isn't meant to be on her own.'

Putting a man ahead of your daughter disgusted Babs but she kept schtum; going into one wouldn't help.

Maggie took a breath. 'She quit the factory because she said she had a new job. She must've told you about it.'

'New job?' Babs muttered under her breath. That's when she remembered what Denny had told her, in this very room, about an interview with Mickey for a modelling job. She'd warned Denise not to get involved with the geezer . . . and now she hadn't come home.

'She never told me a dickie bird about no new job,' Babs lied. Denise's mum was tearing her hair out and Babs didn't want to make things worse by telling her about the Go Go

Girls Modelling Agency. Plus, what if she'd got this all wrong and it had nish to do with Mickey Ingram? Best to keep her own counsel at this stage. She vowed to ask Stan what he knew when she got to work.

Mel sat in her mink coat smoking a cigarette and staring at Pete, just waking up after a long sleep. In an armchair nearby her husband looked grim-faced, like a doctor with bad news sitting by the bedside of an accident victim. Pete struggled up, hampered by his fingers, which stuck to the blanket he was lying on.

Pete used his elbows to lever himself upwards, but fell backwards and only managed to sit up on a third try. He looked shocked to see two other people watching him.

Mickey put his cup down and sneered. 'Good night?'

Pete didn't seem sure. 'I dunno. I can't remember.'

Mel watched as Pete tried to pull his fingers apart. He was in such a state that it was a few moments before he realised why they were stuck. They were caked in blood. He looked at Mickey and Mel but neither said anything. Mel stubbed out her cigarette and lit another one. She watched Pete's glazed and sodden eyes focus and wander around the room. There was blood everywhere. It was sprayed on the wallpaper, dripped on the carpet and puddled on the bedclothes. And most of all, it was up and down his clothes like red paint. Once again, he looked at Mickey and Mel for an answer but got none.

Finally, he yelped, raised his red hands and blubbed, 'What the fuck's going on?'

Mickey avoided his gaze and, with a sad shake of his head, picked his cuppa up again. Mel glared at him. 'I'll tell you what's going on. You remember that girl you met last night in the VIP lounge? Mickey's new model – Denise?'

'No . . .' Then he blinked. 'Yeah . . .'

Mel nodded. 'Well, you killed her.'

It took Pete a while to understand. It took a little longer before he became by turns angry and terrified. His words flowed out in shock. 'Fuck off. I ain't killed no one. Where is this girl? Why would I kill anyone? What's the matter with you? I'm not a killer, I wouldn't hurt a fly. Where's the body? You're taking the piss. What is this – *Candid Camera?*'

Mel gave him a grim smile. 'Right – so what do you make of all this blood then? Do you think someone's spilt a crate of claret? We're not running an abattoir, are we? Mind you, I don't blame you, I blame Mickey . . .'

Mickey was outraged. 'Me? How's it my fault?'

Mel turned on him. 'You were the one who told him to give the girl a hiding. You could see the state Pete was in; you should have guessed what was gonna happen.'

Mickey was even angrier. 'I told him to rough her up – I didn't tell him to beat her to a pulp and leave the pieces on the carpet. What's the matter with you?'

'Oh yes, because giving girls a right-hander is beneath you. You're far too important for that, aren't you?'

'Fuck off, you bitch!'

Mel hissed, 'Are you gonna keep your voice down? Or maybe you want to throw the window open and let the neighbours know?'

The growing ding-dong was interrupted by a knock on the door. When Mickey had confirmed who it was, Cleo walked in. She was still wearing the red mini-dress from the night before. She avoided Pete's eyes.

Mickey whispered, 'Did you sort it for me?'

'Yeah. A couple of the boys took it up the council incinerator.'

Mickey nodded. 'Are you sure they don't know what was it in it?'

Cleo was deadpan. 'Not exactly – I couldn't ask them if they realised it was a stiff wrapped up in carpet, could I?'

Mickey nodded again. 'Sure. OK. They're reliable anyway. Thanks for sorting that for me. I'll make it up to you another time. Get Pete a bucket and mop; he'll have to clear up in here. Then take the rest of the day off.'

Pete came out of his daze and wailed, 'They're saying I did some girl in.' He shook his head furiously. 'I'd never do that. Not me.'

She refused to answer him, only looking at him with anger in her eyes, then left the room. Mel called after her, 'Don't go anywhere yet young lady, I want a word with you after.'

Pete started rocking on the bed, bawling like a small child. 'I want my mum.'

Mickey sighed. 'Your mum can't help you now. Only me and the missus here can. Don't worry about the girl; she was just some scrubber anyway. Trouble is, she might have family and they might go to the law, who might join the dots. We don't want them snooping around. You can flash the cash at the Bill to iron out a few wrinkles but not when it comes to murder. I don't even know if their homicide boys are for hire, I've never had to deal with them.'

Mickey's voice hardened. 'But do as you're told and we can sort this. I'm gonna get one of the boys to drive you to the coast and book you into a B&B under a fake name. Stay there until I give you the nod so you can come back to town and everything will be cushty. If the plod come round, we'll front it out. Although you're not coming back here. This is a respectable establishment. This ain't some fairground boxing outfit where a slip of a girl goes up against a murderous drunk.'

Pete put his head in his hands. 'I need to call Stan. He'll know what to do.'

Mickey was savage. 'Fuck Stan. You're not talking to him. This is all his fault. If he hadn't fobbed his alkie brother on me, this would've never happened. We'll give Stan the full SP later.'

Pete's tears dried a little. 'I still want to speak to him.'

Mel got up and sat beside Pete, taking care to avoid the blood. She squeezed his arm. 'Don't be silly. You know he'd hand you over to the law if he thought there was something in it for him. Leave this to us. Clean the room and go on holiday. We'll call you.'

Pete looked at his hands. The tears had turned the dried blood back into liquid. He began to wipe them frantically on the pillowcase. He couldn't believe Stan would sell him out. But then he remembered what had happened to Stan when they were young and how his brother blamed him for it.

He decided to do what he was told.

Cleo was slumped in her room when the witch Mel came in. She'd never liked Mickey's missus. There was something about her that put Cleo in mind of a dog with rabies. And now she had her fangs in her.

'If Mickey had told me what was in that carpet I'd have run the other way,' Cleo said, every word clipped with anger.

Mel walked over to her. 'Well you're in it up to your neck now.'

Cleo raged, 'Pete didn't kill that girl. I saw what state he was in last night – he was so pissed, he couldn't beat an egg. He didn't kill her. And Mickey didn't either. He's small time. He ain't the got the guts to kill someone in cold blood—'

'Here's a news flash,' Mel growled. 'Pete was a murder waiting to happen. You know that; everyone knows that.' Her tone softened. 'I'll sort you out.'

'I don't want your effing money,' Cleo spat. 'The only reason I'm still sitting here is Pete. If he did do this – *if* – it was an accident.'

Mel sneered. 'You keep telling yourself that. In the meantime, don't think about shooting your mouth off to the plod. They don't have a lot of confidence in the word of a slag like you. Plus, there's already been one bird offed in this house. We wouldn't want another one, would we?'

Mel stalked out of the room, leaving Cleo seething. She weren't scared of Mel or her thicko husband. But Pete . . .

Cleo dropped her head into her hands in despair. 'Pete, oh Pete.'

Twenty-Four

Babs was in a right two and eight by the time she got to the office. She practically bashed the door in. She didn't care; all she could think about was talking to Stan about Denny. She barged into his office without knocking.

'Oops,' she said as he looked at her sharply, none too pleased with her intrusion. She should have remembered that he hated being taken by surprise.

'This better be good . . .' he told her, leaning back in his chair.

Now she had her moment she felt all tongue-tied. But she reminded herself that Denny had said she was going to meet his mate Mickey. She just didn't know when.

'Don't just stand there catching flies,' Stan shot out impatiently. She'd never seen him this grumpy before. 'I'm trying to run a business here . . .' He caught himself. 'Sorry Babs-babe, I got out of bed the wrong side. What's up?'

'My mate Denise has gone missing.' The words shot out of her mouth.

'What happened?'

Babs took a step closer. 'Well, you see . . .'

But before she could finish they were interrupted by a sarky voice. 'Not interrupting a lovers' quarrel, am I?'

Mickey Ingram stood in the doorway with some flash lemon

curd on his arm. The woman was a looker, there was no doubt about it, but Babs reckoned she was all fur coat and no knickers. In fact, she was wearing a fur coat – mink. The woman might've had all the right clobber but it looked cheap on her.

The woman's gaze zeroed in on Babs' belly and then she smirked at Stan. 'You been a naughty boy? Sticking your big camera where it don't belong?'

He ignored her and told Babs, 'We'll continue our chat later.'

'We'll need three Nescafes,' the woman said.

Babs nodded. She headed for the door, looking over at Mickey. She was tempted to ask him there and then about Denny, but decided against it. Better to keep it zipped until she talked to Stan. Plus, Mickey would spin her a load of old cobblers anyway. Babs closed the door, then hesitated, almost tempted to stick her ear against it. Almost. What if she got caught and lost her job? Where would she be then? Not many bosses were willing to take on a girl with a child in her belly. She got on with making the coffee and bided her time.

As soon Mickey and Mel parked their arses in his office, Stan knew they were about to try and piss all over him. He divided the world up into smart people and thick people. Stan was smart. Mickey was thick. But Mel was one of the smart ones. The fact that Mickey was looking pleased with himself didn't bother Stan. The fact that Mel looked like a mink-coated cat with the cream did.

As soon as Babs had set down the three cups of instant coffee and closed the door, Mickey got into it. 'I want that girl out and I want Bev brought back. The girl must be nearly ready to drop her sprog anyway.'

Mel quickly followed on. 'Tell her she ain't coming back afterwards. Our Bev's getting her old job back and she'll be answering to my husband.'

Stan wasn't stupid; he knew the duo having a go at Babs was just them warming up for the kill. He said nothing. He was in no hurry to get them to the point. The more time they spent talking trash, the longer it gave him to suss out what they were up to. It was Mel he was interested in. She was smart in an East End way. In other circumstances, Stan might have found a use for her. But he'd always known that it would come down to a fight. Mickey was a thick thug and gutter pimp. Mel was the nifty one. But Stan was niftier.

When Mickey didn't get a response, he added with menaces, 'Is that a problem?'

Stan took out his silver cigarette case and lit up. He paused to blow a few smoke rings before coolly asking, 'Is there something on your mind? You seem a little put out. Come on, spit it out, we're all grown-ups here.'

Mickey flicked a quick sideways glance at his wife before giving his full attention back to Stan. 'As it happens, there is something on my mind. I've been having a think about the business. I've decided it's better for it to be a one-man operation again. Obviously I'll dosh you up for any contribution you've made. That's only fair.' Mickey seemed to feel he was being eminently reasonable.

Stan lifted an eyebrow as he sucked in a lug of smoke. Breathed out. 'Oh dear. That's a shame. What's brought that on?' He could see Mel was itching to get involved but was restraining herself.

'Oh, you know. In business one head is better than two.'

Stan smirked. 'I dunno; it depends whose head it is, don't it?'

Mel finally started spitting nails. 'OK, let's stop mucking around. You think we don't know what's been going on here? What you've been up to? I was up the land registry the other day and guess what? Some of Mickey's properties have been transferred to your name, including those two houses in Mile End. You slippery little sod.'

Stan let her rip. He knew keeping calm would wind her up. 'It hardly matters; they're all part of the business. Who cares what name they're in? Anyroads, Mickey signed the transfers.'

'Because he signed them without looking at them. Because he trusted you.'

Stan started laughing. 'Ere, Mickey, your missus is accusing you of being too thick to read documents before you sign them. You ain't putting up with that from a bird, are you?'

Mickey's face twisted into open hatred. 'I'll tell you what's going on – you ain't. And if you keep riling me up, I don't care how long I've known you, it's not long enough to stop me kicking you all over Soho. That's a promise.'

Stan smiled back. 'I'm sure. A hard man with no brains, the worst possible combination.'

Mickey rose to his feet, fizzing, his fist tight by his side. 'Come on then. Let's take it outside, you ponce.'

Mel touched his sleeve. 'Sit down, baby. There's no need for any unpleasantness. I'm sure Stan will be reasonable.' Mel took a brown A4 envelope out of her handbag and placed it on Stan's desk.

Stan looked at it and knew he was in big trouble. 'What's that?'

Mel was smiling wide, like she was about to bag a large prize. 'It's a deed drawn up by our brief. You're going to sign over your side of the business to us. And then you're going to transfer all Mickey's property back to him. And then we'll call it quits.'

The stupid bint was having a laugh. But she had confidence in spades, which spooked him badly. 'I don't think so.'

Mel was almost purring. 'Oh, that's right, we forgot to tell

you. We had a bit of a messy incident in Mile End last night.'
Mickey unclenched his fists and sat down again. He was smiling now. Stan was definitely in big trouble.

'A new girl was playing up, so Mickey asked Pete to sort her out. And he sorted her out alright. He sorted her out so well, we had to scrape her off the floor, wrap her up in carpet and tuck it away somewhere. Your big bruv made quite a noise when he was doing it. One of our guests, who we didn't even know Cleo was seeing to, was so upset he ran out into the street in his Y-fronts and scarpered in a Bentley.'

Lord Tilgate drove a Bentley. That explained why he hadn't returned Stan's calls.

Stan's face gave nothing away. 'You're blagging.'

Mel took out a handful of what looked like cards. She spread them out in front of him. Not cards but photos. Various shots of a girl covered in blood. 'You'll believe it when your brother's on trial for murder up at the Bailey,' Mel taunted him. 'Like I said, there's no need for any nastiness. If you sign those documents we could probably make all this go away, couldn't we, sweetheart?'

'I'm sure we could,' Mickey chimed in.

'And where is Pete? I want a word with him.'

'Don't worry about Pete; we're looking after him for you,' Mel said. 'Of course if you don't sign, we'll have to let him back out into the wild and we won't be able to help then. The girl's family don't know where she was, but you know how the street is, the old Chinese whispers. Someone might say something, dots get joined, and the law will be after him. You know what your brother's like, soft as a 99 in the sun. As soon as they start working him over, he'll sing like he's on *Opportunity Knocks*. And we'll have no choice but to help the coppers. It's up to you of course. Your choice. You can keep the photos. We've got plenty more.'

Stan pushed them to one side and picked up the envelope with the documents inside. 'OK. Fair enough. I'll sign. I'll have to get my brief to go over it obviously, and property deeds can't be transferred in a day. It will take a good couple of weeks' – Mickey was helpful. 'Of course. But don't leave it too long. We might get suspicious. Trust is so important in business . . .'

The happy couple left. Stan went over and over it. He didn't know how much was true but it was obvious that those two chancers were confident that their story would survive any sniffing around he might do. And they clearly knew he was going to. Stan suspected there was a dead body somewhere but he didn't believe Pete had killed the girl. He wasn't the sort. But it hardly mattered – his brother was a liability. He'd had his chances, over and over.

He had a couple of weeks to set a chain of events in motion to get him off the hook. But he was confident. Stan had one big advantage in this coming struggle.

They were Mickey and Mel Ingram. But he was Stanley Miller.

Ten minutes after Mickey and Mel were gone, Babs barged into Stan's office a second time. Her boss was sitting at his desk, deep in thought, studying photos. But when he saw her, he hurriedly put them in his drawer.

'Tell me about Denny.' Stan tried his usual smile but it made his jaw seem tense and his features drawn.

Babs got into it as soon as she sat down. 'Like I said, my mate Denny has disappeared and I think it's got something to do with that Mickey.'

'Mickey?' He pulled out one of his Turkish fags but didn't light up, just rolled it around between his fingers. He offered her one, but she declined; the baby always played up after a smoke. 'What's he got to do with your mate?'

'Denny is right pretty and always longed to be a model. I told her about the agency– '

'That wasn't very clever.'

Babs looked shamefaced. 'I know, but she kept banging on about it and I didn't have the heart to tell her to forget it. She's my best mate. She wanted me to put in a word but I kept putting her off. But somehow she managed to sort out an interview with Mickey.'

Stan tutted. 'That was unfortunate. Mickey's not scrupulous. You should have told her to come to me. I would've put her straight.'

'Her mum came around this morning in a right old state and said that Denny went out last night tarted up to the eyeballs and wouldn't say where she was going. No one has seen her since. I'm worried sick about her.'

Stan was staring into the middle distance. 'This girl – what does she look like?'

Babs described Denny. As she did so, Stan massaged the skin around his eyes before whispering, 'I see . . .' Then he looked at her. 'OK. You need to leave this to me. I don't want you worrying. You've got a baby to think about. I'll find out what's happened. Tell the girl's mum not to rely on the law. They won't help; they'll think she's done a runner. You can rely on me. I'll sort this. And if any harm has come to your mate . . .'

Babs' eyebrows flew up. '"Any harm"?'

Stan's jaw tightened some more. 'I'm not saying that it has.' He seemed to be struggling to explain himself. Then he stopped trying and reached over for her hand. 'It's a bad world, Babs. Bad things happen.' When she gulped in horror he went on, 'But not to you. I'll make sure of that.'

She felt safe. Stan would find Denny and everything would be OK. She knew she could rely on him.

Stan moved around to her. He took her hands in his again and pulled her to her feet. She shivered; his hands were ice cold. In a soft voice he said, 'Don't worry, I'll sort everything.' Then he added, 'By the way, I need you to witness some documents for me this week. You know, counter-sign a few odds and ends.'

He'd never asked her to do anything like that before. It made her feel that he trusted her. That she was an important part of his business. 'No problem.'

As soon as the door closed, Stan took the photos out again.

'You stupid bastard, Pete,' he cursed as he stared at the dead body of Babs' best friend.

Then he took out his target list and added two new names.

Twenty-Five

A few days on Babs was getting ready to leave work when Stan slapped some papers in front of her.

'What's this then?' she asked.

Stan plonked himself down on the edge of the desk. Whatever had been troubling him all week must have got sorted because he was back to his usual cheerful, charming self. 'I told you a couple of days back. The papers I need witnessing.'

He shoved a pen in her hand and then turned to the first page. 'Just sign where the pencil mark is.'

Most of the document was covered by the other papers; she couldn't see what she was signing.

She looked up at him, confused. 'What is it? And where's your signature?'

He seemed put out.

'I'm signing it – what's the matter, don't you trust me?'

She felt bad for even asking, so signed in three places and he whipped the papers away. 'Have you found anything out about Denny?'

He simply shook his head before hurrying off to his office. She forgot about the documents and began to worry that Stan knew something he wasn't saying. It wasn't like him. He was can-do. And even if he couldn't-do, he would at least come up with a clever story to cover his rear end. Even in a crisis he always had a line. Once again, she walked into his office without knocking. He looked up in alarm.

She was firm. 'What's going on with Denny?'

'You only told me the other day – I'm looking into it.'

'Have you spoken to Mickey?'

Stan avoided her gaze again. 'Yeah. He said he met her a few nights back and then she headed off to a party somewhere in town. He don't know where but he's asking around for me. That's it.' Then he shouted at her. 'Look – I'm doing my best here. Gimme a break!'

Babs stumbled back, stunned. Stan had never raised his voice to her. 'What's got into you today? If there's something else on your mind, that's fine. But Denny's my best mate and I need to find her. I'll go and find Mickey Ingram myself and have it out with him. I know where he lives.'

Stan jumped up and grabbed her arm. With a huff and shake of his head he released her and put his arm around her instead. 'I want you to really listen to me. You know my view of the world. I don't trust anyone and I've always been proved right. I don't really like people, if I'm honest. But the thing is ...' he ran gentle fingers through her hair, 'I trust you. There's something between us, but I know you need space, not me crowding you. I'm going to be honest with you on one condition: you've got to trust *me*. Don't do anything stupid. Have we got a deal?'

He was so close she could feel his breath on her cheek. She felt warm and safe. God, she loved being in his arms. She nodded. 'Yes, of course I trust you.'

He held her even more tightly. 'Good. I knew you did. So I'll be honest. I don't know what happened to Denny but I'm fearing it might not be good.' She opened her mouth but he put his finger to her lips. 'Now, I want you to go home. I know it's going to be hard to put this out of your mind but that's what

I need you to do. Don't make any enquiries. Leave it to me. I'll tell you when I know anything.' Stan put his fingertips on her belly. 'And look after our little friend in there. They won't want you getting an attack of the nerves.'

'I'm fearing it might not be good.' Babs couldn't get Stan's words out of her head. If anything had happened to Denny . . . She shook the horrifying thoughts from her head. *Nothing has happened*, Babs reassured herself, *nothing*.

Stan hugged her. Babs sank into the comfort he offered, tears rolling down her cheeks. 'I'll get you a cab to take you home.'

Stan stepped back, got her coat and led her down to the street. He hailed a cab and stuffed pound notes into the driver's hand. But before the guy drove off, he cradled her face, kissed her on the lips and whispered, 'Trust me . . .'

Babs stared out of the window on the journey back to the East End. Every time she thought of Denny, she followed in Stan's footsteps: put her fingertips on her belly and thought of her unborn child. He was right. Her baby needed peace and its mother's strong nerves. There was only a month and a bit to go.

But as she watched the world go by, she spotted a black couple walking down Mile End Road. The woman was pushing a pram and the guy was following a couple of paces behind. Babs took the scene in as she passed. Her mouth settled into a grim line.

'Stop the fucking cab!'

The cabbie turned in alarm. 'Alright luv, calm down.'

'I said, stop the fucking cab!'

The driver pulled over and Babs rushed clumsily out, leaving the door hanging open. 'Oi! I want a word with you!'

She caught up to the guy and stepped defiantly in front of him.

That lying, cheating Neville.

The bastard actually had the front to try to sneak around her. Wrong move! Babs used her belly to block his path. 'Which stone have you been hiding under?' she blasted.

Neville was decked out to the nines. He was the kind of guy who dressed up to put the rubbish out; he made Roger Moore look like a scruff. He was dressed in a herringbone suit and a lemon shirt with a black cowboy string tie. The whole rig was finished off with black brogue shoes. And, of course, his most prized possession, his crowning glory, his immaculately shaped Afro. He'd gone crazy about his hair after he'd taken her to see *Shaft*. She was warned not to run her fingers through his barnet under any circumstances. Or, as he put it, 'Don't mess with my Prince'.

'Excuse me,' he said, his voice his Sunday best, obviously out to impress the piece of totty who had wheeled the pram back to stand with him. 'Can you step aside?'

'Step aside?' Babs was furious now, her voice rising loud and clear. 'You weren't saying that when we were tucked up all nice and lovey-dovey between the sheets— ' Her voice ended on a squeak as he grabbed her and marched her down the street, throwing an 'I won't be a second' over his shoulder. His lady was standing with an outraged expression, arms folded.

Babs shook his hand off. 'You've got a lot to answer for, Neville Campbell. Or is it Lewis? Or maybe Morris? There were so many names for you on those letters in that Limehouse flat I thought I'd been going out with Ronald Biggs.'

'Babs?' he asked with mock surprise. 'I've been looking for you—'

'Cut the shit, Nev. I know about Petra, Tania, that poor cow standing over there and God knows how many others. If you didn't want to see me no more, then you should've had the balls to tell me to my face. You know what they say, if you're big enough to put your cock in it, you should be man enough when you want to tuck it away.' She shoved her palm in his face when he started to speak. Now she had him she was going to have her say. 'You left me right in the lurch.' His widening eyes went to her belly. 'That's right, this baby is yours. So what are you going to do about it?' She stabbed her finger into his chest. 'This little one needs a dad about the house. A man who'll put bread on the table. A name.'

Neville must have been proper stressed out. He was actually shoving his fingers in his hair, messing his Prince up big time. 'Why didn't you let me know?'

'What with? A crystal ball? I went looking for you in every hole I knew about like a grade one fool.' She stared at the pram. 'Is that your kid?'

The way he looked nervously over his shoulder answered the question. 'I'm sorry baby—'

'Baby, you got that right. What are you going to do about it?'

He copped another gaze at his lady friend, who was toing and froing the pram in such a hectic motion it looked like it would tip over any second. 'The thing is, I've found myself a really great lady. She loves the ground I walk on but I don't think finding out I'm the proud daddy of some other bird's baby is going to go down so well.'

Oh, Babs knew what he meant alright – that *she* wasn't a great lady. That hurt, really hurt. What a proper moron she had been. She had given this guy everything, *everything*, and all he could chat on about was some other woman like she didn't have feelings. She should've figured out that Nev was a total me-me-me merchant straight away.

She felt like crying, but she ruthlessly shut the waterworks down, fed up of mooning over this man. 'You want to know what your Jack the Lad routine cost me? Everything. I've been called a whore by some old fart of a doctor, had to face down my mum and dad's disappointment, and Denny . . .' Her voice hitched in her throat.

His face became concerned. 'What, Denise who I met at the Reno?'

'Do you know a geezer called Mickey Ingram?'

He looked shocked that she was even uttering Mickey's name. 'I did a bit of . . . let's just call it maintenance . . . on the doors of a brothel he owns around here—'

Babs' eyes bulged. 'A knocking shop?'

He nodded. 'I roughed up any punters who got out of hand and chucked their arses out.' His gaze darted away from the disbelief on her face. 'I'm not proud of it. I washed my hands of that place a long time ago.' He leaned closer. 'If Denny's mixed up with Mickey and his nutty missus—'

His current lady-love rolled the pram up like a tank on a battlefield. She shouted, 'Come on, we've got things to sort out – who is this slag anyway?'

Babs peered into the pram. 'Hmm. Looks like Neville's right. It's not his kid. Your baby really is an ugly little bastard.'

'You little bitch; I'll show you what ugly looks like.'

She swung her open palm at Babs' cheek but it didn't connect. All the anger and uncertainty Babs had been living through burst out like a champagne cork. She threw herself at her wannabe attacker but Neville grabbed her around the waist. Even with his strength, it took Neville some serious work to pull Babs away.

He yelled, 'Knock it off; you've got a baby to think about.'

Babs felt a kick as if her child was silently agreeing with its father. She shrugged him off.

'I hope you have a happy life,' she spat with maximum sark-iness. Then she turned to the angry woman by his side. 'You're welcome to him, luv. A word to the wise, he has a way of leaving his baby-batter all over town.'

As she turned to stalk off, Nev caught her arm and pulled her close. 'Your luck might be in.'

'What are you chatting on about?'

He directed his gaze down the street. 'See that woman over there?'

Babs followed his gaze to see a tall, gorgeous, black woman walking the other way.

'Her name's Cleo. If anyone knows if your mate visited the knocking shop, she will.'

Twenty-Six

Stan's luck was in when he got to the Lancer's Gentleman's Club in Kensington. At the entrance, opening and closing the door for the toffs, was a doorman in a blue uniform. But Stan knew him. He'd guarded dodgy clubs and all-night drinking dens all over London. Now he looked like Cinderella's butler. You had to be flexible in the bouncing game.

'Wotcha, Dan.'

'Blimey – Stan! What are you doing here? Still running that modelling agency? I heard you were thick as thieves with Mickey Ingram these days.' *Wasn't he just!*

'Yeah, I am, sort of. But at the moment I need to get inside.' He dropped his voice. 'I want to have a word with a bloke who lunches and dines here.'

Dan looked wary. 'I dunno. They're a bit choosy about who they let past reception. And you aren't really dressed for it.' He looked at Stan's very natty but very dark red suit. 'If it was up to me of course . . .'

'Of course. But this is urgent, like. Can you get me in round the back? I'll make it up to you and you know I keep my word.'

'I shouldn't really . . . but seeing as it's you.'

Dan took him to the back of the building and after a word with a guy there, Stan was in. He hugged the white walls and followed the whiff of roasted and stewed meat. *How the other half live*, Stan thought when he slipped into the dining room, his gaze taking in the panelled walls, the china and silver and the paintings of blokes in clobber from bygone eras with their noses in the air.

He found Tilgate with a napkin tucked in his collar, staring at his untouched dinner. It seemed that Jack had lost his appetite, but was managing fine with the bottle of vino, already half gone. Stan knew he was taking a risk but at this stage of the game, fortune favours the brave. He crept up unobserved and sat down at the lord's table.

'Alright me ol' mucker?' He gestured at his full plate. 'Nosh in here no good? You should have gone down Nellie's chippie in Aldgate. She would have sorted out a nice pie and mash and thrown in a cheeky smile and a Tizer for free.'

Tilgate was struck dumb but he soon regained his balance. He didn't look best pleased. 'Yes, I might have expected you to turn up here. What did you do? Jemmy open a window with a crowbar? That's how members of the criminal classes usually gain access.'

Stan faked hurt. 'That's a nice way to talk to an old friend. After I arranged a nice African safari for you. That's charming.'

Jack poured himself a glass of plonk and leaned abruptly across the table. 'Can I make a suggestion, Miller? Why don't you make yourself scarce before I call the local constabulary? How does that sound?'

Stan leaned across the table in turn. 'Jack – if there's a problem, you only have to pick up the phone and talk to me. That's what friends do – they don't nurse grudges over dinner at their club. Did the bird not come up to scratch last night?'

The swell's face turned red. 'Come up to scratch? It sounded like someone was being fucking murdered up at that fucking rat hole you sent me to. The place was fucking filthy and as for the girl – she behaved as if it was beneath her dignity to provide a service. And the fucking noise she made.'

Mentally Stan cursed along with the Lord. So Mickey and Mel's story was true. 'Please, Lord Tilgate – there's no need for that kind of barrack-room language. There's ladies present.' In fact, there weren't; women were barred. But Jack looked around anxiously at the curious glances his raised voice was attracting.

'Do you know what would have happened if the police had been called and I'd been found in there?'

Stan knew full well. When they'd discovered who their distinguished suspect was, the plod would've brushed down his suit and called him a cab. 'So what was all the palaver about?'

'I've got no idea. Sounded like a girl was being attacked. So fucking vulgar. And that reprobate you assigned to look after me was as drunk as my Great-Uncle Frederick.'

'Pete was Brahms, then? Do you know who the girl was?'

Jack's voice was going back up again. 'I didn't wait to find out. I made a very quick exit. I didn't even have time to get dressed properly . . .'

Stan started sniggering, imagining Tilgate doing a runner across the square in his smalls.

'You think this is funny?' Tilgate leaned back with a superior expression. 'Our association is at an end. I never want to see you again. Get out!'

Stan had enjoyed taking the piss. The tosspot had earned his ribbing and he'd got some helpful information too. Now it was time for him to play his ace. He took out an envelope and slung it across the table. 'I don't think so.'

Tilgate looked around furtively before picking up the envelope and pulling out the contents. Photos. The blood drained from his face. 'What the hell is this?' he asked angrily.

Stan calmly poured himself a glass of wine and knocked it back in one. 'That, Jack, is a still of you bouncing up and down on a black prostitute in a knocking shop in Mile End. It's from a film, so there's plenty more. And there's also a tape of you making squelching noises and a running commentary of the *ooh ah my dear, yes, that's very good* variety. You know the score.'

Tilgate stuffed the snaps back into the envelope and shoved it into his pocket. 'This sounds like a blackmail attempt.'

'Hardly. It *is* a blackmail attempt.'

'The police take a very dim view of blackmailers.'

Stan picked up the bottle of wine and tipped the remainder down his throat. 'And Fleet Street take a very dim view of randy peers of the realm shagging prostitutes, especially black ones. You're on a losing streak. You know what I want. Give me your name to stick on my stationery, get me into some parties, introduce me to the right people, and you can forget your night out on the wrong side of the tracks, on the wrong side of the bed, pumping the wrong side of a bird.'

There was a pause before Lord Tilgate grudgingly said, 'I'd want the tapes and the film.'

'Not a problem. Wouldn't do you any good though. You know there'll be copies.' Stan dropped his voice to a chilling whisper. 'Come on, cough up and let me get out of here.'

'I wouldn't need to see you again?'

Stan pulled a napkin towards him, pulled out a pen and wrote on it. 'That's the name of my brief. Give him a bell and he'll sort out the particulars.'

Once he was outside, Stan took out his golden list and crossed off the third name from the bottom.

Lord Tilgate.

He took off down the street, a killer smile lighting up his face. Now all he had to do was confirm what happened to Pete and find out where Mickey and Mel had stashed him. And Stan knew exactly who could help him.

'Wotcha, Cleo,' Babs yelled out as she hurried as fast as her large belly would allow her towards the woman Neville had pointed out.

Hearing her name, the woman turned. Up close Babs decided that she wasn't just gorgeous, she was a proper stunner. Cleo was decked out in a caramel-coloured Afro, a long patchwork coat and thigh-high black suede boots.

She looked down at Babs with a hard frown. 'How do you know my name? Who are you?'

'I just need some information—'

The other woman cut her off with a scoff. 'Look, luv, if your old man is one of my friends you need to take that up with him—'

'I'm looking for my mate Denny.'

Cleo stiffened and her dark eyes became jumpy. 'Denny? I don't know anyone by that name. You've got me mixed up with someone else.'

As she turned to make a speedy getaway, Babs caught her arm. 'A mutual friend of ours said you would know if Denny had been to the brothel.'

Cleo tugged her arm loose. 'Brothel?' She stuck her nose in the air. 'Do I look like the kind of lady who would be making her living on her back in a knocking shop?'

But Babs stood her ground. 'Then what was all that talk about your "friends"? You thought I was one of your clients' missuses come to have it out with you in broad daylight.'

Cleo growled and bent slightly forward. 'Naff off. I'm busy.'

But Babs was going nowhere. It was her fault Denny had got mixed up in this in the first place. If she'd taken control of the situation she could've introduced Denise to Stan, who would've warned her off.

'I ain't going nowhere until you tell me the truth.'

Cleo kissed her teeth and started marching off down the road. Babs took off after her, despite the dull ache forming in her belly. 'I know Denny was in your knocking shop with Mickey Ingram.'

Cleo abruptly stopped and swung around. 'Look, babe, I've never heard of your mate. Now clear off before I go and set my dog . . .' Glancing down at Babs' belly she amended, 'my very titchy dog on you.'

Babs hung tough. 'If I do clear off, I'll be back – and I'll bring the law with me next time. And we'll knock on the door of every house until we find this brothel. I know all about Mickey Ingram because he works with my boss Stanley Miller.'

'Stanley . . . Miller?' For some reason that had the other woman nearly in tears.

Babs' heart skipped a beat. Why would hearing Stan's name make this woman nearly cry? And what did it have to do with Denny?

Fearful for her friend, Babs said, between gritted teeth, 'I mean it. I'll bring the Bill down on you.' She rubbed her hand over her belly to try and get rid of the ache that was now see-sawing deep within her.

Cleo seemed to have collected herself. 'This is how it is. Mickey Ingram owns a modelling agency and a girl called Denny went there looking for work. Some of Mickey's girls earn a bit extra by meeting gentlemen, you get me?' Oh, Babs got her alright. 'Mickey brought Denny down to the house where gentlemen meet ladies last night, but there were some crossed wires and she didn't realise what was what. She got upset and threatened to go to the cops. Mickey told her if she did she'd be in aggro up to her pretty eyes. Obviously she got scared and scarpered.' Cleo's voice rose slightly. 'So you can be as sure as eggs are eggs that your mate Denny is hiding somewhere because she thinks Mickey is after her. That's what happened. She'll turn up – OK?'

Babs listened in silence to Cleo's explanation. At least she was admitting she knew Denny, but Babs was far from satisfied. 'Not really. I want to hear it from Mickey.'

Cleo was silent for a while. 'What's your name, babe?'

'Babs.'

'OK Babs, let me tell you something. I can see you've got some guts. But you're in over your head with the wrong kind of people.' She bit her lip. 'Trust me; I know what I'm talking about. Asking questions of guys like Mickey Ingram is never a good idea. Not for Denny, not for you, and not . . .' she patted Babs' belly, '. . . for your young 'un in there either. And Mickey won't be showing his face at our house of introduction for a while. You'll be in the maternity ward before he turns up. And you'd be in another ward if he did . . . Are you alright?'

Babs wasn't. There were spasms in her back and legs. She'd been determined to stay put but when she felt pain shooting up and down her body, she suddenly wanted to be back in her flat. She'd heard all she needed to hear anyway. Now it was just a question of passing the news back to Stan. 'Yeah, I'm fine.'

She tried to walk but her legs folded. If Cleo hadn't caught her she'd have fallen flat on her face in the street.

Cleo's eyes widened in alarm. 'Bloody hell. When's your baby due?'

Very gingerly, Babs pulled herself free. 'Not for another month. I'm alright. We're alright.'

'Here – let me help.' But as Cleo reached for her, Babs waved her away.

Her face screwed up as another pain hit. Somehow she managed to remain standing until the pain passed.

She urgently whispered to her belly, 'You can't come yet. In the middle of Mile End Road? If the other kids found out you'd never live it down.'

'You alright?'

Babs ignored Cleo. Something wasn't right. She somehow made it across Mile End Road. But her belly and legs felt strained and awkward. As she turned the corner onto her estate, a wave of dizziness hit. She had to get to the flat to call the doctor's.

By the time she reached her block she was sweating a second skin. Babs gazed up, almost defeated. She was washed out. Couldn't make it.

'Yes you bloody well can,' she told herself fiercely.

She grabbed the stair rail and took the first step. And another. By the time she reached her flat she was blowing out air like a horse. Babs got inside and closed the door thankfully. She took a moment to steady her breathing. Then she moved towards the phone.

She never made it. A vicious cramp twisted her belly and she groaned as she fell to the floor. Her body burned and then chilled. Her belly seemed to expand and then contract. She tried desperately to get up but couldn't. Then she felt wetness seeping from between her legs.

Twenty-Seven

An hour later, a jumpy Cleo stepped out of the brothel with a floppy hat pulled down over her ears. She drew up the collar on her Afghan hippy boho coat to conceal the bottom of her face and walked down the road. She felt hunted since Babs and her belly had accosted her in the street, even though she knew no one was after her. No one could be. But she felt hunted anyway. Mickey and Mel were in and out like it was their second home. But they had nothing further to say to her. And, of course, Pete was long gone.

Cleo still couldn't believe what Pete had done. It didn't add up. Sure the geezer had a problem handling his booze, but murder . . .? After Pete was gone she'd locked herself in her room and feverishly read the Bible. She read a passage that had given her strength over and over again:

'God is our refuge and strength. An ever-present help in trouble.'

Cleo needed His help but also something extra to steady her nerves. She was heading to the offy to get some brandy to mix with Babycham.

Furtively she looked across the square. Everything was as per usual. A couple of winos and some kids mucking about. No one loitering. No one watching. But her heart was thumping away for some reason. She walked briskly towards Mile

End Road, keeping half an eye on her surroundings. When she was out of the square, she relaxed a little and was caught unawares when a car pulled alongside her. The man at the wheel beckoned to her and asked, 'Hello, sugar, you doing business?'

She didn't answer, pressing on instead. She heard the car accelerate and pass her again. It drew to a halt. The driver had a flat cap like the one Lord Nob had worn the night before. 'I said – are you doing business?'

She caught the briefest of glimpses of the driver but still didn't look at him. 'No. I'm off duty.'

But then she froze slightly. How did he know she did business? She couldn't have looked less like a tom if she'd tried; she was even wearing plimsolls. She felt her breathing speeding up, turned quickly on her heels and began to motor back to the square. The car mounted the pavement in front of her, blocking the way. She took a couple of steps backwards but the guy was out of the motor in a flash. He grabbed her by the collar. 'Get in the car, Cleo. Don't worry about anything, just get in.'

She froze with terror. He knew her name and he knew what she did. 'Fuck off, just fuck off, OK? I'll scream the place down and I've got friends nearby.'

He tightened his grip. 'Mickey's people, you mean? I don't think Mickey's people are going to want to mix it with me.' He used his spare hand to pull open the front of his jacket and show her a pistol pushed into his waistband. 'I don't want to cause you any grief and I don't want to get into any rough stuff. Just get in the motor. Everything's good.'

But Cleo's terror grew. *He's got a shooter. A shooter.* 'I keep myself to myself, alright? I don't know anything about anything. Let me go and this stays between me and you.'

'If you don't get your rear end inside this car, you won't be telling anyone nuthin' ever again.' He opened the passenger door and shoved her inside, then got in and motored off. A few streets away, he pulled up in a darkened street, switched off the ignition and sat back. Cleo saw his face clearly for the first time. If it had been any other situation she would have said he was a looker, but at the moment all she could see was a man with a gun.

'The name's Stanley Miller. I'm Pete's brother.' She couldn't hold her surprise back at that. 'I'm just looking for some info, that's all. I want to know two things. What happened last night, and where Pete is. You tell me that and I'll drive you back to Mickey's place. I can't be fairer than that.'

She looked at the passenger door and wondered if she could leg it before she was shot. 'How do you know who I am? How did you know where to find me? Did Pete tell you to come after me? He's got it all wrong. I never did anything.'

'You worried about the gun? Ere – look.' Cleo flinched as Stan took out his pistol. He unlocked the magazine, shook the bullets into his hand and then threw them out of the open window. 'There you go, you don't need to worry about the shooter. Now, what happened last night?'

Cleo was shaking but she did her best. 'I dunno. There was some kind of fight. Pete was supposed to have attacked some girl. She got hurt. This morning he left in a hurry. That's it.'

'That's it?'

'Yeah – I dunno anything else.'

She knew he didn't believe her. He left a long gap before he said anything else, the way the police did, to make you think they weren't having it. His voice was cold and metallic. 'So when did you last see Pete?'

Cleo's gaze skidded away. 'I didn't really see him last night. He was busy.'

Stan turned her face towards him. 'You know why I picked you and not one of the other girls? – because I know my Pete was a touch sweet on you. Plus, I know all about the specials.'

Cleo reached desperately for the door, but he pushed her back into her seat. 'Oi. Oi – calm down. If you don't know nuthin' else what's the big rush?'

Cleo waved her hand. 'I just do what I'm told.'

Stan half-smiled. 'Come on, a bird like you has brains. You're clever. That's what Pete always said – "that Cleo is a right brain box. She's wasted on the filth that paw her every evening".' His smile slipped away. 'Now, I've heard from a posh little dickey bird that you know more than you've let on. You know him – the toff who came over for a portion last night. Pete was meant to be recording the event for posterity. Daffy got the gear to me as usual. If the toff heard what went on, so did you. Am I right?'

Cleo's expression betrayed her, so he carried on. 'Mickey and Mel would have given you a long and complicated story to remember but you've kept it simple and not left any details that might unravel. Am I right again?' Cleo nodded. 'See, Humpty and that rag doll Jemima on *Playschool* have more brains in their heads than Mickey and Mel.'

'Look, I don't want to get involved—'

'You are involved, darlin, whether you like it or not. You want to get disinvolved? You want out of this disgusting business for good? I'm the man to help you. All you've got to do is say what really happened and what Mickey told you to tell the plod.' He placed both his palms gently on her shoulders. 'And whatever that loud mouth Mickey offered you to stick to his side of the story—'

Cleo cried out in anguish, 'I never took a penny. All I wanted to do was help Pete.'

Stan's face softened. 'That's good to hear. Don't worry

about Mickey and the wife – they'll double cross you anyway. I'm a man of my word.' He leaned in close. 'But if you want out, I've got the cash to make that happen. All you've got to do is help me sort a few things.'

Cheryl Parker had so much booze inside her, she nearly fell flat on her face when she reached her landing.

'Bollocks.' The word ended on a loud burp. Then she smiled. She loved this new estate and its local best of all. The Old Swan knew how to pull a pint. Still smiling, she fumbled in her bag for her key and tried to stick it in the lock. But the lock kept swaying.

'Ah, there you go,' she muttered triumphantly. Then she heard a noise coming from somewhere to the side of her. She cocked her head and listened. There it was again, a whimper.

Cheryl shifted along the balcony until she stood outside her new neighbour's place, that lovely girl who was up the duff. Babs, Cheryl recalled in her drunken haze. She didn't approve of a young girl in her condition being on her own. She should be at home being looked after by her mum, or better still, the bastard who knocked her up.

Cheryl pressed her ear against the door. This time she heard a cry of pain. She might be several sheets to the wind, but she knew when something wasn't right.

The situation knocked some of the booze out of her. She marched quickly to her door and yelled for her eldest boy to get his arse out here.

'There's something up next door. Break the friggin' door down. The girl's not far off having her baby.'

What they found inside the flat wiped the rest of the gin from Cheryl's system.

Babs was on her back, writhing in agony.

'Please ... please,' she pleaded, tears streaming from her eyes. 'I've called an ambulance but it's not here yet.'

Cheryl got on her knees beside her. 'You're alright now, luv.' Then she turned to her son. 'Go and tell the fucking ambulance people to move it.'

Twenty-Eight

The following morning, Rosie Wilson cried out, 'Where's my daughter?' like a woman possessed as she raced down the corridor of Mile End Hospital. George, wearing a worried expression behind his glasses, tried to keep up with her. 'Where's my girl?'

A nurse went over to them. She was old, her face as starched as her uniform. 'Is there a problem?'

Rosie grabbed her arm, nearly dropping the bunch of flowers she held. 'My Barbara, my daughter has had her baby. But the baby weren't due yet. I'm going out of my mind with worry—'

George calmly interrupted, pulling her gently to his side. 'Our daughter has had a baby and we'd like to find out where the maternity ward is.'

As soon as the nurse gave them directions they were on their way.

'What if something bad has happened?' Rosie asked, her voice faltering.

He patted her hand. 'Stop being a worry-wart. Babies come early every day of the week. Anyway, our Babs is from tough stock and so is our first grandchild.'

Rosie's face broke into a smile for the first time since the news had reached her.

They finally reached the maternity ward and found a black nurse at the desk. 'We're looking for our daughter, Barbara Wilson,' George said.

The nurse looked at him in a funny way that had his heart beating like the clappers. If anything had happened to his precious Babs he wasn't sure he could survive it.

'The baby came early,' Rosie pushed in, her husband's grim face making all her worries come into the open again.

'The mother's fine but baby's had a few teething problems,' the nurse said. The way she tilted her head reminded George strangely of when his mum's neighbour had broken the news that his mum had been killed in the Blitz all those years ago. She went on, 'the baby's in the special baby unit but she's improving all the time.'

'She,' Rosie squealed, almost bouncing. 'Oh, it's a little girl.' She looked into her husband's eyes. 'We've got a granddaughter.'

The proud grandparents made their way to bed number nine.

Her mum's voice woke an exhausted Babs. She'd been going out of her mind when the little one had arrived. She blamed herself. If it hadn't been for Cheryl and her boy she hated to think what might've happened. She'd been screaming blue murder when the ambulance had arrived.

Too early, too early. The words had been tearing up her mind as she'd sweated and laboured. Two hours after going into the delivery room her little girl had been born. The doctor had given her the briefest of glimpses . . . there were no words to describe it. She was so tiny, with a gorgeous face and ten fingers and toes. All the heartache she'd been through seemed worth it. Then they'd whipped her child away. Told her that the baby needed special care. Babs had sobbed like she'd never sobbed in her life.

Babs struggled up, wincing from the stitches down below, as her parents almost ran towards her. Her mum was all over her with kisses. 'We got the fright of our lives when the ozzie called.'

Her dad grinned as he pulled off his hat and patted her lightly on the shoulder. 'Well done, my girl.'

'I can't believe my own little girl's a mother,' Rosie said, tears glistening in her eyes. She peered over at the cot beside Babs' bed, which was empty. 'The poor mite, having to be in the baby unit.'

The nurse standing at the bottom of the bed stepped in and explained that the doctor was keeping the baby under observation. But she'd speak to the doctor and see if a brief viewing would be possible. The nurse looked like she wanted to hang around and see the fun. Babs had already decided this particular angel was a complete bitch.

The nurse hurried off to find a vase for the flowers. When she came back, she took up position at the bottom of the bed again. Babs raised her head slightly. 'Not keeping you from your work are we . . .' *Bitch?*

The nurse's eyes narrowed. 'Oh, it's one of the rewards of the job to see grandparents meet their first grandchild.'

Babs' expression turned to hate and she would've mouthed 'Fuck off' if her parents weren't there. With a quick look at her watch, the nurse moved, but she didn't go far. Babs turned away and tuned out while her parents wittered on about babies, difficult labour, responsibilities, life-changing moments and how much joy children brought into people's lives. Rosie made a remark about the father but George cut her short: 'Alright, dear, this isn't the time.'

Her parents' questions went unanswered. Her worried gaze was fixed on where the doctor would appear.

Her mum grew concerned. 'Aren't you talking, Babs?'

'Give it a rest, she's just given birth. You weren't doing a
song and dance act with Babs, were you?'

Babs closed her eyes when she saw the doctor coming. She
heard her parents getting up and the doctor asking, 'Are you
the grandparents?'

Her dad proudly chimed, 'We certainly are.'

'I'm afraid the new addition to the family is a little poorly
at the moment but don't worry, we have everything under
control. I think we can permit a sneak peek!'

Her grinning parents got to their feet. *Go on, tell them, before
they see her. Go on!* But Babs couldn't, she was so wrung out.
Still, she wasn't letting them see her new daughter alone.

'Doctor, can I come as well?'

He frowned. 'You've just given birth . . .' He read the anxiety
in her eyes and nodded.

Babs accompanied her excited parents to the baby unit in a
wheelchair.

'Ah, poor wee things,' Rosie whispered as she looked through
the glass at all the newborns fighting for their very survival.
Two nurses, wearing special uniforms, were also inside.

George turned to the doctor. 'Can we go in?'

He shook his head. 'The room must be kept warm and as
free of germs as possible. I'll get one of the nurses to bring
your granddaughter over.'

Babs steeled herself for what was to come.

A nurse walked over to show off the newest addition to the
Wilson family. Babs' heart lurched with love as she looked at
her beautiful baby. Her eyes were shut in her tiny brown face.
Her hair wasn't, surprisingly, curly, just wisps of dark hair that
looked like they'd been painted on with a fine brush.

There was total silence. Not a gasp. Not a yell. Babs' heart
leapt in hope. Maybe her parents weren't going to see her
baby's skin colour as a problem.

Then her mum burst out laughing. 'I think you've made a mistake.'

The doctor sounded confused. 'No, Mrs Wilson. Is there a problem?'

Her father turned to Babs and said in an emotionless voice, 'I suppose you think this an enormous joke, don't you? Eh? I hope you enjoyed your little bit of fun with your West Indian gentleman—'

'No, Dad. I—'

But he was incapable of letting her have her say. 'You were the apple of my eye and you repay me by spitting in it. We've always been able to hold our heads up and you and your brown bastard are not going to stop that.' George Wilson pulled himself straight. 'You're dead to us.'

And without another word, he turned on his heel and began walking away from them both.

Rosie Wilson turned to her daughter. 'I hope you're pleased with yourself, breaking your father's heart.' Then she followed her husband without looking back.

Babs tried to get out of the wheelchair. 'Mum! Dad!' But there was no life in her body. She started sobbing again, 'I want Stan. Where's Stan?'

Twenty-Nine

That evening, as she lay on the hospital bed with her eyes closed, Babs didn't need a fortune-teller to tell her that her life had hit rock bottom. Her baby was ill, Denny had disappeared like a puff of smoke and her mum and dad had disowned her. And Neville had turned his back on her for the second time.

'Babs?'

She opened her eyes to find Stan standing by the bed. He had a wide grin on his handsome face and a bouquet of roses in his hand. 'Nearly gave me heart failure when word reached me you'd had the kid. Thought you had another month to go?'

She didn't smile. Maybe he was here to stick two fingers up at her as well. But when he leaned over and kissed her cheek, she clung to him. She should've known that Stan wouldn't let her down. He was the only one who had never judged.

When he sat in the armchair, his face was grim. 'I heard about the little one.'

Babs' throat bobbed as she swallowed. 'They won't let me see her again today. She needs to rest.'

He passed her a silver hip flask under her blanket. 'Here, have a bash at that. You look like you could use it.'

'I'm not supposed to.'

He winked at her. 'Doctor Miller's finest. It'll perk you up.'

Babs looked around and then took a couple of sips on the sly. She passed the flask back to him.

He said, 'I saw the baby in the unit. She's in a bad way but I know a thing or two about fighting and that kid's a fighter, I just know she is. She'll go the distance. Probably turn into an athlete or something. Poorly kids like her always do. Now – what are you going to call her?'

Babs bit her lip. 'Someone told me once that you shouldn't name babies born early . . . you know, bad luck if they don't make it.'

'Don't be daft. That fighter deserves a name.'

Stan was so good. 'I've always liked the name Desiree. It's kinda posh and special.'

'A special name for a very special little girl. Have your mum and dad seen her?'

Babs sagged further into the mattress. 'They took one look at her and told me never to darken their door again.'

Stan put a comforting arm around her shoulders. 'I'm not a told-you-so merchant, but I did say that if you weren't straight up with them it was going to make stuff worse.'

'And as if that weren't bad enough, I bumped into two-timing Neville. He was with some woman who's had his kid as well.'

Stan leaned in close. 'Fuck Neville and screw your parents.'

'But Neville knew something about Denny.'

Stan abruptly leaned back, the skin tight around his mouth. 'What did he tell you?'

'He told me that Mickey runs this knocking shop on the other side of Mile End Road. I went and talked to a tart called Cleo. She spun me a story about Denny doing a bunk.'

Stan took out his flask again and tipped it to his mouth. 'This is the first I'm hearing about Mickey and a house of ill repute.' His mouth curled. 'I always knew he was a shifty bastard. That blow-up doll of a missus of his too. I don't want you anywhere near this. Mind you, this Cleo bird might be telling you the truth. Why would she lie?' He patted her hand. 'You've got enough to worry over with your kid, leave this Denny business to me like I told you to. If Mickey's involved, I'll get to the bottom of it.'

'But shouldn't I tell Denny's mum what I found out?'

Stan placed the tip of his finger on Babs' lips to still her words. 'Your problem is you're always thinking about other people. Whatever's happened to your mate, she put herself there, not you. You can't go to Denny's mum with a half-arsed story. All you've got is the word of a tom. If she goes to the Bill with that they'll show her the door.'

She sniffed some of the tears and hurt away. 'You've been great to me. I don't know what I'd do without you.'

Stan cleared his throat. 'You can't go on like this. You're a mum now. You've got responsibilities. You're going to have to sort yourself out to bring that girl up right when she gets out of here.'

Babs shuddered. 'I'm trying my best. I ain't ever done this before.'

'And you're going to need help. I'm going to be plain with you.' He took a deep breath. 'I think I'm the man for the job.'

His hand went inside his jacket. He pulled out a box and laid it on the bed. Babs inhaled sharply.

She gazed at him, wide-eyed. 'Stan?'

He squeezed her hand. 'Me and you fancy the socks off each other. We've already made love and I'll be honest with you . . .' He cleared his throat. 'It's the best I've ever had.'

Babs' face pinked all over. 'Stan, you don't mean—?'

'I do. And I want you to say I do too. Let's get married, Babs.'

She was too shocked to respond. Flippin' hell, she hadn't

seen this coming. Of course she thought Stan was a bit of alright, but getting married to him was another story.

'You know it's the right thing to do,' he coaxed her.

You could do worse than Stanley Miller. A lot worse.

'Alright Stan. I'll marry you.'

He opened the box. Babs gasped when she saw a yellow-gold engagement ring with twin emeralds at the front. He took it out and gently placed it on her finger.

A shattered Rosie was woken from a restless sleep by someone banging on the door. George hadn't uttered a word after leaving the hospital. As soon as they'd got back to Whitechapel he'd headed straight to the boozer. Rosie had known him long enough to know he wanted to be alone. But that didn't mean she liked it. She went home, curled into a ball and bawled her eyes out.

How could Babs have gone with a coloured chap? The only woman she'd heard of with a brown baby was a former prostitute. Oh God, what were the neighbours going to say when they found out? That her Babs was a slag, a tart, easy; that her parents hadn't brought her up right. The shame of it!

The door banged a second time as Rosie uncurled herself, sniffing back fresh tears. She opened the door to find a legless George propped up by two of his drinking buddies.

'He got himself into a right two and eight,' his friend Alan said as she helped get George into the house.

George looked up at his wife with bloodshot, mournful eyes. 'I'm not going to be able to lift my head high ever again.'

His mates shook their heads. Alan said, 'Don't know what the trouble is, Rosie luv, but we thought it best to bring him home.'

She thanked them and saw them out. Back in the sitting room, George had his head in his hands. Rosie knelt by his side. 'It's gonna be alright Georgie, you'll see.'

He lifted his ravaged face. 'Where did I go wrong? I loved our girl like she was an angel sent from God.' His face screwed up. 'I can't get its face out of my head. All that dark skin—'

'Stop torturing yourself. Let's sleep on it and then in the morning we'll go back—'

George shot out of the chair, nearly making her tumble over. His voice was like thunder. 'We're never clapping eyes on her again. You hear me. That woman in the hospital wasn't my Babs. If she comes round here, you're to slam the door in her face.'

Thirty

A week later, the air in the washhouse was filled with sympathy as the women gathered around Babs and listened to her sad story about Desiree having to stop in the hospital. Babs had been discharged two days before and it had broken her heart to leave her baby behind.

Cheryl kissed her on the cheek. 'Don't you worry yourself. That girl of yours is a fighter.'

'My Josh was a preemie,' one of the women announced. 'The ozzie told me if he made it he'd probably have a few problems walking.' Her chest puffed out. 'He's representing his school up at Crystal Palace now, he's one of their fastest runners. Your daughter will come right, just you wait and see.'

Babs smiled a little. She could have kissed every last one of them for trying to make her feel better.

'I just want her home.' Her eyes lit up. 'You should see her. She's got gorgeous hair, a little button of a nose and beautiful brown skin.'

'Brown skin?' someone said hesitantly. "What, is her dad an Italian or something?'

There was an uncomfortable shuffling in the room. Babs wondered what she should say. Of course they would've assumed her baby was white. She caught Beryl's eye and the other woman lifted her eyebrow, making it clear, without words, that this was her story to tell.

Finally she answered, 'No, not Italian—'

'Is her old fella a wog?' Kieran Scott asked as he pushed to the front.

There was such a scandalised intake of breath from everyone else Babs thought one of them would do serious damage to the child. But he was only voicing, in his very crude way, what some of them were too afraid to ask.

'You little bleeder,' Cheryl growled. 'There's plenty of soap in here to wash your filthy mouth out.'

Kieran's eyes grew wide, obviously not having a clue what he'd said wrong.

Babs put a restraining hand on her neighbour's arm. Then she turned a gentle gaze on the lad she'd taken under her wing. 'That's a very bad word and I would be grateful if you never said it again.'

Kieran looked shamefaced as he shuffled his feet. 'Oh, sorry, Babs.'

She raised her voice slightly for everyone's benefit. 'Dee's father is a coloured man. His family are from the West Indies. That's where my girl gets her lovely skin colour from. I'm tying the knot next week.'

A sizzle of excitement swept the room.

'With the father?' someone asked.

'No.' Babs felt shy all of a sudden. 'My fella Stanley.' She showed off her engagement ring to a round of oohs and ahhs. 'I met him after I found out about Desiree.' She grinned like a pure ray of sunshine. 'He's been ever so good to me. I love him to bits, I can't wait to be his wife. For him, me, and my girl to be a real family. We're doing the deed next week.'

'So we've got a wedding to plan.' Beryl rubbed her hands in glee.

Babs quickly burst her bubble. 'No, we want to do it all hush-hush, you know, no fuss. Maybe have a proper reception when we're settled.' She stood up. 'I'm gonna love and leave ya, I'm off to see Desiree.'

Some of the women hugged her and they all wished her and the baby well.

'Can I come with you?' Kieran piped up.

Babs' heart lurched, touched by his kind gesture. ''Course you can.' She held out her hand. He took it and they set off for Mile End Hospital.

As soon as all the other women were gone, Beryl and Cheryl put their heads together.

'Hush-hush and quiet.'

'Not on my watch.'

'She needs cheering up.'

'OK, this is what we're gonna do . . .'

Babs almost broke down as she gazed at her poor baby through the large window.

'She's beautiful, Babs,' Kieran said, just above a whisper. She hadn't asked him to talk so quietly. There was something about being with the vulnerable babies that made you want to keep everything soft and serene. 'She has got a sweet face. And you were right, her skin's a lovely colour.' He squeezed her hand. 'Last time my mum had a nipper, it had a long head and kept dribbling all the time.'

Babs ruffled his hair. 'All babies dribble. You were probably the biggest dribbler of the lot,' she teased, her eyes dancing.

'Was not.' He turned back to look at the baby. 'She looks all tiny.'

'They say she's put on a bit more weight, which is a good sign.'

Her stomach tightened as if it were calling out to her daughter. She was so desperate to hold her. Desiree was doing much better but they wanted to keep her in for one more week at least. Babs didn't know what she'd do if anything happened to her.

Kieran let go of Babs' hand and laid his own flat against the glass. He whispered, 'Keep fighting like Henry Cooper. Your mummy loves you, little one.'

Thirty-One

It was her wedding day, but Babs wasn't really in the mood. All she could think about was Desiree.

'She wouldn't want her mummy to be sad on such a special day,' Babs said to herself as she stared in the mirror.

Although she'd always imagined being decked out in a flowing white gown, trimmed with lace, and a matching veil, she thought she'd done herself proud. She wore a yellow flower-print maxi dress with puff sleeves, a velvet black choker with a cameo of a woman in the middle around her neck and a huge, lilac hat. She'd kept her slap to a minimum, with only a splash of green eyeshadow and a touch of rosy gel blusher on her cheeks. Stan had decided against a church do and gone for a low-key ceremony up at Mile End registry. But that didn't mean she had to turn up looking like some dosser.

Babs sighed. She had written her parents an invite, but then torn it up and slung it in the bin, suspecting that she was wasting her time. Her heart twisted as she thought about poor Denny, who would've been her maid of honour. Stan was still digging away with no joy, but Babs felt guilty that she hadn't breathed a word to Maggie Brooks about what might've happened.

She straightened her spine and said to her reflection,

'Desiree, I want you to know that today is the start of a new life for us, my pretty little angel.'

Five minutes later, humming 'Chapel Of Love', Babs crossed the Essex Lane Estate. Maybe, in time, when Stan's chips came in, they'd buy a house up Leytonstone or Walthamstow way. Not the best places in the world, but they were one step up from Mile End.

Stan was on the steps of the town hall when she reached it. He looked smart as usual in a dark green suit with a white carnation in his lapel.

'Babs-babe, you look a picture; a bloomin' angel,' he told her with a grin as wide as Blackwall Tunnel.

They shared a secret smile as she slipped her arm into his. Inside, they saw a man and woman chatting together. Stan let go of her arm.

'What you doing?'

'Give me a minute, yeah.' Then he walked to the couple, who were eyeing him with suspicion.

'Me and my girl are getting hitched today,' he said. 'We need some witnesses. There's a couple of quid in it for you.'

Half an hour later they became Mr and Mrs Miller, with two strangers as witnesses to their union.

Babs was glowing from head to toe. She gave him such a smacker she thought she'd sucked the very life from her new hubby. But she couldn't help it; she was dizzy with excitement. She'd turned her fortune around and snagged the best bloke in town.

'Steady on.' Stan looked slightly embarrassed. 'We've got all night to christen the mattress.'

Now it was Babs' turn to be embarrassed. 'Ah, that's a bit awkward ... the doctor said ...'

'I get it. No how's your father for a while.' He leaned in. 'Don't stop us from having a good ol' cuddle though.' Then he backed off, straightening his jacket. 'I just need to have a word with someone and I'll catch up with you.'

'But we just got married.' Babs couldn't believe her ears. 'I thought we'd have a little celebration drink at home.'

'And we will, petal. Plenty of time to play mister and missus.' He kissed her quickly on the lips and was off. Over his shoulder he called, 'If you get home before me, get a slap-up bit of nosh on the go. I'm partial to crispy roast taters.'

Babs suddenly remembered she didn't know much about her new husband. What he liked for his tea, what side of the bed he liked to kip on, did he support West Ham or Arsenal. Better be Arsenal! She was not best pleased that he'd more or less left her at the altar, but he had a business on the go and he couldn't just drop everything, even on his wedding day. Babs gazed down at her wedding band and, despite her earlier misgivings, sprang into the air with joy. She was a married woman.

Mrs Miller. Mrs Barbara Miller. Mrs Babs Miller ... She adored her new name; it had such a lovely ring about it. She still felt like she was in a dream. Still couldn't believe that she'd actually married Stanley. He wasn't a layabout but a man who'd worked his way up in the world. When Desiree got out of the ozzie she'd have a proper dad, a man who didn't look at her skin with horror. The only blot on her happiness was her parents. Maybe they'd come around when they knew she was a married woman. They'd already met Stan; it should be easy for them to accept her new situation.

'Oh hello, Babs – how's the baby?'

The surly question made Babs lift her head. She groaned when she clocked Miss Mean and Miss Trouble: the two women on the estate who Beryl and Cheryl had warned her about all those months ago. One was too fat for her own good and the other was too thin. They were both dressed in flared trousers and cheesecloth shirts and the plump one had blonde hair crimped in a frizzy fashion that made her like she'd had an electric shock.

Babs had no choice but to walk their way.

'Fine, thanks,' she replied in a clipped tone.

'Oh good,' said Miss Mean. 'We was wondering if you'd sent her to the jungle to learn how to chuck spears.'

Babs froze. Even though she knew both women had a reputation for rubbishing anyone and everyone, she couldn't believe what she'd heard. 'You what?'

'Yeah,' the other jumped in, 'we heard the hospital left your baby out in the sun too long and she got a bit burnt.'

Both women laughed high and loud.

Babs was outraged. How could they say such things about a sick baby? Her baby? 'It's a shame someone don't send you to the jungle. With a bit of luck you might get eaten. Although, if I was a lion, I'd just have the chips and leave you on the side – you're all fat and gristle.'

'Yeah? At least I ain't some jungle bunny's bow-wow. I've got my self-respect.'

'You ain't anyone's whore, luv. No bloke in his right mind's going to poke you. Even if you paid them.'

Miss Mean gobbed in Babs' face, spit landing on her cheek. Babs was so stunned, all she could do was stand there.

The bitch growled, 'If your kid was here, I'd gob on her too. You wanna be ashamed of yourself, a white woman letting one of them darkies touch you. No white man will touch you ever again.'

And with that, both busybodies walked away.

Babs finally moved, screaming down the street, 'You spiteful pair of witches. I'm going to ring Battersea Dogs' Home to come and put you down.' But the women carried on speeding away.

Don't cry, don't cry, Babs sternly told herself as she wiped the spit from her face. Why was the world such a horrible place sometimes? Why couldn't everyone just live and let live? There was another thought that Babs didn't want to face, that she tried to bury deep. As much as she was disgusted by what those hate-filled women had done, she knew that protecting her precious Desiree was going to be a wagonload harder than she'd thought.

In Bancroft Square, a grim-faced Cleo listened to Mickey grunt and groan for England as he went at it with one of the girls. If his Mel ever found out, he was a dead man. But that wasn't her business. She just had to make sure he was occupied. She'd been waiting for the opportunity for weeks.

She crept downstairs and found his jacket slung over the back of a settee in the VIP lounge. She checked that the coast was clear and started frantically searching through it. It didn't take her long to find what she was looking for.

A few minutes later, she was down the call box on Mile End Road.

'Stan, it's me. I've got the address . . .'

Thirty-One

A deflated Babs walked onto the estate. She felt so dirty after being spat on. She couldn't wait to get indoors and wash the filth off and then Stan could make her feel all better. That perked her up, thoughts of her other half and his lips and his hands ... ooh, what plans she had in store for him.

Babs was startled to hear singing coming from her block.

'Here comes the bride! All fat and wide ...' It tailed off into la-la-la because the singers clearly didn't know the rest of the words. Babs looked up and saw Beryl and Cheryl waving madly at her. What a pair of wallies, Babs thought happily. They both rushed down to greet her in the courtyard.

'Congrats, Babs!' They embraced her with delight.

'Ta.'

'Where's Stan?'

Babs started to cover up for her husband. 'He's coming. He's just got a couple of things to sort out.'

'I hope he ain't got a girlfriend already!' Beryl said with half a wink.

Babs didn't get the joke. 'What's that supposed to mean?'

'Only joshing girl, take it easy.' There was an awkward silence before Beryl added, 'So, you still postponing the reception?'

'Yeah, that's right. We'll have the full works when we've got time and my little one comes home. We thought, let's do the deed, make it all legal and sort out the particulars later on. Stan was terribly eager to get married, so we thought why wait.'

'He must really love ya.' Cheryl gave her a 'you lucky devil' nudge with her elbow.

Babs nodded. Just seeing her neighbours made her feel better after the aggro she'd experienced on the street.

Beryl put her arm around Babs' shoulder and said, 'Not to worry, doll, while you're waiting for the real thing, your ol' muckers have stepped in and organised a little reception of our own.' She stopped as a thought hit her. 'Hang on a minute, how we gonna let your better half know?'

Cheryl turned back to their block and yelled to her eldest. 'Gary,' which came out as 'Gareeeeee'. If you wanted your kids you yelled for them; there was a technique to it. You sang the name rising good and high at the end. Sure enough her fifteen-year-old appeared on the landing.

'Stick a note on Babs' door telling her Stan that he's needed in the washhouse for a knees-up.'

Her kid jumped to it, while a frowning Babs asked, 'The washhouse?'

'Yeah, we've hired it for the afternoon.' Beryl lowered her voice, 'Truth be told, that's a porkie; we've just taken it over. Come on! Everyone's gonna be there!'

That everyone was going to be there and her without her new husband was what Babs was worried about. 'I can't. I need to touch up my make-up—'

'You look a treat. It's a piss-up, Babs, not *Come Dancing.*'

Beryl and Cheryl took an arm each and steered her towards the washhouse, while the bride tried to think of reasons why she couldn't go. She looked at her watch and decided to give it half an hour before slipping away. It would probably only be half an hour before a brawl started anyway, especially if Beryl's sloe gin was on the go.

When they got to the washhouse, she saw balloons pinned outside the door, although several of them said 'Happy Birthday' rather than 'Just Wed.' Everyone was there, mostly the women who used the washhouse, but also folk she hardly knew and a number of others she suspected were merely passers-by who'd dropped in to see what was going on.

But she was tickled pink to see little Kieran Scott there. The benches were covered with an eye-popping piece of lino with drinks on it and near the huge dryers a wannabe DJ had set up a record player and a couple of speakers on an ironing board.

The crowd raised the roof as she came in.

'Speech! Speech!' Beryl and Cheryl cried out, waving at her to come to the front.

Crikey! Babs hated talking in front of people, but she made her way to stand in front of the steam press. As she went she could already hear whispers of, 'Where's the old man then?'

Babs cleared her throat. 'I wanna thank every last one of you . . . for turning out for me and Stan . . .'

Typical knees-up, some people had the bollocks to start jabbering amongst themselves while she was talking.

Cheryl soon put a crimp on that. She stabbed her finger menacingly in the air. 'Effing well shut it or I'll stick you in the dryer and give you the spin of a lifetime.'

Instant silence. Babs swallowed again. 'Stan sends his apologies for being a bit late . . .'

Someone shouted, 'As long as he ain't late in the bedroom department.' That got a huge laugh and broke some of Babs' tension.

She smiled broadly. 'Just blimmin' well enjoy yourselves.'

And that's what everyone did; well, mostly. Over at the drinks table, as the DJ got Slade's 'Mama Weer All Crazee

Now' going, there were complaints that the booze wasn't being dished out fairly. Beryl and Cheryl were being collared with demands for food; when the crowd discovered there wasn't any, grumbles flew left, right and centre.

'Some fucking reception this is,' summed it up.

Right, I'm off, Babs decided. But then she heard a loud, strange voice coming from outside.

'Fuck off, son! Fuck off!'

The room fell silent.

'Fuck off, son! Fuck off!'

The door burst open and a large woman, wearing a hat that resembled a gigantic blueberry and carrying a bird in a cage, strolled, large as life, into the room.

'Fuck off, Stan! Fuck off!' the bird cried, ruffling its feathers.

The woman snapped, 'Shut up, Charlie, stop making a show of yourself.'

Babs wasn't surprised the local nutters were turning up, everyone else had. 'If you're looking for the reception ...' she said kindly, only to be savagely cut down to size.

'I can see where it is, missy, I ain't stupid,' the woman responded. 'And that's despite the best efforts of that little bastard of a son of mine to keep me in the dark. He thinks I was born yesterday. Keep his own nuptials hush-hush.' Her voice went up, everyone looking on with horror. 'From his own mother! This young hussy he's got hitched to ain't much better. She's already knocked out some chocolate drop.' A shocked gasp echoed around the room. Not Babs though: she'd already got a taste of that. 'A fine pair they must make! No wonder the fucking country's going down the toilet. Heaven help us if the Russians invade.'

The penny dropped. 'You're Stan's mum?'

She sniffed. 'I don't like to talk about it, darlin'. What did I do? Seriously. What did I do to deserve a nasty bit of work like that?'

Babs had assumed he'd kept her away from his family because he was embarrassed by her. Now she saw it was the other way around. She held out her hand.

'Hello, Mrs Miller. I'm your son's new wife.'

Mrs Miller was holding Charlie's cage with one hand but her free one remained firmly planted by her side. Her nose wrinkled. 'You know why he's married you? He's trying to wind me up by tying the knot with some slapper wheeling around a pram with a coffee-coloured nipper. Taking his revenge on his own mother – that's the only reason the evil little bastard ever does anything. I suppose you were in on it. Did he offer you a hundred sheets to get knocked up by a darkie?'

Babs did gasp then as she wondered how Stan's mum knew so much about her.

But she didn't get a chance to ask her because Shell Miller's temper went into full flight. 'I thought as much. Well, he's fucked up as usual. I ain't hiding away. I've got my pride; I can show my face anywhere. Always have and always will. Good day to you.'

Charlie added, 'Fuck off, Stan! Fuck off, Son!' and with that, Shell Miller marched towards the makeshift bar.

Dazed, Babs looked down and realised she was still holding out her hand to be shaken. She felt her eyes welling with tears. The gobbing had been bad enough but for her and Desiree to be abused by her brand new mother-in-law – although there was nothing brand new about Shell Miller – was too much. She wasn't having it any more. She was going to give Stan's mum what for.

She turned, leaping out of the way as Stan's mum threw a bottle. It just missed her. 'You call this a fucking bar,' Shell

Miller roared. 'You'd get more booze down a Sally Army sing-a-long.'

That set off another person chucking a bottle, which landed on the record player, putting a shattering stop to the music. All hell kicked off, despite poor Beryl and Cheryl trying to maintain order. Freeloaders piled in to nab booze before it ran out. In the midst of the sea of people crowded around the fast-disappearing drinks, Babs could see a raised hand. On the end of it was an excited Charlie in his cage squawking. 'Fuck off, son! Fuck off, son!' at the revellers. The first punches were being thrown and shouts and threats issued.

Despite being downright disgusted by Stan's offensive mother Babs decided she had an obligation to rescue the old windbag. When she reached her, she attempted to pull her out of the brawl.

The old woman wasn't having it. 'Here me dear, look after Charlie and hold this while you're at it.' She passed her coat to Babs and rolled up the sleeves of her cardie. She pushed a man who was eyeball to eyeball with another wannabe drinker and said to him, 'Did you just pinch my backside?'

The bloke looked at her in disbelief. He gestured at the man he was eyeballing and told her, 'Pinch your arse? I'd rather pinch his.'

It was war. Shell's sturdy arm flew at the guy's face and hit him square. She seemed surprised and disappointed that he hadn't gone down and kicked him in the goolies before punching him again. She reached down, picked up a bottle and began beating him around the head with it. Then she straightened up, yelling, 'Come on then! Who wants some?'

Shell delivered a few random blows to the other fighters within range and even as the sirens began wailing outside she appeared reluctant to leave her ruck. But when the first cops burst in, truncheons drawn, she hurried over to where Babs was standing and took her coat. 'Gotta go, love. The magistrates told me that it was prison next time.'

She took Charlie, who was fluttering around his cage. 'Good do. You can't have a decent reception without a punch-up.' Before she went, she asked, 'Where is my wretched ungrateful son anyway?'

'He had business.'

Sheila gave her a beady look. 'Business is it?' She nodded as if this only confirmed her suspicions. 'You're young, I can see that. You'll find out what he's like soon enough.'

Charlie backed her up by squawking, 'Fuck off, Stan! Fuck off, Son!'

Sheila looked at her mynah with pride. 'You should listen to what my Charlie says. He knows how many beans make five when it comes to Stan.'

As soon as Babs got indoors she headed for the bathroom and scrubbed her face. And scrubbed. And scrubbed. She gazed around the bathroom and thought everywhere looked messy, so she tidied up. Then she did the same to the sitting room, and the kitchen. And then, in a frenzy, she tidied up all over again.

Thirty-Two

Instead of being with his new bride, Stan was in Eastbourne. Clever Cleo had got hold of the address at last. He wasn't surprised to find that the B&B Mickey and Mel had his brother holed up in was a total rathole, all peeling paint and stained windows. He popped on a green tweed hat and pulled it low before he entered. A young woman was at the reception. She was cross-eyed, which wouldn't have been too bad but her unfortunate eyes were magnified by the thick lenses of her glasses.

He gave her his winning smile. 'I'm Frank Fanacapan, luv and I'm here to see Mr Peter Miller. He's expecting me, but told me to meet him in his room.'

As soon as he dropped Pete's name the woman looked jumpy. He didn't need to be told that his brother had already made a nuisance of himself. He went up to the room. When his brother opened the door he looked like a wreck. Stan wrinkled his nose; the stench of booze was strong, stale and offensive.

Pete was already sobbing, slumped on the bed, by the time Stan closed the door.

'You've gone and done it now, haven't you,' Stan said.

Pete lifted his ravaged face. 'I didn't mean to. I don't even remember. It was the drink; I swear on my life.'

Yeah, like it always is. Stan parked himself on the bed near his brother. 'What's done is done. I've spoken to Mickey and his missus and everything is in hand.'

Pete sniffed. 'They've been well sweet, letting me stop here for so long, but I'm going stir crazy. It's too quiet.'

Yeah, they deserve the bloody Nobel Peace Prize. 'The problem is, you really dragged me into it this time. The only way I could make this go away is to become Home Secretary.'

Pete got all distressed again. 'I don't know why I can't remember any of it. My mind's fucking blank.'

'Stop worrying.' Stan tightened his fingers into his brother's shoulder and rocked him slightly. 'What do you say we go for a walk and get some fresh air into you?'

A few minutes later they were in the driving rain, walking towards the deserted Seven Sisters cliffs.

'Remember when Dad used to take us to Brighton?' Stan said.

Pete chuckled. 'Yeah. He'd buy us ice creams and sit us on the beach while he went off to get his leg over with his bit on the side.'

'The dirty old fella,' Stan said, laughing back. It felt good to be having a laugh with his brother again, just like they used to as kids. 'What was the name of that last one?'

Pete chuckled hard. 'Doris Beauregard—'

'Budgie,' they said together, the nickname they'd given her.

'The slapper from hell,' Pete added. 'She was always moaning, lipstick smeared against her top teeth. Looked like she'd been sinking her gnashers into Dad's neck and drawing blood.'

They were silent for a while, lost in the memories of their childhood, some tough and hard, but others soft and gentle.

Pete's joy seemed to trickle away when they got to the cliffs. 'I know you blame me for what Mum did.'

The wind buffeted Stan's face as he moved towards the

cliff's edge, his brother following. The sea looked murky and dark. 'It weren't your fault,' Stan insisted. 'She did what she'd wanted to do for a long time.'

'She does love you,' Pete said quietly, moving to stand beside his older brother.

Stan's mouth tightened. 'It don't matter Pete. Let's drop it.'

But he wouldn't. 'I heard her telling Charlie once that she wished she'd sent you to hospital. A mum who hated her kid wouldn't want to get him medical treatment.'

Stan's rage grew. He didn't doubt that Pete had heard their mum telling her mynah bird all about it, but his brother didn't know the hospital she'd been referring to was a nut house for kids. After the incident he'd gone a bit off the rails and any sane parent would've sat their kid down and found out what the problem was. But, oh no, not his malicious witch of a mum. She'd been thinking of offloading him to the funny farm.

Stan put his arm around his brother's shoulder again and stepped closer to the cliff edge. His voice softened. 'I want you to remember that I love you and I'll love you until the day you die.'

Pete's eyes glowed. 'I love you too, Stan.'

Stan's arm tightened. 'It's getting a bit Baltic out here, let's go back.'

His arm dropped away and his brother turned around, but Stan didn't. He whispered, 'It's time we got this situation sorted out.'

Stan pushed his brother off the cliff. He watched Pete's head smash against the cliff face and finally his body fell, twisted and bloody, onto the beach below.

'I love you,' Stan whispered, the chill of the air seeping into his bones. 'But you were like a dog that needs to be put down for his own good.'

As he walked away in the dark he couldn't hold back the tears.

Where the bloody hell are you, Stan? Babs asked for what felt like the millionth time.

Some wedding night this was turning out to be. Stan hadn't put in an appearance for his reception or his roast tats but she'd convinced herself he'd come home soon enough. What man left his bride on her tod on their wedding night?

Earlier Babs had decided to get all sexy, rigged out in a lacy red negligee with an elasticated back so it would be easy for Stan's wandering hands to get access. She'd waited and waited for her groom but he was a no show. Then she'd come over all worried. What if something had happened? Here she was, flaunting herself like Lady Godiva does the East End when her husband could be in a ditch somewhere. But it was too late to call the office . . . Babs took a slug from the bottle of gin by the bed as her mind raced away. There was eff all she could do. If he wasn't back by morning she'd pop over to Soho.

Babs flopped back on the bed. The mixture of alcohol and anxiety sent her to sleep and she plunged into a nightmare. In it, there was a knock at the door and when she answered it, Desiree was there but she was covered in spit and waving bye-bye to her mother. In her dream, she was screaming at her. Her screams turned into a high-pitched trilling sound. *Trill! Trill! Trill!* The noise coming from her mouth wouldn't stop.

Babs woke, gasping with horror and sweat. The trilling sound was still going.

The phone. It must be Stan.

She legged it into the hallway. The clock on the wall said five in the morning.

'Is that you, Stan?' Her heart was beating so fast. 'What's happened?'

'Mrs Miller?'

Babs frowned. 'Who are you? What are you doing calling at this hour?'

'It's Nurse Chapel from the hospital.' Her voice sounded grave. 'You need to come to the baby unit.'

Babs' heart dropped. 'Is something wrong with Desiree?'

'You just need to get here.'

'Fucking tell me,' Babs yelled.

The nurse paused, then, 'I'm afraid your daughter has taken a turn for the worse—'

Babs slammed the phone down and raced into her bedroom. *Worse.* The word went around and around her head like a whirlwind. She struggled to put her discarded clothes on. She was in such a state she didn't even put the light on. God, her baby, her baby.

Bang! The loud knock sounded like thunder and made Babs jump. *Stan. Please let it be Stan. I can't deal with this on my own.* She belted for the door in her bra, knickers and slip. She pulled it open and froze. Two men were standing on her doorstep.

'Has something happened to Stan?'

One man was tall, with shoulder-length hair. If he'd put the effort in he might have been considered quite handsome. He was chewing gum with a very nasty sneer on his face. The other one was shorter, round and no amount of effort could hide the fact he was an ugly little runt. The strands of his hair had been swept over his almost bald head like rat's tails. He was leering at Babs as if trying to imagine what she looked like in her birthday suit. She self-consciously covered her bra with her hands. She didn't like the look of these two.

'I think you've got the wrong house.' She tried to shut the door but the sneerer slammed his palm against it, sending it flying back.

Babs trembled. 'Get away from here.'

They ignored her and stepped inside. Babs ran for the bedroom. They came after her, not running, but taking long, measured strides. Babs jumped on the bed and in her haste tripped and landed on her back. The bedroom light flicked on. Babs sucked in her breath as the men advanced.

They stopped at the foot of her bed, looking down at her menacingly. Babs tried to draw a breath but no air went in and no scream came out.

The leerer tapped ash onto her bed. 'I'm Cricket and he's Horner and you've been a naughty girl, Babs. Very naughty.'

Cricket? Horner? She'd never heard of them in her life. How did they know her name? Then Babs remembered her baby. 'I need to get to the hospital.'

She lunged up, but Sneerer grabbed her hair and snapped her head back. Terror chilled her blood as she looked into his bloodshot eyes.

He shook his head and tutted. 'Very naughty. Now get your drawers on, sweetheart, we're going for a drive.'

Thirty-Three

Babs got the shock of her life when she saw where Cricket and Horner had taken her – to a police station.

What the effing hell was going on?

'I need to get to my baby,' she begged as they manhandled her out of the car. At least they had let her get dressed.

Neither man took a blind bit of notice of her as they led her into the station. The place was quiet except for a drunk snoring, slumped sideways in a chair.

The officer at the desk said, 'Who have we got here then, Detectives?'

Detectives? Babs' mouth fell open. These two thugs were cops? Now she knew she was in serious bovver. You couldn't trust the coppers; they were a dodgy lot like any other gang. Everyone knew that most of them were as bent as a nine-bob note.

Detective Cricket and Detective Horner of Her Majesty's Metropolitan Police Force dragged her down the stairs. She lashed out at them and begged by turns, 'Get off me; I want my baby, my baby's sick. Please, please let me go. I've got to go to the hospital.'

Horner told her, 'Don't worry about any babies, love ... you're in deep crap ... best place for the kid ... quacks can do miracles these days ... shut the fuck up, will ya?'

They shoved her into a room and slung her into a chair. She made a move to escape but Cricket held her down. Horner produced a bottle of Jack Daniels and two glasses and plonked them on the scratched desk.

Babs screamed, 'I'm entitled to a lawyer.' They didn't even answer her and she wasn't surprised. She knew plenty of people who had been picked up by the coppers, asked for a brief and got a kicking instead.

'I've got to get to my baby.' Tears misted her eyes, her voice hoarse. 'Please.'

Cricket grabbed her hair and turned her face towards his. 'Look, sweetheart, do you want us to call the duty quack and get you pumped full of sedatives? Would that help your baby? How about you pack it in, answer a few questions – and then you can go. We'll give you a lift up the hospital if you like.'

Horner put his feet up, took out his silver box of snuff and sniffed deeply. He let out a satisfied 'ahh' and then took a slug of whiskey.

Babs was shaking and out of her mind but she was so scared, she shut up.

Cricket slowly released his grip. He took out a Manikin cigar and lit up.

Horner winked. 'He's alright luv; he gets a bit grouchy so early in the morning. He'll be chuckling away about this later.' He picked up a file from the desk. 'Now – you know what we're after, don't you? We need to talk about that knocking shop that you've been running down in Mile End.'

Babs realised she was laughing like a mad woman. 'Mile End? Knocking shop? What kind of crap is this? Let me go – please.'

Cricket's cheeks ballooned as he puffed away. Horner was no longer in winking mode. 'There won't be any baby if you wanna play tricky. We want to wrap this up fast and then go for a big brekkie. We know it's you. You've been running a scrubbers-for-money racket out of that place you own.'

Babs felt a trapdoor opening under her but she couldn't understand why. 'Place I own? I can barely afford the rent on my own gaff.'

'Oh dear . . .' Horner opened his file and passed her a couple of documents. 'That's funny – the deeds say different. That's your signature isn't it?'

It was. She stuttered, 'Yeah – I mean, no. I never signed that. I'm being fitted up. All I own is the clothes on my back. Now take me to the hospital!'

Cricket made a tutting sound. 'I told you she'd try and wriggle out of it. Typical Mile End slapper.'

Horner put the deeds back in his file. 'So you had no idea you were running a disorderly house out of your own properties. You expect us to believe that?'

'Properties?' Her eyes bulged. 'Talk to my old man Stanley. He'll tell you. I swear on my kid's life.' Babs teared up, thinking of Desiree in the hospital. 'I swear, I don't know nuthin' about any toms or any houses.' Then she remembered going to see Cleo. 'You mean the house that Mickey Ingram owns—'

Both men burst out laughing, Cricket slapping his thigh in his glee.

Horner leaned in close, whiskey fumes making her nose wrinkle. 'So you're not above trying to stitch up an innocent bloke? You do own the houses; we've just proved that. And we've got statements from some of the poor girls you've been pimping and they put you squarely in the frame.' Babs' mouth fell open. 'You've been living off immoral earnings; you know what that means, don't you? It's a very serious matter.'

Babs begged, 'Please just talk to Stan, he'll tell you. If you have got any statements, they're all verbals.'

Horner looked at Cricket. 'Shall I show her?'

'Well, we shouldn't really. We're officers of the law. It's strictly against regulations. But maybe just this once . . .'

Cricket leered. Horner sneered – and then he reached into the file and gave Babs five sheets of A4 paper covered with closely written handwriting. It was a statement that gave chapter and verse, times and dates and described how Babs had run a prostitution ring. It gave details of the violence she'd used to keep order in the brothel and how she'd supplied the vulnerable girls with heroin to keep them under her control. The words slid like ice over her eyes until she reached the end. There was a signature. It was clear and familiar and had a name printed underneath.

Babs' husband, Stanley Miller.

Perhaps the nightmare she'd woken from wasn't over. Babs was wrung out. She felt barely alive but she managed to whisper, 'No. That's wrong. I want my baby.'

It was Cricket who finally said, 'Baby? You're nicked.'

Cleo was packed and out of the knocking shop as soon as she'd got Stan's call. She couldn't believe it – she was really leaving this life and never coming back. But she hadn't felt right about doing a runner without letting Daffy know. Stan had warned her to keep her trap shut but that woman had been good to her. When she'd told her, Daffy hadn't wished her good luck or said goodbye. She'd simply kissed her on the forehead like Cleo was her daughter.

'Alright, Cleo.' Hearing Stan's voice, Cleo came back to the present.

He walked towards where she was waiting in the darkness under the railway bridge on Coburn Road.

She wanted this done and dusted quickly. 'Give me the keys to my kingdom and I'll be on my way.' She hadn't wanted money from Stan, but a house somewhere far away, her own four walls and roof to start a new life in. It hadn't taken her long to figure out that Stan was a man who knew his way around property.

He dangled a set of keys at her, but as she grasped for them he jerked them out of her reach. 'I need you to do one more thing for me.'

Cleo sucked her teeth lightly. Typical man, always wanting one more freebie. But she needed that house. 'What?'

He told her what he wanted. She wasn't best pleased, but if it kept Micky and Mel off her back . . . She nodded.

'The house is in Forest Gate, not far from the Princess Alice.' He handed her the keys.

Cleo closed her eyes and she clenched her hand around them. They were one of the best things she'd ever felt.

'Just one other thing.' Stan's voice made her open her eyes, irritated.

'I'm not getting down on my knees for a thank you suck. I'm done with that life.'

Stan sent her a crooked smile. 'Nothing like that. Just follow me.'

Cleo stalled. She was in the deserted dark with a man she didn't know from Jack and he wanted her to go to his car. Not bloody likely. He might slit her throat to keep her silent for all she knew.

He reassured her, 'I ain't going to hurt you. I still need you to do something for me.'

He was right. He still needed her help to put Mickey and Mel down for good. She walked with him to his car and waited as he opened the passenger door and stepped back to see what was inside.

'I want you to look after this in that nice, new house of yours.'

Cleo was gobsmacked.

Thirty-Four

Babs rocked back and forth on the floor of her cell, arms wrapped around her knees, out of her mind about her darling Desiree. Her angel was desperately sick in the hospital and those two nut job cops wouldn't let her get word to Stan or anyone else to check what was going on.

'Please God, please take care of my baby.'

There was no one to hear Babs' cry. She'd been stuck staring at these four walls for a week. Since they'd accused her of being the madam behind the Mile End brothel – as if! – the cops had said sweet FA. No interview, no charges, nothing. She knew from TV that they weren't allowed to do that. When Cricket or Horner appeared, as they did from time to time, she demanded a brief.

'Alright love, we'll let you see our briefs if we can have a look at yours.'

Babs had torn into them. 'Fuck off, you pervs.'

'Oh that's charming. We've got an East End tom-runner accusing us of being pervs. Maybe we'll tell the judge, let him know what kind of defendant he's dealing with.'

'You're fitting me up. I want a lawyer.'

'Yeah? And we want Ferraris and we ain't getting them either. Now shut up or we'll put you in solitary. Oh yeah – I forgot – you already are.'

Babs decided the next time they appeared, she was going to play sick and get them to send her to a hospital. Then she'd get help.

When she heard the cops talking outside her cell, she flopped to the floor, clasped her belly and cried out in pain. When the cell door swung open, she cried out again.

'Fucking hell Babs – are you alright?'

She looked up to find her new husband rushing towards her. She stopped crying. She clambered to her feet and slapped him hard across the face, the sound cracking against the cell walls. 'You bastard! You got me locked up.'

She swung manically at him again. Stan swerved his upper body back, trying to grasp her arms, but he missed and she flew at him. Her nails dug into his chin as she screamed, 'You really do think I'm a fucking chump, don't you? You've thought that from the start. You needed a dumb girl in trouble, someone who you could put on the front desk and fend off all your callers. That's it, isn't it? As for the shotgun wedding without a shotgun – fuck knows what was going through your head when you thought that one up.'

Stan caught her arms, the scratches as red as the colour heating his face. 'Babs, you need to stop. I had nothing to do with this—'

She wrenched herself out of his arms. 'So why did it take you so long to get here?'

He yelled back, 'You think I haven't been trying! Those two coppers wouldn't let me—'

'I don't give a fuck about them,' she spat, 'All I want to know about is my baby. What's happening with Desiree?'

Stan gulped. 'That's why I stopped trying to see you. I . . .' His Adam's apple's bobbed convulsively.

Babs froze. She didn't like the haunted expression on his face. 'Tell me.'

Stan shook his head. 'I've been at the ozzie morning, noon and night. I . . .' His mouth moved but no words came out.

'Fucking tell me,' she roared.

'She's gone.'

Babs swayed. 'What do you mean she's gone? Gone to my mum and dad's? Gone to Beryl or Cheryl?'

'We've lost Desiree. She didn't make it. I'm sorry.'

Babs walked towards him in a daze. 'What do you mean – didn't make it?'

Stan rubbed his hand over his mouth, tears glittering in the bottom of his eyes. 'I got a call from the ozzie yesterday. They said Desiree had taken a turn for the worse again and I needed to come in. When I got there, they told me the crisis was over and she was a bit better. I spent the afternoon with her but as time went on, more and more quacks appeared, looking more and more worried and finally at about nine Desiree slipped away. She fought to the end – the kid was a fighter all the way through. They did everything they could . . . but it wasn't enough. She's gone, Babs.'

No, no, no. Desiree couldn't be gone. Not her Desiree. Stan was talking about another Desiree, somebody's else's baby. Desiree dead? No, no, FUCKING NO!

Stan said, 'I'm taking care of the funeral. It's tomorrow.' She flew at him like a banshee.

'You're burying my fucking baby while I'm stuck in jail – the jail you put me in! What kind of a fucking animal are you?'

She beat and kicked at him until he grabbed her arms and twisted her around. He tightened his grip until it hurt her and whispered between gritted teeth, 'what do you want me to do? Leave Desiree in the morgue? Watching her go was one of the worst moments in my life.'

Babs' ears buzzed. Her legs collapsed and she sank to the floor.

Whoever was making that awful howling noise needed to stop. Stop right now before she started beating her head against the hard floor. Babs felt as if her soul had departed her body and she was only flesh and bone. There was nothing inside. She was dead. As dead as her baby girl. Only the tears running down her face showed there was any life in her at all.

Only when she felt Stan's palm rubbing her back did she realise she was the one howling her grief. They lay on the floor for close to ten minutes, Babs clinging onto a man she didn't trust but who had been a comfort to her baby as she took her last breath.

Finally, Stan said, 'They won't let me stay long, so I need to tell you the whole of it. It was Mickey and Mel who stitched us both up.'

'What?' Babs said listlessly.

'I can't prove it but Mickey and Mel . . . they killed Denny.'

All Babs could do was shake her head over and over. Denny gone? She couldn't deal with any more death.

Stan leaned back and wiped the tears from her face tenderly.

'And it's thanks to them that you're here. They're why you weren't with Desiree. They're trying to cover their tracks. Those two cops out there are as bent as a butcher's hook and taking backhanders from Mickey to evict God-fearing families from their homes and anything else he asks them. I never signed my name to any statement, just like you didn't on any deeds. Mel, the bitch, is a dab hand at forgery.'

Babs stared ahead, eyes blank, but asked, 'Why would Mickey and Mel do that? Why drag me into it?'

Stan wet his lips with the tip of his tongue before answering, 'They want me out of the way, to get their hands completely on the business. And they don't care how low they have to go to do it, including dragging down anyone close to me like—'

'Me, Denny and Desiree,' Babs finished in a dazed whisper.

'I need you to be tough, girl. You need to trust me. I'll get you out of here and fix the Ingrams for you, Denny and your lost baby. But you need to trust me.'

Babs finally looked up at him. 'I trust you.'

She flopped in his arms like a rag doll. He gently laid her down on her bunk. She whispered over and over, 'I want my baby, I want my baby . . .'

When she finally looked round her cell, Stan was gone. Hatred filled her and she made a vow. If it was the last thing she did on this earth, she was going to get Mickey and Mel for causing her the worst misery a mother could feel.

Thirty-Five

Stan moved fast after leaving Babs. He pushed some coins into the blower in the phone box around the corner. When the line connected, he told Mickey, 'All the paperwork is sorted and ready to sign.'

'Good lad.' Mickey preened.

'Let's meet at your brief's this afternoon.'

Mickey's solicitor was in the De Beauvoir area of Hackney. It was typical of the idiot to have a lawyer there; the silly sod thought having a legal mouthpiece in a place with a French name made him sound grand. Most of the people Stan knew around that way called it Der Beaver.

Stan carried on, 'Bring Mel with you.'

That surprised his business partner. 'The wife's having her hair done. Again. What does she need to be there for anyway? It's my business.'

'She's going to be as pleased as Punch when it's all wrapped up. There'll probably be a roll in the hay in it for you.'

Mickey cackled lecherously. 'You're probably right. Alright, she'll be there.'

As he put the phone down, it was Stan's turn to laugh.

At four o'clock, Stan rolled up in De Beauvoir. The area had some truly gorgeous houses, but typically of Mickey, his brief was holed up in an office over a greengrocers. Stan found all three waiting expectantly around a table. The only difference he could see in Mel's new hairdo was a bit more bounce, like she was already celebrating her victory against him. The lawyer, who went by the name of Ronnie, was officious and polite and wore a cheap suit and ill-fitting toupee. Mickey was easy and friendly – 'No hard feelings mate!' – but Mel didn't even return Stan's greeting. Instead, she kept her hard gaze fixed on him, determined to make sure there weren't any last-minute strokes being pulled.

The brief got business rolling. 'Mr Miller, if you can sign your copy of the documents and my client can sign his, we can wrap this up in five minutes.'

Stan reached into the pocket of his jacket and produced the A4 envelope that Mickey and Mel had brought to his office. He handed them to Mickey, who turned down his lawyer's offer to give the papers inside the once-over and tried to study them himself. After a few minutes, he looked up sheepishly and mumbled, 'Actually, maybe you better had check. I didn't see a lot of school after the age of twelve.'

Ronnie, who'd had his glasses ready for this moment, shuffled the documents and got reading. He spent fifteen minutes checking each page to make sure Stan hadn't made any changes or set any traps for his clients, before announcing with a professional smile, 'Everything appears to be in order. Shall we all get our pens out and seal the deal?'

He passed the paperwork over to Mickey.

'Hold up a minute.' Mel snatched them from Mickey's hands. 'I want to have a butchers before anyone puts ink to paper.'

It took only a few moments before she ran into a problem. She looked at her husband and then at Ronnie with withering contempt and then turned to Stan.

He played innocent. 'Is there a problem, Mel?'

'I don't have the legal training and years of experience that my husband's distinguished lawyer has.' Her every word was laced with sarcasm. 'But it rather looks to me as if this document has been altered so that Mickey's giving you his share of his business rather than you giving him yours?'

In a right flap, the startled lawyer took the papers and made a good fist of pretending he'd noticed too. Mickey merely looked confused.

Mel snapped, 'What are you playing at, you conniving little git?'

Stan looked up. 'Pardon me?' He tapped his forehead dramatically. 'Oh that's right, didn't I say? There's been a slight change of plan. Mickey's giving everything to me, not the other way around. Come on, let's get a move on, I'm busy.'

Mel turned to Ronnie. 'Make yourself scarce, fella.'

Their brief couldn't get out of the room quick enough.

It was Mickey who led the attack. 'I expected better from you. Sending your own brother down the river on a murder charge? That's bang out of order, even if he is a drunk and as mushy as a bucket of wallpaper paste. I'm disappointed, I really am.'

Stan could see Mickey still didn't get it. Mel was going pale. 'I wouldn't worry too much about Pete if I was you. My understanding is he's already gone down the river – for good, unfortunately.' He interrupted the stunned silence that followed by raising his hands in mock surprise. 'Oh – haven't you heard? Yeah, that's right, tragic story. Apparently, he took a tumble off a cliff on the south coast. He was probably pissed, of course. But then again, maybe he couldn't handle killing that poor girl. Apparently he was staying at a B&B in Eastbourne. Never seen the attraction myself, but he obviously fancied it. Ring the local coppers if you don't believe me. I expect I'll have to get a train down there and do the formals on the body. As you can imagine, that's rather changed the situation. Which means our deal has to change along with it.'

'You murdered your own brother?' Mel gasped, staring at Stan as if she'd never seen him before.

Stan came over all shocked. 'Killed my own flesh and blood? What a thing to say. Really, darlin', wash your mouth out with soap and water. I told you, it was a tragic accident. Of course, you're more than welcome to put the dead girl's body in the boot of your car, run it down the local nick and tell them Pete killed her. You could do that . . . but I've got a feeling you won't.'

Mel picked up the contract, but Stan stopped her dead. 'Hey, hey, hey – what the hell do you think you're doing? You're signing it, not ripping it up.'

The closed window in Mickey's brain had finally opened. 'I'm not signing my share of *my* business over to you, you ponce. Why would I?'

'Because I can help you with some legal problems that I hear are coming your way. I was having a chat with some friends from the vice squad at a cocktail party the other night. Apparently they're taking a very close interest in a knocking shop in Mile End and your name's been floated in connection with it. The pimp running the joint was recruiting girls through a bogus modelling agency in Soho.'

Mickey rose to his feet, fists curled, cheeks flaring red. 'You no-brain wanker, that drops you right in the shit too, seeing how you've been running the agency for the last couple of years.'

Stan knew it would royally wind Mickey up if he smiled, so he did. 'Ah, but that's the thing, I realised when I joined the operation that there was something funny about Go Go Girls, so I put it into liquidation. No doubt you'll remember the papers I gave you to sign to make it happen. It hasn't traded for a couple of years. Of course what happened before I joined I don't know, but the paperwork's all there and I dare say they'll pressurise the toms into giving statements . . .'

Mickey came at him with every street skill he'd ever learned. Stan raised his arm to avoid the right-hander, but felt the full force of the blow from his left. The punch was so hard his teeth rattled, one of his eyes seemed to have gone AWOL and he was spinning across the floor in his chair. More by luck than judgement, he managed to avoid a second bunch of fives as Mickey roared, 'I'm gonna fucking batter you, you slippery fuck.'

As he moved in for the kill, Stan pulled his ace – his shooter. Mickey pulled up in his tracks and Mel shot to her feet. Stan pulled the hammer back.

'Sign the documents,' he ordered. 'Do it now, because I already feel like blowing both your heads off. If you don't sign, that'll tip me over the edge. I've already done one stiff this week; a few more won't make no difference.'

Mickey signed. But as Stan staggered over and picked them up, Mickey warned him, 'You ain't heard the last of this.'

As Stan went down the stairs, every step an agony, he muttered, 'And neither have you, mate.'

Thirty-Six

Babs was rolled into a ball like a baby, still trying to come to terms with the death of her child. She would never see her take her first steps, hear her call her Mum for the first time, hold her hand as she took her to school, smile with pride as her daughter married. Babs' whole body hurt, but she didn't have any more tears to cry. The only thing that gave her a bit of heart was that Stan had been there. Mummy might not have been there but there had been one person present who truly loved Desiree when she closed her eyes forever.

The cell door opened. Babs scrambled off the bunk.

'Right, hop it,' Detective Horner ordered.

Babs almost spat in his dodgy copper face. He and his shit-faced partner had kept her away from her baby. If it weren't for them and Mickey and that fur-coated animal Mel, she would've been there for her little girl. But Babs didn't do that. The first chance she got to fuck over him and that Horner, she was taking it.

Babs slow-walked out of the cell, almost daring him to try and shift her. If he put one hand on her, by God . . .

Babs reached the reception area. The first person she clocked was Stan. He looked like he'd been in a tussle with a lion.

'What happened?'

'I told you I was going to get Mickey and Mel back. I

might've got hurt but our battle to take them down is just starting.'

Babs smiled a grim, nasty smile. 'Good. I won't rest until they're obliterated.'

He kissed her icy cheek. 'That's good, because you're going to have a big part in helping me do it. But let's get you home and get a good piece of nosh down you, you've turned into skin and bone.'

They drove back to their home on the Essex Lane Estate. Stan had laid on the full works for dinner with romantic candlelight.

'I cooked it all myself,' he told her proudly. 'Had a bit of trouble with the gravy, but Beryl came and helped me out.'

Stan rabbited away about cooking up the Ingrams, but Babs was lost in another world. *Her baby, oh God, her baby.* She didn't even realise that she'd spoken aloud until Stan's arms were wrapped around her.

'I miss her,' she sobbed.

'I know you do.'

Babs' bright eyes implored him. 'I need to see her—'

Stan shook his head. 'I don't think now's a good time.'

'I can't rest until I see where my baby has been laid to rest.'

Later, as they cuddled in bed for the first time, she couldn't get her child out of her mind.

After Stan had fallen asleep, she crept out of bed and walked over to the drawer where she'd kept Desiree's clothes. She pulled out the pink and blue hand-knitted booties Stan had got specially made for her baby. She held them tight to her chest, bowed her head and silently sobbed.

It was a beautiful day for the journey to the arboretum. Stan explained as they drove down that he'd arranged for Desiree's plaque and tree to be out in a nice spot in Essex. He wasn't having it in some craphole in the East End where drunks would piss on it. He'd arranged for Babs' daughter to be cremated and had spread her ashes around a cherry tree so she would live on in the leaves and fruit.

They parked in front of the gardens, by stone walls that pretty roses climbed up. The car park was filled with sleek and expensive motors that showed this wasn't a place poor people came to mourn. He led her in and down a gravel path where people were tending flowers and staff were trimming the grass. An old woman could be heard weeping softly as she turned the earth around a tree. They walked hand in hand until he brought her to a halt. It was indeed a perfect spot. They were facing a beautiful plot. A solid cherry tree was already showing its rich green leaves and flower buds. In front of it was a solid bronze plaque.

Desiree Miller
Daughter of Babs and Stan
Another Time
Another Place

Babs took a hanky out and tried to buff the plaque but it didn't need it. It was pristine. She rubbed the thick leaves of the tree between her fingers. They were so healthy; it seemed they'd been waxed. Babs stood for a long time before saying, 'Thanks for doing this. I don't think I could have managed it. It would have been too much. It's totally right for her to be here. It's the right place.'

Stan nodded. 'Yeah, I know. She's at rest now. She fought like a soldier and you can be proud of her.'

'Can I have a few moments alone?'

He squeezed her shoulder. 'Take as long as you like.'

Stan sat on a bench with his hands clasped, looking solemn and watching the passers-by.

Babs cleared her throat. 'Hello my darlin' baby. We've got a nice spot for you and I hope you like it. I hope there are other children for you to play with.' Her face crumpled in anguish. 'I know it weren't my fault, but I should've been there, I should've been there. I would've held you tight while you closed your eyes.'

Babs' shoulders sagged. Oh God, this was killing her. She wanted to lie on the grass to be near her baby. *Stop this. Desiree shouldn't see you like this.* Babs straightened her spine and dried her tears. 'Never forget that Mummy loves you. And will always love you.'

Babs staggered around and stumbled towards Stan. He wrapped her in his arms.

Babs wept softly as he led her to the car. 'It's not fair, it's so unfair.'

Her husband kept pace beside her, holding her, remaining quiet, giving her the space to grieve.

Stan wanted to take her home but Babs insisted that he drop her off in Whitechapel. She'd made up a story about needing something in the market and would meet him at home. Stan hadn't been happy but in the end he'd done her bidding. Babs bypassed the market, crossed the main road and, a few minutes later, walked down the street to the house she'd once called home.

Some people called out her name but she ignored them. She hesitated for a few seconds before she pulled the knocker back on the door.

Her mum opened it. 'Babs?' Rosie was clearly surprised to see her.

Babs' voice was flat and emotionless. 'My baby died—'

Her mother slapped her hand over her mouth in distress.

Babs ignored it. 'I wanted you to know that—'

Her dad appeared beside his wife. 'What do you want?' His face was angry. The street had grown silent as the neighbours looked on.

'George, Babs' baby passed away.' Rosie Wilson's voice was barely audible.

'If it wasn't for you she might be alive today,' Babs accused them, the words hurting her chest. 'She was an innocent child who never did anything wrong to anyone. You rejected her, your own flesh and blood. You were the ones who were meant to love her, protect her . . . now she's gone.' Her mouth twisted as she spat, 'I will *hate you* until my dying day for what you've done.'

And with that, Babs turned her back and walked away.

Thirty-Seven

Six Months Later

'You going to a wedding, Stan?' Beryl asked as he went out on the landing. He was in his best suit, a red carnation in the buttonhole; hair trimmed and splashed all over with Brut. Babs, on the other hand, was green around the gills. She hadn't been feeling herself this morning.

Stan was turning out to be the kind of husband that Babs had been dreaming of all her life – caring, kind, hard working. And he was the lover of the century in bed.

'Sort of!' Stan answered. 'It's going to be a right old knees-up afterwards anyway!'

He couldn't help grinning his pearly whites off. It was his big day. Like a theatre director preparing for the first night of a new play, he was worried that something would go wrong in his big production. He had total confidence in his leading actors; Babs and Cleo wouldn't fluff their lines. But he was worried that the real stars of the show, Mickey and Mel Ingram, would ruin everything at the last minute. All of that hard work could be wrecked by rank amateurs like them.

It didn't take them long to get to North East London, but as soon he parked up, he noticed Babs' head was bowed.

'You'll be alright, darlin'.' Babs had been alarmingly sick before they left, which he put down to nerves.

'Stan, you know I want to do this but I'm scared witless I'll put my foot in it, get it wrong.'

He took her hand and squeezed it. 'No, you won't. Just remember what they did to Denny and that it's because of those two evil twats that you weren't there for Desiree. This is the only revenge you're going to get. You're going to be perfect because you're my wife. Just say what I've asked you to say and everything will be fine.'

They got out of his motor and walked into Snaresbrook Crown Court.

Stan took her to the witness room, where Cleo was already waiting. He gave her a searching look and got a nod of consent by way of reply. After spending a few more minutes reassuring his wife, Stan hurried off to the public gallery to get a good spot for the show.

He made himself as comfortable as he could on the wooden benches and put a bag of wine gums down next to him. He looked out over the court. Everything was in its place. A doddery old judge perched up to one side, various briefs examining their notes, a bored-looking jury who'd no doubt been hoping for a nice juicy murder case and had got this instead, and the two stars of the show; Mickey and Mel Ingram, up on charges of keeping a disorderly house and living off immoral earnings. The only disappointment was that the public gallery was nearly empty. Stan had been hoping for a full house. But even Mickey and Mel's families were unlikely to turn out to support a pimp and his pimpette missus. Stan resisted the urge to smile; the two Ms were on their own.

The two defendants looked very different. Mickey was in a badly fitted whistle with a tie and shirt that didn't match, but looked ready to take on the world to defend his reputation.

Mel on the other hand, had ditched her mink and was in a plain blue maxi dress and matching jacket. She looked the wide-eyed picture of innocence.

Both Cricket and Horner were booked to appear as witnesses for the prosecution but only Horner had made it. Stan smiled, remembering how he'd told his wife that he'd popped a bob or two in the bent coppers' pockets to get them to turn on Mickey and Mel. The two detectives might have turned prosecution but Babs had sworn she would never, ever forgive them for not letting her go to Desiree.

Horner was first on the stand with dramatic, over-the-top tales of car chases and derring-do as he and his colleague Cricket had tracked down the Mile End master criminals. Even the judge looked on the verge of doing an eye roll. He finally cut short Horner with a curt, 'Yes, Detective, I think we get the picture.'

Cleo was far better when it was her turn. Stan actually felt his eyes water as she told the tragic story of being lured into a life of vice by the evil Mickey Ingram and his sinister wife. How she was subjected to various degrading sexual practices by Mickey's sleazy clients. She provided details that seemed to perk up the judge's interest considerably. The only jarring note was that she refused to swear on the Bible, insisting she would affirm instead. But it didn't matter, she was a standout witness.

Finally, Babs came in, clutching her bag as if she longed to hurl it in Mickey and Mel's direction. She faltered slightly as she explained how Mickey had forced her to sign documents putting the houses in Mile End in her name to cover his tracks. Babs constantly looked up at Stan for reassurance that she was getting it right. Mickey was going red with rage. He yelled, 'Bollocks!' and 'This is a fucking joke!' and she shouted back across the court, 'You're a fucking murderer, you bastard!'

Mickey blanched at her outburst, no doubt realising she was referring to Denny. But he didn't get an opportunity to mouth back because he was warned by the judge that if he didn't pipe down, he'd be spending the rest of the trial in the cells.

Babs was told that while everyone understood she was distressed, she must contain herself, especially regarding accusations that had nothing to do with the case. Stan caught Babs' gaze and lifted his eyebrow in warning to leave the business about her best mate out of it.

The defence brief went through the motions but it was clear his heart wasn't in it. When Mickey went on the stand, he hung his head in despair as his client went into one, claiming that the real ringmaster was in fact one Stanley Miller. Cleo and Babs were a pair of bold-faced liars and Horner and Cricket were crooked cops who were a disgrace to Her Majesty's Constabulary. When the sniggering prosecution brief rose, he turned to the judge and told him, 'We've no questions for this defendant, my lord. We think the evidence in this case speaks for itself.'

The judge's eyebrows snapped together. 'Yes, I rather think you're right.'

While Stan had cheerfully eaten wine gums during Mickey's rant, he was frustrated in his desire to see Mel on the stand. She changed her plea to guilty halfway through. She was smart.

It was only after the jury had returned guilty verdicts – Mickey was sent down for six months while Mel got three – that Mickey finally noticed Stan sitting in the public gallery. He jabbed Mel in the ribs and then screamed, 'What's this about, Miller? I thought we had an understanding! You got my half of the business and now this?'

They did have an understanding. But Stan took the view that

defeating an opponent wasn't enough. You had to jump up and down on their grave afterwards to show you'd won. And anyway – the two of them were guilty. All Stan had done was to juggle the facts around to make sure that justice was done.

As Mickey was dragged off by the guards, he shouted, 'This ain't over, mate. I'm going to have you sorted for good, you cunt.'

Stan gave him a smile and a little goodbye wave. Then he rushed to find Babs.

He planted a big kiss on her mouth. 'You done good my girl. I'm right proud of you.'

She looked deep into his eyes. 'I still don't feel right not telling Denny's mum what happened to her.'

'We don't have a body to show her, so if she goes to the Bill it will only lead to a dead end, so to speak. And how's that going to leave her feeling? Worse than she does now.'

'Let's get to the boozer. I need a stiff drink.'

Instead, Stan took out his leather wallet and handed Babs some notes. 'I've got business to see to. Get yourself a cab back home. We'll have that drink later.'

Stan puffed out his chest, walking like the dog's bollocks around the corner, only to find a distraught Cleo waiting for him.

'You murdered him, didn't you?'

Stan arched an eyebrow at her. 'Don't know what you're chatting on about, luv.'

'Pete,' she spat. Her voice cracked with emotion. 'Hearing all that evidence made everything fall into place. And I led you right to him. If I'd never given you that address you'd never have found him.'

'The silly sod either topped himself or the booze toppled him over the edge.'

Cleo stabbed her finger into his chest, her expression

haunted. 'Pete might've been weak but he was a good man. A decent man. All he needed was a chance to find the right path.'

'Without my help you'd still be pumping away for tuppence on your back.' Stan turned his back on her. 'Be seeing you, Cleo.'

She called after him, 'May God forgive you – because I never will.'

Thirty-Eight

While Babs made her way home, her other half went to the Bad Moon boozer in Shadwell. He searched the pub and grinned when he spotted the two men waiting for him.

'Stan, my man,' Detective Graham Horner greeted him with open arms as Stan swaggered over to him and Detective Martin Cricket, who had a Scotch in one hand and his trademark Manikin cigar in the other.

Stan pulled up a pew. 'A job well done, me lads. And here's that little drink I owe you.' He slid a bulging brown envelope across the table, which Horner quickly stashed.

'That missus of yours wants to be glad she's your old girl. I nearly clocked her one after she tried to rearrange my face when we took her down the station,' Cricket said, rubbing the cheek where Babs had clouted him, despite the bruise being long gone.

'You sure she's bought your story about us working for that fucker Mickey?' Horner asked.

Stan relaxed in his chair like the king of the castle. 'Hook, line and sinker. Once I planted the seed that it was Mickey and his old girl who dragged her down the nick, taking her away from her baby, my darlin' Babs has popped them at the top of her "people to hate" list. No way will she think her kind-hearted Stan used her to help stitch up his business partner to take control of the business. Didn't take much for me to nudge her in the right direction after I also let slip how you two have been turfing out good honest citizens on Mickey's say-so.'

They all laughed uproariously at that. Stanley was the dreaded slum landlord of those unfortunate families. Stan had arranged for them to get free sex up at the brothel. Since the day he'd watched two coppers beat the living shit out of a geezer on the say-so of some Face, Stan knew the only way he was going to build an empire was to have a few dodgy plod in his pocket. Cricket and Horner had been on *his* payroll all along, not Mickey's, ready to carry out his orders in exchange for a little drink.

'What I don't get,' Horner said frowning, 'is why you had to tie the knot in the first place?'

Stan just smiled as he pulled his pint towards him. 'Let's just say if she ever finds out the truth in the future, I can control the situation much better if she's my nearest and dearest.'

Horner shook his head as he lifted his pint. 'You're one evil bastard, Stanley Miller.'

'No, I'm a man heading for the top.'

He got out his golden list.

~~Mickey~~
~~Mel~~
~~Joseph Carter~~
~~Lord Tilgate~~
~~Pete Miller~~

He crossed out the final names of the people who had propelled him well on his road.

~~Babs Wilson~~
~~Babs Miller~~

PART TWO: 1978

'Hell hath no fury like an East End woman wronged'

Thirty-Nine

'Now, as we lay our sister to rest . . .'

Maggie Brooks' funeral wasn't packed, but it was a good turnout for a woman who had done her best to put clothes on her children's backs. *Shame she turned her back on her own daughter when her old man tried to fiddle with her*, Babs thought bitterly.

She'd put on a touch more weight in the last six years, as was to be expected after giving birth to two children. Her hair was a flip and fly replica of Farrah Fawcett's on *Charlie's Angels* and her slap a touch brighter with the coming of the disco age.

Babs felt the extra chill around the grave, which had sod all to do with the weather but with the bad blood between some of the people paying their last respects. First off there were the relatives. One or two of them – the ones who didn't look the full ticket – had turned up to see if there were rich pickings to be had in her will. As if! Next up was her lecherous husband Darren, who everyone knew was doing a number as the grieving husband and making a very poor job of it.

Then there was Babs. Her bad blood was standing across from her – her parents. Six long years: that's how long it had been. They were carefully avoiding looking at her, pretending she didn't exist. Babs wasn't doing the same. Her gaze pierced right into them. She shook with rage. If it hadn't been for them, her life might've been so different. Not a word of regret had ever been passed on. Perhaps they were glad Desiree was dead if it saved them embarrassment.

Most of the gathered crowd were family or folk from Whitechapel way but there were a couple of strangers. One in particular caught Babs' eye. A bloke who stood apart from everyone else, huddled in a sheepskin jacket and casual trousers. He had a trendy 'tache and the dark looks of that Ross Poldark character from the show that Babs had been glued to, like the rest of the nation, most Sunday nights. He seemed to be studying the mourners rather than listening to the vicar who, admittedly, had a voice that would cure anyone of a sleepless night.

But no one else seemed to have clocked the guy. Everyone's attention was on the young woman that Darren Brooks had tucked up close to him. He'd introduced her as his 'close friend'. Close friend indeed! The girl had the nerve to parade herself in a leopard-print fake-fur overcoat, patent-leather wedge boots and a skirt so short you could tell where she'd bought her drawers. Babs was standing behind them, so she had a clear view when Darren pinched her bum. Filthy fucker. At his own wife's send-off.

The brazen bird whispered, 'How much longer is this going for? The pubs'll be shut by the time that bloke in the black and white dress finishes droning on.'

Darren murmured back, 'Oh do shut up, show some respect.'

The bold brass hissed, 'The old boot's gorn, ain't she? If you don't show me some respect you'll be reading dirty mags at bedtime instead of copping a feel.'

If dirty looks could kill, Darren might have had a double booking at the cemetery, with the airhead going underground too.

Forty

'Our Babs looked good, but a touch peaky,' Rosie Wilson tentatively informed her husband after the funeral. She spoke as if they talked about their daughter every day of the week. In fact, they'd rarely mentioned her name since '72. Not since the day a distraught Babs had cursed them out on their own doorstep. George wouldn't allow it. He insisted on calling her 'that girl'.

They were in the sitting room by the open fire. Rosie had a cuppa while George pulled on his pipe as he watched the news. Rosie might have a few more grey hairs and wrinkles but her husband hadn't fared so well. He had shrivelled and aged before his time and it worried his wife sick.

'She ain't "our" anything,' George announced. He would never admit it in a million years, but the day he'd put Babs out of his life had nearly killed him. Their girl had been his life and soul. But he couldn't forgive her for what she'd done. Rosie was scared witless that his pain was growing like a cancer inside him and would kill him one of these days. She'd taken what Babs had done hard as well, but seeing her daughter today reminded her how much she missed being a mum.

'She's still our flesh and blood,' she added quietly.

George yanked his pipe from his mouth. 'I've said that girl ain't our anything. How can she be after what she did—'

'She made a mistake,' Rosie implored him. 'And the baby died, for crying out loud.'

'And shamed us in front of everyone.' His body twitched in his armchair. 'You know what someone said to me at work – is it true you had a darkie granddaughter? I nearly clouted him one.' George waved a fist in the air.

Rosie's face crumpled. 'But I miss her so.'

Some of the anger left George. He got up and put his arms around his wife. 'She made her feelings clear six years back. She don't wanna see us, we don't wanna see her. Done and dusted.'

Rosie knew he was right, but that didn't stop her yearning.

For some reason Babs couldn't get Richard out of her mind as she walked onto the Essex Lane Estate. No one seemed to know anything about him and he hadn't known Maggie from Eve, so what had he been doing at her funeral? Mind you, that was the trouble with funerals and weddings, all sorts turned up. Look at Stan's mum, showing her face unexpectedly at their wedding reception and causing all kinds of mayhem. Stan didn't see his mum often, but when he did, Babs stopped at home. There was something about Shell Miller that was plain nasty and it wasn't that she had a screw loose.

Babs' attention was caught by a crowd gathered near the corner shop. No one had to tell her there was trouble. That's all the Essex Lane was nowadays – trouble and strife. The gleaming new estate she had moved onto as a hope-filled nineteen-year-old was falling like a lead balloon. The type of families the council were dumping on it behaved as if their last home had been either Pentonville or Chessington Zoo. And the kids . . . well, it was Babs' strong opinion that some of them should have been put down at birth. No manners, playing out until all hours – what decent parent let that happen?

Babs made her way to the crowd, her nose wrinkling at the smell of burning tyres in the air. Those fucking kids had been at it again, burning tyres in the cemetery like it was some kind of new religion. Babs noticed sixteen-year-old Kieran Scott standing in the distance. He still wore his National Health glasses but had ditched the plaster for his lazy eye. He didn't come around any more, probably thinking he was a big boy who shouldn't be seen hanging around with an old girl like her. Babs worried about him. She suspected he'd finished with school years back. That bloody mum of his had a lot to answer for.

'Oh, Babs,' Beryl wailed. 'It's Cheryl. Fucking animals.'

In the middle of the crowd, lying on her back on the ground, was Cheryl. She had a black eye, one of her shoes was missing and her shopping was strewn all over the place.

Babs let out a gasp as she bent down. 'What happened?'

A dazed Cheryl stared back at her. 'I was just going about my business . . .' She sniffed back some tears. 'I did a bit of shopping and then I went into the chemist . . . Next thing I know, two lads are on me. One grabbed my bag and the other slogs me one in the eye . . .' She shook her head over and over, like she couldn't believe what had happened.

Babs gently embraced her, her mouth set into a murderous line. If she got her mitts on the no-marks who did this, she'd kill them. The walkways that had once looked so posh were now hiding places of lowlifes ready to pounce on anyone walking by. Probably junkies who'd clocked Cheryl coming out of the chemist. Scum, that's what they were, every last one of them. The days when you could leave your door open were long gone.

'Let's get you down the ozzie,' Babs said as she helped Cheryl to her feet.

'I'm alright,' Cheryl insisted. 'Just a bit winded is all.'

'Someone should call the Bill.'

'Nah,' someone threw back, 'they'll do sweet FA unless they're friends of yours.'

'That ain't a bad idea,' Beryl jumped in. 'That commissioner fella who retired – Robert what's his face – cleared a load of them bent coppers out. The plod are all meant to be respectable now, people you can trust.'

Most of the crowd just scoffed at that.

'Essex Lane Estate,' one of them sneered, 'more like Devil's Estate.'

And from then on, that's what the place became known as – *The Devil's Estate.*

As Babs and Beryl helped their friend home, Babs noticed a removals van off-loading furniture into a ground-floor maisonette in another block. Babs hoped this new family were the civilised variety. Then she got the shock of her life. A man and a woman with a little one in her arms emerged from the flat. Mickey and Melanie Ingram.

Mel looked into Babs' eyes and drew her finger across her throat.

Bitch! Witch! Murderer!

The three words bounced inside Babs' mind as she slammed the door to the flat. All she could see was red. That woman had some nerve to put down roots here after what she'd done.

'Babs, is that you?'

'Stan!' Babs practically flew with outrage. 'Stan! You'll never guess who's moved in.'

Babs found her husband with the kids in the sitting room. Tiffany was howling her head off and Jennifer was playing with Mister Silly, her stuffed blue elephant. The girls were her pride and joy. She'd miscarried her and Stan's first, which Babs had taken badly. She'd so wanted a little one to replace baby Desiree. Jennifer had come along in '75 and little Tiffany last year. Her children had given her a second chance to prove she was capable of being a bang-up mum. Although she loved her girls equally, they were very different kids. Jen was a happy little soul, content to play on her own, while Tiff was usually fussing and screaming, demanding her parents' undivided attention.

'It took you long enough to get home,' Stan grumbled as he stood and handed her the baby. Stan was still a suits man but had gone a touch John Travolta in *Saturday Night Fever*, adding white waistcoats to his collections.

'She's wet through Stan, couldn't you at least have changed her?' Babs popped a sweetie cigarette inbetween Tiff's lips. She sucked on it; they were the only things that kept her quiet.

'Don't start. I'm not the kid's mum.'

Stan had never really taken to being a father. He was usually only around long enough to give them a pat on the head. That was the problem with their marriage. Stan was always out and about on business. In fact, there were days on end when he never came home. She understood that he was trying to make a crust, but what was the point in having a family if you hardly ever saw them? She'd had enough. It was time Stan started behaving like a husband and dad.

'Stan—?'

But he cut her off, sensing what she was going to say. 'Gordon Bennett, Babs, I've had it up to here with you giving me earache about work. If I'm sitting on my jacksie all day how the fuck are we going to live?'

'By letting me find something part-time like the other mums.'

Stan looked like he was ready to blow his stack. 'How many times have I told you that I'm not having latchkey kids? The girls need their mum.'

Babs would not be put down. 'So where's the cash from all this business you're doing? We're always on our uppers – except when it comes to your suits and shoes of course.' It was true. They were always scrimping and scraping but he claimed business was booming.

'You have to speculate to accumulate.' He added snidely, 'You change the girls and leave me to do the thinking.'

There he went again, treating her like she was as thick as an MFI plank. He was always doing it, slapping her down. It got Babs mad. Really mad. But before she could say her piece, he carried on, 'I promise that six months from now we'll be moving out of this khazi and into our own house. I might even be able to splash out on the girls' schools. They're not going to be serving in shops.'

It was always the same – *six months from now, a year from now, two years from now. It's coming! It's coming! It's bloody well coming!* Babs was growing tired of it. She clocked the ring on the finger next to his half-finger. Chunky gold, with tiny jewels in the front that looked to her like diamonds.

'Where did you get the cash for that rock on your finger?'

Stan abruptly twisted away and walked towards the bottle of whisky on the sideboard. 'It's on H.P. I need to look a bit flash to impress the people I'm making deals with.' He gazed at her and took a swig. 'That's business, darlin', it's all show. You wouldn't understand. You take care of the home front and leave the serious to me. What was all that noise about when you came in?'

'Mickey and fucking Mel Ingram have moved on to the estate.'

Stan shrugged. 'So what?'

She lifted Tiffany to her shoulder and patted the baby on the back. 'After what we did to them, Mickey might come gunning for you.'

Stan just laughed. 'I ain't scared of that poxy mutt. Anyroad, he knows where to find me. He's small time, he ain't going up against me; he ain't that stupid.'

'Nah, that Mel's still got the right hump with me. She went into the whole *finger across the throat* routine like she's in the mob.'

Stan put his glass down. 'Don't worry about it. Mickey's a bottle job; he ain't got the nuts to come after me, or his missus after you. If you see them, blank 'em.'

Babs gently eased a sleeping Tiffany onto the settee. 'Right bunch of nutters and oddballs at the funeral. Including Maggie's old codger aunt who told me she could *feel* Denny in the wind and waves. She fair gave me the creeps.'

Stan wasn't interested. 'All families have them. She should go on the stage. Pubs have nights with mediums these days. She might make a few quid. There's always some mug who'll pay a fiver to get in touch with the other side.' Stan noticed her silence and burst out laughing. 'Oh, don't tell me you've done it? You really are an idiot. Who were you trying to get in touch with?'

Babs looked hurt. 'There's a woman up Ilford way who does sessions. After we lost Desiree, I went to see if she could get in touch with her.'

Stan shook his head. 'You're only hurting yourself doing stuff like that. Did she make contact?'

A sad expression came on to her face. 'Nah. The medium thought Desiree was a bloke – so I left.'

Stan raised his eyebrows in disgust. 'Perhaps she should have gone outside and spoken to the trees and leaves and they'd have told her. People like that make a mint out of gullible plonkers like you. How could you be so stupid?'

Babs said nothing. Apart from her baby's death, she was forbidden even to mention the events of six years earlier. The few times she'd done it, she soon found out how angry it made him. Stan was not a nice man when he got a cob on. But this time, it was as if there was a force that made her add, 'Strange, though.'

'What is?'

'That they never found Denny's body.'

Stan looked at his wife the way he would at a kitten that had done its business on the carpet. 'Do you get a cheap thrill out of fucking me off?'

Stan walked out of the room. In horror, Babs watched him go, knowing what she and the little ones were going to endure next. Why hadn't she kept her big trap shut? Why had she kept pushing him? She didn't care about herself, but the kids ... Now he was going to punish her for letting her mouth run. Sometimes she wished Stan was one of those husbands who thumped you one and got it over with. But that wasn't Stanley Miller's style. He wanted her to remember it when he thought she'd stepped out of line.

Stan used a spanner to lock off the hot water and pulled the fuse for the central heating. He took the 50ps piled up on the gas meter, knowing she only had loose change in her purse. Then he went out and left his wife and children in the freezing flat, just as his mum had locked him in the cold outdoor toilet when he was young.

Forty-One

'Pack it in or me slapping your legs will be the least of it,' Melanie Ingram yelled at her two eldest children.

Ten-year-old Donna and seven-year-old Tommy were going at it with fists and kicks, scrapping over the Simon Says toy that Mickey had bought them. If Mel heard that toy blare out, 'Simon says' one more time, she'd friggin' well show it what Mel says when she smashed it against the wall.

'We're only mucking around,' Donna responded.

'Don't give me any of your cheek.' Mel emphasised her warning by picking up her slipper. She couldn't stand the sight of her Donna. Her boat had grown to look more and more like her dad's. Mickey idolised that girl and Mel was jealous, pure and simple. Always buying her fancy things, like he used to for Mel back when.

Both kids scarpered, taking their prized toy with them. Mel's face softened as she turned to look down at her baby Stacey tucked up on the sofa near her. The kid was a little angel, delicate and small with fine blonde hair. What Mel liked most about the newest addition to her family was that she was peaceful.

Mel got up and poured herself a generous measure of Bacardi as Mickey came banging into the room. She could smell the cheap perfume coming off him from where she stood.

He didn't even try to hide the fact he'd been screwing the brains off some loose piece. She weren't stupid, she knew that Mickey had been exercising his dinkle away from home more or less since they tied the knot, but at least he'd tried to hide it back then. Now he was out and out blatant; didn't give a monkeys. Mel had always been able to pull Mickey's strings, but that had ended when they got stitched up by Stan Miller and got banged up in Holloway and the Scrubs. Mickey had come out a new man, no longer meek and mild when she crooked her little finger but lording it around like the mutt's nuts, ducking and diving without her by his side. Mel hated the Millers; they had destroyed the grip she wielded over her man. Worst of all, she'd had to flog her beloved mink to put a few more pennies in her purse now she didn't have a free hand in Mickey's wallet.

'Look at the state of ya,' Mickey shot at her, his nose wrinkling in disgust. 'You'd give the winos on this estate a run for their money.'

Mel knew she was a bit of a dog's dinner. Her looks had started going in prison and she'd put on weight carrying Stacey that she just couldn't shift. She was doing that grapefruit diet to shed the pounds. Grapefruit diet? More like piss diet. She was in and out of the bog like it was her second home. Mind you, that was down to the booze too.

'What you going to do about that fucking Stanley Miller, that's what I want to know,' she slapped out at him. Then swallowed a good mouthful of Bacardi.

Mickey swaggered across the room, not taking a blind bit of notice of Stacey; he'd never really taken to the new baby. He bypassed Mel and went for the malt whisky. 'Don't you worry about Miller, he'll be getting his when I'm good and ready.'

Mel shoved her hands onto her hips. '"When I'm good and ready",' she mimicked. 'You've lost your bottle, that's what.

You've had donkeys to sort this out. Instead of shafting them, you're letting them take the piss. You're bricking it–'

He belted her so her head crashed into the wall. Blood streamed from her mouth. The new Mickey liked to raise his hand to her. She could see the pleasure in his dark, moronic eyes. Well, Mel had grown up in a home where getting clumped was a natural part of life, so if he thought that hitting her was going to shut her up, he was mistaken.

He ranted at her. 'I've told you to leave it alone–'

Mel pulled herself off the wall. 'But Mickey–'

'No,' he yelled. 'Alright, so we lost the business and got banged up; it's over. And it needs to be over – because if he ever even gets wind of what really went on between his brother and that girl, he's going to come after us with all he's got.'

Mel knew what he was saying was true, but she couldn't let it go. Her life wouldn't be the total shithole it was if it weren't for them fucking cunt Millers. As she wiped the blood from her mouth, she vowed she was going to make them pay.

Mel Ingram started doing what she did best – plotting and planning.

Forty-Two

Both baby Tiff and three-year-old Jen were crying the place down the following morning. It was so cold. The girls had slept in their coats tucked up next to Babs with all the blankets heaped around them. But they'd woken up to a freezing flat. Of course Stan wasn't around. *I bet wherever the bastard is, he's nice and toasty*, Babs thought bitterly.

She couldn't understand why he punished her and the girls this way. She'd never heard the like. Sure, she knew of families where the man's fist did most of the talking, but cutting the hot water and heating off – what the fuck was that about? And she had sixteen pence in her purse, not enough for the gas meter. She couldn't put the kettle on or even boil some water because the cooker ran on gas. She had to give Jen some Robinsons orange squash and bread and jam and Tiff, Farley's Rusks mashed up in cold milk.

There was only one way to get the heating and gas working – go begging to the neighbours for a few coins, which she hated. Carrying Tiff, and holding Jen's hand, she knocked on Beryl's door.

'Well, hello, my lovelies,' Beryl cooed to the girls.

Babs felt so embarrassed. It wasn't the first time she'd come begging, but it didn't make the shame any less. 'You couldn't see your way to giving me a couple of quid and a few fifty p's? Only it's—'

Beryl smiled. 'Of course luvvie. Be back in a jiffy.'

To Babs' surprise she came back with a Campbell's tomato soup tin, minus its lid.

Babs gazed at it as she lifted Tiff higher on her shoulder. 'What's that?'

Beryl just smiled and handed it over. Babs' breath caught when she saw fifty-pence pieces piled almost to the top. She shook her head. 'I can't take your stash—'

'It's not my anything. I had a little win on the gee-gees so I says to myself, "I'm gonna give that nice girl with the lovely kids on my landing some gas money so that when that dick of a fella of hers takes the money and turns the heating off she'll have some put by."'

The blood drained from Babs' face. 'How did you know?'

'Walls have ears. My old da would sometimes take the coal away and lock us in our rooms to freeze our bollocks off. A fella bashing up a woman isn't the only way he can make her life a misery. When the kiddies are old enough, you find yourself a little bit of work.' She leaned in close, her expression dead serious. 'It's not good for a woman to have to lean on a man all the time.'

An hour later Tiffany was in the land of nod and Jen was organising a tea party for Mister Silly and her dolls in the lovely warm flat. The blower went. Stan kept the purse strings tight but he insisted they have a phone; said he needed to be available for business.

'Who is it?

'It's Doreen, Maggie's neighbour.'

Babs resisted the temptation to slam the old dog down. Doreen McAlister was a busybody of the first order who loved to jar about everybody else's business but her own. What the hell could she want?

'Maggie had a good send-off,' Babs said. 'It was nice to see so many people turn out.'

'It was good of you to show your face; I know she would've appreciated it. By the way – did you meet that bloke, Mark, at the graveside?'

'Nah.' Babs frowned. 'Who's he then?'

'Well, that's the problem, no one seems to know. Only he popped round mine later and was asking all kinds of questions about Denny. Did we know where she was, he wanted to get in touch with her, stuff like that.'

The awful memories of her best mate's end came flooding back. Babs shuddered. 'I hope you told him to do one. Maggie wouldn't have wanted people nosing around.'

'Told me he was a friend of the family and wanted to catch up. But if he was a friend of the family he'd know she vanished like a puff of smoke in '72. And that most folk think she's a goner.'

'Did you tell him that?'

'Yeah. He said he'd been abroad for a while. When I asked him how he knew the Brookses, he came over all airy-fairy and didn't really say. Strange.'

Babs had a bad feeling. 'What did he look like?'

When Doreen described him, it was obvious who she was talking about. 'He told me his name was Richard.'

'Don't surprise me. He looked more like a gangster's heavy than a friend of the family. He gave me the right creeps. You don't think he's anything to do with Darren, do you? I don't want him round here again.'

Richard/Mark had certainly been a bit tasty chasing off the toughs who'd given Darren a kicking. He'd also been a bit tasty . . . Babs wiped the last thought from her mind. 'How's that child molester doing?'

'Cracked ribs and a fractured skull, the way I heard it.'

'Serves the perv right. Should've broken every last one of his fingers to remind him to keep his mitts off young girls.'

There was a long pause and Babs guessed there was worse to come. 'Thing is, this guy was asking after you as well.'

Babs nearly dropped the phone. 'You what?'

'He asked a ton of questions about you. He asks me, *do you know this Babs who was Maggie's daughter's best mate? Do you know where she lives?* Thought he was gonna ask what your fave tipple was next. And he asked after Stan and where he was these days too.'

'And what did you say?'

'I showed him the door and told the geezer to mind his own.' Her voice lowered. 'He looks a bit handy, know what I mean? Thought it best to tip you the wink.'

As soon as the call was done, Babs was on the blower to Stan. The last thing she needed was some hard merchant asking about 1972. But she got the same old same old palaver on the phone – Stan was nowhere to be found. The girl running his office said he was 'out' and couldn't be contacted. But Babs thought otherwise; she knew all of his tricks.

From the early years of their marriage, Babs had got fed up with him always being out when she rang him at work. Plus the fact that she didn't actually know where he worked. All he'd say was that he was 'in property'. What that property looked like or where it stood was a bit of a mystery. When pressed, he got on his high horse and fumed, 'I'll tell you what – when I ask you about the hoovering you can ask me about my work – OK?'

In the end, she'd given up calling. But this time it was urgent. She left a message about Richard, which the bored woman on the other end seemed a bit pissed off that she had to take down. 'Mr Miller is a very busy man, but I'll pass it on if he comes back.'

'Don't come the madam with me. I know how busy he is; I'm his wife, remember.'

Babs popped a couple of Annies – one for her head, the other to steady her nerves – then made herself a cuppa with a finger of gin and began to fret about the guy at the funeral. It was at times like this she really needed Stan around and, sod's law, it was times like this he never was. Moments later though, Stan was on the line. When Babs had told him about Maggie's funeral, he'd grunted, but now he was very interested indeed.

'Alright, ring Maggie's neighbour and tell her if she sees the geezer again, she's to call me at once. I'll make some enquiries at my end.'

Babs couldn't help being sarky. 'What's the point? You're never there.'

'I've said I'll ask around.' With that, he put the phone down.

She called Doreen back, muttering curses.

'I was just about to call you,' the other woman whispered excitedly. 'The guy's back again. He's sitting up the end of the road in a Ford Granada.'

Forty-Three

Babs decided to find out in person what this Richard fella was about. She borrowed a couple of nicker from Beryl's gas money, dropped the girls off at Cheryl's and took the tube down to Whitechapel. Since '72 she'd tried her hardest not to come back to her old manor. The place was chocka with sad memories.

She passed the Blind Beggar and Blue Anchor pubs and turned into the street where Maggie Brooks had done fuck all about her old man trying to molest her daughter. Babs didn't realise she was shaking until she spotted the Granada parked up on the pavement. She decided this was work for Stan, not her. She'd get to Doreen's and give Stan a bell.

But as she passed the Granada, she couldn't resist taking a gander at the driver. Her heart skipped as there was a quick blast on the horn. She kept walking and heard a shout behind her. 'Hello again!'

Babs turned and saw the guy leaning out of the driver's window. 'Remember me? I'm Richard – Richard Smith – we met at Maggie's funeral.' His hair blew easy in the breeze and Babs saw his eyes were a soft grey.

He seemed a lot more cheerful than he had been at the graveside. Babs looked up the street at Doreen's house and began to slowly walk back to the car. After all, it was daylight and she had a good pair of lungs on her if it came to screaming.

'Hello. What are you doing here? Keeping the place under surveillance like Starsky and Hutch? Or are you more the Huggy Bear type?'

He chuckled. 'I've been trying to track down Maggie's relatives but no one seems willing to help.'

She arched her eyebrow. 'Why are you doing that then?'

'I told you at the funeral, I'm a friend of the family.' When he saw the look on her face he changed tack. 'Alright, I can see you're a smart girl and I'll level with you. That's a cover story.'

'You don't say.'

'I'm actually a private detective. I've been asked by Maggie's lawyer to track down any surviving relatives with regard to her will. Apart from her old man that is – of course he's not getting a penny. She left quite a lot of money behind and Denise would get a sizeable portion of the dough. But no one seems to know what happened to her.'

Babs could see right through this chancer. 'If you were a real private detective, you'd know Denny is probably dead.'

Richard Smith gave her a look of pure innocence. 'Yeah, so everyone keeps telling me. But there's no record of her death. Strange, eh?'

'Maybe. But not as strange as the idea that Maggie Brooks left a legacy. The only thing she'll have left behind is a pile of empty bottles.'

He pulled a face. 'You'd be surprised how much Mrs Brooks managed to squirrel away over the years. Quite a pretty penny. She liked to keep a shilling or two under her mattress, if you get my drift. How else do you think she paid that muscle to do over her old man?'

True enough about those bully boys, but the rest of it . . .

Nah! Pure bollocks. Babs turned to go but he got out of the car and called after her. 'Don't rush off, Babs.'

She froze to the spot. Then did a slow motion turn and whispered, 'How do you know I'm Babs?'

'I told you, I've been making enquiries. I was hoping to drop by and have a word about Denny. Amongst other things.' What other things? What was he going on about? 'I know all about Stan as well. Have you seen him lately?'

She didn't like any of this. Sounded like he was giving her a warning.

Babs drew close. 'I've got a bit of advice for you, mate. Go back and tell your gaffer you're out of your depth. You don't know who you're dealing with.'

He looked just like he had when he'd chased off snooker cue guy at Maggie's send-off – not frightened of nobody. 'Maybe. We'll see. Do you mind if I drop by and ask a few questions about Denise?'

Babs hissed, 'Are you deaf? Word is she's six feet under. And don't even think about trying to track me down – or you might be too.'

Babs set off at an even pace and Smith made no attempt to follow. But when she reached Whitechapel Road she began running, desperately looking for a phone box.

'Mr Miller, there's a call for you. It's your assistant. She says it's urgent.'

Stan told the waiter, 'I'll call her back.'

'She said it was about the Whitechapel deal.'

Stan was irritated. He was up to his elbows with some important clients. They were buying property. Or maybe they were selling it; Stan couldn't keep his head on the matter at hand. He was worrying about this bloke wandering up and down the East End asking questions about the Denny girl.

These sorts of situations were like a woollen pullover. Start pulling at one thread and the whole thing was likely to unravel. He'd end up with a pile of wool and some awkward questions about his late brother.

Fucking Denise. He hated thinking about her; it brought back memories of Pete. And then he'd recall what he'd done and he didn't like that, not one bit.

He'd told the girl at his office that if Babs rang with any information about someone called 'Richard' or 'Mark', she was to say it was about the 'Whitechapel deal'.

'I'm sorry, gentlemen, but could you excuse me for a moment? I need to take an urgent call.'

Stan went behind the bar and picked up the phone. The girl at the office passed on the news from Babs. His wife had clearly been all over the place but she did include one vital titbit. She'd written down the registration number of this Richard Smith's motor. And that was all Stan really needed. He was such a good customer at the Italian that the manager allowed him to use his office to make a private call.

'I need to speak to Detective Graham Horner.'

The days when Cricket and Horner were up for a wrinkle had become few and far between. Now they were 'busy' or 'unavailable'. Horner had explained how it was over a snifter a few months earlier. His voice had dropped, as if he feared prying ears.

'This new crowd that have taken over the Yard, they're more interested in nicking us than the criminal fraternity. It's got right out of hand, I'm telling you. Honest thief takers being sacked, retired, sent to the sick bay or even . . .' – he recoiled in horror – ' . . . stuck in the slammer with guys they helped put away. Totally out of order – and for what? Helping people out when there's a drink in it for you?'

So the hunt-the-bent-copper racket up at the Yard was

lapping around his former associates' feet and they were lying low. But Stan wasn't totally sorry to hear it. He had more than enough info to torpedo their careers and he'd decided to hold the threat in reserve until he needed it.

Now he needed it.

Horner finally came on, his voice tight and furious. 'I thought I told you not to ring me at the office. Naff off, will you, I'm busy.'

Stan was jovial. 'Yeah, we're all busy, but I'm sure you can manage a couple of hours for an old mate in need. Especially as it's business related. Or should I say; your former *freelance* business?'

There was a pause. Horner said, 'I ain't got a clue what you're talking about.' He said it loudly, like he wanted his whole office to hear. This Robert Mark geezer, the previous commissioner, might be retired, but his ghost still had everyone running scared and covering their backs.

Stan didn't give two fucks. 'The Bad Moon today at four?'

'The pubs are closed then, Miller.' He was back to whispering again. 'I would've thought a law-abiding citizen like you would know we've got licencing laws in this country.'

Stan could do menace as well as Horner. 'The landlord holds lock-ins for his special friends, of whom I have the honour to be one. Just knock on the door and mention my name. That way we get to have a drink and a chinwag where walls don't have ears. And this does need to be in private, believe you me. Oh – and call that runt Cricket and get him there too.'

Rosie Wilson fussed around the house for a good fifteen minutes, then put on her coat. 'I'm just going to pick up a few pieces down the market,' she told her husband.

George had his head in a newspaper and his pipe on the go. He looked up at her and he frowned. 'But it's brass monkeys, pet. You don't want to catch a cold again, you nearly ended up in the London last year.'

She tied her headscarf tight around her chin. 'Stop fussing. A bit of English cold never hurt no one.'

He folded his paper and put it down. 'Well, I might come and stretch my legs with you.'

'No,' Rosie almost shrieked. She steadied her voice. 'No need for that. I'm ... I'm ...' Her gaze darted away. 'I'm meeting a few of the girls for a quick snifter after. I won't be long.'

Then she was gone, the front door banging after her. George slowly eased into his armchair, worried. His Rosie hadn't been right since they'd seen Babs at the funeral. He knew she missed their daughter but he wasn't having *that girl* anywhere near this house. The shame of it! George had come a long way from the lad with no shoes on his feet and no one, including his daughter, was going to take away his respectability. He mourned not having his friend Daffy to talk to any more, but she was off in a new life, having finally set up her boutique in the West End. Mind you, she'd only tell him to forgive and forget and George Wilson was not in the mood to do that. He would never forget what his daughter had done to this family.

Rosie walked briskly through Whitechapel Market but didn't stop at any stalls. She kept up her pace until she reached the tube.

Forty-Four

'Oi, darlin' – you got anything worth nicking?'

The two lads sitting on a wall looked serious as Babs walked back onto what people were now openly calling The Devil's Estate – or simply, The Devil. Babs was tempted to tell them to get stuffed, but when they jabbed their elbows into each other and started sniggering, she stopped feeling threatened. She despaired of this next generation.

She raised her arms. 'Does it look like it?'

The boys stared at her clothes. 'Yeah, you do look a bit trampy.'

She gave him the 'V' sign and honour was satisfied.

She'd meant to avoid the block where Mickey and Mel had moved in but she was so lost in thought, sorting out what she was going to tell Stan, that she only realised she was a couple of yards from the Ingrams' flat when she almost collided with the back of a Ford Granada. She walked around it . . . *Hold up, she recognised that motor.* Richard Smith's motor. She felt ice in her veins. He was on their estate already, only hours after he'd told her he was making 'enquiries.'

Babs looked around nervously. That wanker must be following her. Then her gaze fell on the door to the Ingrams' and she realised she was wrong.

He was standing at the gate and seemed to be having a

set-to with Mel. Babs darted behind the car and crouched down to see what happened next. She heard Richard Smith call Mickey's name and a few moments later, the swaggering no-brain tub of lard appeared on the doorstep and saw his missus off with a wave. The two men shook hands, which made Babs' heart drop. It appeared they were well in with each other. Richard Smith went into the flat and Mickey stood for a few moments, looking up and down the estate. Babs crouched even lower. When he'd finished checking there was no one spying on him, Mickey went inside.

Babs got to her feet. She could feel her heart beating. Something serious was going on and she needed to speak to Stan urgently. But how could she find a husband who never seemed to be around?

Someone poked her in the back.

'You breaking into cars now, Babs?'

Startled, Babs spun around. It was her mother.

'We didn't mean nuthin' by it.' One of the teens who'd given Babs the verbal was shitting himself as he gave Kieran Scott an account of his disrespectful actions.

Sixteen-year-old Kieran was top dog of the tearaways on the estate. He'd seen the two prats giving it the big 'un with Babs, so he'd had them dragged to his little hangout.

'What I saw didn't make me happy.' He raised his fist, ready to use the knuckleduster he'd made himself from corrugated sheeting dumped in the cemetery. But he stopped short of the lad's cringing face. 'I'm giving you a message to spread far and wide. Anyone even looks at Babs Miller the wrong way, I'm coming after 'em.'

'I'll make you a nice cuppa,' Babs told her mum and without waiting for an answer, she left her unexpected – and unwanted

– visitor in the sitting room and fled into the kitchen. She was still brimming with anger at what her mum and dad had done to her and Desiree, but unlike them, she would never slam the door in anyone's face. So she'd taken her mum upstairs. But what could they say to each other after all these years?

Babs downed a couple of Annies and picked up a dishcloth to clean the kitchen, which was already spick and span. Cleaning was her little tic when she was anxious – in times of stress everything must be in its place.

'Barbara Wilson,' her mum said sternly from the doorway, 'stop hiding. You were the same as a little girl, always hiding away in your bedroom rather than getting something sorted out.' Rosie Wilson spoke to her daughter as if there wasn't six lost years between them. 'And we've got a lot to sort out.'

Babs drew in an uneven breath as she turned. God, her mum still looked the business after all these years. The grey in her hair and the new lines on her face couldn't take away from that no-nonsense expression.

'It's Miller,' Babs finally said. 'Barbara Miller. I got married to Stanley, the one you met that Sunday. We've got two young ones now.'

Her mum's expression made all the tired lines on her face show. 'I was so, so sorry about your baby—'

She turned on her mother in fury. 'Oh, you mean the innocent baby who broke my dad's heart for having the cheek to be born?'

Sorrow clouded Rosie's face as she stepped fully into the room. She wrung her hands. 'It was the shock of it all. You should've told us, warned us. You made fools of us. And once it all kicked off, there was no turning back.'

Babs strode across the room until she was in her mum's space. 'I was just a kid and so was my daughter. You know – a human being – you wanna try being one some time.' A dam broke. She sank onto a chair, her face in her hands, tears running down her cheeks.

Rosie took charge. 'Alright, have a good cry, you've earned it. I'll make a cuppa.'

A few minutes later, they faced each other across the small Formica table. Babs broke the silence. 'Dee was too small and she didn't make it.' Then her voice rose slightly and she added in a bitter voice, 'I wasn't there when she passed.' When Rosie touched her daughter's hand, Babs looked at her in fury. 'Don't say perhaps it was for the best – or I'll kill you.'

'I wasn't going to say that. We're very sorry.'

'We?' Babs scoffed. 'I bet Dad isn't. Why did you come, Mum?'

Rosie's fingers tightened. 'Because I missed you. I've missed you for years, but your dad . . .' She shrugged and Babs got the message loud and clear about where her father stood. 'Since the funeral . . . I just had to see you.'

They were interrupted by a bang on the front door. Babs stood up. 'That will be my neighbour with the kids.'

Cheryl bustled in with the girls, her face still marked with the bruises. Rosie went all dopey-eyed over the children, especially Tiffany who was sucking madly on her sweetie fag. 'They're adorable,' she told Babs.

Babs couldn't help but think – *it's a bit late now, I'm afraid*. But instead she whispered, 'I know. I'm glad you like them.'

While Rosie played with her grandchildren, Cheryl pulled Babs aside. 'I'm leaving. For good.'

'You what?'

'I can't hack this place no more, what with being walloped senseless the other day. I put in for a transfer with the council and they've fixed me up with a nice spot near my sister in Romford.'

Babs was crushed, no two ways about it. Cheryl and Beryl

had been a lifeline to her. What was she going to do without her dear mate? No more days of sitting on the balcony chatting and laughing over a sloe gin. The friends embraced.

'We'll have a leaving drink for you before you go,' Babs said when they pulled apart.

'Not at the Knackered Swan.' Cheryl shook her head as she mentioned the estate's boozer. Everyone called it the Knackered Swan because its polish had rubbed off a long time ago. 'Word is someone's pushing drugs there. I don't want no part of it. Come around to mine for a cuppa and some Gordon's.'

Babs watched her friend go. As her mum had walked back into her life, one of her best mates was leaving.

'What's the matter, pet?' Rosie asked. She held Tiffany while Jen looked through her *Bunty* mag. That girl did like looking at Bunty's clothes.

Babs popped on a fake smile and she nodded. 'Life's what the matter is, Mum, just life.'

For the next hour they nattered away, catching up with each other. Then Jen conked out over her *Bunty*.

'I'd better be off. Your dad will be wondering where I got to.' Rosie self-consciously smoothed her hand down her dress. 'The children are beautiful, but watch little Tiffany. Someone once told me that a baby who fusses all the time will grow into a right handful.'

'She'll be alright.'

'Can I come back?' Rosie asked, so quickly Babs wasn't sure she heard right.

'Of course you can. I missed you something rotten too.' Then they were hugging the life out of each other.

'I'm so sorry,' her mum said, the words muffled in her neck. 'Everything just went too far and ran away from us.'

'What's done is done. It's the future that matters.'

Her mum eased away from her. 'We're gonna have to keep

your dad in the dark for now. But he'll come round eventually.'

A happy Babs escorted her mother to the stairwell and waited to make sure she got across the courtyard safely. Even being an older woman was no defence on the estate.

As she walked back towards the flat, she realised someone was following her. Close behind. Babs thought of that bitch Mel Ingrams, hurried back to her front door and tried to slam it behind her. But she was too late. A well-buffed leather shoe was already jammed in the doorway. Behind the half-closed door she heard a voice say, 'I thought I'd pop around for that chat.'

It was Richard Smith.

Forty-Five

The foot was well wedged and the door wasn't closing. Babs tried blagging. 'If it ain't Tricky Dickie. I'm so glad you paid me a visit. My old man Stan wants a word with you. Wait there a moment; I'll get him.'

Babs made herself sound confident as she went back inside. 'Stan,' she called out like a damsel in distress.

Babs anxiously bit one of her nails as she waited for the man at the door to do one, fearing her irate husband would give him a proper hiding. She waited. And waited. But she didn't hear footsteps retreating along the balcony. At least he'd made no effort to come inside.

When he laughed and said, 'Yeah, you do that Babs – go and get Stan,' she knew she was sunk. He knew full well Stan wasn't there. Babs went back to the door and swung it open.

He reached into his pocket. 'Apologies for dropping by like this. Very rude, I know, but as I was visiting friends on the estate—'

'Yeah. I saw.' She lifted her brow knowingly.

Now it was Richard Smith's turn to falter. He was silent for a moment before going on, 'And I thought, as I was in the area, I'd drop by and leave you my card.'

As she took it, their fingers briefly touched, sending an electric heat through Babs she hadn't felt in years. She shook off the sensation and took the card; she knew Stan could use it to find out who this character really was. 'I'll pass it on to my husband.' His arch look said he didn't believe her.

'What makes you think I wouldn't?' Babs didn't know why she was prolonging a convo with this git.

'Come on. I'm a private investigator; I know you and Stan have split up.'

Split up? He might have been private but he clearly wasn't much of an investigator.

She huffed. 'Is that what your small-time friend Mickey told you? I've got news for you; my husband and I are still very much married, as you're going to discover when I have a little word in his ear about you. As for your friend Mickey,' she sneered his name, 'he's an ignorant little prick.'

Smith seemed to understand that he'd dropped a ricket. 'I'm not interested in your marriage; I only want to find Denise.' All of a sudden he seemed to be in a hurry to get out of there.

Babs yelled after him, 'Sure . . .' Then she plastered a satisfied smile on. She'd seen him off. Should really take off one of her shoes and throw it after him. Instead, she closed the door and stared hard at the card. There was just a name and a London number. Curious, she went into her front room and called it.

A woman answered. 'Hello, can I take a message?'

'No, luv, I want to speak to Richard Smith.'

'I'm so sorry, I'm a temp, I don't know everyone's name yet. Can I take a message?'

Babs was sure she could hear voices in the background. She slammed the phone down by way of a message and propped the card up on the mantelpiece. Why on earth had Mickey Ingram told Smith that they'd split up, when he of all people would know it wasn't true? She knew Stan was going to be very interested in her caller.

But as usual, she couldn't get him on the blower.

At four that afternoon, in the deserted saloon bar in the Bad Moon in Shadwell, Stan, Cricket and Horner sat around a table talking business. Althea and Donna's 'Uptown Top Ranking' played away in the background. The new landlord knew the drill and had made himself scarce; the blinds were drawn to keep out prying eyes. Stan skipped the small talk and got straight down to the matter at hand. He explained about the mysterious Richard Smith and his enquiries into the equally mysterious disappearance of Denny Brooks six years earlier, leaving his brother's name out of the mix. The two cops, who were suspicious at first, became confused.

'OK. So some bloke's going round asking questions about some bird we've never heard of. How's that got anything to do with us?'

Stan lit a Havana. They went better with his new upmarket image than the Turkish fags. 'You see, boys, that girl is connected with Mickey Ingram and his former knocking shop up in Mile End. Which, in turn, is connected with that fit up we did on Mickey Ingram and his missus up at Snaresbrook. As well as you both getting your end away there at my expense, you understand?'

They finally twigged about the problem. 'I need you two boys to do me a couple of favours. For a start, you can find out who this jam jar belongs to.' Stan gave Horner a scrap of paper with the car registration number Babs had taken. 'And secondly, have a rummage through the filing cabinets and see if your boys collected any info on the disappearance of Denise Brooks back in '72.'

The piece of paper in Stan's hand was left hanging in the

air. Neither of the two cops made a move to take it. Cricket explained, 'It ain't happening. We don't care about some bird from six years back. We can't help. It's too risky.'

Stan knew he had them by the goolies. One word from him and that anti-corruption mob would have them. He waved the paper at them. 'May I remind you that we're all in this tub together. And if that tub should spring a leak, we're all going to drown together.'

Cricket's face darkened. 'What's that supposed to mean? I'm sure you know better than to threaten us.'

Horner took the scrap of paper from Stan and put it in his wallet. 'No problem mate – we'll do that for you–'

Cricket's rage exploded. 'Have you lost a screw?' But his former partner sent him a pointed look.

Horner carried on. 'And we'll see what we can find out about the girl.' He ignored Cricket's dirty look. 'I've got to say, it seems a bit unlikely that this could cause us any problems.'

'Unlikely?' Stan scoffed. 'I've built a career by catering for the unlikely. Al Capone getting nicked for tax evasion was unlikely. I want that information back to me pretty lively.'

Stan wasn't fooled. He knew Cricket and Horner would do to him what he'd helped them do to others. He didn't even blame them really. He'd never trusted people who weren't looking out for number one. He was also pretty sure the memory of what the three of them had got up to in '72 would soon come back to them. They would be looking for a chance to stab him in the back. But there was a difference. He'd been ready to stab them in the back from the beginning.

Forty-Six

Two days later, it took the woman in the jewellers in Bishopsgate ten seconds flat to spot the row of white gold diamond rings. She was dressed to impress, in a long black cashmere coat, shades, and stiletto heels. Her shiny brown hair bounced down her back.

As soon as she reached the counter she slowly pulled off her sunglasses. She glanced at one of the shop assistants.

'You,' she said with all the airs and graces of someone with money to burn. 'There's a ring I wish to see.'

The assistant walked over. As the customer swept her hair back with both hands, the assistant couldn't help but notice the three gold necklaces she wore. All different lengths, nothing showy.

'The third from the left,' the woman instructed.

After seeing those necklaces, the shop assistant couldn't get her keys in quick enough. She figured she was on to a big sale. She set the tray of rings carefully on the glass counter.

'May I suggest Madam try this one.' Of course it was the most expensive.

The woman did. She twisted and turned her finger in the light.

'Madam, if I may say, it truly complements your colouring.'

The high-pitched door buzzer went off. The assistant looked over to see the postman with a few letters in his hand.

'Just one moment.' She hustled over to the door.

As soon as he was in, the postman said, 'You're going to have to sign for this one.' She rushed him over to another counter and bent down to find a pen. She quickly signed for the letter and took the three others he handed her.

As soon as she'd finished, she noticed that her customer was nowhere in sight. *Where could she have . . .? Shit.* She rushed over to the ring tray and noticed two empty spaces – one for the ring she'd encouraged the woman to wear and the next expensive one of the lot. She started trembling. She went over to the letters and opened the first one. Blank paper inside. There were blank papers inside every one. She'd been set up.

Fifteen minutes later, in the public lav on Commercial Street in front of the white Hawksmoor Church, the woman ditched her wig and the postman dumped his disguise. She dumped the three necklaces as well; pure toot from the Roman. The three-necklace trick was a speciality of hers. Wearing three necklaces of different length screamed money, much more than one trussed up in diamonds.

There was no need for chat. She passed him his 'drink' money by way of the second most expensive ring and the other one she palmed herself.

When he'd shifted himself, Mel Ingram turned to the mirror, fluffed out her hair and grinned. Now she had all she needed to sort that slag Babs Miller out.

Two bloody days. That's how long Babs had been trying to get hold of Stan. He gave her a bell just before her mum arrived to take them all to see *Grease* at Mile End Cinema and then off to Vicky Park.

'Alright, Babs, what's happening?' He sounded bleary and vague, as if he'd just got in from a bender.

That got her back up. 'I dunno. Why don't you come back and find out before the girls start to confuse you with the milkman.'

There was a long sigh before he explained, 'Give it a rest; I have to work. I'm doing it for my daughters, ain't I? I can't come back at the moment; I'm down in Cornwall looking at some sites for a project. I'll be a couple of days.'

Properly put out, she switched the phone to her other ear. 'Is that so? I suggest you put your project on hold and get your aris back here; you've got a more urgent one.'

Stan yawned. 'Can't, luv – too much money at stake.'

'I think you'll change your tune when I tell you about the visitor we had.'

'The grim reaper?'

Was this guy for real? 'Yeah, that's right, you have a laugh – still think it's funny when I tell you it was that Richard Smith again? I thought you were sorting him out! How did he get our address?'

Stan wasn't laughing. 'I am sorting him out; I'm waiting for a call about it. What did he want?'

'What he wanted last time, to know about Denny. And another thing, he seems to think we've split up. He got a bit of a shock when he discovered we hadn't. Who is this bloke?' There was a long silence at the other end of the line. Babs broke it by saying, 'And there's another thing. I saw Smith snooping around the estate. Guess where? He was coming out of the Ingrams' – looking very pally with Mickey.'

Stan flew into a rage. 'Mickey Ingram? Why the hell didn't you tell me?'

Babs was tart. 'Oh, I tried – but you're never available, are you?'

The phone nearly vibrated with Stan's anger. 'Alright, I'm coming back. I'll sort Mr Smith and Mr Ingram. I'll see you about two-ish.'

'This afternoon? I thought you were in Cornwall?'

But he'd already hung up.

Cornwall my arse!

Forty-Seven

Babs was right. Stan wasn't in Cornwall but he was near a phone. He called Horner as soon as he'd finished with his wife. 'What's going on? I thought you was looking something up for me. I told you I needed it sharpish.'

'I have. I left a message with the girl at your office. Didn't you get it?'

Stan realised he'd been careless. He hadn't checked in. 'Just tell me.'

'The car registration you wanted? It's good news and bad news. The bad news is the motor's registered to a dentist in Huddersfield, so we're talking a fake set of plates. But I've asked around and apparently this Richard Smith character goes after people who've defaulted on loans. In Maggie Brooks's case, she's got out of paying it back by using the old trick of dying. So Smith's on a commission to get the money back from the relatives. That means her kids. The other kids have got sweet FA, so he's set his sights on Denise. 'Course, everyone's telling him the girl's dead but he don't believe it – well, you wouldn't, would you? That's why he's sticking his beak in.'

Stan wasn't convinced. 'So what's this geezer's real name? I'll go and pay him a visit, just to be on the safe side.'

Horner was steady. 'No need. I'm going to put the frighteners on him. You relax. We'll take care of it.'

'I'd rather speak to him myself.'

Horner was getting the needle. 'What's the matter with you, Stan? You're getting paranoid. I've taken some big risks on your behalf and now you're getting the hump about it? I've told you – I'll fix it. I'll get the paperwork for the loan out of him and we can meet up for a drink and you can have it. That'll prove I'm not taking you for a ride.'

There was a long pause. 'Alright mate. You fix it and we'll have a meet.' Stan put the phone down and thought about what he'd heard.

It was plausible.

It was too plausible.

Cricket was sitting next to Horner, listening to his call with Stan. After the receiver went back Cricket smiled. 'He don't believe you.'

'Of course he don't believe me, the suspicious little sod. Don't worry; he'll soon have a lot more to worry about than the mysterious Mr Smith.' He picked up a file. 'We're going to put Miller out of business for good.'

He laid the file back on the desk so his one-time partner could see the name on the front.

Peter Miller.

'What's got you stewing, luv?' Rosie Wilson asked her daughter.

They were in Victoria Park near the lake after having a lovely trip to see *Grease*. They'd had a grand time, grand-mother, daughter and granddaughter singing along to 'The One That I Want'.

Jen loved coming to Vicky Park. It had loads of space to run around. Babs sometimes took her to the lido, but had decided against it today. Miffed, her bottom lip sticking out, Jen had sulked all the way until she'd got here and decided to have the time of her life. If only it were always that easy to forget your troubles. There were just a few people around, including a woman lying on a blanket, which was a bit odd because the sun wasn't out. Oh well, each to their own.

Babs considered her mum's question as they sat and watched the swans swimming. She didn't want to tell her the full SP about this Richard Smith character but she could certainly put in a few bad words about her other half. 'If you're talking about me and Stan, we've got our problems like any other couple. Mostly we're alright, but sometimes—'

Rosie rocked baby Tiffany. 'Sometimes it can be a real uphill struggle keeping your marriage alive.'

'Peek-a-boo,' Jen shouted as she pushed her head out from behind a tree. She rattled her blue elephant, Mister Silly, at them.

'I see you,' Rosie replied, making Jen laugh. Babs grinned. She was as pleased as Punch that her mum was back in her life and getting on so well with the girls.

She turned her attention back to her mum. 'I didn't realise that you and Dad had your ups and downs.'

'Every couple does. It wouldn't be a marriage otherwise. There was this fancy piece he used to see ...' Babs couldn't help the gasp of surprise. Her dad, George Wilson, cheating on her mum? Never. 'What you're thinking is exactly what I thought,' Rosie continued. 'One of the girls at the sweatshop made it her business to tell me he saw a woman every couple of months at his work—'

'Peek-a-boo,' Jen and Mister Silly said again.

'I see you,' Rosie said and then got on with her story. 'So I went down one night and caught them at it. Caught him teaching her to sew. Turns out this woman wanted to set up her own boutique and needed someone to teach her the ropes.' She smiled as she remembered. 'I did give him a cuff around the ear for not putting me in the picture.'

'I don't think Stan's two-timing me, I just wish he was home more. I always imagined that married life would be me, him and the kids having dinner at the table every night. Says he's away in Cornwall—'

'Cornwall.' A dreamy look covered her mum's face. 'I loved that Poldark. He made me wet my knickers.'

'Mum! I've got children within earshot.' They both burst out giggling.

Rosie continued her free marriage guidance. 'Fair play to your husband, at least he's a worker. Those first few years are hard, because you're trying to set yourselves up for the future and that often means putting in long hours. Your dad worked all the hours God sent so we could afford the rent.'

Babs sighed as she watched two of the swans rubbing their beaks against each other. 'But he goes to all these posh dos and meets some really important people and I wish he'd take me with him. You don't think he's ashamed of me?'

Rosie cuddled Tiffany closer. 'Don't be daft. I only met Stan that one time years back but even then it was as plain as day he was really taken with you. You want to hang on to a man working that hard.'

Babs felt the drops of rain. 'Better get going before the heavens open.' She scanned the park and couldn't see her daughter.

'Jen,' she yelled. 'We're off.'

No answer. Babs stood up. 'Jen, we'll play peek-a-boo with your nan when we get indoors.'

Still no answer. Babs took a few steps forward and really started to look. There was no sign of Jen anywhere. Her heart began jumping.

'Jennifer! Jennifer!' she shouted.

Rosie put Tiffany in her pram. With her hands on her hips, she yelled, 'Jennifer Miller, get here now.' No Jen appeared. At the stricken expression on her daughter's face she calmly said, 'No need to panic, she's around here somewhere.'

But Babs was panicking. 'But where? Where is she?'

She left her mother and started running around the park. Five minutes later she was back, in floods of tears. 'I can't find her anywhere.'

'Stay calm. Let's find one of the park keepers . . .' Her voice dribbled away when they saw a woman and a child walking towards them. Babs' panic turned to rage as they came closer. It was Jen alright, holding onto the hand of that bitch Mel Ingram.

Babs didn't wait for them to reach her but stormed over, fists clenched, ready to commit murder. 'What are you doing with my daughter?' she growled. She picked Jen up and held her close.

Mel smiled smugly. 'I was lying on my blanket minding my own business . . .' – Babs glared hot and hard – 'when this gorgeous little girl came up to me and said she needed to go for a number one—'

Babs sent her child a furious look. 'How many times have I told you not to speak to strangers, eh?'

Jen's face creased up and she started bawling.

'But we're not strangers,' Mel announced sweetly, 'we've got such a long history, me and you.'

Babs got right in her face. *Oh, she wanted to slap her.* 'You stay the fuck away from my kids.'

Mel shook her head. 'Tsk! Tsk! Is that any way for a mum to speak in front of her daughter? You wouldn't want people to say she's being dragged up.'

Mel was packing confidence in spades. What was she up to? 'You followed me, didn't ya?'

'It's a free country.' She turned her back on a fuming Babs and started walking away. Then stopped. 'I nearly forgot, here's Mister Silly.' Mel handed the stuffed elephant back to Jen. 'You're a little cutie, ain't ya?' She patted the child's nose. Babs swung Jen away as if her kid might catch some fatal disease.

When Mel had gone, Babs sternly twisted her tearful daughter to face her. 'What did she do? Did she hurt you?'

Jen shook her tear-stained face, her mouth wobbling. Babs didn't comfort her. Her child had to learn to never, *ever* go near someone she didn't know.

Babs watched her hated enemy disappear into the distance. That bitch had followed them here; she just knew it. That vindictive excuse for a woman was up to something.

Forty-Eight

When Babs got home with the exhausted girls, two coppers were waiting by her front door. Something told her this had to do with that malicious Mel, but she didn't know what. She kept it all peaceful.

'Mum, take the girls in while I find out what these nice gentlemen want.'

Rosie sent her a fretful look but didn't say a word.

The tallest officer spoke. 'We've had a report that a crime has been committed and we need to search your property.'

'What crime is that then?'

'Robbery,' the other cop said simply.

Babs just laughed. 'I don't know who you've been talking to, but I can guess.' She glared across the estate to where the Ingrams lived. 'Be my guest.' She waved her hand at the door. They were going to find fuck all in her place. Probably Mel had called them with some bogus tale just to aggravate her. She wasn't giving the nutter the satisfaction.

Her mum looked properly worried as the coppers moved into the sitting room where she was dealing with the girls.

'These gentlemen just want a bit of a butchers,' Babs said quickly, 'why don't you take the girls into the kitchen for a bite to eat.'

Both of the cops were staring hard at Jen. Now Babs was worried. Why were they looking at her little girl like that?

''Ere, what's going on?'

Her mum tried to shield Jen from the unwelcome visitors, but one of the coppers stepped towards her. 'Miss—'

'It's Mrs Wilson to you,' Rosie snapped.

'Can you please hand me that toy.' He pointed at Mister Silly, dangling from Jen's hand.

Babs couldn't get her head around it. Why would he want Jen's favourite toy? Before she could think it through, her mum reluctantly passed it over. This didn't go down well with Jen. 'Mister Silly, Silly, Silly,' she sobbed.

The officer pressed the toy and turned it this way and that. Eventually he said. 'There's nothing here.'

An angry Babs cut in, ''Course there's nuthin' there, it's a bleedin' stuffed elephant. That crazy woman from across the way has put you up to this.'

The officer held the toy out to Jen. 'I can only apologise for this—'

But before Jen could take the toy, the other cop grabbed it, sending her into crying mode all over again.

'I think there's one place we missed,' he said, slyly.

And there was. Mister Silly's hollow trunk. He stuck his finger all the way up it. Grinned. Pulled out one of the most gorgeous rings Babs had ever seen.

She shouted, 'I've never seen that before in my life.'

Most people on The Devil's Estate were a tad shy about stepping foot in a cop shop and Babs was no different. But she didn't have much choice this time.

'I'm telling you, I was set up by this Melanie Ingram. Perhaps you're in on it!'

The two plods ignored her. Babs kept up her loud

protestations of innocence as the sergeant at the desk booked her in. When she got out of here – if she ever got out of here – she was going to batter Mel until even her mother couldn't recognise her. Fancy using a kid to do her dirty work. Just the thought of that moo near her beautiful daughter made her sick to the stomach.

'I wanna call my husband,' she yelled. But she didn't say it twice. Cornwall or not, he was never around anyway.

Once again, they ignored her. One of them opened a door and the other one pulled her through. What was she going to do? Was she meant to call a brief or something? That other time the disgusting Cricket and Horner had ignored her when she demanded a lawyer and then slung her in the slammer. She couldn't be banged up again. What would happen to her girls? Last time she'd ended up losing her firstborn.

All these thoughts made her mind whirl and she began to tremble.

'I'm under the quack,' she pleaded. 'I need my medication.' She needed one of her Annies badly.

But they just took her down a long, narrow corridor with closed doors on each side. A door opened just as they reached it and a man stepped outside and bumped into Babs.

'I'm sorry,' he said as he grabbed her arms to steady her. Then his hands fell away, as if he'd been burned.

Babs' mouth dropped open. She was face to face with the good looks of Tricky Dickie Smith. In a police station?

'You?' she blurted out.

The cop holding her arm greeted Richard Smith with a nod and a 'Detective–'

Richard Smith swiftly cut in before any more was said. 'May I ask what this woman is doing here?'

Babs was in a daze. *Detective? Fucking hell, he was a*

copper. Her tummy started turning. Had he been playing another part so he could find out about Denny's murder? She couldn't think straight.

Richard Smith pulled one of the officers aside and whispered for a while in his ear. The officer nodded, turned to his colleague and beckoned him over, leaving Babs standing on her own. But she wasn't on her own for long. The two Bill who'd detained her disappeared, and Richard Smith joined her.

'This is all a bit unfortunate.'

'You don't say.' She should've twigged ages ago. Babs gave him a crafty smile and he had the decency to shift his gaze away. His ears and cheeks went beetroot red.

'I might have guessed. Cut your hair and shave your 'tache off – it's obvious. You're still a fine-looking man–'

He gave her a gorgeous smile that she would've appreciated on any other day.

What are you thinking; a fine-looking man, my arse! He's an effing copper!

Babs carried on dissecting him. 'You've got those policeman eyes . . .' Her emotions were riding sky high. 'Is that what you were doing round the Ingrams' the other day? Fitting me up?'

He touched her arm and Babs got that electric shock again. She shook him off.

'This is nothing to do with me,' he said calmly. 'And to prove it, I'll get the charges dropped . . .'

There was bound to be a *but*.

'But only if you have lunch with me and hear me out.'

Mickey slapped his wife across the face.

'I told you not to stick your oar in,' he spat.

Mel touched the cut on her lip and looked back at him defiantly. He didn't scare her. 'She had it coming. Both of those twats have been making a proper Jerry outta you. One of us had to do something about it.'

Mel had gleefully confessed how she'd stitched Babs Miller up as soon as her husband had come in, but instead of a pat on the back, he'd clouted her one. *That's thanks for you.*

He raised his hand again, but she didn't flinch. She pulled herself off the wall and turned to the gawping children. 'What are you lot staring at? Think this is a puppet show? Get out of my sight.' Donna and Tommy didn't need telling twice and Donna took snoozing Stacey with her.

She turned back to him and softened her voice like she used to in the old days.

'I was only thinking of us. Restoring our self-respect.'

Mickey took a deep breath, calming down. 'So she's down the nick. What if she starts blabbing about that girl? It wasn't until she started mouthing off about that Denny in court back in '72 I clocked she even knew the girl.' He tapped the side of his head. 'Fucking think, will ya. Before we know it the plod will be at our door wanting answers to questions they should know nuthin' about. And what happens if Stan finds out, eh?'

Mel wrapped her arms around herself. For once her nitwit of a fella was right. She'd been so intent about getting at Stan she hadn't thought it all through. It had still been a real treat seeing the coppers take that bitch away, though.

Mickey's voice intruded on her thoughts. 'We've already had Richard Smith sticking his snout in.' He grabbed Mel's mouth and twisted it. 'Keep that shut.'

Forty-Nine

Babs should have walked. Blanked him, like Stan had told her to. But she was too shocked. She was also relieved. Now she wouldn't have to rely on Stan to find out who the guy was. She thought bitterly about how little she trusted her husband.

She didn't need to worry about the girls because her mum was looking after them. At first she insisted Richard take her for a nibble down Hackney way; being seen breaking bread with a plod was not a good look on The Devil. But he promised her he wasn't stationed in the East End and no one knew him there, so she agreed to go to a local greasy spoon. The music playing on the radio, Bill Haley's 'Rock Around The Clock', matched the Rockabilly hairstyle of the old geezer who owned the place.

She asked for a cuppa but after seeing him order the full works thought, *sod it, he's paying*, and decided to have the most expensive thing on the menu. A slap-up breakfast – toast, fried bread, three sausages, two rashers of bacon, bubble and chips. No way was she going to be able to scoff that lot, but that wasn't the point. As long as he was out of pocket, that would keep her nice and chirpy. While they waited, Babs tried to work him out. He still looked like Poldark to her. A very good-looking Poldark indeed.

As soon as their food arrived, he got down to business. 'Since you know who I am now, I'm going to be frank with you. I'm a detective working out of Scotland Yard in a special department with specific duties. My name isn't Richard Smith, but you can call me that anyway.'

Babs mumbled, 'Tricky Dickie, more like.'

Her disdain didn't deter him. 'I'm currently working on a difficult case but I can't tell you what it is. I'm not even telling my colleagues at the local police station what I'm up to. They think I'm doing a traffic survey. But I'll tell you straight off, I'm not interested in, nor am I after, your husband, Mickey Ingram or your good self. I'm not interested in Denny, either. But you've got some information that would help with my enquiries. It's about what happened at Mickey and Mel's trial in 1972.'

Babs stiffened. She wasn't mad keen on facing a perjury charge. 'I dunno. I just gave evidence. Why don't you talk to the judge?'

One of his eyebrows arched as he smiled at her. 'That wasn't what I had in mind. I need to look at the broader picture. You know – get some background, a bit of light and colour.'

Babs knew she had to be careful. She took it for granted that this cop was lying to her because she took it for granted the cops were always lying. But in this case she assumed it even more. She'd seen Richard go into the Ingrams'. It made sense that he'd enlisted Mickey's help to untangle what had happened. But had Mickey played along to stuff up Stan and get his revenge? What didn't make sense was why Smith thought she'd help him shaft her own husband. But what she didn't share with him was that over the years – since Stan had started behaving like a proper twat – she'd begun questioning Stan's whole

story about Mel forging her name on those house deeds
and his on that police statement. If it was forgery, it was a
bloody stellar one. She was too old to be anyone else's fall
girl, even her old man's.

'Sorry, Tricky Dickie. It's not happening.'

'I can understand why you're not eager to help.'

He knew something. He was playing her. She decided to
play detective herself. 'Tell me, Richard – what on earth makes
you think I would tell you anything?'

He studied some chips he'd forked before admitting, 'I
messed up there. My understanding was that you and Stan had
split up in some acrimony and I thought you might be willing
to help. But it seems I was given the wrong information.'

Not that 'they've split up' bollocks again. 'Who's been
bending your ear with that codswallop?'

His soft grey eyes were deadpan. 'Just something I turned
up.'

'I see. And is Mickey Ingram helping? I saw you go into his
gaff.'

Richard looked pained. 'I was in discussions with a view to
him helping me out. But he seems to have changed his mind.
Are you sure you don't want to help? I've told you, I'm not
after Stan.'

'I'm not helping the law, I don't care who you're after.'

'I admire your loyalty, Babs. But it's misplaced. Stan doesn't
tell you everything.'

'What do you mean by that? What things?'

He said nothing for a moment, but then: 'It's in your interest to tell Stan nothing about our meeting. You need to stop
thinking about your husband and think about your children's
future instead.'

That sounded like a threat if she'd ever heard one. But what
worried her more were these 'things' she didn't know about.

What was he not telling her? And why did it feel like he was sure he had a way to get her to talk?

Stan was back from 'Cornwall'.

Babs gave him chapter and verse about what had gone on with Mel at the park, but he didn't seem that interested. He waited until her mum had gone before showing where his real interest lay. 'Right – what did this Smith bloke say when he came round the other day?'

It had taken Babs ages to get her mum to believe that the Bill weren't pressing charges. Then and only then had Rosie been willing to leave, after she'd given her granddaughters huge kisses and hugs.

Babs didn't answer Stan straight away. She couldn't get those 'things' she didn't know out of her head. She inspected her old man. Stan was in his trademark three-piece suit but she noticed it was of a higher quality than usual, tailor made. Her dad had taught her all about the difference between off-the-peg and made-to-measure. He was also wearing a gold disc watch and a flash bracelet. She gave him a chilly stare. 'Come into some money? And might your daughters be seeing some of it?'

Stan got defensive. 'I hired the clobber. I'm in business, looks count . . .'

'Have you found who this Richard Smith is yet?' she asked innocently, playing it dumb. The mask was off now. She didn't trust her own husband any more. He hadn't been in Cornwall and she didn't believe he was borrowing his flash clobber either. *Stan wearing someone else's clothes like he'd been rummaging around in a charity shop? You must be joking.*

'I've heard things but my enquiries are ongoing. That's why I'm back.'

'What things?' Babs was coming to despise that word.

'Never you mind.'

Here we go again, treating me like a mutt only fit for a pat on the head. Babs had to restrain herself from twisting her mouth. She told him about Mel Ingram's little caper with the ring but skipped the part where Richard had got her off. Instead, she wanted to know what he was going to do about it. Stan didn't answer her. He went to their bedroom. Babs was in the middle of downing some pills when he reappeared in workman's trousers and boots, a ripped turtleneck and a donkey jacket. He stood in front of the mirror and adjusted a flat cap, which he pulled down low over his forehead so his face was partly concealed.

She frowned. 'Stan, what are you doing?'

'I'm going to see a man about a dog.' He went into the kitchen. She followed him. He took a bread knife and headed for the front door.

The blood drained from her face. 'Stan, what are you planning on doing?'

But he ignored her, heading out across the estate.

Fifty

Stan picked up speed as he approached the Ingrams' front door. He wanted to get this over with. He hammered with his fist. Mel answered, and looked at him with a mixture of surprise, fear and contempt. 'Well, look who dropped off the back of a lorry.'

Stan looked her up and down. 'Blimey babe, you've let yourself go, ain't ya? I remember when you were a peach. Now you look like a potato that's been left in the sun too long.'

'Fuck you.'

She tried to shut the door on him but he was too quick. His steel-toed boot wedged in the gap and he began to push it open. 'Is the old man in, Mel? I need a word. By the way, that was a bit naughty, you and the ring.'

She tried desperately to keep him out, but he was too strong. 'He ain't in.'

'You won't mind if I have a quick butchers around then?' He put his hand in her face and pushed her backwards.

Mickey was in the front room, watching the racing, apparently oblivious to the commotion. He looked up in shock. 'What the fuck are you doing here? I thought we'd cleared things up. I've shown the missus what-for for playing silly buggers with Babs, no harm done I hope. I'll go down the nick myself and get her off the hook.'

Stan took a seat. 'Babs is back home. You wanna keep that missus of yours on a lead. Nuthin' would make me happier than to leave it at that. But that was then and this is now and we need to clear up a little misunderstanding.'

Mel glowered at him. 'Kick him out Mickey; he's probably here to grass you up again.'

Stan shook his head. 'That's nice, ain't it? I come round to clear the air and his missus is mouthing off like her husband still counts for something. That's charming. I'll tell you what, droopy drawers, why don't you go and organise a nice cuppa and some gingernuts. That's if you haven't eaten them all, which judging by your figure you have.'

Mel turned to Mickey. 'You gonna let this cocky cunt talk to me like that?'

Mickey looked at Mel and then at Stan before saying quietly, 'Go and make some tea Mel. I'll sort this out.'

She slammed the door behind her. Stan looked around the front room and felt almost sorry for his old sparring partner. Once Mickey had been the top geezer and he had been his side-kick. Now look at him, living in a piss-poor flat with run-down furniture and cheap rugs to cover the holes in the carpet. Stan had heard that Mickey was mouthing off about how he was still a big shot but there was no evidence of it in his drum. He made a mental note that while Mickey had once been a wiry fighter, he'd become a bit of a pudding like his wife. Stan, who spent his spare time in boxing gyms, knew he could take him now. There would be no repeat performance of the hiding he'd taken in the solicitor's office. He could work this fat slob over.

Stan picked up a fake porcelain figurine of a shepherdess sitting on a glass coffee table. The glass had a crack in it and the paint on the figure was flaking. Stan turned it over to find 'Made in Taiwan' printed on the bottom. Fancy being reduced to living surrounded by tat. It was tragic really.

'Alright, what's the problem? Let's sort it out.'

Stan clasped his hands together. It was obvious that Mickey knew what the problem was. It was all over his face. 'Don't play the silly girl with me, bruv. You know what the problem is. And I've got to say I'm disappointed. Very disappointed. I know we've had our differences but I thought you was better than this. I really did.'

Mickey avoided Stan's eyes. 'I don't know what you're going on about. Talk some sense and I'll help you out.'

Stan picked up the figurine again, intending to drop it to make his point. But it wasn't valuable enough. He put it down again. 'What I'm talking about is your new friend. What's he calling himself round here? Richard Smith? Napoleon Bonaparte? Don't really matter.' Mickey's eyes were darting around like a pinball machine but he kept silent. 'Oh – you didn't realise I knew? Let me tell you something, my friend; you better believe I know most things round here. I can afford a lot of friends and they keep me posted.'

'I don't know no Richard Smith.'

Stan massaged his fingers together. 'I know you're bitter, Mickey. I understand that. You don't want to be a good loser, that's your business. But this is going too far. You know that – you're a geezer.'

Mickey finally caught his eye. 'This has got nish to do with you. It's just to help me out. I ain't taking you on, I'm playing him. It's all part of the game.' Then he added grimly, 'You should know, you've played it often enough.'

Stan rose to his feet, knocking over the coffee table as he did so. 'I ain't getting through to you, am I?' He patted the knife in his breast pocket to make sure it was still available. He'd been looking forward to this moment ever since '72. It was the one thing he'd been denied when he'd taken his former friend down. The opportunity to beat the living crap out of him. He clenched his fists. 'Perhaps I can get it through another way.'

Mickey jumped out of his chair. 'Stan, you've got it all wrong. Smith is in the gambling racket. I think he's interested in making a move on some of your properties, you get me? I ain't got a clue what he wants them for.'

Stan's face lit up with fire and fury. 'You're forgetting who I am if you think I'm taking the bollocks you're shovelling my way. Who the fuck is Smith?'

Mickey ran out of the flat, knocking Mel out of the way. Stan took off after him. Mel was screaming. The kerfuffle attracted the attention of passers-by and neighbours. They stopped to watch at windows and on balconies. There wasn't much in the way of entertainment on these estates and Stan was determined to put on a good show. And to make it very clear what the consequences of crossing him were.

Mickey was already faltering and gasping. He called out, 'Get the Bill down here, I'm being attacked.'

They didn't seem inclined to do so. Stan broke into a trot and soon caught up with his pathetic quarry. He grabbed hold of his vest and pulled him backwards. 'You need to decide whose side you're on. Let me help you make the right decision.'

He leaned back and then head-butted Mickey's nose. He felt the soft flesh crush and the bone behind absorb the full force of the blow. Stunned, Mickey staggered backwards but the shock seemed to keep him on his feet. He sneezed and puffed blood. Stan landed a right on his left cheekbone. It landed badly and it took a second, better-aimed blow to the right before Mickey toppled over like a sack of spuds. Stan looked up and around, hoping the gathering crowd would give him some credit. But they seemed to feel they'd been short changed by such a one-sided scrap. People started shouting out:

'C'mon, Mickey! Show some life, mate, for fuck's sake.'

'Where's the law? I've got a tenner on this bout and I've been ripped off. It's a fix.'

'What division is your old man supposed to be in, Mel? He looks like a super-fat-fuck heavyweight to me. He needs to lose a few pounds.'

As Mickey tried to get to his feet, two female arms wrapped themselves around Stan's neck, accompanied by screaming. He wrapped his hands around Mel's wrists and pulled her off. He was tempted to give her a slap but decided that wouldn't go down well. He shoved her to one side and turned back to his ex-friend, now on his feet but completely out of it. Stan knew the sporting thing to do was call it a day and help him back to his flat. But this was business. He slammed another right-hander across his face and it was clear he wouldn't be getting up any time soon. There was scattered applause from the windows and balconies.

'That's enough, Stan.' Only when he heard Babs' stern voice did he realise she had a ringside seat too.

But it wasn't enough. He delivered a savage kick to Mickey's ribs, then knelt down and whispered so no one else could hear, 'Who is Smith?'

But Mickey was too senseless to answer.

Fifty-One

Stan swaggered into the Bad Moon. A jukebox in the corner was playing Blondie but it wasn't a very good one. The needle was stuck and Debbie Harry kept repeating, 'Denis . . . Denis . . . Denis . . .' until the landlord kicked it into silence.

Stan said, 'A glass of red plonk.'

His upmarket life had introduced him to red wine and he was becoming quite a connoisseur; well, that's what he thought.

The landlord creased up. 'Red wine? 'Ere, Stan, are you turning a bit funny?' Then he nearly jumped two feet in the air when he realised what he'd said. He raised his hands in surrender and begged, 'Just ribbing you, no need to take offence.'

Stan ordered a pint instead and sat alone near the window, which had once given a view out on the docks. The days when the area had been a constant flow of people and vehicles, of ships' horns and clanking chains, were over. The docks were long finished and pubs like this were ghosts of the places they used to be. The night sky looked naked without the cranes and the air was still without the noise from warehouses and ships.

He remembered the evening at the strip show when he told Lord Tilgate the East End would rise again and it was just a question of buying up and waiting. As he looked out over the shadows and desolation, he couldn't help wondering how long the wait was going to be. The property company he ran that Lord Tilgate had agreed to front had bought all over East London and he had the key points covered. He was making a lot of money from rent and various other property wrinkles but he wasn't the tycoon he'd been planning to be. When he saw Lord Tilgate, the canny old goat would say, 'Oh hello, Miller – is Mile End like Chelsea yet?' He still needed Tilgate on the company's letterhead so he resisted the temptation to say. 'Dunno – are you still screwing black tarts?'

But what really needled him was that it was true. The East End hadn't risen again. Rather the reverse, it seemed to be sinking fast.

'Hello, Stan, glad you could make it. We know you're busy.'

He looked up to find friendly neighbourhood bent cops Cricket and Horner.

'Hello, boys. Park your bums. I'll get you a drink.' He gestured at the landlord. 'So what's got you in such a pickle?'

Horner looked at Cricket, who looked back at Horner. They were acting like they were about to break the news that a child had been found brutally murdered.

Horner did the talking, as per usual. 'We're here to give you a steer. Word at the Yard is that you're in big trouble.' He checked to see no one was listening. 'Apparently, there's a case review going on down in the murder department.'

Stan studied the men carefully. He knew them. He knew all their tricks. 'That's interesting. And what's my steer?'

'You're in the frame, mate. It seems they're going over the murder of your brother Pete and your name keeps cropping up. Nothing to do with us obviously, but we thought you'd like to know.'

Stan sighed. 'That's a bit strange, because he wasn't murdered. He committed suicide. Or maybe it was an accident. Have they seen the coroner's report?'

Cricket leaned over the table. 'They've seen it but they don't believe it. The lead detective is a right bastard called Ericson. Once he gets his teeth into a case, that's it, he don't stop. He's already interviewed the receptionist at the B&B where Pete was staying. Pete had a visitor the day he was murdered but the receptionist claimed she couldn't describe him. After Ericson slapped her around a bit and showed her pictures of you, she's playing ball. She's willing to testify you're the guy. You're deep in the crap here.'

Stan drummed his fingers on the table. 'Is that so?'

Horner took over. 'Right in the crap, mate.'

'So, tell me, why would this Ericson be investigating a suicide from six years ago?'

'Who knows? Ericson's the ambitious type. He ain't had a collar in ages so he's probably gone back over the files and decided you're his man. A respectable businessman like yourself, he gets you up the Bailey and puts you away and he's moving up the ladder. You might have read that the Met's been cleaned up but there's still characters like Ericson around, willing to bend the rules.'

Stan's smile widened. 'Well, quite – they're still employing you two farts for a start.'

Horner swallowed the insult. 'We can help but only if you level with us. He was your brother; you must have known where he was. We're not saying you killed him, that's ridiculous. But tell us what happened. Did you arrange the B&B? Maybe went down there and said hello?'

It was what Stan had always feared. Pete was still messing things up, despite being brown bread for six years. Stan had no idea whether there really was an inquiry into Pete's death going on. He'd made a mistake in beating Mickey so badly he couldn't tell him who Richard Smith was. He wasn't sure he could believe him even if he had. Something was going on, though, and he needed to know what. But one thing was certain; these two pricks were there to screw him over. That was the great thing about Horner and Cricket, they were so reliably unreliable.

'Alright, lads, you've been honest with me and I'll be honest with you. I need to unburden myself about Pete. I feel gutted about it. I'm to blame. I'll tell you what really happened.'

Cricket and Horner looked at each other in shock. 'This is strictly between you and us. You're among friends.'

Stan's face dropped. 'Pete told me he was going away but he didn't say where. He seemed on top of the world. I couldn't see how much pain he was in and I should have done. When I heard he topped himself, I felt terrible. I should have been there for my brother and I wasn't. I'll have to live with that for the rest of my life.'

Cricket and Horner sat back in disgust. It was Cricket who finally said flatly, 'Yeah. That's terrible.'

Stan seemed nearly in tears. 'I'm sorry, boys, I've got to go and have a weep.'

Horner hissed, 'We understand. Look, we're seeing Ericson for lunch tomorrow, we'll get an update. Let's say we meet here later tomorrow so we can let you know what's what.'

'That's good of you.'

Stan walked off. The walls were closing in but he was still Stan Miller. And if the walls were being pushed in by the likes of Cricket and Horner, he didn't have too much to worry about.

Inside the Gents, Cricket was frothing at the mouth like an angry dog as he griped, 'I really thought he was going to give us something there. Fucking waste of time ...'

Horner stretched his lips in a cruel smile. 'You heard the man, he's meeting us tomorrow. We get him talking again. Push him a bit more—'

'The bastard's too smart,' his former partner cut in.

Horner's smile deepened. 'But this time I'm going to make sure he cracks. And we'll come wired for sound.'

Cricket frowned. 'What do you mean?'

'I'll stick a portable cassette in my jacket to record every last one of his incriminating words.'

'Mum, why are you sad?' Jen asked Babs.

Jen was such a sensitive soul. She could always tell when her mum was upset. Babs still felt distraught after the stroke Mel had pulled and Stan brawling with Mickey in front of the whole estate. What a show-up. She didn't want them to be one of those families who let their dirty laundry blow in the wind for all to see. Why couldn't he have beaten the shit out of the fat fuck behind closed doors? Naturally, as soon as he'd done a number on Mickey, Stan had been off – an important business dinner this time.

At least she'd made a decision about the copper. Richard Smith might press her buttons but she wasn't telling him a dickie bird. When Stan got back she was telling him the lot. A wife did not grass up her old man. Final.

'Nothing, baby.' Babs tried to brush off her misery for her child's sake. She still had two kids to bring up and what was the point in getting down in the dumps? Time she snapped out of it. In a cheerful voice she said, 'Shall we pop some new clobber on Bunty?'

Jen leapt down with a shout of joy. If there was one thing she loved, it was dressing Bunty up in the cut-out clothes she came with. They spent the next half hour on the sitting room carpet. Bunty went on a picnic. Bunty went swimming in the lido in Vicky Park. Bunty went shopping down the Roman.

A gleeful Jen announced, 'I like this.' She pointed at the long, red maxi dress Bunty was togged out in.

'Where's she going in her knockout dress?' Babs felt a million times better.

But before an excited Jen could answer, a fist banged at the front door. 'Keep it down,' Babs shouted as she got up, 'you'll wake up the baby.' Then she realised *she* was likely to wake up Tiffany with her yelling.

She could've committed murder when she saw the cop from hell, Richard Smith. 'This is the second time you've come knocking at my door. Don't you understand what "no" means?'

In a loud voice, so any and everyone could hear, he informed her, 'Barbara Miller, I'm arresting you for perverting the cause of justice.'

'You what?' Babs could only gape at him. 'You're having a laugh.'

He whipped out a pair of handcuffs. 'I won't use these if you come peacefully.'

Babs shook her head, raging. 'I'd like to see you and whose army try.'

He reached for her and Babs let fly with a right hook that glanced off his cheekbone. He winced but kept on, grabbing her arm and twisting it behind her back.

''Ere, what the heck's going on?' Cheryl cried out from her doorway.

'Get your bloody hands off her,' Beryl screamed from the other side.

Both women rushed at him like avenging angels, but he pulled Babs in front of him and snarled, 'I'm an officer of the law. If you touch me, you'll go down for assault.'

Both women held back, but their anger was at boiling point. 'What's she done?' Cheryl demanded.

He ignored them as he cuffed Babs and dragged her along the landing. Babs could hear Jen crying her eyes out and

Tiffany howling a storm. 'Take them to my mum's,' she belted out. 'Stan . . .' But Richard Smith didn't allow her to finish as he dragged her away.

With the whole estate looking on, Richard Smith dumped Babs into the passenger seat of his car.

Fifty-Two

'I don't know what you're up to, fella, but you're making a massive mistake.'

Richard said nothing. He'd taken the cuffs off as soon as he'd locked the car doors. They'd been driving for ages. But he kept it zipped, just like he had with all the other questions she'd flung at him. The geezer was obviously losing his marbles, dragging her off like that on a bogus charge. Then Babs' heart fell. Unless he'd found out about them stitching up the Ingrams years back ... But that just didn't make sense. Why would a cop give a rat's arse about those lowlifes getting banged up? There was something else going on here and she had the right to know what.

'Tell me what's going on, matey.' No answer; no surprise there.

Babs shivered. She'd been taken away from her children, just like the last time she'd been banged up. She couldn't go through that heartache again.

'I don't know what you want!' she screamed. Then she noticed the sign on the road for Canonbury.

'What are we doing in Islington? I thought you were taking me to the cop shop?' She was getting scared. 'Mister, if you try and do anything—'

'Put a sock in it,' he finally said. 'Just relax and enjoy the ride.'

Cheeky beggar! Knowing she had no alternative, Babs kept it shut until they rolled into a gorgeous Georgian square. He cut the engine and warned her, 'I don't want no more earache, you got it? All you've got to do is wait and watch.'

Babs scrunched her face up. *Wait for what? Watch for who?* She didn't like this one bit but knew she had no choice.

Nearly fifteen minutes later, a flash shiny red Merc stopped outside one of the houses. Babs moved closer to the window. A young woman stepped out of the car, laughing. She was dressed to the nines in a lace blouse under a sleeveless vest and a cranberry-coloured skirt that blew in the wind. She looked like she was having the time of her life. A man appeared, his head down, looking at the baby he held in his arms. He wore a bulky cardie and flared tartan trousers. The woman whispered in his ear. Whatever she said had him laughing out loud. He raised his head.

Babs' heart stopped. 'Stan?' She twisted to the man next to her. 'What the fuck's going on?

'That, Mrs Miller, is your husband's other wife and child.'

'Wife?' Babs stared at Richard as if he'd lost his mind. She rammed her fingers into her chest. 'I'm his missus. You ask anyone—'

'Of course you're his wife—'

'Then what are you rabbiting on about?'

He took a long breath. 'She's his other wife. He married her after he married you.'

'No – no, no.' Babs wasn't having this. 'You've got it all wrong.' She laughed like a crazy woman. 'Stan with another wife? He can't even deal with the one he's got. Pull the other one.'

She had been paralysed by overwhelming shock. Now she was going into denial. Her Stan a . . . What was that bloody word? *A bigamist.* Stanley Miller tying the knot with someone else while he was married to her? *Nah. It's a wind-up. This Richard is playing me for a proper mug.*

'He's probably helping out the dopey cow.' Babs could live with an affair. That was what some blokes were like. But not another marriage. Not another kid.

Richard held out a piece of paper. Babs stilled. Wouldn't touch it. There was something about it that put the frighteners on her. She knew it was going to change her life forever.

Defensively, she folded her arms. 'What's that then?'

Richard's voice softened, but it wasn't gentle. 'Read it.' He dropped it like a grenade into her lap as he got the car back on the road.

I don't have to do this. I don't have . . . Babs picked it up, her mouth set in a stubborn line. She unfolded it. The large words across the top jumped out at her:

CERTIFIED COPY OF AN ENTRY OF MARRIAGE

A marriage certificate. Babs' mind flashed back to the day she and Stan had received their own. She looked at the names.

Clare Fullerton-Green
Stanley Miller

Babs' heart nosedived. It can't be true. No way. She gritted her teeth as she read the rest of the information. Then her lips stretched in a grim smile.

Babs chucked the paper into Richard's face, wishing she was belting him a good one instead. 'The age of the groom's all wrong. It says he was thirty-one when this marriage took place. My Stan is thirty-one now. You've got this wrong big time, Tricky Dickie.'

Richard seemed impatient. 'Use your brain, Babs. If he put his proper age it'd be easy to track that he was already married. This is how bigamists operate. They change a little bit here, a little there—'

Babs shook her head. Shit, she needed an Annie. 'You're trying to pull a fast one, make me do what you want.'

Richard wouldn't let it go. 'It makes sense from his point of view. He's in property, a man of business. He needs to wine and dine clients at home. He can't do that at your place. What message would "The Devil's Estate" send out? He needs some-where to take them to. Hence the house. The second wife's dad is loaded and he paid for it.'

'He can only have the one wife and that's me!'

Richard ignored her. 'And he needs the right wife to act as hostess. With the greatest of respect, Babs, that isn't really your thing. Is it? Entertaining toffs? But, she's got breeding, she can play the part. I see it all the time. A nice attractive girl like you marries a bloke and thinks they know them. Years later they find out they don't know them at all.'

'Bollocks,' Babs snarled. 'If he wants another wife, why are we still married? Why's he had two kids with me? Why's he keep turning up? If he wanted another woman, he'd throw me overboard, no problem. I know him.'

He shook his head as he swung his motor in a tight right. 'Stan can't just kick you to the side. You know where the bodies are buried – so to speak. He wants to keep you sweet in case you go to the law in revenge. And of course there's an added advantage – you can't force a wife to give evidence against her husband. You don't think he knows that? Stanley Miller is always two steps ahead.'

Babs could feel even her miserable life slipping away from her. 'More bollocks – he knows I'm not a grass. He doesn't have to worry about that whatever he's done.'

Smith sighed. 'Maybe – but the Stan Millers of this world think, *why take the risk?* What do you want me to do to prove it? Kick in their bedroom door and take photos?'

'Shut up.' Babs couldn't take much more of this. Her head felt like it was coming off her shoulders. She needed a pill badly.

'Face it – he's thrown you aside. But he's not throwing you out; he's not stupid. If you help me . . .'

Babs lashed out at him, making the car zigzag along the road. He pushed her back with one hand as he settled the steering wheel back into his grasp. Babs reared up and clobbered his ear. The car veered onto the pavement as she let fly, hitting him any which way she could. He tried his best to restrain her, but she kept at him. He took a sharp turn that had Babs tumbling back into her seat. The car slammed to a stop.

Babs lunged back up, but Richard grabbed her by the wrists. They twisted together, Babs pushing at his chest, Richard shoving her back down. Babs' blouse slid down and skirt up, exposing her bare thigh. He managed to lock his leg around her, holding her in place. Both breathed heavily, their eyes only inches apart. They moved at the same time; Babs up, Richard down. Their lips fused in a hungry, almost angry kiss. Babs thrust her fingers into his hair as their tongues tangled. Her hands moved desperately to his trousers and fought with the zip. He pushed her skirt up. Babs kicked her knickers away and they went at it like young lovers who had been desperate for a long time. Babs threw her head back, her mind in turmoil.

You shouldn't be doing this, you bloody idiot . . . but it's so good.

Babs clung onto him for dear life as they came together. Richard collapsed against her. Babs stroked his hair as their breathing settled down.

Babs said mockingly, 'Typical man, aren't you? Serve it up on a plate and out comes your knife and fork.'

'Well, I hope you enjoyed my cutlery.'

He eased off her. She sorted herself out. They turned their heads to each other and simply stared.

In unison they blurted, 'That shouldn't have happened.'

Silence. Then Babs said, 'I still don't believe a word about Stan.'

Richard sighed heavily. 'You know I'm telling the truth. Stan goes away on business for long stretches of time, right? Now you know where he goes. He's a clever bugger to have pulled it off for so long. He's making a monkey out of you and you can get him back. Help me.'

Babs squeezed her eyes tight, feeling burned out. Plus she'd just done the dirty. Not just with anyone, but a copper. She would not allow herself to believe what he was saying. 'Drop me off in Whitechapel, so I can pick up my kids from my mum's.'

Richard could see from her face that there was no point talking more about it. They both stayed schtum until they were parked outside her parents' house.

Richard grabbed her hand when she reached for the door. 'You know what you've got to do, Babs. He's off in North London having a whale of a time with his fancy floozy while you and your girls are scraping to make ends meet in the back end of nowhere. I like you.'

She knew the last had sod all to do with Stan.

'I'm married,' she shot back.

'So is your husband. Twice over.'

Babs wrenched free, opened the door and moved as quickly as her legs could take her. She heard him call out, 'Do the right thing, for you and your children.'

Fifty-Three

Babs knocked urgently at her parents' door as Richard's motor disappeared in the distance. *Can't believe I just had it off.* A tiny smile played on Babs' lips. She'd give Richard Smith one thing; he knew how to use his truncheon.

Her parents' door opened. Unfortunately, it was her father.

Startled, they stared at each other, struck dumb. The old animosity bristled between them. They were both up for a row, regardless of who might be earwigging.

Her dad's fingers grew white around the doorframe. 'I thought we'd made it clear you're not welcome here.'

He tried to close the door, but Babs pressed her hand against it. 'Believe me, I wouldn't be here now if I didn't have to.' She puffed her chest out. 'I've come for my kids.'

'Your kids?'

'What's this kerfuffle?' Rosie cried out behind George. Her face softened when she clocked her daughter. 'What's up, luv?'

George Wilson did his nut. 'You've been seeing her against my wishes, haven't you? I told you—'

Both women cried out, 'Oh, go inside and suck on your pipe.'

George's mouth flapped open. He took one look at his missus' stern face and did an about turn.

Rosie waved her hand. 'Don't worry about him. He's all bark and no bite. Come on in.'

Babs hesitated. It felt like betraying Desiree to go inside. Her dad clearly still wouldn't accept his granddaughter even though she'd been in the ground for six years.

Babs stayed where she was. 'I'll wait here. Bring them—'

With an exasperated sigh, her mum took her arm and pulled her into the house. Rosie stared right into her daughter's eyes. 'Both you and your dad are as stubborn as each other. One of these days you're both going to have to get this sorted.'

Babs tightened her lips. Maybe her mum was right, but what her dad had done was wicked. She had enough troubles without adding more. 'Mum, I just want to take the girls home.'

Rosie frowned. 'The girls? Why would I have the girls?'

Babs was worried. 'Never mind. Cheryl's probably still got them. Can I get on the blower to double check?'

'Stay for a cuppa, love, you look worn out.'

'Not until I know the girls are alright. Plus, I'm not stopping where I'm not wanted.' She gazed pointedly in the direction of the sitting room.

When Babs got off the phone, she looked in a worse state.

'What's up?' Rosie didn't like the paleness of her daughter's skin.

A grim-faced Babs was heading for the door as she answered. 'Cheryl doesn't have them. She says she brought them around here but you and Dad weren't in—'

Rosie nodded. 'We must've still been around Cousin Phil and Kate's.' Seeing the terrible, stricken look on her daughter's face, she urgently added, 'What's the matter?'

'Something happened.' She waved her hand; no way was she telling her mum about Tricky Dickie and Stan. 'I told her to bring the girls here. Seeing as you weren't in she got a bit muddled about something I said and took them somewhere else.' Babs recalled saying Stan's name but never finishing the sentence because Richard Smith had started dragging her off.

'Where are my grandbabies?' Rosie tentatively asked.

'Around Stan's mum's.'

'Well, that's alright then.'

'No it ain't. Her place is the Miller House of Horrors.'

Shell Miller laughed her head clear off as she watched *George and Mildred*.

She stared down at her baby granddaughter. 'I do love it when he calls her Mildew,' she told her. She'd been surprised when some woman dropped the kids off. Stan wouldn't have her near his kids. Nor that slapper he'd married. She'd only seen the eldest girl once and this was the first time seeing the baby. She hadn't even known they had a new nipper. What was the world coming to when your own son wouldn't let you in spitting distance of your grandbabies?

Shell groaned as the telly zipped off. She didn't fancy getting up – her old legs weren't as good as they used to be – but she needed a coin to get it up and running again.

'Fifty p! Fucking fifty p!' Charlie squawked.

'Shut up, you daft bird, you'll wake the little one.' Her eyes filled with tears as she gazed at the baby sleeping beside her. How could Stan have kept her away from this little angel? The woman who'd left her said she could make a bit of a fuss, but the mite hadn't let out a 'boo' since she'd been here.

'Fifty p! Fucking fifty p!' Charlie kept at it. Bloody hell, she was going to strangle that bird.

Shell struggled out of her chair, huffing and creaking all the way. As soon as she was on her feet, the front door went. She smacked her lips together; probably Stan or that Babs come to get the kids. Well, she had a few choice words for them!

She staggered towards the door.

'Oh, it's you,' she sneered. 'My son too chicken to face me?'

Babs pushed past her. 'I want my children.'

'Not even a thank-you-very-much for looking out for them,' Shell grumbled as she followed her daughter-in-law into the main room. She saw the way Babs' gaze took in the dirty carpet and bottles of Guinness and cider strewn on the floor. Judgemental moo. It wasn't her fault that she didn't have the energy to take care of the place. Her next door said she should get one of them home helps. Go begging to the council? Never.

When Charlie saw her daughter-in-law he fluttered his wings and squawked, 'Stan! Stan! Stan!' Babs had only been around here with her son; no wonder the mynah expected him to come through the door. And the only reason her boy came around, she thought resentfully, was to make sure that Charlie was doing alright. What would he do if she boiled the old bird up in a pot one day? That stretched her tight mouth into a smile.

Babs spotted Tiffany on the settee, but got flustered when she couldn't see Jen.

'Where's Jennifer?'

Shell harrumphed. 'The little madam was giving me a load of cheek. Kept boo-hooing and making a right racket—'

Babs got right in her face. 'Where's my daughter?'

'There's something wrong with that kid. She needed a good dose to teach her some manners.'

Babs grabbed the front of her dress. 'If you've touched my little girl—'

'Khazi! Khazi! Outdoor khazi!' Charlie blared.

'Shut up!' Shell shouted.

Babs let go of her, her eyes nearly coming out of her head. 'So help me Shell if you've ...' She never finished, as she rushed towards the back of the house.

A panicked Babs heard Jen's sobs as soon as she reached the nasty outside loo. She wrenched the door open to find her precious little girl holding her flaming red arm. The toilet stall itself meanwhile was as cold as ice. What person would do this to a tiny child? Sheila Miller was as batty as a fruit and nut bar.

'Baby,' Babs said, lifting Jen tenderly into her arms. She held her tight and soothed her.

'I never . . . did . . . nuthin'.' Jen's little body shook with each word.

'Shh! Shh! We're never coming back here again.'

Rage almost blinded her. She re-entered the loony bin to get her other child. She almost let her mother-in-law have it when she saw her sitting as snug as a bug back in her chair, guzzling Purple Guinness.

Babs picked up her baby. 'You're an evil old crone, doing that to a small girl—'

Shell couldn't see what the problem was. 'The kid fell over and hurt her arm. Then she wouldn't stop blubbing. I put her in the loo to teach the little missy a lesson. If you were any kind of mother, you'd know about that. Once you let kids take liberties, they've got you wrapped round their little finger like a noose around your neck.'

No wonder Stan had turned out the way he had. Despite his supposed second wife, Babs even felt a slight flicker of sorrow for him. But all she cared about now was protecting her kids. 'If you ever come near my children, ever again, for any reason, I will kill you! And I mean it – I will put you in the ground!'

Shell peered at her over the rim of her glass. 'I don't think you will, dear. I know how to look after myself. I could take you – and my son – no problem.'

'You're a monster!'

Shell snarled back, 'You have to grow up tough round here. How's that kid going to survive in the playground if she starts blubbing every five minutes? She'll be eaten alive. She'll end up no better than my Stan. Whinging about losing his finger because he was locked in the toilet all night. What a poof!'

Stunned, Babs could only stare. 'I beg your pardon?'

Shell smirked. 'I bet he didn't tell you that. Too ashamed. I bet you he told you some cock-and-bull bollocks about losing it in a fight.'

Babs couldn't speak.

Stan's mum had enough words for the both of them. 'Whining about a little bit of frostbite after a night in the bog – what kind of man is that? Fine lot of use he'd have been in the war.'

That was where Stan had learned his idea of punishment. Leaving her and his children in the freezing cold. Babs was too staggered to do anything but repeat, 'If I ever see you anywhere near my children again, you're dead . . .'

She pushed the pram out of the door while Shell roared, 'Spare the rod, spoil the child!'

A few streets away, Babs stopped the pram and examined Jen's arm. She sucked in her breath. It was swollen and very red. Babs hoped against hope that it wasn't broken.

'It hurts!' Jen sobbed.

'I know, don't worry. If it's not better in the morning I'll take you to the . . .' She couldn't bring herself to say 'doctors'. Since her baby had died, Babs found it so painful to deal with doctors. She'd had to, of course, when she gave birth, but other than that she kept well away from them. She fobbed her daughter off. 'Don't worry about that evil old woman, you won't be seeing her again.'

Her eyes still wet with tears, Jen said, 'I didn't fall over, Mum. She hit me.'

Fifty-Four

The next morning, Babs stood under a murky sky in front of the house in Islington. She hesitated before giving the brass knocker a good old rat-a-tat-tat. A woman could be heard coming down the hallway. She was shouting in a very clipped voice, 'Don't get familiar with me or I shall ask you to be about your business.'

'Stan married to a posh bit like that,' Babs scoffed. 'No effing way.'

Confidence bolstered, she waited for the door to open. The woman Babs had seen the previous day looked down at her.

Even in her workaday clothes, you could see her hourglass figure. Even without make-up and with a kerchief wrapped around her barnet, you could tell she was a stunner. Babs, who already hated this woman, hated her even more.

'Yes? Can I help?'

Well, could she? Richard Smith had insisted this tart was married to her husband, but Babs didn't believe it. In spite of all the evidence, she couldn't believe it. She had to see for herself. But now she could think of nothing to say.

The woman repeated, 'Can I help?'

An idea occurred. 'I . . . I used to live in this house when I was a little girl. As I was passing, I couldn't resist . . .'

'Oh, I see.' Mrs Posh looked doubtful. 'I suppose you're hoping to have a little walk down memory lane?'

If this was the East End, the woman would've assumed it was a scam and slammed the door in her face. But Babs was hoping her good manners would get the better of her. She begged, 'If I could have a little peek at the old place, it would help me so, Ma'am.' She wasn't quite sure why she sounded like Oliver Twist but it seemed to work.

'It's a little inconvenient; I've got workmen in but . . .' Babs tried to look like her kids when they wanted sweets. Mrs Posh smiled. 'Oh very well, just for five minutes.'

'Oh, thanks!'

When she was through the door, Babs began scanning the place for evidence that Stan had just been paying a visit.

'My name's Clare – and yours?'

'Er – Karen.'

'OK, Karen. Could you wait in the hall a minute? I've just got to put my builders straight on a few things.'

Babs studied the hall. She could see no sign of Stan. None of his hats or coats on the rack. None of his shoes lying around. Her hopes rose. Meanwhile, Clare was in a fair old ding-dong with her builder. He was telling her, 'What you want's a bit tricky, luv. And it's going to cost a fair bit of poke.'

Clare obviously resented the suggestion that money might be an issue. 'Don't worry about the *poke* and don't call me *love* either, I'm not a bus conductress. Just give me a quote and don't roll me over. My husband's in the business and he'll be having a look at it.'

Her husband was in the business? Babs' heart sank again.

Clare came back and led Babs into her main room. 'Do you remember this? It was probably something else in your day.'

The room was clearly Clare's pride and joy. Wooden floors and panels with original fittings and furniture. Even the paint looked like it was sourced from the sort of company that provided original colours. She explained, 'It's all completely authentic!'

But Babs wasn't interested in how it had been tarted up. Her eyes roamed over the mantelpiece and furniture for any sign of *him*. There wasn't any. She couldn't believe her old man would actually sit and watch telly here. It looked like an expensive hotel. Stan might have his airs but he was a meat-and-two-veg guy, not the sort of ponce who would feel comfortable in a room like this.

Babs said, 'It's so beautiful. Been here long?'

'About two years, since my husband and I got married.' Clare beamed. 'It was a complete wreck then so we've had to do a fair bit of work but my husband is in property. He'd had his eye on the house for quite a while. Islington might have been a dump but it's getting back on its feet now.' She quickly added, 'No disrespect obviously, I'm sure the people were very nice in your day too.'

There was no sign of Stan in the dining room either. Babs' hopes began to climb. 'Is your husband from Islington?'

'No, he's from the east side of town.' She grinned. 'Bit of a barrow boy made good, if we're being honest. But no one cares where you're from these days, do they? Apart from my snob of a mother; but she'd have thought Prince Charles was beneath me.'

Babs closed her eyes briefly. Why couldn't this dopey bint have said her old man was from Scotland? Or anywhere but the East End? 'What did you say his name was?'

'I didn't.' Clare was curt. Babs wondered if she was pushing her luck. Clare folded her arms in a way that was clearly meant to suggest Babs' visit was over. 'Thanks for dropping by.'

'Oh – could I have a little peek upstairs? That's where my family lived, on the second floor. The house was divided into flats.'

Babs could see how uncomfortable her host was but she had to find the truth. The bedroom was the best place.

'I suppose so.'

As they went up the stairs, Babs asked, 'So how did you meet your husband?'

She knew this was starting to sound like an interrogation and the answer was short. 'Oh, you know, just socially.'

Babs headed for the first room she saw. It was a nursery with a small baby lying in a cot. Babs knew how creepy she seemed but she couldn't stop herself. Clare was right at her shoulder, obviously anxious for her to go. But her good manners won out.

'And this is Florence. We call her Flo. Actually, I think it's time for her feed.'

Babs wasn't listening. She stared and stared at the little girl. The baby wasn't that much younger than her Tiff.

Clare had had enough. 'I hope this visit has helped bring back a few memories but I really need to be getting on.'

Babs awoke from her trance. 'Sure. I'll just have a quick look at my old room.'

She darted out of the nursery and rushed down the landing to a large bedroom. An uncomfortable Clare looked as if she was planning to throw Babs out. 'Karen, I don't want to be rude but I'm going to have to ask you . . . Karen?'

She rushed after Babs. 'Are you alright? Are you crying?'

The tears were flowing down Babs' face, in muffled sobs that soon broke into shrieks. She was holding a wedding picture showing Clare in a beautiful and obviously very expensive bridal gown. Her arm was linked through her husband's, Stanley Miller, wearing an equally expensive suit, with a pink carnation in his buttonhole.

Clare jumped back, terrified, as Babs dropped the photo, fled the room, belted down the stairs out onto the street.

Rage shook Babs' body as she ran. *I'll fix you! You cunt! You wanker! And that fucking posh bitch with a stick up her arse! I should have decked the slag. And that wedding gown she was wearing ... I was in a cheap Roman outfit for a five-bob wedding in a registry office, in some beige council building that looked like a prison.* He'd had a kid – Flo, what kind of name was that? – the same age as Tiff, with someone else while hers were just this side of wearing rags. Fucking Stanley Miller. He'd had his last laugh at her expense. And the money he'd spent on that stuck-up slapper. That gown alone had cost more than he'd given her for clothes in six years. And what was much, much worse, far more than he'd ever provided for Jen and Tiffany.

'I'll give him Cornwall when I see him.'

She heard a horn sound and a car pulled up. Richard Smith was at the wheel. 'Do you believe me now?'

Conscious of the tears staining her cheeks, Babs hurriedly wiped her face. He was the last person she wanted to see her in a state. 'Where did you come from?'

'Been parked up since breakfast time, waiting for you to show.'

She tried to keep a brake on her emotions. 'OK. Well, you were right – well done. Now if you'll excuse me, it's payback time for my lying scumbag of a husband.'

He looked at her sadly. 'Get in a minute, Babs. I want to talk to you.'

She pulled open the passenger door and plonked herself down with her arms folded. He leaned over and kissed her. Babs tried not respond, but this man was offering her something warm and her blood was running so cold. She got deep into it.

Richard pulled back at last. 'No point getting mad, Babs. Get even. I've told you how you can do it – by helping me out.'

She turned on him. 'You just don't get it, do you? People like me don't help people like you. We don't grass.'

'He's made a complete plonker out of you – a laughing stock – isn't that enough for you?'

Her mouth twisted. 'Don't you worry about that. I've got something lined up to sort him out . . .'

She went to climb out of the car but he grabbed her arm. 'Er – about yesterday . . .'

'Oh, fuck yesterday . . .'

'Well, exactly, that's what I wanted to talk to you about.'

She pulled her arm away. 'I ain't got time, mate.'

As she walked away, he called after her, 'I'll ring you later.'

She looked back. 'You're a trier, Tricky Dickie, I'll give you that. I ain't grassing.'

'I'm not talking about grassing. I'm worried about you. Please don't do anything stupid.'

But she was already gone.

Fifty-Five

Do anything stupid? Chance would be a fine thing; the bastard never came home. As she went to pick her children up from Cheryl's, Babs devised ever more spiteful revenges. She considered trying the Maggie Brooks approach of having him beaten up. It would be a brave man who took on Stanley Miller, though. She considered beating him herself; she was angry enough. But she'd be lucky to land a blow before he shut her down. Making a scene in front of his clients? She'd have to find out where he worked first. Perhaps Richard had been right; grassing him up was the best option.

But she wasn't prepared to do that, now or ever.

When the anger ebbed away, she was surprised to find what she really felt.

Relief.

For years, she'd struggled with what to do about Stan. He was no kind of husband and no kind of father. Yet, he was still her children's dad. She didn't feel she had the right to take them away from him. She didn't want to have to account to them when they were older and asked about him. She'd struggled on, hoping things would get better. Perhaps it was selfish to expect him to be around every day helping out. Maybe the scrimping and saving would be worth it in the long run. Now, she could kick the bastard out with a clean conscience.

Perhaps she even owed Clare for taking the little wanker on.

When she got to Cheryl's her problems got worse. Poor Jen was in a right two and eight. Her arm had started hurting again. When she'd got the girls home yesterday, Mummy had kissed it better and put a bandage on. She promised Jen that it would be fine in the morning. Instead it looked worse; swollen and painful. Babs put a silent curse on Shell Miller's head for hitting her own grandchild. By rights she should go around there and make Shell think twice about whacking another kid. But the very thought of going near that loony bin sent chills through her.

Cheryl looked worried. 'You'll have to take her down to the quacks.' She tutted in sympathy as she stared at poor Jen. 'She's such a brave girl, aren't you?'

Babs knew she was right, but she dreaded going down to the doctor's. As far as she was concerned, doctors meant death.

But Jen was biting her lips so hard that Babs knew she didn't have a choice.

'I don't think it's anything to worry about, Mrs Miller,' Dr Phillips informed her, 'but to be on the safe side we'll run her down the hospital for an X-ray.'

Babs swallowed, scared. 'The ozzie? But you said it was nuthin'!'

He looked at her as if she was an idiot. 'No, I said I thought it was nothing but we'll need an X-ray to be sure. It's a perfectly safe procedure – hospitals do it every day. What happens is . . .'

Babs cut him short. 'I know what an X-ray is, I'm not missing a brain.'

The quack was puzzled. 'So what's the problem?'

Babs held Jen tight. 'Nuthin'. There's no problem.'

She walked from the surgery at a grim pace and went to the bus stop. And walked right past it. She couldn't take Jen to

Mile End ozzie. The place was filled with a wagonload of sad memories. The thought of being in the place where Desiree had died nearly crippled her. She was terrified that if she took another one of her kids there they wouldn't come out alive.

Babs asked hopefully, 'Is your arm still hurting? Is it feeling better?'

'No Mummy, it's worse.'

Babs gazed over her shoulder and saw the number 25 bus in the distance. With a huge sigh, she headed back to the bus stop. 'Don't worry, sweetheart; we're taking you to the hospital.'

At the entrance to the casualty wing of Mile End Hospital Babs couldn't seem to put one foot in front of the other. In her head, all she could see was her darling Desiree in the special baby unit, her tiny chest moving slowly up and down. Then her chest stopping as her eyes shut forever. Oh God, she couldn't do this.

'Are you alright, luv?' Babs snapped out of it to find a concerned nurse standing in front of her.

'Yes,' she responded weakly.

'What's the problem?'

It was Jen who answered, her lip trembling in pain. 'Hurt my arm.'

Before Babs could say anything, the nurse scooped Jen into her arms. 'Right, let's get you sorted out.'

Then she was marching into the hospital. With a sick feeling, Babs followed. The nurse took charge and in a jiffy a doctor was seeing to Jen. He flatly refused to allow her to stay with Jen while she was X-rayed and Babs' heart beat fast all the time her girl was out of sight. As soon as she came out, Babs gathered Jen up in her arms.

The doctor pinned the X-ray up. 'No bones broken, I'm happy to say, it's just a nasty knock. No games or anything until the swelling goes down.' He turned to Jen. 'Will you do that for me?'

Jen nodded, wide-eyed.

Babs hurried down the corridor as fast as possible. She passed a staff nurse, who seemed to be staring at her. As Babs raced towards reception, the woman called out, 'Miss Wilson?'

When she turned, the woman was coming back down the corridor. 'Babs Wilson, isn't it?'

Babs' eyebrows creased. 'It's Babs Miller now. Do I know you?'

The nurse was cheerful. 'Of course it's Miller, I remember your husband Sid ... No, Stanley. You probably don't remember. I was on the team that looked after your daughter. Desiree, right?'

Babs felt like her heart had been pierced. And then she realised this sick bitch was smiling at her. 'No. I don't remember. I'm surprised you do.'

Now the nurse was laughing at her. It was only her whirling head that stopped Babs from punching her out.

'We don't get many half-caste ...' the nurse corrected herself, 'mixed-race babies in our unit. And it was quite a fight to keep her with us. She's always stayed in my memory. There were plenty of times we thought we were losing her. But she was a fighter!'

'Yes, I know.'

'So how is Desiree? She must be at school by now.'

Perhaps this dumb cow had been off the night they lost her baby and they hadn't told her? Either that, or her memory wasn't as good as she thought. Babs put Jen down. 'She's dead – didn't you hear?'

The nurse's face dropped like a stone. 'Dead? I'm so sorry. What happened?'

Babs looked at her. She seemed honest enough. 'She was too small, I suppose. Why don't you ask your colleagues up in the maternity unit? They were the ones looking after her; I'm surprised they didn't tell you.'

The nurse's eyes were misty. 'I'm sorry, I don't understand.'

Babs felt the ground giving way under her feet. She looked up towards the floor where her baby had fought and lost her battle. 'She died up there . . .'

The nurse stepped back in shock. 'Your daughter didn't die, Mrs Miller.' Babs stumbled backwards, the blood draining away from her face. 'I remember the day your husband came to pick her up. We all formed a crowd and gave them a round of applause when they left. He said you were confined to bed under doctor's orders.'

'I'm sorry, Mrs Miller, but if you don't leave immediately we'll have to call the police.'

There was a crowd around the maternity ward's reception. It included Babs, a howling Jen, several nurses, admin staff and a burly doctor who'd been summoned to offer support.

'You'll have to call the fucking army, love – I'm not going anywhere until you tell me what happened to my daughter.'

The receptionist gritted her teeth. 'As I say, we have procedures and we can't—'

'Fuck your procedures. Tell me what happened to my baby and I'll go.' Babs knew how she looked and was surprised at how calm she felt. She was on a mission.

The receptionist looked at a colleague and mouthed, 'Call the Old Bill . . .'

A kindly-looking senior doctor appeared. 'What's the problem?'

The receptionist explained. 'This lady – a Mrs Babs Miller – wants some medical records. As I've told her, we can't do that. She can't even prove who she is.'

Babs gestured at the nurse she'd met downstairs, who was standing anxiously in the background. 'She knows who I am.

And she knows who my baby was. Now get me my fucking records or I'll fucking wreck the joint.'

The doctor took Babs by the arm. 'OK, Mrs Miller, I understand your distress. Why don't you take a seat in my office? I'll speak to my colleagues and we'll see what we can arrange.'

Babs' nostrils flared. 'You're not going to fuck me about?'

'I'm a doctor. We don't – as you put it – fuck people about.'

Babs sat in the office with Jen on her knee and waited. She kept up a constant stream of chat to stop herself thinking about what the nurse had said. That Stan had come here and taken Desiree home. They must've got her baby mixed up with someone else. She needed one of her Annies so bad she thought her mind was going.

Twenty minutes later, the doctor returned with a file under his arm. 'You're Barbara Miller and your daughter was Desiree. Is that correct?'

'Yes,' Babs mumbled, her grip tightening around Jen, but careful not to hurt her arm.

The doctor pushed his glasses higher on his nose. 'I shouldn't really be doing this but according to our records, Desiree was discharged into the care of your husband Stanley on . . .'

Babs didn't hear the rest. She felt as if she'd had a stiff drink on an empty stomach and then had the air sucked out of her lungs.

'Mrs Miller, do you suspect foul play? If so we'll need to call the police . . . Mrs Miller? Mrs Miller?'

Babs felt herself falling. She heard Jen shouting, 'Mummy! Mummy!' The quack raced to the door and yelled, 'I need some assistance please.'

She came to briefly when the doc slapped her cheek. 'Can we call someone?'

'Yes. Richard Smith.'

Then she fainted.

Fifty-Six

When Babs awoke, she saw Richard by the side of her bed. She sprang up. 'Where's Jen?'

Richard gently pushed her back down. 'Jen's with the nurses. They've told her you're tired and need a little sleep.' He asked, 'What happened?'

Her voice sounded to her as if it belonged to someone else. 'Stan murdered Desiree—'

Richard's face grew alarmed. 'Slow down. Who's Desiree?'

Babs' mouth started racing. 'I was expecting when I met Stan. Her dad was a coloured fella, but I weren't with him no more. She was born early and had to stop in the ozzie here.' Her voice rose. 'Stan took her away while I was in prison for the brothel thing. Ask the quacks here. Then he murdered her and told me she'd died in hospital.'

He patted her shoulder, trying to calm her down. 'How do you know he murdered her?'

Her hands flew in the air. 'Where is she, then?'

Richard said, 'I'll get in touch with my colleagues and they'll ask him.'

Babs shook her head. 'Don't do that. He's not stupid enough to kill a kid without having a rock-solid cover story. Don't worry about him. I'll get him for this, you see if I don't. He's a child killer. We know how to deal with them in the East End.'

'You need to get out of that flat. Leave a message saying you've gone away for a few days,' Richard told Babs as they drove towards her parents' place. Both Jen and Tiff were conked out in the back. 'I'll get in touch with my colleagues and they'll start an investigation. In the meantime, you're to sit tight. On no account take the law into your own hands. Are you listening, Babs? Babs?'

She was listening but she wasn't taking any notice. 'Sure.'

'I mean it. If you do something stupid, I can't help you. My colleagues will get in touch and we'll take it from there. OK?'

'Sure.' But she already had a plan in mind. 'I'll move in with my parents until you've sorted things out.'

'Would he look for you there?'

Babs didn't answer. Richard dropped them off at her mum's and gave her a final warning, pointing his finger. 'I mean it; this is a police matter now. Stay out of it.'

She watched him drive off and whispered to herself, 'A police matter, my arse.'

Rosie Wilson got the surprise of her life when she found her daughter and her two little ones on her doorstep.

'Babs, luvvie, I didn't know you'd be dropping around.'

She glanced back into the house. George wasn't going to like this.

Babs hustled her children inside. The baby was sleeping like a dream and Jen was gazing around.

'Mum, I've got to go somewhere. Can you look after the kids for me?'

Rosie didn't like her daughter's face. She looked pale and strained. 'Of course I will, pet.' She took baby Tiffany and cradled her. 'Is everything alright, you don't look yourself.'

Babs smacked her lips in irritation and reached for the baby. 'No problem, Mum, if you can't look after them—'

Rosie shuffled out of Babs' reach. 'I just told you I would. I don't know what's got a flea in your clothes, but you can tell me all about it over a brew.'

Babs shook her head. 'No time for that.' She bent down and looked into Jen's eyes, so like her father's. 'You listen to everything Nanna Rosie tells you. And be a good girl for me.' She looked up at her mum. 'Jen's hurt her arm—'

'My other nan hit me,' Jen piped up.

'You what?' Rosie was clearly outraged.

Babs straightened. 'Not now, yeah. I just need to use the lav and then I'll be gone.'

Rosie beckoned Babs towards her, and lowered her voice. 'Your dad's in. I don't know what he's going to say about this—'

'Y'know what, Mum, the way I'm feeling now, he can fuck off.'

'Babs Wilson-Miller.' Rosie was scandalised and let it show.

Her daughter grabbed one of her hands and held on tight. 'I'm begging you.' Then she was rushing up the stairs to the loo.

'This generation . . .' Rosie mumbled to the children. 'Well, it's about time you met your granddad.'

She waltzed the children into the sitting room. George frowned. 'If this is who I think it is—?'

Rosie had had enough. 'You listen to me, you cantankerous old fool. These are your grandchildren and they will be staying here tonight. If you don't like it, I suggest you get a room at the Seaman's Rest.'

But George wasn't listening. He was looking at the baby in her arms. His heart did a flip; the baby was a dead ringer for his Babs. His Babs – he hadn't thought about his daughter like that in years. Just then the little mite woke up and started fussing and crying. George Wilson's heart melted. He opened his arms at the same time as his daughter shut the back door.

Babs knew Richard would be parked nearby to see if she made an attempt to leave. She peeked around the back wall. There he was. About fifty yards down the road. He was going out of his way to help her, but this was her problem. She was going to deal with it on her own.

She caught a bus back to the estate. From below she checked there were no lights on in her flat and her murdering bastard of a husband hadn't put in an appearance. But of course he hadn't. Probably too busy knobbing the posh bitch in Islington and telling her money was no object. When she went into their home, she shivered, not just because it was cold. This was the lair of a child killer. She didn't know why she felt in her bones that Stan had snuffed out the life of her little girl. But if he hadn't done that, where was Desiree?

Babs left her bag behind in the flat. She had one aim and one aim only now; to take care of Stan. For good. Her steps were confident as she walked across the estate and a few minutes later she tapped on a door. When it opened, Babs was greeted by a shocked face. So shocked, the door wasn't even slammed shut again.

'Hello, Mel. Can I have a word?'

Fifty-Seven

'What the . . .?'

Babs didn't let her arch-enemy finish her sentence. 'Don't worry; I'm not here to cause any bovver. Stolen rings, knocking shops, even Denny – I couldn't give a fuck. I just need some information. Is Mickey in?'

Mel's features turned nasty. 'You've got some kind of nerve . . .'

Babs' voice was nearly a whisper. 'I told you – I don't want any trouble.'

Mel stepped outside the flat to see if she was alone. Then she relaxed slightly. 'I don't know what your game is, but there's no point in playing it. Now sod off, before I decide to fix you good and proper.'

Babs nodded. 'I understand. I felt the same until this afternoon. But things are different now. I bought into Stan's version of events back in '72. But I might have been wrong all along. I just need some help.'

Mel shook her head. 'No can do. It's too late for that now.'

The door was closed in Babs' face. She walked away, not sure where to go. But then she heard a shout. It was Mel again. 'Oi – come here a minute.' Babs went back.

'What did he tell you?'

'Who?'

'Stan – what did he say?'

Babs smiled at her 'What is it the boys say in the changing room? *I'll show you mine if you show me yours.*'

Mel pursed her lips. 'Mickey's down the hospital, thanks to the hiding your Stan dished out.'

'He's not *my* Stan any more,' Babs growled, her body shaking.

'I see. Alright then, come in.'

In the living room, Mel poured herself a Bacardi. 'Do you want one?'

'I do as it happens. A large one.'

The two women sat facing each other. Mel was still sizing her up.

'I just want to ask you a couple of things.'

But Mel was more interested in her own questions. 'What did he tell you? He didn't try to blame us for the girl, did he?'

'The girl?'

'Yeah – Denny. We only realised you knew the bird during the court case in '72. Did he tell you we put his brother up to it?'

'No. He told me you and Mickey killed her.'

Mel was outraged. '*We* killed her? What the fuck?'

'Yeah. And that you fitted me up for owning the brothel.'

'And you believed him? What kind of an idiot are you? Surely you know he lies for England?'

'Yeah, I know that now. But I didn't then.'

Mel calmed down and topped the pair of them up. 'It was his brother Pete who killed the girl.'

Mel stared at the ceiling. Babs realised there were tears in her eyes. 'What happened?'

Mel's head dropped back down, crying properly now. 'I can't say. I was to blame, really.'

'I told you, Mel, I'm not here to cause trouble. I've got troubles enough of my own.'

Mel bit her bottom lip for a time, then said, 'If I tell you what's what, you can't go blabbing to Stan.'

Babs crossed her heart. 'Whatever you tell me stays inside this room.'

Mel took a hard swallow of rum. 'We needed to get Pete out of the business. He was always pissed, a menace, but Stan wouldn't have it. He was a sucker for his brother. So when Denny turned up on the scene, we saw a way to get rid of Pete.' She shook her head. 'The strange thing was, I really got to like her. We told her we'd make her into a top model. Pure bollocks of course. Anyway, we got her down to the knocking shop by telling her there was a showbiz bash going on.'

Babs wanted to speak but kept quiet. 'She was such an innocent. Celebrities in Mile End, give me a break. We made sure that Pete got blotto and we got him into one of the rooms upstairs. Then I pulled Denny aside and told her about our plan—'

'Which was?'

'We were going to put pig's blood all over Pete's room and tell him that he'd offed the girl. At first Denny didn't want any part in it, but I told her we'd get her a job on a cruise liner. She was desperate to get away from that disgusting stepdad of hers.' Mel polished her drink off and slapped her glass on the table. 'So she comes in to help us spread the blood around but then she gets cold feet.' Mel's eyes grew wide. 'I tried to stop her. Grabbed her. She sidesteps me and the next thing I know she's falling . . .'

It was like Mel wasn't in the room with Babs any more as she recounted the story.

'She hit her head on the corner of the fireplace. She was gone. There was nothing we could do. So me and Mickey went on with our plan, except this time we really did have a dead body.' Mel chucked her glass violently across the room, where it shattered into pieces. 'You wanna blame me? Go ahead. I blame myself, it was my idea.' Mel was jeering, but Babs could hear the emotion thick in her throat. Her worst enemy was on the point of cracking up. 'The first time I met her outside the modelling agency I told her to go home . . .' Mel shook her head tiredly.

'What a fucking mess. You can call me many things, but I'm no bloody murderer. Nor's my Mickey. Stan's been pulling your tail all along. He thought it was his brother who killed her. The only reason he'd have fingered us was to get you to do his bidding.'

'Stan said you put my name on the deeds to the knocking shop. That's why I got banged up.'

Mel swept her hand restlessly through her hair. 'Neither me nor Mickey ever clapped eyes on your signature. How the hell could we make a good copy?'

Babs wasn't even stunned to hear what Mel was telling her. Stan had probably been yanking her chain from the get-go.

Mel carried on, 'Your old man's the one who stitched us all up.'

Hadn't he just! 'That was a terrible thing you did with Denny and she – God rest her soul – paid the price. But another terrible thing happened. When all this business was going on, I was pregnant, you remember?'

Mel nodded.

'When my baby was born, it was touch and go whether she'd survive. While I was in the cells, Stan came and told me she had died. But it wasn't true. He took her out of the hospital. Did you or Mickey ever talk to him about that?'

'Give over. We were too busy trying to stuff each other up

to swap small talk about babies.' Abruptly her tone changed. 'Why? What are you saying?'

Babs' whisper had a rasp in it. 'He killed her.'

Mel gave her a grim smile. 'Bollocks. He's a sicko but he wouldn't kill a kid. Not even for money. Not his style.'

Babs gave the same answer she'd given to Richard Smith. 'Where is she, then?'

Mel got out another bottle of booze, drank straight from it and thought for a while. 'I dunno.'

'Can you think of anyone who might be able to help?'

'Not really. Hold up a minute.' She put the bottle down. 'You could ask that black tart Cleo, Cleo Clarke, who helped Stan nail me and Mickey at Snaresbrook. She was supposed to be working with us but Stan obviously made her a better offer.'

Babs remembered the gorgeous black woman from the trial, the one who hadn't wanted to let her into the knocking shop when she was searching for Denny.

'And where do I find her?'

Mel shrugged. 'Fuck knows. She liked the East End, so I doubt if she moved far. And there was another thing – she was very religious. Always reading the Bible, that's what Daffy told my Mickey. Strange, eh?'

The two women regarded each other. Mel was first to break the tense silence. 'Stan or no Stan, you still did a badness to me and my old man. Stay away from my family.'

'The feeling's mutual.'

Then, Babs was gone. The name *Cleo Clarke* turning over in her head.

Back in the flat, Babs tried to figure out how to track down Cleo. The only clue she had was that the tart was a religious woman and religious people went to church. She got out the Yellow Pages and started calling church after church after church like a mad woman. She got more and more stressed and eventually slammed the book shut. No way was she going to find the woman with this method. Besides, didn't Bernice, a black woman in her block, say that her church was in the back of a barber's on Sundays? The Yellow Pages wasn't going to list that type of gathering.

Babs got up, took a slug of gin and popped a couple of Annies. She gazed down at her bag. She didn't have time to find Cleo. She had to deal with Stan now. It was time he understood that hell hath no fury like an East End woman wronged.

Fifty-Eight

Babs went to the part of The Devil's Estate people usually kept well clear of – the underground car park, aka Neverland. It hadn't taken residents long to figure out if you wanted to get your motor nicked, this was the best place to park it. It also attracted a wagonload of lowlifes – druggies, kids bunking off and crooks who wanted to do deals in the shadows.

Babs started down the long, concrete slope and soon found herself in a dark underworld that sent shivers through her. Many of the wall lights were busted, but a few still shone a thin, ghostly light around a world of concrete, dumped cars and shadowy figures. She knew who she was looking for but didn't know where to find him. She had no alternative but to ask someone.

Babs went towards a group of men sitting on top of a burnt-out car, but moved swiftly past them when she smelt the tummy-wrenching stink of meths.

'You alright, doll?' one of the winos called. 'Take your drawers off and come and keep me company.'

That got a laugh from the onlookers. It almost made Babs scarper, but she kept her nerve. She kept her feet moving until she saw a crowd of teens. Two had plastic bags over their mouths and noses, inhaling deeply. If Babs was Catholic, she would've crossed herself because she knew what they were doing – sniffing glue. What was the world coming to?

'You shouldn't be down here, Mrs Miller,' one of the lads said, detaching himself from the group.

'Frankie Lloyd,' Babs answered with her best mum voice. She wanted to tell him his mother would be turning in her grave if she could see him now, but that would only hurt the boy. His mum had been taken prematurely six months ago. Breast cancer. Poor Mr Lloyd took it bad and wasn't coping, his children running wild. Instead she asked, 'Know where Kieran is?'

He didn't look surprised. Frankie knew once upon a time she and Kieran Scott had been close. He pointed at one of the closed garages at the end of Neverland.

This is nuts, Babs thought as she knocked on the steel garage door. You can still turn ... She stumbled back as the door flipped up and out. It was opened by a boy of about sixteen but the garage was what grabbed Babs' attention. It looked more like a room in someone's house. A room full of knock-off gear. Tellies, radios, parts of cars, even a switched-on set of Christmas lights stuck up on the back wall. In front of that was a small desk and the person sitting behind it, smoking a fag, was sixteen-year-old Kieran Scott.

He looked at Babs slowly, his lazy eye moving in the opposite direction from his good one. Goosebumps popped out on her arms. Kieran wasn't handsome, but he had something that kept you looking. He switched his gaze to the other lad and gave him the nod to leave. Then he lazily eased to his feet.

The door shut behind Babs with a clang that almost made her jump.

Kieran dragged hard on his smoke. 'What do you want, Babs?'

He looked at her as if she were a stranger. How sad! Her

heart did a funny flip inside her chest. Poor sod had probably had all the feeling beaten out of him.

She remembered why she had come. 'I need you to get something for me.'

Fifteen minutes later, the deal was done.

'You're a true sweetheart,' Babs told him, embarrassed and grateful at the same time. He was the last person she'd wanted to involve, but what choice did she have? Stan's mug was well known in the boozers around these parts, so going to a pub to sort out her problem hadn't been an option.

'A favour for a favour, Babs.'

That startled her. The way his good eye was roaming over her like she was some tart up on Commercial Street freaked her out.

He closed in on her. 'What the fuck, Kieran?'

He whispered, 'I'll have to come over when it's dark. We can't have anyone twigging what's what.'

He wasn't suggesting . . .? Him and her? Sod that. Babs pulled herself straight. She was putting a stop to this right now. She prepared to give him back what he'd got for her. 'If you think I'm desperate enough to let you hump—'

He put his finger on her lips. 'I want you to teach me to read.'

In the dark, heavy night, Stan drove onto The Devil. As if the mysterious Mr Smith wasn't enough glass on his toilet seat, Clare had told him about her visitor – the equally mysterious 'Karen'. He'd laughed it off. A nutter. But when he'd asked for a description, Clare had become suspicious.

'Please – tell me you don't know this mad woman?'

So he'd dropped the subject without finding out anything – apart from the fact that she was 'frightfully common'.

There was no way it could have been Babs. Stan was a

master of keeping his various lives apart. But he couldn't be sure. And even though Babs was as dumb and as soft as a rice pudding, he didn't want to have to deal with his double life being exposed.

As he turned into the dark courtyard for his block he saw a bloke standing by another car. The fella must've been feeling the cold. He was rigged out in a fedora like a cartoon mobster, a muffler pulled over the lower part of his face, gloves and what looked like a pair of strides from a smart suit. Stan would've ignored him, except the fuckwit took a few steps that put him slap bang in the path of his motor.

Blimey O'Reilly! 'What's this Herbert up to?' he muttered.

He sounded his horn and slowed. The idiot had his hand stuck deep in his pocket and seemed to be struggling with something.

Stan leaned out of his window. 'Get outta the way, you prick, or I'll iron you with my wheels.'

The geezer didn't move an inch but his hand finally emerged with something deadly in his hand. *A shooter.* Stan went on high alert as the fella tried levelling his weapon at his car. Bollocks. He threw the car into gear, rammed his foot on the accelerator, threw the lights on full and pressed his thumb on the horn. Blaring away, the car flew forward like an angry bull. Instead of letting his trigger finger go crazy, the assassin dived for cover. Stan felt the car judder and thud as two bullets hit the bodywork. When he hit a bollard, he escaped, hanging low and going round the front to take cover. Two more shots ripped through the night air. One blew out a tyre, the other wailed like a cat as it struck the brickwork of the old washhouse.

This cowboy was coming over as a rank amateur.

In the Blitz, they said, you never heard the bomb that killed you. In the underworld the rule is you never see the man that shoots you. Stan had always taken every precaution to avoid a hit, but you could never be sure. He had enough pride to think he'd only piss off serious people who could afford to get the job done properly. The idiot trying to shoot him was more like a school leaver who'd lasted a week on a hitman's access course and been told to try shelf stacking instead.

Stan peered over the bonnet and saw his guy emerge from behind a van. Instead of making a swift getaway, the prat was knocking around, trying to see what the deal was. He obviously wanted Stan dead badly. *Not if I catch you first.*

Stan ran towards him at high speed. The gunman twisted around and belted it. Stan motored after him. The geezer was nippy and obviously knew the estate. He led Stan a merry dance along walls and walkways, through playgrounds and gardens, always managing to keep about twenty yards ahead. Whenever Stan was closing, the guy would switch direction or go through gaps that took Stan longer to wriggle through. Soon he realised he'd been led in a circle, right back to the scene of the shooting.

But when he came round the corner into the courtyard that fronted his and Babs' block, he saw his bird had flown. The yard was empty, with no way he could have avoided Stan seeing him. Puffing away like mad against a wall, he listened for the tell-tale sound of a vehicle starting nearby but heard nothing. Stan looked up along the block, checking the balconies for any sign of the fugitive. When he saw nothing, he walked back to his car. As he locked it, it suddenly hit him – what if the killer was making his way to Babs and the girls? Stan bolted towards his block.

Fifty-Nine

Rosie was still smiling when she left the bedroom. She could hear Jen's happy giggles as her Granddaddy George played with her. It almost made her weep to see him with his grandkids. All these years wasted, when they could've been a happy family. Well, they were one now and that's all that mattered.

The phone rang downstairs. She got to it on the third ring. 'Rosie Wilson,' she said quietly; she didn't want to wake the baby up.

'It's Stan. Are Babs and the girls there?'

Rosie frowned. The children were there, but why would he think that Babs was?

He carried on before she could say anything. 'I just got in and there's a note saying she and the kids are spending the night at your place.'

'Yes, that's right, Jen and Tiff are here . . .' But not her daughter. She didn't know what was going on, but the last thing she wanted to do was drop Babs in it. 'And Babs.'

'Can I speak to her?' Her son-in-law's voice sounded stressed and he was breathing heavily.

Rosie thought quick on her feet. 'She's lying down. Had a bit of a headache, poor dear. I don't wanna disturb her.'

'Fair dos. Tell her to give me a bell first thing.'

After he rang off, Rosie held the receiver against her chest, worried. Where was Babs? She knew there were a few hiccups in their marriage but she hoped her daughter wasn't playing away from home.

Babs was shaking when she finally reached Whitechapel. Her clothes stuck to her body with sweat. She was still shocked by the enormity of what she'd tried to do – murder her own husband. Blast Stan far enough into kingdom come to show him what a murdering bastard he was. He didn't deserve to live, not after snuffing out Desiree's life.

When she'd dropped the girls off, Babs had sneaked into her mum and dad's bedroom and nabbed some of her dad's clothing. She'd gone to see Kieran and got the Browning pistol. Then she'd waited for Stan to appear.

But it hadn't gone to plan. She'd pulled the trigger alright, but had been so nervous her shots had gone wild. And when he'd started running after her . . .

Babs was at breaking point as she reached for the door in front of her.

George was disturbed by knocking. He turned to Rosie, but she was sound asleep. The knocking came again. Bollocks. He didn't want the noise waking up his beautiful granddaughters. He quickly got up, popped his dressing gown on and went barefoot downstairs.

'Who's there?' he asked, his mouth close to the door.

All he got back was the sound of soft weeping. He didn't like the sound of this, but he opened the door.

'Dad?' Babs said. She was in a right old state, her eyes red-rimmed from crying. She was wearing . . . Hold up!

'Is that one of my suits?'

There was a choking noise at the back of her throat. 'Dad?'

George ushered her inside. He might've had a problem with

his daughter for what she'd done years back, but he didn't like seeing her in this mess. 'What's the matter, luv?' he coaxed her.

Babs stared at him, her eyes wild. 'My baby . . . Oh God, my baby.'

In that moment, all the hate in his heart disappeared. He held out his arms and she collapsed into them. He drew her towards the stairs to sit down. She laid her head on his chest as she gently wept. He caressed her hair.

'Shh! It's gonna be alright. I'm so so sorry that your little one died. I should've stood with you.' There were tears in his eyes too.

She looked up at him. 'I need you to phone someone called Richard Smith. He's to come and get me. Tell him I'll tell him everything.'

George felt his wife sit down on the step above them.

Rosie said, 'We'll do that in a minute. Let's get you sorted first. Cleaned up and changed into some of your clothes we still keep in your old room.'

Babs laid her head back on her dad's chest as her mother leaned down and put her arms around both of them.

The first thing Richard Smith did when Babs got in his motor was search through her bag, one of the beautiful ones her dad had bought her years back. She was too washed out to protest. He pulled out the gun.

'How did you know?' she asked.

'What would a vengeful person do in your situation? Simple – go gunning for the man they thought murdered their daughter.'

Her dad had been scandalised that she'd left in the middle of the night, but Babs needed this sorted now. She couldn't go on like this.

Richard took her to a small hotel in Finsbury Park. Once the door was closed, they stared at each other. Babs was the first to move. She walked right up to him and wordlessly began to take off his clothes. Soon they were making the type of tender love she needed to feel whole again.

Afterwards, as he held her close, she whispered, 'Stan doesn't have the right to be breathing air while my baby's dead—'

'We've got no proof that he killed her.' Babs tried to pull away but he held her tight. 'A couple of my mates on the murder team looked into it and they came up with nothing. I've got a funny feeling if you tell me what you know, we'll find out what happened.' He eased her gently to the side and stared at her. His face was dead serious. 'I work undercover at the Yard in anti-corruption.'

Babs froze. She hadn't been expecting that. She thought about all the stuff a while back about them trying to get rid of bent coppers. It was about time someone did something, though she wasn't sure she wanted to be part of it. But if it meant finding out about Desiree . . .

She stared up at the ceiling.

Babs' fingertips touched his arm, giving him his answer.

'There were two crooked cops in the vice squad who were hand in glove with Stan. We've got most of the bad guys but these two slipped through the net. I need to find anything I can so we can put them in chokey or kick them off the force. You'll know them – they're called Cricket and Horner.'

Cricket and bloody Horner. The same dodgy cops who had kept her away from Desiree. She hated them with a passion. They'd been working for Mickey and Mel and . . .

Babs urgently turned to the man by her side. 'Stan told me they were working for Mickey and Mel. But it's not true. My first day in Stan's office, he gave me a list of important people.

If they came in or called I was to put them straight through. One name was C&H—'

'Cricket and Horner,' he finished off. 'Tell me about 1972. Everything you can remember.'

He scooted off the bed in his birthday suit, giving Babs an eyeful of his trim backside, and got a notebook and pen. He perched on the bed as Babs sat up and wrapped the blanket around herself. 'The first time I met Cricket and Horner was when they dragged me outta my home on my wedding night. I was in a right state because the ozzie had called to say Desiree had taken a turn for the worse . . .'

She told him the lot – from Stan offering her the job in Soho, to the tragedy of hearing her baby was dead. Babs' breathing shuddered.

'You're a strong woman to have survived all that.' His voice was quiet.

'I had a harsh teacher.'

Richard looked at his notes. 'I'll be frank with you. The big problem is that all the paperwork has conveniently disappeared. And they'll say – which is unfortunately true – that you lied in court. That's always the problem we face. Bent cops can always claim the people informing against them are liars and crooks. I've found plenty of verbal evidence that Cricket and Horner were on the take, but I can't prove anything. They were on a number of criminals' payroll but as crooks they wouldn't last five minutes in the witness box.' He gazed grimly at his notes. 'Your husband really is a piece of work.'

'Yeah. So I've noticed.' She frowned. 'I don't get why he got hitched to me.'

His mouth twisted. 'If his schemes went wrong you couldn't be forced to give evidence against him. He wouldn't want to make an enemy of you. You know too much.'

Babs looked forlorn. 'Well, he made a mistake there. I don't know nuthin' more than I've told you.'

His frustration began to show. 'You must do. Think about it. Is there anyone else I could speak to? Someone solid and reliable? We need a respectable citizen; tough enough to take the heat in the witness box. There's got to be someone.'

Babs sat back. She remembered her talk with Mel. 'Mel Ingram said there's someone who might be able to tell me what happened to my baby. Her name's Cleo Clarke.'

Richard slipped on his shirt and left Babs alone in the room for fifteen minutes. When he came back, he wore a jubilant expression. 'I found her. We'll go talk to her tomorrow morning.'

He gazed at her solemnly. 'When my investigation is complete, we can't see each other.'

She understood. And if the truth be known, as soon as Stan was gone she didn't want another fella hanging around. She was done with blokes for good.

Babs let the blanket slip down from her naked body. He walked towards her.

Sometime in the early hours of the morning, Babs crept quietly out of the bed. She tip-toed over to Richard's jacket and retrieved the pistol Kieran had given to her.

Sixty

'Yes! Yes, yes, yes! Let me hear you sing!' Cleo Clarke yelled the words with joy and glory.

The thirty-strong choir raised the tempo even higher as they sang Boney M's version of 'Rivers of Babylon'.

'Joy! Joy!! Joy!'

The choir bashed their song out at an even higher pitch. There was no music, and Cleo was beating her baton completely out of time with the rhythm. But it didn't matter, they knew the words and they were eager to praise all that is holy.

'Will I hear a sound like this again before I'm promoted to glory?'

The stone walls and stained glass of the old Wren church soaked up the volume. The flowers vibrated in their vases.

'Final verse! Let the East End of London hear the noise. All the way from Bow Bells to . . .' She wasn't quite sure, so she cried out, 'Dagenham Causeway! Let me hear you sing, let me hear you sing.'

The choir were determined to finish their practice on a high and made one last frantic effort to push the dial up. But then a strange thing happened.

Cleo's baton, which had been whirling like a propeller, slowed down as if its engine had turned off. The gleeful laughter on her face turned to ash. By the time their song was over, she was motionless, her attention elsewhere.

There was no joy in her voice when she murmured, 'Brethren and sistren, that was beautiful. Pat yourselves on the back.' She got down from the prayer stool she'd been standing on and added, 'If you'll excuse me for a moment.'

She hurried down the aisle, wearing an expression more suited to a funeral than a choir practice, until she reached the two people sitting on a pew at the back.

They stood up when Cleo reached them. 'It's Babs, isn't it?'

Babs nodded. 'That's right.' They were both remembering their stormy encounter that day in Mile End. 'Stanley Miller's wife. And this is Richard Smith, Cleo.'

'It's Sister Cleo now. I've given my life over to the Lord.' She looked suspicious.

Babs frowned slightly. She didn't get why the other woman had a cob on. Sure, they had a tense history but they weren't enemies either. 'Mr Smith is a policeman, leading an investigation into all that bovver back in 1972.'

Cleo stepped back as if someone had slapped her face. 'I don't want to know. By all means stay here and be uplifted by the divine majesty of God, but my past is dead to me.'

Richard got tough. 'I don't think so. One way or another you're going to answer some questions, even if I have to lead you away in handcuffs while the good members of your choir look on.'

Cleo sounded once again like a working girl on the make. 'Cuff me up? For what, you crafty rozzer? I ain't done nuthin'.'

He pursed his lips. 'I dunno what I could pull you in for, Sister. But my experience leads me to believe that you can always find something if you really want to.'

Cleo turned and looked at the choir. They were staring at

her with curious faces. 'Alright, five minutes. We'll go to the vestry.'

As they passed the choir, Cleo called out breezily, 'People! You don't need anyone's permission to sing songs of praise! Let me hear you sing!'

The singing began again. It could still be heard when they reached the musty-smelling vestry. For poor Cleo, the songs of praise were like a wagging finger to remind her she'd been a terrible sinner. 'I don't know what you're after, but I can't help. That period of my life is over. I prefer not to remember. What happened . . .' She quickly corrected herself. 'I mean, what *may* have happened, is dead – and I am now alive.'

Smith picked up a book lying nearby. 'I see.' He opened it at random and began flipping through the pages. 'Do you know what this book is?'

Cleo was startled. 'Yes, of course. It's the Bible.'

'That's right. The Bible. Now, I admit I'm not an expert or anything but I know it says a fair amount about truth and justice. I'm pretty sure it contains the line: *let your yea be yea and your nay be nay.* And I'm also sure it says a lot about giving false testimony.' He closed the book and stared at Cleo. 'That's right, isn't it?'

Cleo was cornered by her own beliefs. She said nothing. Instead, she looked at Babs for support. Babs said, 'If you're worried about grassing Stan up, don't be. In fact, the deeper you drop him in it, the more I'll like it.'

Smith smiled. 'So you see, Sister. Your duty is clear and the way is straight. I can see you're the kind of girl who won't compromise where the truth's concerned. I need to know what went on in that brothel, I need to know about Mickey and Mel Ingram, Stan Miller and Denise Brooks and if you've ever heard of two bent police officers called Cricket and Horner.'

Babs explained, 'Richard needs evidence to send them down for good. And I thought you might know something.'

Cleo sank into a chair. She fixed her gaze hard onto Babs. 'You're sure there's nothing else that you're here for?'

Babs was puzzled by Cleo's attitude. 'You're not the only one who wants to leave the past behind.'

Clearly satisfied with this response, she turned to Richard. 'Yes, I knew Cricket and Horner. I had to give them freebies because of the work they did for the boss. I thought it was Mickey, then I found out it was Stan.' She stood up. 'I've got something to stop those spawns of Satan alright.'

Dennis Brown's reggae classic 'Money In My Pocket' was blaring from an upstairs room in Cleo's house.

'Bernice,' Cleo yelled, 'turn that devil music off.' With an apologetic look, she turned back to her visitors. 'That's my younger sister. She hasn't quite found her way to the Lord yet.'

Cleo ushered them into the sitting room. 'Please take a seat. I need to get something from my bedroom.'

Babs whispered to Richard, 'Cleo was a right piece in her day, with a gob on her.'

Richard curled his fingers around hers. 'I don't want you to get disappointed if she can't help find out about your baby.'

Before Babs could respond, Cleo came back in the room and handed Richard an old shoebox. 'Me, Stan and his brother Pete – may God forgive me – had a little wrinkle going where we filmed certain clients. They didn't tell me why we were doing it, but I figured it was a blackmail racket. I know for a fact Stan destroyed the lot. Except this one, which was my own little scheme.' She took a breath. 'It's Cricket and Horner, doing the dirty with me and a whole lot more.'

'Thank you very much,' Richard said.

But Cleo wasn't finished. 'There's one other thing you

should know.' She looked him in the eye. 'I think Stan murdered his brother.'

Babs seethed. 'I told you that bastard was a murderer.'

Richard held his hand up to stop her and turned his attention to the lady of the house. 'Tell me exactly what you're talking about.'

Cleo spoke for the next ten minutes with tears in her eyes. 'It was all my fault. If I hadn't given him the address ... I pray for forgiveness every night.'

'It's not your fault,' Babs tried to comfort her. 'It's not only you Stan's conned, it's muggins here as well. Do you know anything about my baby, Desiree?'

Cleo's mouth dropped open. 'What?'

There was a noise in the passage. A younger, cheekier version of Cleo popped her head around the door. 'We're going to the park . . .' She twisted to talk to someone else, who Babs couldn't see. 'No! Your mum has got visitors. No . . .'

There was the sound of childish laughter and a gorgeous, brown-skinned girl of about six, with masses of corkscrew hair, bounced into the room. 'I want to give Mum a kiss before I leave.'

She threw herself into a dumbstruck Cleo's arms. Then she turned to Babs. And Babs found herself looking into the same green-brown eyes as her father's.

'I want my Desiree back,' Babs yelled.

'She ain't your anything. And her name's Dee,' Cleo threw back, equally furious.

They were in a furious stand-off. When Babs had clocked that Cleo's daughter was her lost baby, she'd felt utter relief that Stan hadn't done away with the girl. But then stark raving anger had set in. No wonder Cleo had been giving her the evil eye from the start. Realising what was going on,

Bernice, Cleo's sister, had quickly shooed Dee into the kitchen.

Richard was on his feet as well. 'Ladies, you need to keep it down or Dee . . .' he caught Babs' raging glare, 'Er . . . Desiree will hear. We need to calm down.'

Cleo was the first to give way, Babs following.

Cleo shuffled forward urgently. 'This is what happened, as God is my witness. The night I left the knocking shop for good, your old man asks me to testify against Mickey and Mel and then says he wants another favour. I go over his car and there on the seat is a basket with a beautiful baby in it. He asked me to look after her.'

'He hands my kid over like she's a Christmas pressie and you don't think that smells fucking fishy?'

Cleo got defensive. 'He told me that Dee—'

'Desiree,' Babs growled.

'That Dee was his missus' baby. Swore she was a drunk and druggie who put it about with so many men she didn't even know who the father was.' Babs gasped in dismay. 'And when the kid was born black she didn't want to have nuthin' to do with it.'

Babs stormed, 'That's a bollocks lie.' Richard touched her arm to allow Cleo to carry on.

'At first he said it was for a couple of months, tops. Then one day he comes over and said you didn't want her back. "She don't want no black bastard running around the place", he said.' Babs let out a noise like her heart was breaking. 'I took him at his word.' Cleo placed her palm over her heart. 'I would give up my life for that girl. She's part of me. Part of my family. I'm not going to get married; I've had it up to here with men telling me what to do. Dee is the only child I'll ever have.'

Babs shook her head. 'But's she's mine. Mine. I carried her

for nine months. Gave birth to her. Stood by her when my parents turned their backs. I want to take her home.'

Babs' wrenching plea hung in the deathly silence that followed. Cleo said calmly, 'You're right, you're her blood mother. But she doesn't know you. I've been her mum for six good years. This is her home. Are you really going to rip her away from all that?'

Babs couldn't think straight. All she wanted to do was snatch up her daughter and run as fast as she could. But could she really take her away from this good woman? A woman who had given her love and a home? The last point Babs didn't want to admit, but she had to – a woman who was the same colour as Desiree. Babs shuddered as if that racist woman's spit was hitting her skin all over again.

As if reading her mind, Cleo's sister spoke from the doorway. 'The other day, some guy called Dee a very ugly name and Cleo grabbed him by the balls and put him right. It's not easy for us some of the time, but we stick up for each other.' She was holding a photo album. 'We don't have many photos of her because we don't have the money for a camera, but one of our cousins does.'

For the next half hour, Babs devoured pictures of her baby. As she turned each page, she knew she had to make a life-changing decision. When she closed the book she turned to Cleo's sister. 'Can you bring Desiree in?'

A single sob broke from Cleo's mouth but her sister did what Babs asked. Babs' throat clogged with emotion when her child shyly entered the room.

She called her over. 'I'm your Auntie Babs . . .'

As Babs got into Richard's motor fifteen minutes later, she tried her hardest to put the past behind her, but she couldn't forget the face of her child. Just couldn't. What a rotten world.

Richard Smith took one look at her and opened his arms. Babs fell into them, softly weeping, her heart breaking all over again.

He vowed, 'I'm going to bring Stanley Miller down if it's the last thing I do on this earth.'

Sixty-One

'Shall I be honest with you mate? I reckon our friend's kippering us,' Horner said, his palm running over the pocket where the portable cassette recorder was hidden.

Horner and Cricket were tucked away in a snug corner in the Bad Moon. There was no sign of Stan Miller. They'd promised him they had stuff he really needed to hear.

Cricket tapped ash onto the sticky wooden floor. 'Nah, I don't think so. He said it himself – if he goes down, we go down. But if we go down, he goes down too.'

'Miller's a slippery sod. He always was. He knows we're up to something. And we're sitting here like coconuts at the fair. That's what I reckon.'

'Give him ten more minutes. He'll be here. You're a bottle job, mate.'

Horner seized his colleague by the lapels. 'I'm a what?'

The door to the saloon swung open. They turned to see who'd come in. It was a young man in his thirties, smartly but casually dressed. He ambled up, taking a chair as he went, and parked it, to their surprise, at their table. 'Having a row? In a nice pub like this? Shame on you.'

Horner let go of Cricket's jacket. 'Are you a friend of Stan's? Because if you are, we're coppers. So you better take a walk before you get hurt.'

The stranger seemed puzzled. 'Coppers? That's odd. I'm one myself and pretty sure we haven't been introduced. The name's Richard Smith.'

Cricket and Horner jumped up. 'Sit down,' the stranger ordered. 'This pub is surrounded by so many vans of uniformed you'd think Millwall were playing West Ham.'

They sank uneasily back down. Horner started to spin a line. 'What are you playing at? We're just about to arrest a suspect for killing his brother. Now he'll have seen you lot and run for it. You're looking at a disciplinary.'

Smith looked serious. 'I'm assuming you're talking about Peter Miller?' They were gobsmacked. 'I've been looking into it myself and thought Stan might have murdered his brother.' Richard dropped the sarky tone. 'There was no chance Stanley Miller was going to come here. He might be a murderer but he ain't stupid.'

Horner fought back. 'I don't know who you've been talking to but if it's Miller, the geezer's a crook. We've been after him for ages and he don't like it.'

Richard laid a photo on the table. It was a still from one of Pete Miller's films, showing Horner with Cleo astride him at the Mile End brothel.

Horner studied it. 'So what? Sex ain't illegal.'

'No, of course not. Unfortunately, there's tapes as well. Audio of you sharing all kinds of pillow talk. You're very frank about backhanders, fit-ups and even some of those evictions you took part in. Stan never trusted anyone; the knocking shop was wired for sound. It was a regular *Debbie Does Mile End*.'

The two bent cops were stunned. 'And I've dispatched some cars to pick up Stan Miller at the house he owns in Islington.'

Cricket launched himself at Horner, battering him with a

glass in one hand and his clenched fist with the other. 'You prick, you fucking prick!'

They were pulled apart by Smith and two colleagues, who'd been posing as customers at the bar. As they were cuffed, Richard put his arms around them and said in triumph. 'As they say in *The Sweeney* – put your trousers on, boys; you're nicked!'

Stan was in a position he'd never expected to be in – running for his life. With only the full moon for company, he crept along the landing towards his home. What a fucking all-time moosh he'd been. He should've figured out Richard Smith was undercover, trying to find dirt on Cricket and Horner. And instead of getting out of the way – he had zero love for the pillocks – he'd bloody got himself stuck in the middle. Now his past had caught up with him. A wagonload of Bill had turned up at his and Clare's to take him, but he'd managed to do a bunk through a window. He needed to get up and out of here as soon as.

He reached his door. Took out his key, and stuck it in the lock.

'Babs! Babs!' he shouted.

No reply. Good, he didn't need the stupid bint giving him a load of earache. First stop was the kitchen and then the bedroom for a quick change of clothes. The kitchen was dark; he left it that way so no one outside could see him. He headed for the gas meter and felt around the back for his stash of cash. He pulled it out.

The light flashed on, startling him. He spun around.

'Finally come home, Stanley?' Babs said.

Her face was hard as she stared at her husband. But she had to burst out laughing at what he was decked out in. A woman's short silk dressing gown, a pair of Y-fronts, a vest and sodden fluffy woman's slippers. His hair was all over the shop and he was half shaven. The untouchable Stanley Miller didn't look so mighty any more.

'Left somewhere in a hurry?'

For the first time ever, she saw Stan blush. 'Yeah, that's right, have a good laugh. Get me a drink.'

'There ain't any. I drank it all.' She was done taking orders from him.

He sighed. 'Fan-fucking-tastic.'

Babs waved at the cash in his hand. 'What the hell is this?'

'It's my emergency stash. Everyone's got one.'

'Right. So every time I've needed a few quid extra to clothe and feed the girls . . . How could you do that to your kids?'

'Don't make a fuss, you silly cow. I'm in a spot of bovver. Old Bill raided a place I've been using in Islington. I was in the bathroom having a shower and I had to go out through the window.' He looked down at his clobber. 'Hence the unusual get-up. I've had to run all the way. I expect it's nothing but I didn't fancy answering any questions. The wife weren't too chirpy about it either.'

The out-and-out cunt. 'The wife?'

He turned away, but she saw how pale his face had gone. 'Just a figure of speech–'

'You're a filthy liar, Stan,' she chucked at him, letting her fury boil to the surface. 'I know all about your posh piece of snatch. Two wives on the go.' She tutted. 'You have been a bad boy.'

'I don't know who's been filling your head with that bollocks–'

'I have, that's who. I saw you with my own eyes. And you've got another kid.' She wanted to throw something at him, but restrained herself. 'Why did you marry me, Stan?'

His lip curled slightly, then he plastered on his trademark charmer's smile. 'Because you're the only girl for me. We're good together—'

'Wrong again. Tie the knot with muggins here and she can't say nish about your evil dealings; because she can't be forced to testify. And, of course, playing me like a fiddle to stitch up Mickey and Mel.' She sneered, 'All your little secrets are out now. Second wives? Other children? Child abduction? Oh yeah – and you killed your brother.'

He moved forward. Babs' hand flew out from behind her back, holding the shooter Kieran had got her.

He began laughing, a chilling sound. 'Woah! Hard girl! Waving guns around like your effing handbag now?'

'I should fucking shoot you dead right where you stand for making me think my girl was dead all these years. You gave her away to another woman. Cunt is too good a word for you.' Her voice broke slightly. 'Why did you take my baby away?'

'Whoever said that is a full-time liar.'

Babs shook her head, furious. 'I saw her. I'll tell you why you did it – you wanted total power over me, and that wasn't going to happen as long as I had Desiree. That's why you got me this flat, weren't it?'

'No, I did that because I was trying to give a girl in a bad situation a break.' His face turned nasty. 'As for that brown bastard baby of yours, did you really think a man in my position would be seen down the shops with some darkie? I don't think my business partners would've got that.'

She hitched the pistol higher. 'Get out.'

He opened his arms wide. 'Go on then. Let's see how many nuts you've really got. It's easy to pull a trigger and you can always tell the law it was self-defence. Go on – I dare ya.'

She turned the pistol to the side. The flat shook as she shot out a window. And a second time when she shot out another one. The cash dropped from Stan's hand and fluttered to the floor. She turned the gun back. 'Maybe you're right. On the other hand, while the plod won't turn out here for a burglary, I'm pretty sure they will when the neighbours tell them there's been shots fired. If I was you, I'd be about my business sharpish before they get here.'

The way the estate was going, she couldn't be sure the neighbours would call the police. But as a resident of Islington these days, he wasn't to know that.

He let his hands drop. He was still smiling. 'Fair enough.' Babs trained the gun on him as he walked past. He gave her a little salute and said, 'That was quite a clever move; I didn't think you had in you. I'll get changed and then I'll go.'

'No, you won't. Out. Now.'

He hesitated. 'That's nice, that is.' But time was short. There were sirens in the distance. It probably wasn't for them but it was a useful reminder that the coppers would be there shortly. 'Alright, I'll go – what about a hundred nicker from my emergency supply? Just to tide me over? You can keep the rest.'

'Fuck off.'

He went out into the hallway. When he got to the door, he paused and begged. 'It's chucking it down. At least let me have my cap.'

She took it from the coat rack and slung it at him. He put it on at a jaunty angle. 'Alright Babs, so long. I'll see you later.'

He disappeared into the night.

It turned out he was right. He did see her later.

Twenty-five years later.

PART THREE: 2003

'He's back to spread evil.'

Sixty-Two

Babs could hardly contain her excitement as she picked up her granddaughter's birthday cake. She couldn't believe that little Courtney was ten. It seemed like only yesterday she was rocking her in her arms for the first time.

They were holding Courtney's party in one of the houses Babs cleaned in Mile End. The management company who ran the place had said no problem to her holding the birthday party here. In all the years she'd worked for them, they'd never given her a blind bit of trouble.

Babs had wanted somewhere special to hold the party. Courtney was her Jen's eldest and everyone was gathered together for a right old bash. They'd had their trials and tribulations over the years, more than most, but they'd come through all of that and were a solid family now. Including Dee. It still bought tears to Babs' eyes knowing that her firstborn was openly acknowledged. Their reunion hadn't been the easiest of roads – Dee had had to tell her point blank not to call her Desiree – but they'd got there in the end, understanding each other a little bit more every day.

Babs' own birthday would be coming up in three days' time. She was turning the big five zero. Instead of piling on the pounds, like many of her mates over the years, she was thinner than ever; probably down to the gin she still guzzled too often. She didn't want a shindig to celebrate her half-century, just a nice bit of nosh 'n' slosh with her three girls. She was chuffed about being the head of a family of three daughters, three grandkids, including Dee's adopted boy Nicky, and two sons-in-law – one of whom was an out-and-out git who'd had the decency to leg it. She still missed her parents and was eternally grateful they had made up. Her dad had been such a strength for her. He'd loved his Jen and Tiff to death. Beryl had gone the same way as Cheryl and moved out Essex way. And Richard . . . Babs had never set eyes on him again. But that was life. And life was cracking. If Babs was a churchgoing woman she'd thank God for it every day of her life.

The music stopped, giving Babs the signal to bring the birthday cake on through. They'd got a gorgeous pink and white cake with Courtney's name written across it in gold and silver glitter. Ooh! What a treat the girl was in for. Babs headed happily to the party room. She thought it was a bit strange she couldn't hear Courtney's mates running around and letting off steam. Those bloody girls had better not've told everyone to shut it, which would give the game away to Courtney that the cake was being brought in. She couldn't wait to see her grand-kid's face.

When Babs saw the man standing near Courtney and Jen, she realised why it was so quiet. The cake slipped from her hands and crashed to the floor. Everyone gasped. Except for him.

'Babs, I can't believe you never sent me an invite to my own granddaughter's birthday,' announced Stanley Miller.

Horrified, Babs couldn't speak; couldn't utter a bloody word. *This is a nightmare. I'm still tucked up in bed, not at Courtney's party.* Babs squeezed her eyes shut, shook her head and desperately re-opened them. There he was, like the devil come to collect his due. Fucking Stanley Miller. He was leaning on a cane with a silver top that matched the sprinkled strands in his blond hair and, typical, he was suited and booted. Every soul was quiet as they looked at her, even the kids, but Babs saw none of them. She only had daggers for the rotten bastard of an ex-husband she hadn't seen in twenty-five years.

'What the fucking hell do you think you're doing here?' Babs raged, her hands tightening into fists.

'Mum!' It was Dee, of all people; she usually cursed a blue streak, regardless of the company. 'The flamin' kids.'

Babs wasn't having none of it. She stabbed her finger at Stan. 'I want him out. Now. Get that two-faced, two-timing—' She couldn't go on. She felt as if she was going to keel over. She desperately needed one of her happy pills, though she'd been trying so hard lately to cut down.

Jen rushed to her distressed mother's side and put an arm around her shaking shoulders. Tiffany turned, ready to defend her mother. 'I don't know who the heck you are, matey, but you wanna sling your hook.'

She was confused when he just smiled at her. There was something about that smile she couldn't put her finger on . . .

'Flippin' hell.' He peered at Tiff with such wonder she took a step back. 'Tiffany. You've grown, girl—'

'Of course she fucking well has, you muppet,' Babs screamed. 'What did you think? She was still going to be in nappies twenty-five years on?'

Babs saw the truth dawn on her three girls. She whimpered.

'Is this—?' Tiffany started.

'Our flippin'—' Jen continued.

'Stanley Miller,' Dee finished.

One of the mums dragged her kids out of the party. Babs

knew that the word that Stanley Miller was back in town would be around The Devil's Estate in five minutes flat.

'Right, kids,' Dee's fifteen-year-old, Nicky, jumped in with an upbeat voice. 'Who's up for a dance competition?'

Bless his kind soul, thought Babs, trying to distract the kids from the major-league aggro. Her Dee had brought that boy up right. The children let out a big cheer when he hit the music system. When Sugababes' 'Round Round' beat filled the room, they started jumping and prancing all over the place.

Babs, her girls and her boomerang ex gathered in a corner. Up close, she saw how yellow his skin appeared and how thin he was. Her Stan had never been a fat sod but he'd liked his nosh. *Her Stan? Are you off your rocker! This man is nuthin' to you.*

Stanley leaned on his walking stick and reached out to touch Jen's cheek. An outraged Babs batted his hand away. 'I'll break your fingers. I'm warning you . . .'

'Mum, cut it out,' Jen said as she saw her father stumble and try to right himself.

Babs snorted. What an all-time drama queen! She'd had enough of this. She pointed her finger at him again. 'Right, me and you, outside.' She turned to her anxious children. 'Stay put—'

'But, Mum,' Tiff cut in, eyes only for her father, 'I want—'

Babs shook her head savagely. 'I mean it. Stay here. Cut some cake for the kids.' She turned and marched out of the house, keeping up a mad pace, not giving a shit if her one-time old man could keep up. She was glad he looked like death warmed up. Glad he had to be propped up by a walking stick.

They stopped on the top step of the three-storey house in Bancroft Square. Babs didn't even need to look behind her to know her daughters were playing twitchy curtains, trying to get a butchers.

She got straight into his face. 'I don't know what disgusting hole you've crawled out of, but you need to jump right back in it. My girls have done fine without you for twenty-odd years.' Her mouth twisted. 'After I divorced you, I suppose you married that flash cunt up Islington way. Properly, that time.'

Stan let out a rattling cough that made his thin frame shake. Babs hardened her heart.

He took out a silk hanky and wiped his mouth. Babs was surprised he still carried one. Old habits died hard.

Finally he said, 'I only wanted to come back and see the kids. Is the black our Desiree?'

'*Our* what?' She erupted. Was this man living on another planet? She lowered her voice so no one heard. 'You told me she was dead, remember, you filthy bastard.'

'Did you tell her that?'

'Of course not. I don't want your evil anywhere near her.'

Stan started back to the open front door. Freaked out, Babs grabbed his arm. 'What are you doing?'

He looked at her and she was stunned by the pain in his eyes. 'I've got to tell her. She probably blames you and that ain't right. I can't live with myself any more.'

Babs' mouth drooped. She might've been a pushover then, but he was going to learn the hard way that life had toughened her up 'Keep running your mouth, Stanley Miller. I don't believe a word of it.'

'But it's true, Babs-babe—'

'Don't call me that.' The nerve. Trying to sweet talk her with the patter from the past.

'I'll admit it took me years to face the wrong I'd done you. Done my kids.' He patted his chest. 'I couldn't look at myself in the mirror no more. I swear.' His face crumbled in anguish. 'All I want to do is make it up to you.'

She folded her arms. 'And how are you planning to do that?

Get Mr Spock to beam us back to 1972 and do it all over again, with you playing the perfect hubby this time? If you're so guilt-ridden what took you so long?'

He settled himself more evenly on his stick, his shoulders sagging. 'Nearly came back in '95, but I chickened out. Figured you'd only think I was here to cause trouble—'

'Don't put none of this on me.' Babs' scorn was piercing. 'I'm so over you, Stanley. Do me a favour – shove right off.'

He clearly wasn't shoving off any time soon. 'I'm a minted man now. I've done well for myself, properties in Spain and a couple of other countries.' He pulled out two photos and handed them to her. She stared at snaps of a gorgeous villa in the sun and a swanky yacht. 'That's my place in Spain,' he explained, 'and the other's my floating palace. I don't want to cause bovver. I just want to use my money to give my daughters and grandbabies a better life. Ease their way.'

'So you've still been living it up, while I was here on The Devil trying to keep it all together.' She looked him up and down. 'You sicken me.'

That made him laugh sadly for some reason. 'If you want me gone, Babs, I'll go.'

'First good thing you've said. Yeah, I want you gone.'

His skin went even paler. 'I'll be gone, alright. In three months' time. I'm dying.'

Sixty-Three

'Right, I want everyone to listen up and I want everyone to listen good, because I'm fucking serious.'

A ripple of shock went round Babs' living room. She never swore in front of the kids. She had a rule about it. But since her ex had reared his unwanted self she was making a habit of it.

Jen wasn't happy. 'Mum, cut it out – Little Bea, Courtney and Nicky are here.'

'I know they are. It's them I'm thinking about.'

Babs had moved quickly after the reappearance of her ex-hole. *Dying, my arse!* And even if he was pegging out, that had fuck all to do with her. Stan was up to no good, she just knew it. Babs wouldn't let him sink his poisonous fangs into her family. He was a fast worker and she needed to move faster. She'd ordered her brood up to her flat straight after Courtney's shindig.

Dee, Jen and Tiffany sat looking expectantly at their mum, hovering by the electric fire. Nicky was amusing Courtney and Little Bea, Jen's youngest, with a computer game. Babs gazed at them. They were so different. Dee was the glamour-puss of the outfit; long, sleek legs encased in skin-tight leather trousers, huge platinum hoop earrings and a short-layered hairdo with buttermilk streaks. While Dee was in your face, Jen carried herself and her clobber more quietly. She wore a short denim miniskirt with an off-the-shoulder electric-blue top. And Tiff didn't give two effs about elegance. She'd always been a trouser girl. Today she was in three-quarter cargo pants and Nikes. Her hair – which had once been as blonde as Stan's – had long ago been cut super short and dyed midnight black. So very different, but Babs loved them all the same. That was why she had to do what she was about to do.

She didn't beat about the bush. 'Listen up, ladies. Not a dickie bird until I've had my say.' Her daughters waited. 'We all had a bit of a moment when the old man turned up. Tiff and Jen, I don't wanna badmouth your dad but there's three things you need to know about him. First thing is that he's a deeply evil man. The second is that he's deeply evil. And the third is that he's the kind of deeply evil geezer who will never change. Trust me, I know. Been there, done that, got the effing T-shirt.

'I can see how you might be fooled by his frail old duffer act. But that's all it is – an act. He can't go for a piss without faking. It's in his nature. You want to know why he's back – I'll tell you. To spread evil around. To cheat, to lie, to scam and to steal. How do I know? Because that's what he does.'

Jen opened her mouth but Babs slapped her down with a wave of her hand. 'No speakee from any of you until I'm done.' Jen clamped her lips tight. 'I'll tell you what he's going to do. He's going to start paying you all visits and using this smarmy charm to worm his way into your lives. He's very good at it. What are you going to do? As soon as he shows his slippery skin, you're gonna tell him to slither off. Don't get into any kind of chat; that's what he wants, that's how he operates.' Babs' voice cracked. 'If I see him do to you what he did to me, it would break what's left of my heart.'

She cleared her throat. 'I ain't figured out what he's actually up to, barging his way into our lives after all these years. I don't know and I don't care. We're not going to give him the chance to set whatever con he's running in motion.' Babs folded her arms. 'Anyone got anything to say?'

Dee shrugged and Tiffany shook her head. Jen broke the silence. 'Evil's a bit strong, innit? He just looked like an old bloke to me. Maybe he does want to make up. That's reasonable.'

It was Jen that Babs was worried about. Despite her difficult years with her nearly ex-fella, Nuts, she had a soft heart. It made her a juicy target for someone as brutal as Stan. Tiff was a chip off the old Miller block, learning the hard way about life from hanging out with the wrong crowd, although – thank God – those years were long behind her. And Dee could see a BS merchant coming a mile away. Jen, she couldn't be sure of.

'I'm not saying he's not up to something. It's just, you know, he might be on the level.'

Babs stood in front of her middle kid. 'The only time your old man will ever be on the level is when he's six foot under. I want you to promise me you'll cut him dead.'

Jen was getting upset. 'Yeah, but—'

Babs shouted at the top of her voice. 'Promise!'

Her grandkids looked at her, shocked. Nicky turned to the girls. 'Let's take our game into Nanna Babs' bedroom.'

When they were gone, Jen muttered, 'Alright, blimey, don't jump out of your pram. What's he supposed to have done anyway? I never understood why he left.'

'We don't need to get into that. After all, whatever he's done, he's still your father.'

'Who we're not allowed to talk to?' Tiff said sullenly.

Babs let out a heavy-duty sigh. 'Jen, hun, you don't want to know, you don't need to know. You'll just have to take my word for it. He's a very bad man. I'm not going into details. Sometimes secrets shouldn't be told.'

Dee surprised everyone by shoving to her feet and grabbing her Gucci bag. Her dark eyes brimmed with fire as she hissed, 'Yeah, that's the trouble with this family; people hide way too many secrets, especially you.' She kissed her teeth long and hard in irritation and headed for the door.

Babs cried out in alarm, 'Where are you going, luv?'

'Outside. All the secrets in this room are doing my head in.'

Dee whipped out a B&H and lit up, totally furious. This family had more secrets than Aladdin's cave and it was stressing her to the max. Sometimes she wished she'd never bothered to contact her mum. She hadn't been fool enough to think it would be all easy breezy, but this mess, she'd never seen coming.

'Dee, babe,' her mum let out hesitantly.

When she didn't answer, her mum walked over and put a comforting arm around her waist. 'I've been wrong to keep the past from you—'

'Bloody straight you have,' Dee hurled back. 'Do you know what it felt like growing up without a clue where you really come from? About your parents? Not knowing you've got blood family out there? I do, and it ain't right, ain't right at all.'

Babs tightened her arm around her eldest. 'Stan told me you were dead.'

Dee's mouth opened, an outraged 'What?' on the tip of her tongue, but she was too stunned to say it. Babs took a deep breath, and the whole tragic story poured out.

'You've got to understand,' she finished, 'I married a monster who came knocking at my door like a prince. I was easy pickings. Your dad—'

'Who is . . .?' Dee had asked this question so many times without a response, she'd finally given up.

Babs gripped the edge of the balcony. 'His name was – *is*, I don't know if he's alive or dead – Neville Campbell. He was just a lad out looking for a good time.'

Neville Campbell. Dee had to steady her breathing. Just hearing her father's name was a big deal. She would've been Dee Campbell if life had gone differently.

'When you refused to say a word about him I figured there was some big drama to tell. You know, he was married with a couple of young 'uns already, or you had a one-night stand and couldn't remember his name. Even maybe that he'd kicked the bucket before you could get married.' She twisted her head to gaze at her birth mother. 'I never once thought it was that simple – he just didn't want to know.'

'But I wanted to know,' Babs said strongly. 'Even when my parents turned their backs on me for having a coloured baby – that's the word we used back then, coloured – I was determined to keep you.' She had a fierce, faraway look in her eyes. 'Even after I got spat on—'

'You what?' Now it was Dee who turned fierce, her hands pumping into fists. 'You tell me who the fuck gobbed on you and I'll go around and show them what it's like.'

Babs put a restraining hand on her arm. 'It was back in '72. A totally different world. White women who had brown babies didn't get an easy time of it.'

Dee pushed away from the balcony. Bloody hell. Spitting on mums? It didn't get any lower than that in her book. The fuckers wanted stringing up. Sure, Dee had experienced racism as a nipper, but gobbing on people was taking it way too far. If anyone *dared* spit on her Nicky they wouldn't need to worry about doing it again; she'd rip their effing head off.

Dee felt a wave of shame. She'd given her old mum such a

rough ride since making contact with her. All she'd done was bombard her with me-me-me questions. She'd had no idea her mum had been duped into thinking she was a goner. What a shitty bastard this Stanley Miller was. Babs hadn't even had her mum and dad to lean on. At least Dee had Bible-bashing Cleo to look after her.

'How did a God-fearing woman like Cleo get mixed up with your old man?'

Babs turned away. *Ah, more secrets.* 'It ain't for me to tell. You'll have to ask her.' She caressed her daughter's cheek. 'I will be forever in her debt for bringing you up. I wanted to take you back when I found you, but I couldn't do it. You were already calling her Mum and she loved you to bits.'

Dee frowned. 'Why didn't you come back and see me?'

Babs sucked her breath in hard. 'Pretend to be your Auntie Babs? I couldn't do it. I'd have ended up in the nut house. I left it up to you, hoping and praying that you'd try to find me.'

Dee got angry again. 'But I . . .' She bit her tongue and held back her frustration. Her mum had been through one of the hardest things a mother could ever experience and she was about to give her a hard time too. She couldn't do that and sleep well tonight.

'It feels good to hear the truth. Why don't you tell Jen and Tiff all about Stan? It's killing me seeing how sad they are. Secrets hurt, Mum, they hurt bad.'

Babs took Dee's hands urgently. 'Stan's a master shit stirrer. I'm not letting him near my girls because they're going to end up hurt worse than they are now, believe me. He's a bold-faced liar and a cheat.' She pulled out the photos Stan had had the nerve to give her, pushing his cushy life into her face. 'He's been living it up while I've had to scrape every penny I could.'

Dee studied the pictures. 'Where's this, then?'

'His place in Spain.'

Dee held onto the photos. 'I'm gonna hang onto these. It's making you upset. Don't let him get to you. You've got a very special birthday coming up this week and we want you to have a bollocks-good time. That's all you should be thinking about.'

'But don't you get it?' Babs pleaded. 'He's after something, and nothing, not even his own flesh and blood, is going to stand in his way.'

Babs looked so tortured that Dee pulled her into a tight embrace.

'You've got to promise,' Babs begged, 'that you'll watch your younger sisters' backs. That evil fucker will be coming after them.'

Sixty-Four

'You're jerking me, I ain't going in there.' Nicky had been too busy chatting on his new flip-top Motorola to notice that his mum wasn't driving them home to Essex. He only realised where they were going when she parked up outside Auntie Cleo's, her foster mum's.

'Stop with the earache and exit the motor,' Dee told him sternly.

Nicky began dialling another number. 'I ain't going in to see the mad bird. I'll wait for you here. Oh, and put the radio on for us.'

Dee grabbed her son by the ear. 'I'm upset. You know what that means. Do you want to make me fizz some more?'

He put his mobile away sulkily and got out of the car. 'What have I got to come for? I've got a gig tonight . . .' But when he caught his mum's eye, he shut it.

Dee pressed the bell on the door of the house in Forest Gate, where she'd grown up. Cleo Clark opened the door with a joyful smile. Cleo might be fifty-odd but her brown skin was wrinkle-free. She wore a very respectable dress over a still-trim body.

Cleo held out her arms. 'It's an answer to prayer! Only last week our emergency prayer group held a special meeting for all those who might need some help. I put Jimmy up and here he is! A lost sheep gone to the bad who needs leading home!'

'My name's Nicky, not Jimmy . . .' The poor lost sheep struggled as Cleo wrapped her octopus-like arms around him, 'and I ain't gone bad either. Well, not really.'

Cleo ignored him, showering him with kisses and praises to The Almighty. Then she clocked the look on Dee's face. 'Is there a problem? Is your lost sheep a drug addict?'

The question brought back all the reasons why Dee had done a runner when she was sixteen and cut ties with her for years. Cleo had been the kindest, most caring mother a person could want, but her unwavering religion had made her overprotective. A young Dee wasn't allowed to do this, do that, couldn't see this person, that person, until she'd felt like she was suffocating. When she'd taken up with a lad Cleo condemned as a 'bad seed', Dee had had enough. She packed up her shit and scarpered without leaving any clues. She'd felt rough; she knew her foster mum would be worried sick. But she'd had to do it or Cleo would've come after her and dragged her back, quoting the Lord's word every step of the way.

Cleo had been right about that lad, but Dee hadn't cared. She was free. Free to pursue all the things Cleo said were the devil's work; money, make-up, dancing – yes, dancing! – and booze. It was only after Cleo had appeared outside John's club in Soho that Dee had begun to think about reconnecting with her. Back then, she'd been trying to do the same with her biological mother. She'd decided, *one mum at a time*. She'd waited till she was truly sure of her relationship with Babs before knocking at Cleo's door.

Dee said, 'No, he's not the problem. It's another lost sheep that's turned up.'

'Come on through – Dominique's here.'

Dominique, Auntie Cleo's friend, had been a regular visitor

during Dee's childhood. Dee had wonderful memories of playing dress-up in the gorgeous clothes she'd bring her from her up West boutique – though Cleo had given many away, proclaiming them too wicked for a decent girl to wear. On any other occasion Dee would've been happy to see her, but not today. She needed some time alone with her foster mother.

Dominique sat comfy on the sofa, her walking stick propped up by her side. Dominique's bobbed hair was completely silver now and the skin on her face had grown slack with age. She smiled with pleasure when she saw them.

'Desiree,' she cooed. Dominique was the only person who insisted on calling Dee her full given name.

Cleo assured her, 'You can say anything in front of Dominique. A problem shared is a problem halved. Now, what's up?'

Dee pointed her finger at Nicky without looking. 'Put the phone away.' She sighed. 'Stan's back.'

Cleo flicked a quick glance at Dominique and set a puzzled expression on her face. 'Which one's Stan?'

'Remember, I told you that Babs' ex is this Stanley Miller geezer.' Dee never called Babs 'Mum' to Cleo; it felt disrespectful of the woman who'd brought her up. 'He turns out to be a right piece of work. Dumped his family donkey's years ago. We've just come from one of Babs' grandkids' birthday bash – and he turns up bold as, like he's just back from popping down the shops.'

Cleo painted on a shaky smile. 'Yes, I know the name – Babs' ex, of course!'

Dee noticed the uncomfortable glances the women were exchanging. She was no fool; something was going on. She leaned forward, her gaze stabbing them one after another. 'You two know him, don't you?'

Cleo gave Dominique a final look, which Dee suspected was

to tell her to keep her mouth shut. 'I told you we know the name. Anyway – that's good, isn't it? The family back together again? Praise be!'

This was too much for Dee. Her anger ricocheted around the room. 'Family? Back together? Do you know what Babs just told me? The little fucker put his ring on her finger and told her I was dead, like I was trash. And I reckon he'd have been just as happy if I'd ended up in a weighted sack in the river!'

Cleo avoided her eyes. 'Dee, this was all a long time ago . . .'

'Why didn't you tell me any of this?'

Cleo tried to rally. 'My understanding was that Babs couldn't cope and I was asked to look after you – which of course I was only too happy to do. You brought so much joy into—'

Dee rose to her feet. 'Cut the crap!'

Cleo gave up the ghost. She raised her eyes to the ceiling, as if calling for help, but finally looked across at the woman she loved like her own daughter. 'That's more or less what happened. Stanley Miller is a bad seed.'

Dominique broke in. 'An evil seed.' She looked at Cleo. 'You – we – should tell Desiree the full story.'

Dee's mouth fell open. 'This involves you as well?'

It was Cleo who answered, her voice as weary as her face. 'It's not pretty.' Her gaze wandered to Nicky, which Dee took to mean she didn't want him earwigging.

'Listen to that Missy Elliott CD I gave you,' Dee ordered her son.

'I've gone off her,' he said, clearly more interested in the revelations to come.

Cleo said, with a mischievous twinkle in her eye, 'I've got a great gospel CD you can listen to.'

Nicky quickly took out his CD portable and put his headphones in.

Cleo started her story. 'You know I was always going on at

you about being rebellious. Well I was the same when I was a girl.' She cast her gaze at Dominique again, who nodded encouragement. Cleo took a deep breath. 'I ended up like Mary Magdalene before Christ took her hand. I became a prostitute.'

Dee's mouth tumbled open in shock. She nearly started hyperventilating when Dominique added, 'I was her madam. Called Dorothy back then, though most called me Daffy.'

Bible-basher Cleo a tom, and that little old lady running a brothel? Dee didn't believe it.

'But I never forgot the truth and the light that is the way of Christ.' Cleo pulled a chain with a key on it from around her neck. 'This opened the drawer in the brothel where I kept my Bible so no one could nick it. The place was run by a man called Mickey Ingram—'

'Bloody hell.' Dee had got Mickey banged up when the cops took down her husband John's car scam op back in '93. She still had nightmares about him finding out her part in that, and in what had eventually happened to Chris, John's right-hand man and Nicky's real father.

'Sounds like you know him?' Cleo asked.

Dee brushed her off. 'Not really. His missus lives on Babs' estate and they don't see eye-to-eye.'

'Stanley Miller was mixed up with it all,' Cleo continued. 'I wanted out.' Tears appeared in her eyes. 'On the outside I was tough, but inside I was crying. I was so ashamed.'

Dee flew over to her foster mum and put her arms around her. She'd known a few girls who'd ended up on the game. No way was she condemning the woman who'd fought tooth and nail for her. And who was she to talk; she'd made some pretty dumb choices in her time. Ones she hoped John and Nicky never found out about.

Cleo sniffed. 'Stan had a brother I was close to. His name

was Pete. Total tank head and all mouth, but he wouldn't have hurt a fly. There was some story about him and Mickey and Mel.' From the way she avoided making eye contact, Dee figured there were some things she still didn't want to reveal. 'Anyhow, Stanley offered me a way out—'

'Was that taking care of me?'

'Sort of. It started out as one thing and ended up with you living here.' Her voice became fierce. 'Stan told me some bollocks story about Babs not wanting you. It was a different world back then.' The exact same words her blood mother had said.

'Is that why you never told me about Babs when I was little?'

'I was scared. Frightened that you'd leave me once you found your mum. I didn't know if Stan was still around and I didn't want you anywhere near him. I never once regretted having you.' Cleo caressed Dee's cheek. 'You brought salvation into my life. I'd been living in such a dirty world and you made me feel clean again.'

A lump formed in Dee's throat. No one had ever said something like that to her.

Dominique spoke, and for the first time Dee heard the steel in her voice. 'I knew your Grandfather George. He got me started in the fashion world, which meant I could leave the trade in women behind. He was a good man—'

Dee spat bitterly, 'That bloke turned his back on Babs when she needed him. He's no granddad of mine.'

Dominique replied, 'Both him and Babs realised their mistakes later. The point is, if Stan's back, it means big trouble.'

Cleo's face turned gloomy. 'Whatever dirty pie you can stick your finger into, you'll find Stanley Miller's digit there already. Blackmail, violence, theft, extortion – the story is he finally had to leg it because the Old Bill were after him for the murder of his own brother.'

'Murder?'

Cleo became vague again. 'So they say . . .' There was a long pause before she added, 'He really is the spawn of Satan.' She kissed the key around her neck, as if to ward off evil spirits.

Dee rose to her feet, her face determined. She snapped her fingers at Nicky to follow her. 'If he's looking for trouble, then I'm going to give him some.'

Dominique thumped her walking stick on the floor. 'You can't go up against Stanley Miller. That man has an extra gene that's called toxic.'

Dee stood proud. 'That bastard screwed me over the moment I was born. And now he's going to pay. In full.'

Sixty-Five

The old place sure has changed, Stan thought as he limped into the Knackered Swan. The pub was packed and noisy, with the Black Eyed Peas' 'Where Is The Love' softly playing in the background. As more people clocked who'd walked through the door the place got quieter and quieter. Eventually there was total silence.

The landlord greeted him as soon as he reached the bar. 'Well fuck me sideways, Stanley Miller. Thought you were a goner.'

They shook hands. 'Alright, Jacko. Takes more than rumours to put me down.'

Jacko gave him a pint on the house. 'So where you been ducking and diving all these years?'

'Ducking and diving? Not me, mate. Strictly legit is my middle name these days.'

Jacko leaned in close, bushy eyebrows pushing together like a pair of caterpillars cosying up to each other. 'No disrespect intended but you don't look too bright—'

'Yeah, that's why I'm back.' Stan took a drag of bitter. 'Gonna be cocking up my toes soon. I needed to make peace with Babs and the girls.'

Jacko tutted, like he'd heard this story one too many times in his establishment. But Stan was no longer listening. He'd spotted a familiar face. 'Well, well, well,' he muttered. He left his pint behind and took himself on a little trip down memory lane.

'Fuck. Off,' Mel Ingram greeted him.

'Is that all the love you've got for me after all these years?' Stan didn't wait for a response. He sat down opposite her. She looked bad: really bad. It wasn't that she was fat – Stan was into big and beautiful, like most men – she was a total mess and reeked of stale sweat and booze. Worst of all was the dead look in her eyes. It was like she was just waiting to be put six feet under.

'I heard you were back, you miserable rat.' She took a slug from her rum and black. 'I says to myself, "Stanley fucking Miller, back! That cunt must be after something."'

Stan gazed at her sadly. 'Why does everyone keep saying that?' Mel scoffed and polished off her drink. 'Can't a guy just wanna return to the bosom of his family?'

She laughed so hard her triple chins looked like they were dancing. 'The only family a geezer like you has is himself. You might be able to pull the wool over the eyes of birdbrain Babs, but I know you too well.'

'So where's Mickey, your knight in shining armour?'

'Don't give it the old innocent one, you know the fucker has been making babies with his new senorita—'

'Thought he was in Portugal.'

Mel sniffed. 'That's what he wants the world to think. I know different.' Her sharp gaze pierced Stan. 'That's the thing about me – I know all of it. Every deal we did, every paper we signed, every player we took down. So what are you really back for? You'd better tell me, coz I'm gonna figure it out anyway. And when I do,' she leaned over to him, 'you better watch your back.'

Stan appeared to take not a blind bit of notice of her warning. 'Listen,' he said, a slow smile spreading across his face.

At first Mel appeared baffled, then her face creased into a smile when she heard what he did – David Cassidy's 'How Can I Be Sure' playing softly.

"Member that tune, Mel, babe? '72. First time I heard it was with you and Mickey in the Lilac Room.'

Mel's face lit up, making her look like she was a young woman again. She started to sway. 'Ah, yeah. I had my mink coat on.' Her hand moved as if she was wearing it still. 'We had two bottles of Bolly and steak.'

Stan held out his hand. 'May I have this dance?'

'Don't be bloody daft–'

'Come on, you silly moo.'

A giggling Mel placed her hand daintily in his and he pulled her up. With faltering steps, Stan slow-danced her around the pub. People started clapping and some of the older folks sang along.

'Fuck Mickey,' Stan whispered in her ear, 'you're still a woman who knows how to have fun.'

Mel's face came over all like a kid at the funfair. 'You fancy coming over to mine for a snifter?'

Stan rubbed her back. 'Ah, wish I could, but I think my missus would take that the wrong way.'

'You blokes don't hang around, do ya?' She was back in bitter mode again. 'Mickey gave me the old heave-ho as soon as a new model came on the scene.'

'That's his loss.' He gave her considerable bum a considerable squeeze. The punters laughed so hard it nearly took the roof off. Mel took it in her stride and laughed along as well. When the dance was done, they bowed to their audience.

'Nice seeing you again, Melanie,' Stan said, leaning on his stick. 'You take care of yourself.'

The Annies had long since been replaced by a new breed of pill. Babs popped another Benzo. She washed it down with a good mouthful of gin and started scrubbing the spotless cooker. Since that effing wanker had showed his ugly mug today, she'd been popping pills left, right and centre. She knew if she didn't stop, she'd probably end up getting her tummy pumped. But her nerves were shot to pieces and the memories . . .

Babs gritted her teeth as her cleaning intensified, vicious, manic strokes that sent pain shooting up her arm and scratches into the steel. Why did he have to come back? Why couldn't the toerag leave them alone? Her mind was about to shatter. She threw the Brillo pad down. She was going to stop him in his tracks and she had a secret weapon.

Babs settled her shoulders back before picking up the phone. 'Kieran, is that you, luv?'

'Babs? What you doing phoning so late? Is something up?'

Kieran Scott had gone from The Devil Estate's bad boy to one of London's up-and-coming Faces. He even had a club behind him; at least that was what Babs had heard. She never asked him what he did, because she didn't want to know. Whatever it was, Kieran was living the high life; as far away as you could imagine from the dirty boy she'd met all those years ago.

Kieran growled. 'If anyone's hurt you . . .'

Most folk saw him as a thug, plain and simple, but they would think again if they saw the way he handled Babs. Kieran would lay down his life for her. He'd been protective of her since she'd taken him under her wing. Babs had almost called him up to sort out that worthless shit, Nuts, Jen's soon-to-be ex. She was tempted to tell him Stan was back and bothering her. That was all it would take to get Kieran moving. Probably to drop Stan off a building.

'Just wanted to know what you were up to,' she said at last. She didn't want to drag Kieran into this. She was going to have to figure a way to shut Stan down herself.

'You sure?' he asked. 'Because ...' Kieran let out the last word on a long moan of pleasure.

Babs was disturbed. 'You alright, son?' Then she heard a woman giggle. Another moan from Kieran. Babs' face grew hot with embarrassment. 'Sorry . . .'

'No, it ain't you that needs to be sorry . . .' His voice was rough, but gentle. 'I've got a bit of company, that's all.'

That got Babs smiling. It would warm her heart no end to see Kieran settled. After the horrors of his childhood he needed a good woman to make him the centre of her life.

'You want me to come around?'

Definitely not. As soon as he saw her face he'd know something was up. 'I just wanted to hear your voice. Take care, luv.'

Babs slowly put down the phone. Fancy that: Kieran with a lady friend. She leaned against the wall and let out a long, weary sigh. Why was Stan back?

Babs downed some more gin and took another Benzo.

A pissed Mel left the boozer to weave her way home. That old fart Stan had bought back memories she'd thought long buried. Worst of all, the fucker had made her feel young again. Fancy taking her hand like she was the Queen and getting her to have a bop in front of everyone.

Mel started singing 'How Can I be Sure' under her breath and twirling around like she was back in bad boy Stan's arms again. Back in '72. Back in her mink.

One, two, three. One, two, three, she chanted as she twirled and twirled and twirled . . .

Something hit her solidly in the forehead, shoving her to the ground. She cried out in pain.

They hit her over and over again, until she was an unmoving bloody mess.

Sixty-Six

'Hello, darlin', any chance you could give me engine the once-over?'

Tiffany wasn't surprised to hear her dad's gruff voice the following morning. She'd been expecting a visit sooner or later from mister lowlife.

'No,' Tiffany said, not looking up from under the bonnet of a GTi. She still did the odd spot of work down Richie's garage, despite the windfall she'd come into recently. She couldn't let anyone know about that, after all.

Tiff bet her life that Little Richie, who ran the place with his bellend brother Ron now their old man was retired, was observing all the goings-on as he usually did. Sure enough she heard, 'Tiffany, my girl, that is no way to speak to one of our customers. Why don't you—'

She hitched her head up to look at him, the small puffed-up penguin. She wouldn't have to take his bullshit much longer.

'It's personal,' she told him. She saw her father from the corner of her eye. He looked happy, leaning out of the window of a battered hatchback, but he looked even more knackered than he had at the party. His face was like a skull with a sausage skin pulled over it, dusted with mustard. If it hadn't been for the smile, she might've thought about calling 999.

Instead she folded her arms. 'Alright, Big Ron, I've got this.'

When he disappeared, no doubt to earwig from the office, Tiff turned her full attention on her father. 'Hello, Stan, what a nice surprise.'

'Call me Dad, Tiff. You owe me that, surely?'

Tiffany tapped her spanner in her palm. Owe him? Was he high or something? He came hobbling back into her life after doing a bunk for most of it and this arsehole thought she owed him? Was going to start calling him Dad?

'I've got my hands full here . . .' Something crossed her mind. 'How did you know I was working here anyway?'

Stan switched off the engine and got slowly out of his motor with the help of his stick. 'I asked around. I still know Faces around these parts. You know what they say, you can take the geezer outta the East End but you can't take the East End outta the geezer. Thought you'd be married with a parcel of nippers by now.'

Tiffany let out a slow, mocking smile. It was time to shock Stan out of his pants. 'Probably would've if I had a thing for fellas. I like my other halves nice and curvy, like my motors.'

To her irritation he didn't even blink. 'One of that lot, are ya? Knew a few back when.' He smiled wistfully. 'Aww, those were the days. Soho . . .'

Tiff cut her eyes at him and then got back to work. 'I've got nish to say to you. You can save your breath. You look like you could use all the breath you can get.'

She sneaked a glance at him and caught him looking down, his face forlorn. 'As I expect your mother told you, things ain't looking too clever for me.' When she didn't reply, he let out a sour cough. 'She didn't tell you, did she?' He shook his head. 'That's nice, that is. Not telling her own daughter that her father's only got three months to live? Charming . . .'

That shook Tiff up slightly. Then again, maybe it was one of those Stanley Miller specials her mother had warned her about.

Anyway, so what if the geezer wasn't long for this earth. He hadn't been there for her when she was growing up, so sod him. 'I'm sorry to hear that.'

'We've all got to go sometime,' he said. 'When your time's up, it's up. It does mean I need to get my personal affairs in order before I go. Make sure my family, especially my grandbabies, have in death what I couldn't give them in life.'

He was deffo scamming. Tiff was sure of it. She was supposed to rattle off some sympathetic questions now. But it wasn't going to happen. She knew his type – she was one of them. Conning was second nature to her. Now Tiff knew where she got the gene from.

When she stayed schtum, Stan released a knowing, cold snigger. 'Babs ain't told you about that either, has she?' She could see he'd clenched his fists. He fumed, 'Your mum's really done a number on you and your sister. She hates me – I get that, maybe she's even right to. But to take it out on you two? That's properly out of order.'

Tiffany was careful with what she said. She would bet her life he was a fake, but then again, if he really was a crook he might be leaving a few quid behind. A girl could always do with a few dollars more. It would be a bit of compo for all she and her sister had never had out of him.

She pulled herself straight and gave him the eye. 'OK, Stan, you wanna leave me and big sis and her kids a few sobs in your will – give yourself a pat on the back, we ain't gonna stop you. Just don't bother us, alright?'

His laugh started small but grew louder and louder like she'd told him the best shaggy-dog gag in the world. 'A few quid? You're having a proper joke, babe. It's a few mill. And that's just the cash; that don't include my properties, cars, wine and the rest of it. I'm a very wealthy man.'

At the mention of millions Tiff's heartbeat jacked up, but she made sure it didn't show on her face. He could still be conning the overalls off her. 'Fair enough. Just split it fifty-fifty between me and Jen and maybe we won't spit when we hear your name.'

Stan drew closer to her. He looked haunted. He searched the garage as if worried someone might overhear. 'I wish it was that simple. Trouble is, it ain't. I'm trying to set up a trust fund for Jennifer's girls. A little bit of that, just over half a mill, I've set aside for you, your sister and your mum as a way of saying sorry.' He pointed his finger at her. 'Make no mistake, the majority of the money is for my grandkids. But I want you, your sister and your mum to be the trustees to make sure Jen's daughters get that money when I'm gone. All it'll take is a couple of minutes signing the paperwork.'

Despite not being able to get the words 'half a mill' out of her head, Tiff said, 'If you want to leave Courtney and Little Bea your golden egg you're going to need to find another way of doing it. I'm telling you straight, me, Jen and Mum won't be signing dick. In the meantime, I'm working, so piss off – and don't come back. We're not interested.'

Her dad's face turned tragic. 'Fair enough. I suppose after all the crap your mother's poured into your ears since you were little, it was too much to hope you'd take me at my word.' He gave her a card. 'I'm staying there. If you change your mind, call me. But I promise you this – one way or another, I'm going to make sure you all get something for the heartache I've caused.'

'Whatever.'

He got back into his motor and started the engine. 'Speak to your sister and then give me a tinkle. Help me out by helping yourself out.'

He drove out of the yard. Tiff looked at the card. Imperial

Hotel, Park Lane. She knew the place; it was frequently name-checked in the tabloids as the place where the showbiz big nobs stayed. It looked kosher, but as Tiffany knew, you can get cards printed anywhere.

She went back to work but couldn't settle; those bloody three words kept fizzing around her head. Half a mill. Half a mill ... *He's probably scamming you. Yeah, but what if he's not?* It wouldn't leave her alone. She sat, staring into space, in a flash Japanese Range Rover for a solid five minutes, before getting out her Nokia.

'Jen, I need to speak to you, like, now.'

'Could I pop over and have a word with you and John?' Babs asked her eldest on the phone.

She felt like the walking dead; she hadn't managed to get much kip last night. Her tongue felt dry from too much gin and her head was a touch off-centre from the pills. But it was the only way Babs could deal with her bastard of an ex roaming around, just waiting for his opportunity to wreck her family a second time. Not on her bloody watch.

Dee seemed surprised her mum was asking, but said, 'Depends when you want to come?'

'Now?'

Dee didn't answer straight off. 'I suppose so, we ain't doing anything.' Babs' relief faded fast when her daughter added, 'as long as you don't want to chat about return man Stan. I never wanna hear about that bloke again.'

Babs' heart sank. 'Well ... I was hoping ...'

'It ain't happening, OK.' Babs could almost see her daughter wagging her finger in the air. 'John already knows something's up. If he tumbles what that baby-dumping-fucker done, he'll go gunning for him. I can't have that; we're a clean-living family nowadays. Did I tell you we're involved in the harvest festival? I don't want "church-goer butchers bloke" in the local parish newsletter.'

Babs couldn't imagine Dee at a harvest festival. She'd probably end up chucking a can of Heinz soup at anyone who dared not listen to her. 'Please, luv. He's come back to destroy us. I know him, that's what he's does.'

'No, Mum.'

'I just want to know where he's been for the last twenty-five years. Your John knows people; he can ask around. Stan must've been up to something.'

There was a long silence before Dee said again, harder, 'No. If you mention him chucking me overboard when I was a baby, John'll fly off the handle. You've never seen him go ballistic. Believe me, it ain't a pretty sight.' Dee's tone softened. 'You should have your feet up, think about your birthday. Don't worry about Stanley Miller; he'll get what's coming to him.'

A dejected Babs put down the phone. She should be looking forward to her girls taking her out for her fiftieth, but she couldn't muster up any pleasure. While Stanley remained at large all she could feel was something awful looming.

Dee punched her mobile off as John put a comforting arm around her. They were in the main room of their plush house in Essex. John had held her all night after she'd told him how Stanley Miller had destroyed her childhood. Dee hadn't wanted her mum to know she'd dished the dirt. She wanted her to stay well out of it. If anyone was going to sort Stan Miller, it would be her.

'You OK, babe?' he asked.

Dee laid her palm over his. John had blown a fuse when he heard the story. He'd wanted to find Stanley and blow his fucking brains out. But Dee had made him cool off. She was going to make Stanley Miller rue the day he'd been born, but they had to play this one carefully.

'We need to find out what that arsehole has been up to all these years. That means contacting someone in Spain.'

John poured himself a brandy and Dee a glass of Bolly. 'Uncle Frank will know what's what.'

Uncle Frank was a former Face, now retired and lapping up the sunshine in Spain. He wasn't John's blood relation, but when things had got tight when John was a kid, Frank Reynolds would see him right.

Dee sipped her fizz while John got on the blower to Uncle Frank in Malaga.

Sixty-Seven

'What about these?' Jen asked her younger sister.

Tiff looked at the birthday banner in Jen's hand. 'Don't be daft, that says, "Happy Birthday Princess". Mum's turning fifty, not five.'

Babs thought they were going off up West tomorrow, but Tiff and Jen had got together with Dee to organise a surprise birthday bash instead. Hitting fifty was one of the great markers in life and had to be celebrated properly. Dee was sorting the booze and grub and they were getting stuff to decorate the Knackered Swan, The Devil's local. Dee had wanted the party to be somewhere swish and upmarket, but Jen had persuaded her that Babs needed to feel nice and comfy on her big day.

'I just thought they would be a nice touch,' Jen said. 'You know, make her feel ultra-special since Dad had the nerve to show his mug again.' She saw the stubborn look on Tiff's face and dropped them back on the shelf.

Jen wheeled their well-stocked trolley to the next aisle as Tiffany said, 'Talking about Dad—'

Jen put the brakes on with a screech and turned in irritation. 'Don't go there, Tiff. I don't wanna know. That man caused our poor mum a bellyache of trouble and we agreed to have sod all to do with him.'

'But he came to see me—'

'He what?' Now Jen was really narked. 'I hope you told him where he can stick his walking stick.'

Tiff looked her sister right in the eye.

'Mum never told us everything—'

Jen sneered, 'Un-bloody-believable. He's already got you wrapped around his crooked little finger—'

'He's bloody dying.' Jen gasped. She hadn't been expecting that. She might despise the old duffer, but dying . . . 'He says he told Mum at Court's party, so why didn't she tell us?'

Jen banished her sympathy for a bloke who had never been any kind of a father. 'Listen to ya. Mum must've had her reasons. The prick's probably yanking your chain to make us feel sorry for him.'

'Come on, Jen, you saw his face. Looked like it had been dipped in custard. He's got three months to live.'

Jen's eyelashes fluttered uncontrollably, her mouth wobbling. She had zero love for the father who had abandoned them, but three months left to live . . . that was a hard thing for anyone to swallow. She felt cold.

'He's loaded,' Tiff revealed. 'Got a fuck-off villa in Spain and a friggin' yacht. He wants us to go and have a chat with him in his Park Lane hotel.'

'Park Lane?'

'He says he's set up a trust for Courtney and Little Bea. He's put aside a little dosh for me, you and Mum, but the real money is for your kids.'

Jen smacked her lips together. 'And you believe him?'

Tiff shrugged. 'Dunno. But I tell you what, if there's money coming my way, I'm willing to hear him out.'

Jen should've guessed Tiff's motivation – hard cash. Her sister had nearly wrecked their lives when they were younger, ducking and diving with the wrong crowd for more poke to shove in her pocket.

'I don't want nothing to do with his money, even if he says it's some trust – whatever that is,' Jen declared and almost bumped into Tiff as she started angrily wheeling the trolley.

'Think of the girls.' Tiff was dug in like a pesky mosquito that wouldn't give up until it was sucking on blood. 'You work all hours at that supermarket and I know you take in ironing on the sly to get some extra pennies.' Jen's face pinked. She didn't like people knowing about the ironing; made it sound like she couldn't take care of her kids. Mind you, it was better than dossing off the social.

'Think about what Court and Little Bea's lives would be like if you could get your hands on some cash any time.'

Jen picked up a decorative, plastic tablecloth roll. 'I think we should take some of this—'

Tiff grabbed it and chucked it back on the shelf. 'Think about it. Courtney can have those swimming lessons she's always wanted. Little Bea can attend those gymnastics classes. And what about you? Maybe you can find some work in the fashion industry again.'

The same thoughts had flashed through her head when Tiff mentioned their dad's money. The teacher at school said Little Bea was a natural gymnast, but Jen didn't have the readies for extra classes. Sometimes you can only buy your kids' dreams with money. And what about her own dreams? She was only twenty-eight for crying out loud, plenty of time to get back to the career she'd always yearned for. But she also felt guilty. Their mum had moved heaven and earth to create a good life for them, all on her own. And what was Babs going to think if they took even a penny of his money? She knew what – she'd blow her friggin' top!

'Come on Jen,' Tiff coaxed her, 'all he wants is a sit-down, to meet us proper like. What you do after that is up to you.'

Did she really want to meet the bloke who had kissed her

off when she was young? Jen couldn't even remember him, but she recalled how bloody cold their home was sometimes. What was that about? Jen realised she had a mountain of questions for him.

'Alright, but I ain't letting my girls have a penny of his dirty dosh. And let's keep this to ourselves. Mum's been hurt enough already.'

The shag pile carpet in the Imperial Hotel was so deep it nearly came up to Jen and Tiff's ankles as they walked to their dad's suite. When they reached his door, Tiff whispered – it was the kind of place where a couple of Mile End birds felt they had to whisper – 'One thing's for certain, the old man weren't lying about the money he's supposed to have. This place must cost a bomb.' But when she looked around, her sister wasn't there. She was twenty yards away and she wasn't moving. Tiff hurried back. 'What's the problem?'

'I've changed my mind. We should never have come. Mum was right, he's a crim.'

Tiffany rolled her eyes. 'How do you know?'

'Because only a wrong 'un could afford to stay in a gaff like this.'

Tiff took her sister by the arm. 'So much the better for Courtney and Little Bea. That means they're in line for a big pay-out when he pegs it. Now come on.'

Jen protested, 'Mum's gonna kill us when she finds out.'

'I'm not telling her and neither are you, so she won't be killing anyone.'

The two women were still hissing at each other when the door to the suite opened and their father welcomed them in. Tiff shook his hand. Jen tensed as Stan hugged her tight. 'I can't tell you what a treat it is to see you here. I know it can't have been easy. I know what your mum would say. But if it means anything to you, you've brought a little ray of sunshine into a dying man's last days. There's a drinks cabinet over there, help yourself. I can't join you; doctor's orders.'

Tiff helped herself to a large voddy and her sister chose a miniature Coke. Like the room, the drinks cabinet stank of money. Even the juice bottles looked like they came from a French vineyard. They took seats on the plush antique chairs, looked down on by proper pictures, with real paint and everything. Their dad sat on an ottoman and put his legs up. After a silence only interrupted by Stan's hacking cough, they got down to business.

Tiff's first question was about his dough, while Jen wanted answers about the past. Stan seemed more interested in helping Jen.

'Look, love, I don't want to drag it all up again. All I'll say is that me and your mum were very young. We were stupid, the way young people are. We gave it a go and it didn't pan out. I'm not going to pretend I was husband of the year. I did some hurtful things and I'm really sorry about that. I'll never forgive myself for walking out on you two. It should never have happened but it did. I've lived with it every day. The important thing in life is to move on. I have but she hasn't.'

Jen's lips thinned, obviously pissed at the swipe at her mum. 'I don't really remember you, but I remember our house was freezing. Why didn't you look after us properly?'

Stan coughed into his handkerchief. 'I don't want to badmouth your mum or anything, but I'd give her dosh to pay the bills and sometimes . . . Well, she liked a bit of a roll down the bingo.'

Jen got upset, her voice rising. 'That's funny, Mum used every last penny from her cleaning job to see us right. If you're going to keep blaming her, I'm outta here.' As if to emphasise her words, she gripped the side of the chair, ready to get up.

'I ain't blaming anyone,' Stan insisted. 'I'm saying the past is the past and we should look to the future.'

Jen's gaze hardened. 'So where have you been holed up all these years?'

Tiffany was proper fed up with this episode of *This Is Your Life*.

Instead of answering, Stan said, 'Get us a glass of water.' When Tiff handed it to him, Stan took out a transparent bag full of white powder.

She sniffed. 'Doing a bit of the old Snow White?'

He half-grinned back at her. 'Coke? Not bloody likely! This is one of the meds the quack's got me on.' He mixed it with the water and knocked it back. His face screwed up. 'That stuff's nasty.'

Tiff and Jen were both silent as they stared at him, as if seeing him for the first time. Seeing his illness. Their dad was up the creek without a paddle.

'Dad . . . err . . .' Jen stammered, 'you don't have to answer—'

He waved her words aside. 'It's alright, babe, you've got a right to know.' He put the glass down. 'What happened was this. I was running my own property empire and I pissed off the law. It was partly my own fault; I know that now. Anyway, when you piss off the cops, they don't forget. They're always on the lookout for something to do you for. Then my brother topped himself.'

Jen broke in. 'You had a brother?'

'Your mum never told you about Pete?' It was the first time he'd got angry. 'I know she ain't got no love for me but she should've told you about your family. Everyone has the right to know about their flesh and blood.'

Seeing the stormy look on Jen's face again, he waved his frail hand in the air to stop her tearing a strip off him. His eyes grew misty as he talked about his brother. 'Your Uncle Pete was my big brother. He looked out for me when we was grow-ing up.'

Stan shook his head. 'I can't tell you when it happened exactly, but suddenly it was like I was having to prop him up. He was a troubled man and decided to end it all. Of course, the law thought this was their big chance and tried to pin it on me.' His voice became fierce. 'Like I would do that to my own brother. It broke my heart when he died.'

His head dropped into his hands as he fought with his emotions. The sisters looked at each other, not sure what to do. Finally, Jen said, 'Dad, maybe you should lie down. We can have our chat some other time.'

His head came up. 'I'm alright, darlin'. I don't like chatting about the past. It's not all about your mum. There were other people involved. I've got my own scars as well.'

Whatever she thought of him, Jen didn't like seeing her dad laid low. She got up and poured him another glass of water.

'Cheers, pet. Anyway, two-twos, I had to leg it abroad until it blew over. As soon as I got the wink I was going to come home, even after your mum officially divorced me, which I only found out about once I decided to come back to Blighty. But the Bill wouldn't let it go. When the plod are out to get you, they're out to get you, know what I mean? So I sold all my property here and reinvested it in Spain. I couldn't get in touch, in case the coppers were watching. I hated the situation but what could I do?'

Tiff spotted the snag in his story. 'But you're back here now under your own name, right?'

For just a second she was sure there was a steely look in his eyes. But then they went soft again. Had she imagined it? Had she just glimpsed the real Stanley Miller?

'I hired a lawyer in London who made enquiries at the Yard. Turns out they've got nish. It was all bollocks. There is no case against me and there never was, so I was free to come back.'

Jen kept plugging away about the past. Tiff drummed her fingers on her armrest. Her ears pricked up again when her father said, 'Look, babe, I'm not going to say my property business was totally on the level, no business ever is. It had a complicated structure under a lot of different names. But since the quacks told me the shutters are coming down, I've been working night and day to make sure it's all legit.'

He paused. 'I need the trust for your girls to be airtight. Which means I want you, Tiff and your mum to look after it until the girls reach eighteen. But that needs all three of you to sign the documents my lawyer has drawn up . . .'

Tiffany scoffed, folding her arms. 'Trust for your grand-kids? A little dosh put aside for all of us? I don't believe a word of it.'

Stan went red. 'Do you know what happens when someone tells you you're dying?' His fingers were bone white on the arm of the chair. 'Every last fucking thing you can remember flashes before you. And then, whether you like it or not, every last wrong thing you did takes a turn sitting next to you and keeps poking and poking until you give an account of your-self.' Stan looked Tiff directly in the eye. 'I have to come to terms with what I did to you. The only way I can do that is to make sure my grandbabies are taken care of.'

His voice lost its emotion. 'You don't want to know – fine, get up and leave. I ain't stopping you. But know this, on my heart, I'm going to set that trust up if it's the last thing I do before I close my eyes.'

Jen stood. Her chin trembled slightly as tears sparkled in her eyes. 'I think I'll just powder my nose.' She fled to the state-of-the-art bathroom. Stan and Tiff were left alone.

He studied her. 'Still sitting on the fence, darlin'?'

She opened her hands. 'Dunno, Stan. Maybe.'

'I understand. But I'm too old to play games. And I'm nearly too dead anyway. You'll see when you get to my age. Now, if you'll excuse me, I have to go neck some of the hundred and one pills I've been issued with. Fuck knows why, I'm a goner anyway.'

He used his stick to slowly ease up. Tiff didn't know whether to help him or not. For the first time since meeting her dad her instinct was to help, but she didn't move. She felt guilty at her attitude and wondered why she wasn't interested in the old man's life like Jen.

The door to the suite burst open. A young woman stepped inside. She was dressed from head to toe like a Kelly Osbourne mini-me, hauling shopping bags from some of the city's most exclusive stores. When she saw Tiff, she whipped off her DKNY sunglasses and threw them across the room. Her bright blue eyes lit up like icy fireworks. She seemed ready to thump someone. She dumped her bags and screamed, 'Who the fuck are you?'

Tiff was so stunned by this bat out of hell that she could only say, 'I'm Tiffany.'

'And what the fuck are you doing here? You look like you should be in some low-rent Goth convention.' The woman marched over to her. 'Get the fuck out.'

Alerted by the noise, Stan came out of the bedroom. 'Oh hello, luv, I weren't expecting you back this early.'

Her false lashes flickered like crazy as she turned her attention to Stan. The glow from her eyes seemed to blast him backwards. 'Obviously fucking not. As soon as my back's turned you move some fucking slag in.' This woman was East End to the core. When a red-eyed Jen appeared, her voice went stereo. 'I don't fucking believe it, here's another one, except this one is done up like Tweedledum. You having a bit of girl-on-girl action without inviting me?'

Both Jen and Tiff gasped, but Stan held them back with a raised hand. He hurried to the woman as fast as his spindly legs would let him, as if he feared she was about to attack. He explained in an undertone, 'They're my daughters. I told you I had daughters. Keep it down. This is a posh hotel and I don't want any complaints.'

'Fuck the neighbours. I want to know what they're doing here.'

Stan's eyes were haunted when he looked at Tiff and Jen. 'They've dropped by to catch up, that's all.'

The firecracker sneered, 'Oh, they've just dropped by to catch up, have they? You fucking prick! They're here on the take! What's the matter with you? Get 'em out. If I find out they've been here again, I'll show you what it's fucking like.'

'They'll be off in a minute. Look . . .' He pulled out his wallet and took out a gold card. She snatched it, her poisonous stare fixed on Tiff and Jen.

Stan begged, 'Get yourself off up Bond Street and buy something fancy. Something that sparkles.'

The woman swivelled to face him, her mad hair flying to the side. She ranted, 'Oh, I will. But if I find out that you've ever, *ever*, spoken to these two scrubbers again, then so help me . . .' She pointed a finger in turn at Tiff and Jen. 'And let me give you two ladies a bit of advice. I'm from Hackney, right? I know people. Proper people. If I find out you've been chiselling Stanley, I'll have the pair of you taken out. And don't think I'm joking.'

She cuffed Stan around the head as if he was a little kid and marched out.

As she went Stan reminded her, 'Don't forget about dinner tonight, lovecake.'

'Fuck your geriatric mates!' She slammed the door so hard the walls shook.

Head bowed, Stan shuffled over to the ottoman and sat down.

Tiffany said casually, 'Was that a friend of yours?'

Stan pulled his head up. He seemed close to tears. 'In a manner of speaking.' Then he added, by way of an apology, 'She's my wife.'

Sixty-Eight

'Fucking hell Stan,' Tiffany said with distaste. 'Are you for real, bonking a nutter like that?'

Jen chucked in, 'How old is she? Never thought I'd live to see the day my *old* dad was robbing the cradle.'

'Yeah, yeah, I know. There's no fool like an old fool.' He shook his head in despair. 'You know what the worst of it is? When I met her in Malaga, what struck me was how laidback she was. And she was, right up until we flew to Vegas for the wedding. I got engaged to an angel and married a monster. No getting away from it, I've been a mega prat. Here Tiff – get me a drink, will you? A big one.'

'I thought you weren't allowed any.'

'I'm not and that's why I'm having it. With a bit of luck, it'll kill me stone dead.'

Tiffany fetched her father a Scotch, although she put a lot of mixer in it. He gulped it down eagerly. Jen looked even more upset at the idea her dad had been trapped by such an obvious gold-digger. 'You need to divorce that bitch. And you need to do it now.'

This suggestion cheered the old man up. 'Divorce? You're kidding. I'll be a pile of bones by the time her solicitors have picked me clean. Which brings me to the delicate matter I was hinting at earlier. My wife is labouring under the illusion that she'll be inheriting my assets, a not-unreasonable thought in the circumstances. But that's not gonna happen. My grandkids are getting it.'

Jen wasn't interested. 'We can talk about this another time. Pack a bag; you're coming home with me. I'll look after you.'

Stan burst out in a loud chesty cough. 'No chance. If she comes back and finds I've done a runner, she'll be manning the guns. We can't talk about this later – there's no time to lose. If I go before all this is sorted out, that mad bird will get the lot. I'm not having that. I've let you down enough already.'

Jen shook her head. 'You're not safe here. That woman is one stop short of East Ham.'

Stan beamed. 'Barking? You got that right. I appreciate the thought but you don't need to worry about your old dad. He can look after himself.' The hacking cough he launched into suggested otherwise.

Then his mobile went off. He pulled it out. 'Yeah . . . that was quick . . . right . . .'

He rang off. 'My brief says all the paperwork is in order. He wants us to sign at two tomorrow.' He grabbed Tiff's hand in desperation. 'You have to get your mum to sign. If she don't, Courtney and Little Bea get sod all and my fucked-up missus gets the lot.'

Babs tried her best to get the demon she'd once married outta her nut as she left to go to work cleaning two houses in beautiful Bancroft Square. Getting her hands on the job had been real jammy. She hadn't even applied for it. Back in '89, a note had come through her door looking for a part-time cleaner. She'd assumed the notes were going through all the doors on The Devil, so she knew she'd have fierce competition. But she'd given the number a tinkle, and ended up getting the job.

And what a cushy number it had turned out to be. The

houses were occasionally leased but more often than not both properties were empty. It was a bit odd, but at the end of the day she was getting her dosh so she kept it shut. When there wasn't much dusting to be done, Babs would mostly kick up her heels and knock back a few jars.

As Babs turned to shut her front door, one of her neighbours, Sally Rigg, rushed over. Babs liked Sally well enough, but it wasn't the same as having Cheryl and Beryl there.

'It were awful,' Sally informed her, shaking her head dramatically.

'What was awful?' Why did Sally always start her tales in the middle? Babs was forever having to draw her back to the beginning to make sense of it.

'The body.' Sally made the sign of the cross.

'Is this an early Christmas pressie? Has my old man finally done the decent thing and died?'

Sally moved closer. 'Someone battered Mel Ingram. It looks like the ten tonne bitch is a bloody goner.'

That did get a gasp out of Babs. She hated the vindictive old bag with a passion, but hearing Mel might be dead really rocked her. As far as Babs was concerned, after a nuclear attack there would be two things left in this world – cockroaches and Melanie Ingram. It was really strange, but Mel's existence was one of the things that gave Babs' life order. First Stan turns up like a rotten penny and now Mel was done for. She felt like her control was slipping.

'The ambulance people said she's hanging on by a thread. They've taken her to intensive care at the Mile End. It's lucky they haven't shut the A&E there yet.'

'Cheers, Sally.' Then she went back in and slammed the door shut. Babs couldn't explain what was happening to her. By rights she should be skipping merrily around and singing 'Ding Dong! The Witch Is Dead' at the top of her voice. But the news brought back every last bad memory she wanted to forget – her parents turning their backs on her, spit hitting her in the face, the last time she saw Dee as a nipper, pointing a shooter at Stan. The memories tumbled over and over until Babs was forced to down a couple of Benzos to make them go away.

She was grateful when the phone went off. 'Dee hun, is that you?'

'Sorry I ain't been in touch. Me and John have been making enquiries about Stan in Spain–'

'Spain?' Babs was confused 'Even though I asked you and John to ask around you said forget the past–'

'Hell, no!' Dee's voice roared down the phone line. 'Do you really think I can forget what that arsewipe did to me? The nightmare he put you through? No effing way. I just didn't want to worry you, that's why I never said nuthin'. John's got a good contact in Malaga. Stan's been feeding you a load of bollocks. He doesn't live in the villa from the picture. The guys in there are East Europeans. No one's heard eff all about him there–'

Babs' rage pushed her forward. 'I knew he was stringing me along as soon as he opened that lying trap of his. Dying, my bloody back foot–'

'Hold up Mum, he might be getting ready to pop his clogs,' Dee cut in. 'I haven't finished. John's contact heard a story about a Stanley Miller and some young girl up the coast in Alicante. People think he might have married her, but that's not definite. I reckon he's loaded.'

'Why?'

'Come on, be honest, can you think of any other reason why a young chick would want to hook up with a dying Billy Goat Gruff type?'

Babs bit her lip. 'That poor girl.'

Dee let out a sharp laugh. 'Hardly, she won't be poor if she's really married him. I should know . . .'

Babs didn't like the sound of that. 'What you saying? That you tied the knot with John because he was flush?'

Dee swore. "Course I'm not. It's just . . . well you know how these young girls are.' She coughed. 'Anyhow, we aren't chatting about me. I wouldn't lose any sleep over Stan's kindergarten missus.'

But once the call was over, Babs couldn't help repeating, 'That poor girl . . .'

She remembered being an innocent girl, knowing only a little about the world when Stan had targeted her. He'd stuck a bullseye right on her heart, taken aim, and reeled her in. Babs couldn't help feeling sorry for the young thing. She probably thought she was taking Stan for a ride, when all the time he was the one at the steering wheel.

Babs knew she shouldn't do it, but she couldn't sit by and watch Stan crucify yet another innocent. She had to give this girl a nod. She went into the kitchen and ransacked the pedal bin to find the card Stan had given her.

'Right,' she said. When the line connected, the hotel reception put her through to his room. If Stan picked up, all she had to do was slam the phone down. If his wife did, nothing was going to hold her back.

'Hello?' someone answered.

It was a woman alright, but the voice made her see red.

'Tiff, is that you? What the flying fuck are you doing in your dad's hotel room?'

Sixty-Nine

'Mum, we need to talk.'

Babs sized up her betraying daughters straight off. They'd come over and found her cleaning Number 9 Bancroft Square. It was clear they'd decided that Jen was the spokeswoman while Tiffany lurked in the background. Babs guessed that they thought it would be better to have Jen's gentle touch instead of Tiff's in-your-face-twist-your-arm method of persuasion. But it didn't matter. Even if they had the Pope fronting the operation she weren't agreeing to nuthin'.

But she'd always taught her kids it was important to give people a fair hearing. 'Go on then – talk away.'

Jen turned to her sister for support, and got an eye roll back. 'It's about Dad's will . . .'

Babs cut her short. 'You mean Stanley Miller's will. He's not your father. Surely you understand that. You know what a real father is, don't you? It takes more than a roll in the hay.' Babs got back to cleaning.

Jen put on the fake sympathetic look she used with her own children. 'We know how you feel. We feel the same, don't we, Tiff?' Her sister merely mouthed *get on with it*. 'We hate the no mark too. But this is serious. If he really is a high roller, then we'd be stupid not to cash in when he goes. He owes us. He owes you, come to that. It's gotta be worth a shot, hasn't it? What have we got to lose? Please – come with us to his solicitors tomorrow to get what belongs to us. That's all we need. If you want us to ignore him after that, no problem. We'll dance on his grave if you like.'

The various surfaces were getting a furious cleaning as Babs' anger welled up. On the living room wall, an antique mirror hung in the frame of a door that had once led to the neighbouring house. Babs kept it polished as smooth as a skating rink. She could see her two girls in its reflection, both heavy with greed as they thought about the fortune they were only three signatures away from.

Babs took a deep breath, screwed her cloth in her fist and turned to face them. 'He's really taken you in, hasn't he? You're like a pair of fat fish on his hook and he's sitting on the riverbank watching you wriggle, pissing himself laughing. What a pair of mugs.'

Jen's voice went shrill. 'Laughing? Mum, he's dying, which you failed to mention. He's got sod all to laugh about. He's got to be on the level, he'll be dead in three months.'

Babs went back to rubbing the mirror. 'Will he? He seems to be getting around all right. Perhaps we should get a second opinion?'

'Mum! He's dying! And he's loaded! How can you be so fucking selfish?'

Jen and Tiffany followed her into a reception room. Babs got to work on another mirror as Jen shouted, 'Are you listening?'

'I can't help it, with you blaring like a demented foghorn. It's you two who aren't listening. Dee and John have been checking out his story and guess what – he don't own that house and yacht he's touting around—'

'He explained all of that,' Tiffany cut in. 'He had to get rid of some of his assets—'

Babs stared incredulously at them. 'His fucking assets, my arse. Your old man's on the take again, don't ask me how or why, but it's true. If he really was dying and really was loaded, he'd be on the blower to Satan to put his stash in one of hell's safest vaults.'

Tiffany pushed her sister aside. 'Alright, Mum, we get it; you're a bitter old woman warming her hands around her own spite.'

'You what?' Babs yelled.

'Fair dos, I don't blame you. I'd probably feel the same in your position – take it out on him if you like, but that doesn't give you the right to take it out on Courtney and Little Bea!'

Tiffany shrank back in fear when her mum let rip. 'Who do you think you are, coming in here and shouting the odds at me? You really are your father's daughter, aren't you? I hope when you finally realise what a chimp he's made outta you, you'll at least have the decency to feel ashamed of yourself.'

The silence that followed was broken by the sound of the front door creaking and a man whistling as he came in. All three women were startled. Babs shouted, 'Who's that?'

The whistling stopped abruptly but there was no answer. Babs picked up a poker and went out to confront the intruder.

She gave a wry smile when she clocked who it was. 'Let me guess, you just happened to be passing and decided to drop by. Offer a little support to your two saps here.'

Stanley Miller stood in the hallway. For a few moments, he seemed at a loss for words. Then he turned on the charming smile that had sealed a thousand deals and admitted, 'Busted . . .'

Babs squinted at him. 'How the hell did you get in?'

'The door was open. I don't have to knock to talk to my own family, do I?'

Babs thought the door had been closed but she'd been so

upset she couldn't be sure. It hardly mattered. 'You're wasting your time, dick brain. I'm not signing nuthin'. Why don't you go and book a plot at the East London Cemetery instead?'

Stan sighed. 'I'm glad I've caught all three of you together. We really do need to make that signing tomorrow. My quack's told me to come back pronto. There's some last-ditch operation that might squeeze out another couple of weeks of life for me.' He looked forlorn. 'I'm sure you wouldn't begrudge me that. Even you, Babs.' With a flash of his eyes he asked, 'Are you gonna help out, my dear?'

'Fuck right off.' Babs flared up. She flew at him and started whacking him around the nut with her cleaning rag. Stan stumbled back.

'Mum! Mum!' both Tiff and Jen cried out.

Babs tried to fling them off, but Tiff held her arms tight. She wailed, 'I lived with that man for six years and if I told you—'

'Go on then,' Stan goaded softly. 'Tell them. How you stuck a shooter in my face—'

'What?' Tiffany's hand fell away from her mother. 'That pistol in the house was yours?' The one Jen had taken when that business with Nuts kicked off. 'We thought that was Dad's gun from years back.'

Babs shook. She wasn't ashamed. She'd shoot, stab and hang Stanley Miller if it meant he stayed away from her kids. 'He'll crucify the both of ya.'

Both her daughters looked shocked that she wasn't denying it.

Stan sighed again. 'Sorry, girls. Don't sweat it, I'll liquidate some assets and make sure you get a few quid. It won't be much but it'll keep you and my grandbabies warm through the winter.'

Babs was more convinced than ever that he was lying. She

was the one trying to look after the girls, not him. 'OK, you've had your fun, now do one.'

He went, leaning heavily on his stick. Tiffany and Jen blanked their mum as they followed him out, slamming the door behind them.

For a few moments, Babs felt butterflies in her belly. She straightened up. He was lying through his teeth. She was sure of it. It was all he knew. The girls would see that eventually.

She went back to work but first she checked the lock on the front door. Opening and closing it, making sure the latch sprung. It was fine.

Babs frowned. She could've sworn she'd closed the door after the girls came in.

Babs was watching *Who Wants To Be A Millionaire?* when there was a loud knock at the door. She stiffened. Better not be Tiff or Jen; she was still miffed with them. Mind you, if she carried on having the hump, that would split her family apart and then Stan would've won. Hoping to make peace, Babs put down her glass of gin and opened the door.

'Alright, Mrs Miller.'

The last time Babs had spoken to Stacey was ten years back, to warn her to stay away from her Tiff. The girls had been secret best buddies but both Babs and Mel had put a stop to that. Babs couldn't help feeling sorry for Stacey. The girl was a total mess, her body sucked to skin and bones by a very nasty heroin habit. Babs thanked God every day that her Tiff hadn't gone the same way.

'My mum wants to see ya,' Stacey went on, her body trembling slightly.

'I heard she was at death's door in the ozzie.' Babs didn't invite her in; skag heads could run masterclasses on pinching stuff.

Stacey sniffed and nodded. 'Mum's tough. It'll take more than a good kicking to put her down. Anyway, she wants you to pop in.'

Mel Ingram wanting a word with her? The last time that had happened was in '93, in a ruck down West Central Police Station. Since then they had an unspoken rule – *you stay on your side of The Devil's Estate and I'll stay on mine.*

'What's she want to see me about?'

Stacey shrugged. 'Dunno. Just passing a message on.'

Babs didn't want to ask Stacey of all people, but she needed to get a message to her Dee. 'Do you have a mobile I can use?'

No questions asked, Stacey whipped out a phone with a cracked screen.

'Look, luv,' Babs said, embarrassed, 'I ain't ever used one in my life. If I tell you what to write will you send a text for us? And put one of them sad faces at the end.'

Stacey did what she asked without any questions. And surprised Babs by not wanting a fee for services rendered.

Then Stacey made the fatal error of asking, 'How's Tiffany?'

Babs reared forward and pointed her finger like a deadly weapon. 'I've already told you, I don't wanna hear my girl's name in your mouth. Is this what this is all about—?'

'Nah,' Stacey croaked back. 'Just wanted to know what she was up to—'

'Fucking. Stay. Away. From. Her.'

Stacey rushed down the landing. At the end she turned back. 'Mum still wants to see you.'

Then she was gone. Babs didn't know what the effing hell was going on, but that drug bunny had better stay away from her youngest child. Meanwhile she needed to make up her mind – was she going to see her enemy?

Seventy

'What are we going to do if Mum don't turn up tomorrow?' Tiffany asked Jen as they sorted through the decorations for Babs' surprise fiftieth party.

Jen's front room looked like a wreck, with banners, streamers, party poppers and plastic tablecloths strewn all over the carpet. Jen's girls, Little Bea and Courtney, were having a whale of a time giggling away as they tried to fill the balloons.

Jen swept her hair back off her face. 'She's going to turn up to her own party, although no one had better have blabbed to her about it.'

'Not the party, stupid,' Tiffany huffed, 'turn up to sign Stan's papers.'

Jen sighed and sat next to Tiffany. Her sister had a big photo album in her lap, full of snaps of Babs in her heyday. Dee had come up with the blindin' idea to use the photos as part of the party.

'I don't feel good about strong-arming her to sign.'

Tiff tutted. 'Not you as well. Stan owes us big time. Now the geezer wants to hand over a ton of cash to your kids and all you and Mum do is bleat about it. Plus, you heard him, Mum had a fucking gun in our home. He's not the only one holding back about what went down.'

Jen lowered her voice so her daughters couldn't hear. 'But what if Mum's right and he's stringing us along?'

'As far as I'm concerned, he can lead me anywhere if it ends in a pile of wonga.'

Jen shook her head in disgust. 'Why does everything come back to money with you?'

'Simple. I don't wanna be poor.'

The door knocker banged before Jen could think of a slap-down. Sure, money was important, but it wasn't everything. She didn't understand how her baby sister couldn't see that.

Jen was alarmed to see her mum when she opened the door. Her gaze jerked back into her flat. Bollocks, if her mum came in, the surprise party would be rumbled. Jen held on tight to the doorframe. 'Alright, MUM.' She practically shouted the word so Tiff and the girls could hear. Jen moved onto the landing and stood in front of the door.

'What are you doing here, MUM?' She spoke in stereo again.

Babs frowned. 'You gone deaf? What's with all the yelling?' She tried to get to the door but Jen blocked her. 'What you doing?'

Jen's mouth opened but nothing came out. Then she managed, 'Courtney's got a bit of a bellyache. She's lying down. I don't want to disturb her.'

Now it was Babs' turn to look concerned. 'Poor thing. I know what will put her right . . .' Babs tried to get to the door, but once again Jen stopped her. Her mum put her hands on her hips. 'What's going on, Jennifer?'

'I just told you. Courtney—'

'If you spin me that line one more time I'll clout you a good 'un, knock some truth into you.' Babs twisted her mouth. 'Your bloody dad's in there, ain't he?'

'You what?' Jen shook her head furiously. ''Course he ain't—'

Steam was practically coming out of her mum's ears. 'It ain't enough you go around to see him, now you're having him over for dinner and a chat.'

Dismayed, Jen put her hand on her mum's shoulder. 'Mum, straight up, Dad ain't here, alright?'

'Then why are you making me stand out here like a bottle of milk?'

Jen took a deep breath. 'Me and Tiff had a bit of a tussle earlier about this biz with Dad. It got a bit out of hand and now the sitting room is a total tip. And if I'm honest, I just want some "me" time.'

'Oh, luv,' Babs said sympathetically. 'This nonsense with Stan has bent us all out of shape. That's why I told you to stay well away from him. He's pure trouble—'

'Maybe,' Jen shot in, 'but at least I finally got to meet my father at an age I can remember what he looks like. And I'm going to sign his papers tomorrow.' She shook her head. 'Not coz of the dosh. He's dying, Mum.' Her voice choked. 'Dying.'

Babs took her daughter in her arms. 'I remember what it was like when your granddad was near the end, it wasn't an easy thing to watch.'

Jen pulled herself from the comfort of her mum's embrace. 'Then sign the papers tomorrow. Just bloody well sign them. Then Dad can have the peace he deserves before he leaves our lives forever.'

Babs still didn't know what she was doing in Mile End Hospital as she reached Mel Ingram's ward. She hoped it wasn't another deathbed confession; she'd had a bellyful of them. She walked into ICU and almost ran smack into Stacey Ingram and her thirteen-year-old cousin Dexter.

'Alright, Mrs Miller,' the boy said respectfully. He was such a beautiful, well-mannered kid, it was hard to believe he belonged to the Ingram clan. Courtney was sweet on him, but it was a no-go situation as far as Babs and her mum were concerned. She was not getting involved with an Ingram. Besides, Babs suspected that Dexter wasn't their cousin but something else entirely, and she didn't want her granddaughter mixed up in that.

'I *am* really Sorry to hear about Mel,' she said. And she really was. What was the world coming to when a woman couldn't walk home without being beaten to the ground?

'Glad you came,' Stacey said with a skittish expression. She could clearly tell what Babs thought about her. 'Be seeing you, then.' *Not if I see you first!*

Once she was alone, Babs turned her attention to her old enemy. Mel was hooked up to a machine and had tubes coming out of her. Babs couldn't help gasping at the state she was in. One eye was shut tight and her face was battered black and blue. Whoever had clobbered her hadn't been mucking around. Babs thought back to the first time she'd seen Mel in the Go Go Girls Modelling office. She'd been so full of bluster, prancing around in a fur coat. Babs took no pleasure in the state she was in now.

Mel's one good eye was bloodshot and rheumy.

'I hear you wanted a word,' Babs said.

Mel's cracked lips opened and she croaked, 'Eight . . . seven . . .'

Babs' eyebrows dipped in confusion. 'You what?'

'She's groggy from the medication,' a pretty nurse told Babs.

Mel started speaking again, this time with an urgency that seemed to be upsetting her. 'No eight-seven . . . nine . . . ten . . .'

'Maybe you should come back later,' the nurse advised.

Babs didn't have a clue what Mel was going on about, and she wasn't coming back later. 'I'm off–'

Mel's hand shot in the air and the machine started going bonkers. 'No . . . ten . . . nine . . . nine . . .'

Babs had had enough. She started for the exit. All the way she could hear a drugged-up Mel almost pleading, 'Nine . . . ten . . .'

Babs was grateful for the peace. She was sitting on a bench dedicated to Councillor Joseph Carter – whoever he was – for services to the community, near the disused building that had once been the washhouse. Back in '85 the council had turned it into what they called a 'partnership hub', a place where residents could 'interface' with the council more easily. What a crock of crap that had been. After that initiative had slid its way down the sewer the place had stayed empty and unloved. Babs often came here to remember what this estate had once been. The laughter, the women, the kids, the jokes. The way mums would yell for their children to come home. The children laughing and crying when they took a tumble in the adventure playground that had been pulled down years ago. They'd even had a caretaker back then. What happened to the community that would help out if there was a problem that needed sorting? They didn't have money, but that didn't make them animals. It weren't like that no more. Everyone shut their door instead of going in and out of each other's homes. Everyone waited for the council to clean the stairs instead of clubbing together and doing it themselves.

Babs pulled out a miniature vodka and raised it high. 'Here's to the good old days.' Then she hesitated, remembering being spat on.

'Here's to some of the good old days,' she amended and downed the lot.

Seventy-One

Fucking creep making your sisters sign tomorrow at 2.
Save yr sisters. :(

The text from Babs only reached Dee the following morning. Her mobile had been playing up. She almost ditched the useless thing. The tomorrow in the text was now today. She didn't have any time to lose. She drove her metallic silver Corvette to the Imperial Hotel. She and John had been talking to those in the know about Stan, but no one knew a dickie bird. So if the mountain wouldn't go to Dee, Dee was going to the mountain, hoping the mountain was not in his room.

In the reception, she explained to the smartly dressed girl on the desk that she was a new chambermaid reporting for duty.

As soon as she heard the word 'chambermaid', the woman got all sniffy. 'The first thing you need to know is that chambermaids don't come into reception. Ever. They present themselves at the staff entrance round the back.'

I'll present you with my fist, Dee thought, but kept it to herself. She followed the woman's directions, and found what she was looking for easily enough. A young woman in the standard maid's rig, who already appeared bored with her life, sat perched on a pile of pallets, smoking a ciggy.

Dee walked up. 'Hello, babes. How'd you like to do a girl a favour while bumping the width of your purse.'

She looked Dee over with sharp, brown eyes. 'Dunno. Depends what it is.'

'I just need to borrow a maid's outfit and get a master key for the suites.'

The girl burst out laughing. 'You're joking. I don't mind being sacked but I ain't going to prison.'

Dee wasn't deterred. 'Two fifty?'

The girl looked around for prying ears. 'Five hundred. And my break lasts half an hour. If you're not back here by then I'll go screaming to the management that some tough bird has nicked my key.'

Dee got her purse out and told her, 'You're wasted here; you should be running a protection racket. Find out which room a Stanley Miller is staying in.'

The chambermaid headed off to reception and was back in a jiffy with the information about Stan's room. She took Dee through a side door and down to a changing room where she found her some ill-fitting overalls. She was equipped with dusters and polish and pointed to the service lift. Finally the girl gave Dee her master key with the warning, 'Half an hour, tops – otherwise I'm screaming the place down.'

Dee went up to the top floor and padded her way along the lush carpet to Stan's suite. She knocked gently on the door. She assumed that he would be out and about as it was the day for the docs to get signed. She had no plan B if he answered. But there was no sound within. She went inside. She could see he was already preparing to do a runner. Suitcases were neatly arranged on the floor and the dressing table had been cleared. Dee hurried to the bedroom. That too was spotless. There was no sign anyone had ever stayed there. In the bathroom she finally found a trail pointing towards her slippery fish. On the shelf was a half empty box of Slim-o-matic, a popular dieting product.

On the side of the box was the usual blah-blah about weight loss heaven and a picture of a woman in a bikini to prove it worked. Apparently if you mixed a sachet in a glass of water you were so full afterwards that chips and cakes held no attraction. Along with testimonials from satisfied customers was the slogan, 'Lose weight without even noticing!'

'No wonder the bastard's so skinny,' Dee mused aloud.

Then she found something else.

A single pot of M.A.C. yellow eye shadow called Bright Sunshine. Next to it was a shaving brush whose bristles were stained the same colour. Dee applied some to her face. Despite her dark skin tone, she acquired something of the pallor of a dying woman.

Of course, it was possible that Stan was slimmer of the year and had taken to wearing slap. But Dee thought it more likely that his demise was less imminent than he'd been leading people to expect. 'The crafty little bastard,' she muttered.

She looked at her watch and realised her half hour was moving on. She took the slimming sachets, the eyeshadow and the brush and stuffed them into her pocket. After one last sweep, she headed for the door. But as she did so, she heard voices on the other side and a key in the lock. Desperate, Dee looked around. Like a lover who'd been rumbled by an unsuspecting spouse, she flung herself under the bed.

The door swung open and two people came in. She recognised Stan's voice straight off. 'Alright darlin, let's get sorted. I'll get one of the penguins to take the cases downstairs and you go and settle up. Bring the car round and wait for me out front. You can run me over to my brief.'

But Dee didn't recognise the woman. She had one of those little girl voices favoured by posh girls from North London.

Dee could see her pricey kitten heels from under the bed but nothing else. The girl squealed, 'What makes you so sure they're going to sign, Pops?'

Pops?

Stan was confident. 'They'll sign, Flo, you'll see.' Who the heck was Flo? 'My two birds are greedy, like everyone else in the world. Babs ain't greedy but she won't have any choice if she wants to keep her daughters. You'll see. Your old man's got it all worked out nifty-jifty like always. Now – move your tush.'

The girl drawled, 'Popsssss, you're so vulgar.'

His daughter? Babs had never said Stan had any other sprogs, especially some la-di-da bit. Dee looked at her watch. Only ten minutes before the chambermaid went on the warpath.

Stan was still talking. 'And after the lawyers, I'm going for a steak and chips. That fucking slimming food really was killing me. 'Ere – are you sure your mum's credit card will cover the bill?'

'Of course it will; Mummy's loaded. That spineless creep she married pays it all off anyway. He's got so much money he won't even notice. Don't stress about it.'

Stan sounded outraged. 'Clare married again? You never told me–'

'I thought everything was on a need to know.'

'Who's this fella then?'

'Someone she met at a boring auction house. His name's Crispin Chapaux – you might've heard of him?'

'Nah. You don't tend to meet blokes called Crispin in the boozers I go to. I can't believe your mum married someone else.'

'Well, a girl's got to live.'

Stan grunted. 'I suppose they do. And he settles her bills?'

'I told you, she'd have to be putting six figures on her plastic before his pockets would feel any lighter.'

Stan was rueful. 'You're a lucky girl. If I'd half-inched my mum's credit card it wouldn't have covered the chocolates the hotel put on the pillow.'

Dee looked at her watch again. Five minutes left. The door swung open. Another voice entered the conversation, to Dee's surprise; she hadn't heard anyone else come in. But from the sound of it, they were a right slag from down Dee's way.

'Come on you old fucker – get a fackin' move on!'

Stan chuckled. 'You really are a credit to your old dad.' The girl squealed with laughter. Dee realised Flo and the East End slapper were one and the same.

'Are you sure your other daughters will come?' Dee could hear the tension in her voice. Oh, so posh bint didn't like sharing Daddy.

'The smell of hard cash is like flies on shit to people from the East End. They'll be here alright.'

'And your ex-wife?'

There was a pause. 'That bitch will follow her brood.'

The door closed and the sound of their footsteps faded away in the corridor. Dee got out from under the bed and slipped out of the room. She flew down the stairs to where the chambermaid was waiting.

'You're five minutes late. I'm in trouble. That's got to be worth another oner.'

Dee took off her overalls and pushed them into the girl's arms, along with the master key. 'Here's a word to the wise. The important thing in a criminal career is knowing when to call it a day. Learn from the mistakes Stanley Miller made.'

The girl was blank. 'Who the hell is Stanley Miller?'

But a fuming Dee was already marching away.

Seventy-Two

'She won't come, will she?' Jen predicted, her fingers intertwined like a cat's cradle.

She seemed to have forgotten that her main interest was getting to know the father she'd never really had. All she could think about was having extra pounds for her girls.

Tiff was confident. 'She'll be here. Mum's already lost a husband; she ain't going to kiss goodbye to her two daughters as well.'

Jen was outraged. 'She's not kissing me goodbye. She'll still be my mum. Sign or no sign.'

Tiff smiled at her. 'She'll still be my mum too. But it won't do any harm to think we'll cut her off if she don't put pen to paper.'

They were sitting in the lawyer's plush office. Normally clients were expected to wait in the reception room, but Stanley Miller was obviously top drawer here. The brief sat at his desk. He looked as if he was going over documents but Tiff suspected he was really doodling. Every time there was movement outside, the two women stiffened slightly. The door swung open and the office junior appeared, a skinny young man in a suit that looked too big for him. 'More tea, ladies?'

Tiff looked down at the purple concoction she was sipping. 'If you've got any proper Rosie Lee, I'll have some.'

The junior didn't get it. 'Proper tea? That is proper tea.'

Tiff handed him the cup. 'No it isn't, it tastes like aftershave that's been stewed in fruit. I'm thinking more PG Tips with a drop of milk from a real cow with a spoonful of sugar – that's tea down my way.'

The junior looked like he'd been asked to draw up a multi-million pound contract. 'I'll see what I can do.'

Jen twiddled her thumbs. 'She's not coming.'

For the first time, Tiff began to wonder if Jen was right. 'No . . . There's no sign of the old man either. I'm just beginning to wonder if we've been *Punk'd*. If some creepy guy comes in with a film crew, somebody's going to get decked; you mark my words.' She turned to the lawyer. 'Excuse me, bruv – any word from our dad?'

Without looking up, he told her, 'Mr Miller is a very busy man. It's not unusual for someone in his position to be out of sync with the clock.'

'Thanks.' She didn't add that he was a pompous twat or that he'd soon change his attitude when the Miller girls became millionaires. They'd probably get a decent cuppa as well. Tiff eyed the papers they were supposed to sign, piled up on the desk. She noticed Jen was staring at them as well.

Her sister whispered, 'We should have got our own lawyer to check those contracts.'

'Yeah, we should. Except until we've signed those docs the only lawyer I can afford is Nick the Brief from Plaistow and he has trouble reading and writing.'

'Perhaps we should read them ourselves?'

'Face it, Jen, they're legal documents not Mills & Boon. What chance have we got working them out?'

The door swung open again. Tiff's heart skipped a beat. But it was only the junior again, empty-handed. 'We don't have any PG Tips. Would you like a latte instead?'

'Have you got any booze?'

'I'm afraid not, no.'

He was lying. On the lawyer's desk was an ice bucket with a bottle of champagne ready to go pop after the signing. But it was starting to look like the bottle was going to remain unopened. But as the junior left the office, Tiff saw her mother, framed in the doorway and looking like murder. She stared at them with cold hard eyes. 'Girls – I want a word – in private.'

The two young women hurried like two naughty children. Babs whispered, 'I'm going to make one last appeal to you. As your mother, and I hope as your friend. I'll admit I haven't always been the ideal mum but no woman is. But I'm begging you, don't sign. Trust me for once. I know Stanley Miller, you don't. I can't even begin to fathom what he's up to but there will be something. Please. Don't sign.'

Tiffany avoided her mother's eyes and saw Jen was doing the same. At that moment Tiffany hated herself, but she'd come too far now. After a long silence, a resigned Babs uttered, 'Very well. There's nothing more to be said.'

When the group turned, they saw Stan had arrived. His face looked more waxen and jaundiced than ever. He rested on his walking stick, out of breath. But he had a gentle smile on his face. He hobbled up and the family was reunited. Stan put his spare hand on Babs' shoulder. She shuddered as if a rodent had run across the room.

'Babs! Glad to see you've finally seen sense!'

She took his hand off her jacket and let it drop as if she was brushing bird droppings away.

'I saw sense long ago. It's these two who haven't.' She took a deep breath. 'But I'm going to sign.' At the jubilant look on her ex-husband's face she quickly added, 'Not because of you, but because my grandkids mean the world to me. If you—'

Stan's lawyer appeared outside his office. 'Ah, Mr Miller,' he said when he saw Stan. 'Something's come up. I'll need half an hour to sort it out.'

Stan didn't look pleased. 'Can't one of your associates do it?'

'Afraid not. My apologies.' He was already motoring away. When he saw his office junior he said, 'Go and buy some PG Tips at the Waitrose around the corner.'

'I need information and I need it fast. I've checked the Yellow Pages with no joy. Can you access the electoral roll?' Dee asked John. She was sitting in the back of a cab speeding towards the grander parts of North West London. Dee wasn't sure where she was going yet but she thought that would be the right area.

His response was sarky. 'The electoral roll? Yeah, I think I've got a copy in the can.'

Dee lost her temper. 'You'll be getting a copy of the back of my hand if you give me any more lip.'

'Fine, I can ring around. Who do you want to look up?'

'The guy's called Crispin Chapaux and he's got a wife and possibly a stepdaughter called Flo.'

'How do you spell Chapaux?'

Dee's temper wasn't improving. 'How the hell do I know? But he's obviously loaded.'

'Alright, leave it with me. I'll ring some guys. London, is it?'

'I fucking hope so.'

Dee ordered the cabbie to take her up to Hampstead. As she waited for John to call back, she began to wonder if all this chasing around was worth it. Then she summoned up the image of Stanley Miller telling her mother that baby Dee was dead, and her lust for revenge took the wheel.

John called back. 'I spoke to an old mate of mine on the force and he looked up your friend Crispin. There's four names depending on how you spell it, but I'm pretty sure your guy is the one who lives in Islington. I know the area and he'll be worth a few bob. He lives with a woman called Clare but there's no sign of any Flo. Hope that helps.'

Crispin. Clare. *Bingo!*

Dee went to Islington. John had been right; Mr Chapaux was obviously worth a few. Short of a sign saying 'Poor People Keep Out', the square he and Clare lived on couldn't have been any posher. The cars parked around the patch of green in its centre belonged in a luxury car showroom. Dee mounted the steps of a three-storey house with black iron railings and a grand oak door, still unsure what her line was going to be. She hit the heavy knocker and waited a long time before a woman appeared in paint-smeared overalls and a multi-coloured bandana wrapped around her hair. 'Yes?'

Without thinking Dee said, 'Good afternoon, Madam. I'm Detective Inspector Dee Hater.'

She left it at that but that was enough. The woman's hand flew to her face. 'Oh no . . . what's she done this time?'

It had to be Flo. 'It's quite serious I'm afraid – perhaps you'd prefer to discuss it indoors so the neighbours can't hear?'

'Yes, of course, that's very considerate of you, Sergeant.'

Dee was needled at being demoted. 'Detective Inspector.'

'Come in. I'm Clare by the way.'

She led Dee into a large room on the ground floor, which had been converted into an artist's studio. There were canvases everywhere and paint slopping around. Dee didn't know much about art but she knew what she liked – and it wasn't this. If the people who sat for Clare's paintings really did look like this, they needed to see a plastic surgeon, not to mention a skin specialist to sort out their green faces. Clare pointed to an armchair in the corner and pulled up a stool. 'Would you like a drink, Inspector?'

Dee knew from the TV shows that she was supposed to say, 'not while I'm on duty', but she decided that she wasn't on duty. 'I'll have a large brandy, Madam.'

Clare found a decanter half filled with cognac and sighed. 'Alright, what's happened?'

'I'm afraid it's credit card fraud and for quite a large amount.'

Clare lit a cigarette and inhaled fast and deep, like she was on the verge of a nervous breakdown. 'Been stealing purses again? I might have guessed.'

Dee tried to look serious. 'Yes, I know that's her usual MO but I'm afraid this time it's a bit closer to home.'

Clare pricked up her ears. 'What's that supposed to mean?'

'I'm afraid to tell you that we believe she's been using your credit card.'

Clare jumped off her stool in horror. 'My card!'

'Yes, I'm afraid . . .'

But Clare had run out of the room. Dee picked up the fag that the outraged woman had dropped, took a couple of drags and then stubbed it out. Clare was soon back, emptying her handbag on the floor. 'She's stolen my fucking credit card, the conniving little bitch! I'll fucking kill her.'

Dee was shocked by the salty language coming from this upmarket arty type. 'I understand your distress, Madam, but I need to ask you some questions.'

But Clare wasn't listening. 'Is she down the station again? She can fucking well stay there. I'm not bailing her out, not this time.'

Dee was firm. 'Madam, I'm sorry but I really do need to clarify a few points. Are you familiar with a criminal associate of Flo's who uses the name Stanley Miller?'

Clare exploded, lashing out with her foot and tearing the canvas showing the face of a woman too blue to be really healthy. 'Stanley fucking Miller. No wonder the bitch has descended into the criminal classes, I thought she'd just got in with the wrong crowd. Where is he? You need to arrest him immediately, he's pond life, complete scum.'

It seemed pointless to ask, but Dee did anyway. 'Do you know him?'

'Of course I know him; he's the girl's father. How come you didn't know that? What kind of fucking detective are you anyway? I was married to the bastard.' She let out a maniacal laugh. 'Or at least I thought I was. Florence is our daughter.'

Dee was starting to get a little scared. She'd never met a woman who kicked off more than her before. She decided to skedaddle before any more paintings got trashed.

'Florence is claiming that she's someone else at the moment. Would you have a photo we could confront her with?'

Clare was still seeing red. 'My fucking credit card.' Dee jumped as she overturned several easels.

On the wall she'd spotted several photographs, including one of Clare standing next to a sulky-looking girl. Her eyes had a fox-like look that reminded Dee of Stan. She unpinned the snap and headed for the door. 'We'll be in touch.'

Clare was crying so many tears that Dee tried to help. 'Perhaps, as this is a family matter, we might be able to drop the charges.'

'Drop the charges? Stick the bitch in Holloway and throw away the key.'

'That's another alternative, of course.'

Dee ran out. She hailed her cab and told him to take her directly to Stan's lawyers. But two o'clock had already come and gone. She was probably too late . . .

Seventy-Three

The atmos in the lawyer's office was more like an execution than a signing. Stan paced back and forth, waiting for his brief to come back. Babs kept herself to herself, staying well away from the man who had once charmed her with a pair of baby's booties.

'Why did you never marry again?' Stan suddenly asked.

Babs huffed, still refusing to look at him. 'And end up with another leech like you? No, thank you.'

Tiff and Jen sat there listening, but left them to it.

Stan gave his former old lady the once-over. 'You've still got it going on. Maybe settling down again would rub that vinegar look off your face.'

'Right.' Babs stood up.

'Mum, please,' Jen cried. Then she turned to her dad. 'Why are you stirring everything up?'

'Just a bit of fun.'

Tiff looked angrily at him. 'Well, cut it out. We . . .'

Mercifully, the door swung open and the lawyer came in. He appeared harassed, but gave everyone a professional smile. 'Apologies again, Mr Miller.'

'That extra time had better not appear on my bill.'

The lawyer got the papers ready. 'I think we'll get Tiffany to sign—'

Stan cut him off. 'Don't they teach you lot manners? The mature ladies always come first.' He waved his hand in Babs' direction.

Mature! She'd give him effing mature. But she got up and took the seat opposite the lawyer.

'I've put some post-it flags exactly where you need to sign.'

He slid the thick document over. Just as well he'd marked it; it was so big she wouldn't have been able to find her way around it.

Babs picked up the pen. She could feel Stan nearby like a croc waiting to snap up his dinner. She leaned forward. A commotion outside the office made her pull back. Jen and Tiff jumped to their feet.

Everyone heard the office junior shouting, 'You can't go in there,' followed by a louder voice saying, 'Fuck off out of my way or I'll knock you spinning into next week.'

It sounded like that was what was happening until the door burst open. Dee was holding Flo by her Harvey Nicks dress. The girl's cheeks were red and her ear was swollen. Dee had clearly been to work on her and now she seized control of the office. She pushed Flo towards Stan and warned her, 'Stay there and don't cause no bovver or I'll give you another portion ... oh – and your mum wants a word with you. Something to do with a credit card?'

Flo sounded like a posh girl talking common or a common girl talking posh. 'Oh fuck . . .'

Stan wasn't going to give up without a fight. He put a protective arm around Flo's shoulder and shouted, 'Have you assaulted my wife?'

Dee sneered back, 'Oh blimey, he's been caught bang to rights and he's still trying it on. Although given the way you carry on, it wouldn't surprise me if you did end up marrying your own daughter.' Dee turned to the shocked faces in the room. 'Oh yes, people, Stan had a daughter with another wife along the way and now she's pretending to be his scary baby-missus.' Dee enjoyed her moment of triumph. Only Babs didn't seem surprised. 'He thought you two muppets,' she peered with disgust at her half-sisters, 'would feel more sorry for him if you thought he had a wife ready to pick him clean. I found little miss Flo–'

'Flo?' Babs cut in. 'I saw you as a baby–'

Flo snarled back, 'You took him away from Mummy–'

'What the effing hell is this about?' The tone was classic Tiffany, but it was Jen who'd actually spoken.

Babs straightened her back. 'I was wrong to shield you from the truth about your dad. I'll tell you the lot later on. But for a start, he married some other bird while he was still married to me.'

'Shut up,' Tiff let out in astonishment. Jen just shook her head.

Dee got on back with her tale. 'I found Flo down the road, sitting at the wheel of the getaway car. With a little bit of encouragement ...' Flo was touching her cheek. ' ... I persuaded her to admit her and Stan cooked up this scheme together. She was in for half the money, although she's claim-ing she doesn't know what the scam is. And funnily enough, I believe her.'

No one said anything. Stan sighed and took his arm off Flo's shoulder. He obviously knew that the game was up.

Dee pushed the lawyer out of the way and stood centre stage. She produced the Slim-o-matic packets from her hand-bag and put them the desk. 'So let's see what's really been going on here. Item one – slimming powder that you mix up in a glass to make those pounds fall off. Sounds a bit hocus pocus to me but it obviously worked for Stan. Hence that just-dying look. Item Two. Yellow eye shadow. Put that on your chops and your thin face won't look too clever either. Our friend here isn't pegging out at all. He's probably healthier than we are.'

She scanned the shocked expressions, including Babs'. 'Me and Flo have been having a bit of a natter and she tells me her old dad is flatty broke with his arse hanging out of his trousers. There's no legacy. Never was one. He was quite the little property magnate when he fled the country twenty-five years back. But since then he's frittered it away on wine, women and song. He's been through more WAGS than a footballer with a hit record. So he's not dying and he's got no dosh. That only leaves one question. What's the scam, Stan? Why are you so eager for these ladies to sign this telephone directory?'

Stan grinned. 'OK. It's a fair cop. I might have exaggerated things a little but only to help the girls here. I have got a large estate to leave behind. Flo doesn't know everything about me. I've simplified things.'

Dee picked up the contract. She waved it at Stan. 'The truth's in here somewhere. I'm going to take this away with me and find out what it is.'

'Madam, you can't do that,' Stan's lawyer stuttered, making the mistake of getting in Dee's way.

'You got any kids?' she asked sweetly, cocking her head to the side.

He appeared confused. 'One. A son.'

'Well, if you're planning on having any more you'd better shift it – before I boot your tackle so far across London you're gonna need a sperm donor to get your wife up the duff.'

He swiftly got out of her way.

She crammed the document into her Burberry bag. 'Come on, Mum, you shouldn't have to deal with this shit on your birthday.' She stabbed her hot gaze at her half-sisters. 'Your other daughters can take themselves down a burger bar and think about what they've done.'

After Dee and Babs had left, Stan said, 'Why don't you two girls join me and Flo for lunch? Get to know each other?'

'You've got the nerve of the devil,' Tiffany said at last

He raised his hands by way of apology. 'You'll get your money. And a free lunch.'

In a rage fit for a heavyweight bout Jen rushed across the office, ripped his stick out of his hand and belted him so hard he went crashing.

His daughters marched out. He turned to his remaining child and growled, 'Don't just stand there; help me up.'

With a sulky expression, Flo did as she was told. Stan pulled his clothing back into order. Then he turned sweetly to her and asked, 'Have you still got your mum's credit card?'

Seventy-Four

'Right, birthday girl, it's time for you to get your gear on,' Jen told her mum with a wide grin.

Babs smiled back. Jen and her sister had turned up at her door, sheepish at having the wool pulled over their eyes. But that's what happened when some folk waved the promise of a wodge in your face. Babs had welcomed them back with open arms, although Dee had given them the evil eye. None of them could figure out why Stan needed those papers signing; they couldn't make head nor tail of the paperwork.

But who cared? All that mattered was that Stan was out of their lives. Although Dee had said one thing that still rang in Babs' head. 'That effing nut job of a daughter of his is proper trouble. I don't think we've seen the last of her.'

Babs forgot about Stan's daughter and looked at her own in turn – Desiree, Jennifer, Tiffany. Her heart filled with pride. They'd come through so much together . . . and survived. Stan had thought that he was coming back to the same ol' Babs, but he'd been wrong. He hadn't figured out she wouldn't be standing alone. She had three bolshie daughters for backup.

Although Babs was smiling, she was bloody tired. All she wanted to do was put her head down and sleep for a year. 'Do we have to go out tonight? Can't we do something or other at the weekend?'

All her daughters were alarmed. Dee put her straight. 'Are you off it? You're fifty today, not Saturday or Sunday. Plus, we've booked that fancy restaurant. You're gonna love their bolognese.'

'I can get one of them in the freezer section down the supermarket,' she said with a wink that got all of them laughing.

Eventually she got up. 'Alright, I get it. I'll go and get ready—'

'In the meantime,' Tiff interrupted, 'we're going out to get some supplies in for when we get back—'

Babs frowned. 'What, all of you?'

Instead of answering, Tiff planted a kiss on her cheek. Then they were all gone, leaving Babs alone. She sagged back onto the settee. She'd been trying to hold it all together, keep it all cushty so her girls wouldn't get worried about her. Now the full realisation of Stan trying to tear her family apart hit. Babs bowed her head and cried and cried. Five minutes later she wiped back her tears, went into her bedroom and pulled out a suitcase dating back to the 1970s.

For once in its life, the Old Swan really did look like a swan. The pub was gleaming, decorated with balloons, streamers, banners – including one with 'Princess' written across it – all sorts of food laid out, sparkling glasses and a ton of champagne ready to pop. It looked like it was waiting for royalty, which of course it was. One of The Devil's Estate queens, Barbara Miller, had hit her half-century and the residents had turned out in force.

Babs' old gang were all present – Cheryl and Beryl and many of the other women who had met, laughed and gossiped in the old washhouse. It was like the old spirit of the Estate had come back.

Dee, Jen and Tiff surveyed the boozer with pride. They'd all clubbed together to make sure the night would give her memories to last a lifetime.

'Listen up, everyone,' Dee told the gathered crowd, 'we want to make sure that this is a surprise, so when you see the signal you better keep your gobs shut. Jen's Courtney is going to go and get Babs and my Nicky will keep a lookout. As soon as he raises his hand, keep schtum. Got it?'

Despite everyone nodding, Dee squinted menacingly. 'Anyone who slips up will answer to my fists.'

She passed some photos to Courtney. 'You know what to do with them?' The ten-year-old nodded. 'Good. Then get your nan straight after and bring her over. And remember . . .' She placed her finger across her lips, 'not a word about the party.'

Courtney grinned with excitement and went on her way.

Babs twirled around her sitting room singing, 'Leader Of The Pack'. She wore a bright white maxi dress she'd taken from her old suitcase. Her dad had given it to her back in '72. It floated around, making her feel like she was on cloud nine. She'd never actually worn it; she'd been saving it for a blinding occasion. Then tornado Neville and hurricane Stan had hit her life and there had never been a right moment, so she'd just tucked it away. But now she was fifty, she wanted to feel like a young girl again. Wanted to recall what it felt like to be full of promises and dreams.

Babs waltzed past the ironing board she'd put up to run the creases out of her dress. She laughed as she tried to make the motorbike noises in the song. Ah, she felt so flippin' good. The door knocker went. The girls. They were going to do their nut when they saw her outfit, especially Dee, but sod 'em. This was her night and she was gonna wear what she wanted.

She opened the door and immediately wished she hadn't.

'You didn't think I was going to forget my Babs-babe's birthday,' said Stanley Miller, with his killer smile.

Before she could react, he'd shoved her back and slammed the door behind him.

Ten-year-old Courtney had one more piccie to go. Her mum didn't usually let her go out on her own, but fetching Nanna Babs for her surprise party was special. Though her mum had told her point blank that she was to hurry and if anyone looked at her the wrong way she was to scream her head off. *As if!* She was a big girl now . . .

'Court,' someone called, freezing her in her tracks. Her mum had also said that if anyone tried to talk to her she was to keep walking.

'Court.' The voice was louder and more insistent this time. Her gaze darted around. All of a sudden her braveness deserted her and she almost scarpered back to the Old Swan. But she didn't when she saw who it was. Her mate Dexter Ingram, who had gone to big school a few years back. Courtney started blushing. He was such a heartthrob, kind and clever too. She didn't get why her mum and Nanna Babs always told her to stay clear of him.

'You alright, Court,' he said as soon as she reached him.

He was skinny, with hair in zigzag cornrows and a skin tone similar to her Auntie Dee's. A portable CD player peeped out of the front pocket of his low-riding jeans and the ch-ch-ch sound of music came from the earphones around his neck. They were soon sitting in the shadowed stairwell, sharing his earphones, bobbing furiously away to Sean Paul's 'Get Busy'. She loved, loved, LOVED this tune. Proper bassline, people!

Mum and Auntie Dee had said go straight to Nanna Babs' . . . but a couple of minutes wouldn't do any harm.

Seventy-Five

'What are you doing here?' Babs asked her former husband as she stumbled backwards into the sitting room. He matched her step for step. 'Thought you were on a flight back to Spain.' Her heart was drumming away like crazy.

He ignored her question. 'Not going to offer me a brew or anything?' He tutted. 'Is that any way to treat the man who gave you two beautiful girls?'

A cold chill ran along Babs' spine. 'This ain't a good time. The girls will be here soon to take me out—'

'And no one invited me,' Stan said with mock sadness. 'That breaks my heart. Oh well,' he shrugged, 'I suppose I'll learn to live with it—'

Babs wasn't having it. 'Cut the bollocks. Why are you here?'

Stan pulled out a bunch of papers. 'Sign it. My lawyer's clever, see, he had another copy.'

'Fuck you,' she spat back.

She tried to get around him but he grabbed her arm and slammed her into the sofa. She wasn't taking this. Babs jerked herself forward and up. 'You need to fuck off outta here before I call the Bill.'

Stan watched her coldly. 'When you've signed it I'll piss off into thin air, never to be seen again.'

'Maybe I will . . .' He stepped triumphantly towards her, but stopped when she added, 'When you tell me what I'm signing.'

He laughed like a mad man. 'You still don't get it, do you? All these years it's tickled me something silly to think of you on your knees, scrubbing them houses.'

Babs stumbled back again. 'What's that got to do with you?'

He curled his lip. 'That was always your problem, never could figure out what was right in front of you. I really did fancy you in the beginning—'

'And then I became just another tool for you to get what you wanted, that fucking business of yours.'

'Clever girl.' He flew at her and crashed her into the wall. Babs fought hard but he wouldn't let go. 'If you don't sign, so help me—'

Stan's words choked in his throat as Babs slammed him a good one in the nuts.

Stan doubled over, groaning in pain. 'You . . . fucking . . . bitch.'

Babs didn't hang around. She ducked to the side and belted for the front door. She opened it . . .

'Owww!' Her head jerked back so violently she thought it was going to rip clean off. Stan had her by the hair.

'Let me bloody well go.'

He twisted her to face him. Babs was petrified by the expression on his face. Pure evil. Waves of rage came off him like heat from a volcano.

He threw her on the floor. The corner of her head caught the skirting board. Dazed, she looked up at him. Stan loomed like her worst nightmare.

'All you had to do was sign the papers.' He grabbed her by the hair and dragged her into the sitting room. Babs tried to fight back, but she felt so limp and drained.

Somehow she made her mouth move, her words coming out

slurred and slow. 'You're the mug here. Pete never killed Denny.'

'What?' She couldn't see his face clearly but heard the shock in his voice.

'Mickey and Mel took you for a proper mug. You topped your own brother for nothing—'

'Shut up.'

Babs twisted the knife. 'Mug! Mug!'

He shoved his face close to hers. 'I've warned you—'

'Mug! Mug! Mug!'

'Shut up!' he bellowed. But she wouldn't.

'I'll shut that fucking trap of yours for life.' Stan closed his hand around her throat. Pressed down and squeezed tight. The air stuck in Babs' chest.

Can't breathe. Can't breathe.

Babs tried to lift her arms, but nothing happened.

'Bye-bye, Babs-babe.'

Babs didn't know where she got the strength from but she managed to raise a hand, aiming for his eye but getting her nails deep in his cheek instead. He growled as he swung her to the side like a rag doll. Babs' hand flopped back. Dark lights started flashing in her vision. Her breath was coming short. She was dying and there was nothing she could do about it.

'I'll teach you,' he snarled. Blood was dripping from the scratches, but he was grinning like a demon.

Stan increased the pressure, making the air bubble away in her chest. *I haven't said goodbye to my family. My wonderful girls. Little Bea and . . .*

What happened next was a blur. A spray of blood hit Babs full in the face. Stan looked down at her, blood pouring from his head and a stupefied look on his face. He toppled over to the side to reveal a wide-eyed and terrified Courtney holding her grandmother's steam iron. Courtney hit her granddad's head again and again, until he stopped moving.

The iron tumbled from Courtney's hand as she looked, horrified, at her grandfather's body.

'Courtney . . . sweetheart,' Babs rasped.

Courtney dropped to her knees. 'He was . . . he was . . .'

With her last bit of strength, Babs pulled her granddaughter into her arms. Courtney started sobbing against her chest.

Babs eased her up. She drew air noisily into her body, gasping as she met her former husband's wide unseeing eyes. Courtney had killed her grandfather. *Oh God.*

Think, think, think. Babs got to her feet as quickly as she could, swaying slightly. She drew Courtney to her side. 'I don't want you to worry about a thing, baby.'

Courtney's eyes were wild. She was trembling. 'I had to come and get you for your surprise party at the Knackered Swan. Auntie Dee gave me photos . . . they're a surprise as well.'

Babs knew she had to think on her feet. She checked her granddaughter over. 'Let's get you cleaned up.'

She took Courtney into the bathroom, making sure she kept Courtney's gaze averted from Stan. First thing she did was remove Courtney's bloody coat. There was no blood on her clothing and Babs scrubbed her face clean.

She took Courtney into the passage and got on her knees. 'You have to listen to every word I'm going to say, OK, love?' Courtney nodded, her face frozen in fear. 'You're going to go back and say that you saw me, but I told you I was coming over on my own. Say that you didn't tell me about the party, just that your mum and your aunties were waiting for me down the local.'

Courtney nodded again, so Babs carried on. 'You didn't see your Granddad Stan—'

'But—'

'No, listen.' Babs shook her slightly. She hated doing it but her beloved Courtney had to understand. 'You didn't see him, only me. I only let you come in the hall. And tell them I took your coat because you fell on the way and got it dirty. You got it?'

Courtney just nodded, the tears threatening to fall again. 'This isn't your fault, baby,' Babs reassured her. 'Whatever questions anyone asks, you've got to stick to our story. If you don't things will get worse. Much worse.' She drew in a fresh breath. 'Granddad Stan was a bad man. A very bad man. If you don't stick with our story, his badness will stay with us. You don't want that, do you?' Courtney shook her head furiously. 'Good girl. Now off with you and tell everyone I'm on my way.'

Her granddaughter flung herself into her arms and they hugged tight.

'I love you, Nan.' Then Courtney rushed off.

Babs slumped against the wall, her hand covering her mouth. She couldn't let anyone know what her beautiful, brave Courtney had done. She was only trying to defend her. The child was so young, just ten years old. If anyone knew what had gone on, Courtney's life would be ruined. Babs wasn't going to let that happen. She went into the sitting room and made herself look down at her dead ex-husband.

'May you rot in hell,' she spat. Then she put her hands in his blood and smeared it over herself.

Babs' heart beat like a manic drum machine as she made her way to the surprise party. She kept her head up so she didn't have to look at the blood on her clothes. When she got inside the lift, she nearly crumbled with emotion when she saw the first photo; a black-and-white snap of her and Denny at school, their arms around each other. She half smiled as she noticed the elastic bands her best mate always wore to keep her white socks up.

The next photo was on the door of the former washhouse. A formal studio portrait of her with her mum and dad on her mum's thirtieth birthday.

The photos went on and on.

Dee in two plaits, missing her two front teeth, smiling like mad into the camera.

Babs in Mile End Hospital maternity ward staring down adoringly at newborn baby Jen.

Babs with Beryl and Cheryl drinking sloe gin on the landing.

Babs with Jen and Tiff and Nanna Rosie in Vicky Park.

Babs holding her first grandchild Courtney.

And there they all were at Courtney's birthday bash the week before – Babs, Dee, Tiff, Jen, Nicky, Courtney and Little Bea.

Babs didn't even realise she was sobbing her heart out. Her gorgeous girls had created a wonderful walk down memory lane. A tribute to her life. And now that life and theirs was about to fall apart.

Seventy-Six

'What's taking them so long?' Jen asked her two sisters impatiently.

Tiffany shrugged. 'You know Mum, she's probably still putting on her slap.'

Their half-sister, Dee, was watching the increasingly restless crowd. People had been waiting for things to kick off for quite some time now.

'Oi,' she called, spotting someone she didn't know. 'Get your mitts out of the mini sausage rolls. No one starts on the nosh until she gets here.'

The person quickly whipped their hand away; Dee Black was a woman who didn't stand any nonsense.

Dee turned back to her sisters. 'I told you we should've had it at an upmarket venue. Somewhere plush and cultured.'

Tiff rolled her eyes. 'Bloody hell, you're not still rabbiting on about that? Give it a rest will ya.'

Dee blinked her false eyelashes at her, furiously. 'Everyone's so low rent here. Look at 'em.'

The crowd was a motley crew of people, mainly from The Devil's Estate.

Jen said, 'This is where a lot of her mates are.' She leaned forward and whispered, 'It must be that surprise we laid out on the way that's keeping them. I bet Mum's gobsmacked.'

They all looked as pleased as Punch with themselves at the thought of the surprise.

Nicky, Dee's boy, who was keeping lookout, suddenly and dramatically raised his hand, signalling for silence. But then he frowned and said, 'Hold up.' He peered through the window. 'That can't be right . . .'

His mum snapped, 'What are you going on about? It's either them or it ain't.'

'It's . . .'

Before he could finish, the door opened and Jen's daughter Courtney came in. Alone.

'Where's your Nanna Babs?' Jen asked. Then she looked closely at her daughter and scowled. 'Where's your coat?'

Courtney swallowed, her face pale. 'I fell . . . it got dirty . . . Nanna Babs kept it.'

'So where's your grandmother?' Dee asked her. 'Are you alright? You look a bit peaky.'

Courtney swallowed again as she nodded. 'Nanna said she's just coming over.' She looked up at her mum. 'Can I use the loo?' She scarpered without waiting for an answer.

Jen stared after her. 'She didn't look right. Maybe I should—'

'She's coming! She's coming!' Nicky called out excitedly.

The lights popped off and they fell silent.

Half a minute later, the door opened. The lights flew back on and the crowd gathered at Babs Miller's surprise fiftieth joyfully cried, 'Happy birthday!'

But the happiness was sucked out of the room at the sight of the blood on her face and white dress.

'Something terrible has happened,' she said, 'someone needs to call the coppers.'

'Let go of my fucking mum,' Dee screamed as the police led a handcuffed Babs to their panda. Her husband and son held her back.

Tiff and Jen looked on, shocked and tearful. Courtney had her face muffled against her mum, bawling her eyes out. The people on The Devil were used to the badness in life. But no one could get their heads around this one. Our Babs murdering her ex-husband Stan? Never. But his bloody body pointed the finger squarely at her.

'I won't let them take her,' Dee carried on, almost beside herself with fury and grief. 'My mum was taken from me once before, it ain't happening again.'

'Shush babe, shush,' John soothed her. 'We're going to get her the best brief there is.'

Babs turned as she reached the cop car. 'I'm gonna be alright. I don't want none of you to take this on.'

The crowd shook their heads sadly as she got into the back of the car.

As the car pulled away Babs met Courtney's eye and mouthed, 'Remember.'

Two hours later, the door to Babs' holding cell door opened and a cop stepped in, ramrod-straight, like he was on his best behaviour. He cleared his throat. 'You've got a visitor.' Then he turned to the visitor and respectfully said, 'Sir.'

A man decked out in the belt, braces and brass of a top cop walked inside and closed the door. His hair had turned iron grey and was clipped short, but Babs would still recognise him any day of the week.

'Tricky Dickie?'

The man Babs had known all those years ago answered, 'Commander Patrick Johnson.' *Patrick*? So that had been his name. He sighed and sat on the bunk next to her. 'You can still turn a fella's head.'

Babs blushed like she hadn't done in years. 'I don't think there'll be any fellas where I'm going.'

He took her hand, just like old times. 'What happened? I thought Stan did a flit years ago.'

'He turned up like the bad penny he is. And before you ask, I did kill the rotten bastard. I'd do it again in a heartbeat.'

He placed his finger on her lips. 'Whatever you do, don't say that to anyone. Don't say a word until your lawyer gets here—'

The door opened again and the same cop stood there with a bloke in a suit. 'Not another word, Mrs Miller,' he warned.

'This gentleman says he's your lawyer. I thought you were using the duty solicitor?'

Babs hadn't let herself cry yet, although she so wanted to. *You've gotta do this for Courtney, you've gotta do this for the family,* she told herself over and over. This brief was obviously a proper lawyer. He had a proper suit, a proper briefcase and was wearing proper aftershave.

Commander Patrick Johnson stood up. 'We'll talk later,' he promised.

When they were alone, the lawyer sat down on the bunk. She spat, 'Who the hell are you? I don't need another lawyer. I've admitted killing Stan and that's all there is to it. Now hop it.'

The suit cleared his throat. 'So I understand. Although that's a shame. If you'd waited a few hours before making a statement, I'd have been able to help. You missed out some rather important information that might have influenced which charges the police preferred.'

'Cry me a river.'

The brief raised his eyebrows. 'It's up to you of course. But we can sort this out.'

'Indeed. Now why don't you go and top up your eau-de-cologne?'

But the lawyer wasn't done. 'That's not why I'm here

anyway. I do the legal work for Mr and Mrs John Black and Mrs Black asked me to look over some documents for you.'

Babs felt reassured to hear Dee's name. Mind you, she was sticking to her guns. She'd done Stan in and that was the end of the matter.

The lawyer opened his briefcase and produced a folded and creased copy of the contract that she'd been expected to sign earlier that afternoon. It seemed a very long time ago.

'I think I've identified what the late Mr Miller was up to. On page 53, in amongst a lot of jargon, it seems he was hoping that you would transfer ownership of two properties in Mile End.'

Babs sniffed. 'You know what I think? That crapster was off his rocker, good and proper.' She scoffed. 'Me, own properties. As bloody if!'

The lawyer pressed on. 'I've already checked the land registry. You own them – since 1972.'

Babs felt the ground move beneath her feet. 'Hold on.' She started pacing. Her mind rewound furiously. She spun around to face the lawyer. 'There was this one time when my name was on some documents, but it was a forgery . . .' That's what Stan had said about the deeds to the knocking shop. Back in '78, Mel had sworn neither she or Mickey had done it. Probably Stan playing her for a fool right from the start. Didn't matter, it was still a fake.

'I can assure you they aren't forged,' the lawyer said.

Babs folded her arms in frustration. 'They must be. I never once signed anything . . . Blimey . . .' She slumped on the bunk. It's funny what you can recall. She remembered like it was yesterday. The day she'd seen Neville again. Stan was perched on her desk in the Go Go Girls Modelling Agency . . .

'What's this then?' she asked.

Stan plonked himself down on the edge of the desk. Whatever had been troubling him all week must have got sorted because he was back to his usual cheerful, charming self. 'I told you a couple of days back. The papers I need witnessing.'

He shoved a pen in her hand and then turned to the first page. 'Just sign where the pencil mark is.'

Most of the document was covered by the other papers; she couldn't see what she was signing.

She looked up at him, confused. 'What is it? And where's your signature?'

He seemed put out.

'I'm signing it – what's the matter, don't you trust me?'

She felt bad for even asking, so signed in three places and he whipped the papers away.

No wonder he'd covered the paper, the lying fraud; he'd been making a total kipper out of her. Babs' mind slammed back to Stan's attack. He'd laughed his head off, claiming she was a fool for not figuring it out. Was it these houses? He was having revenge on her from the grave.

In desperation Babs spat out, 'I never realised what I was doing. I didn't know they were knocking shops. He had me over a barrel. I never—'

The lawyer placed his hand on her arm to calm her. 'I don't know about any knocking shops but the properties are in your name. May I ask you another question?'

Babs nodded reluctantly. 'You were the cleaner for two houses in a Bancroft Square in Mile End?'

Babs nodded.

'I've discovered that the owner was a management company—'

'Yeah, I know that. Hardly anyone lived there, but I didn't care as long as I got my wages on time.'

'That management company was owned by Stanley Miller.' Babs felt sick. 'Oh, I get it.' She gritted her teeth. 'He said he got a sick thrill knowing I was on my knees scrubbing the floors of the houses. *His houses.* That's why I got the job, just so my ex-hole could laugh his twat off at me still grafting on his say-so.'

The lawyer shook his head. 'We've established that the signature on the deeds is yours, yes?' Babs nodded. 'You need to hang onto that. OK?

'Stanley Miller may have given you the job to laugh at you, but there was something much deeper going on. The houses were his insurance policy if he ever needed money, which we now know he did. Getting your two daughters to sign was just a cover. It was your signature he needed. Your signature, which would sign both houses back to him. Once that was done, he could sell them and get the money.'

Babs wiped her hand against her forehead as things started slotting into place. Mel saying nine and ten in the hospital. Those were the numbers of the houses she cleaned. Had Mel been trying to tell her what Stan was after? Had Stan attacked Mel to shut her up? That was how Stan had got in while she was having that ding-dong with Jen and Tiff; the bastard had a key. Flippin' hell.

This was doing her head in. 'I'm not in more trouble, am I?'

He quickly reassured her. 'No. Quite the reverse. As you of all people will know, both houses are substantial Georgian properties in a very sought-after square ...'

Stan had been right after all. The East End had risen again.

'And very valuable.'

Babs turned to him in disbelief. 'Valuable?'

'Mrs Miller, you may be facing a murder charge but you're also a millionaire.'

acknowledgements

To my Hodder sisters, Ruth, Rebecca, Alice, Fleur and Keshini. What a team we are! And where would I be without my agent, Amanda? Nowhere! She's a force of nature. A huge shoutout to the bloggers and reviewers who have taken the time to put my work on the crime map.

Thank you!

Thank you for reading *Blood Mother*. I'm keeping my fingers crossed that you enjoyed it. If you did I'd love to hear about it – you can get in touch with me by:

Email: dredamitchell@yahoo.co.uk

Twitter: @DredaMitchell

Facebook: Dreda Say Mitchell

I always love to be linked to reviews and ratings on your blogs or online!

If you enjoyed BLOOD MOTHER, look out for the gripping
new novel in the FLESH AND BLOOD trilogy

BLOOD DAUGHTER

They say blood is thicker than water . . . but that's not going
to stop it being spilled.

Coming August 2017

HODDER